# CHILDREN OF THE DAWN

## PATRICIA ROWE

S0-BNV-586

WARNER BOOKS

A Time Warner Company

WARNER BOOKS EDITION

Cover design by Diane Luger
Cover illustration by Mel Grant
Hand lettering by Carl Dellacroce
Book design by Elizabeth Sanborn

Warner Books, Inc.
1271 Avenue of the Americas
New York, NY  10020

Visit our web site at
http://pathfinder.com/twep

W A Time Warner Company

Printed in the United States of America

First Printing: September, 1996

10 9 8 7 6 5 4 3 2 1

Dedicated to Don
—who makes everything possible—
on our 25th anniversary.

# CHILDREN OF THE DAWN

# FOREWORD

N INE THOUSAND YEARS AGO, ANCESTORS OF THE
Plateau Indians flourished in southern Washington State.
Hunter-gatherers who were led by women, the People of the
Misty Time left a legacy of artifacts, legends, and petroglyphs
carved in black basalt.

From high on a windswept cliff, a woman's haunting stone
face looks out over the mighty Columbia River. Her large
solemn eyes are gracefully ringed. Owlish horns perch above
curved eyebrows. She Who Watches, known as the Moonkeeper, Ashan (Ah-Shan'), is the heroine of an ancient legend:

*A woman was chief of all who lived in this region. That
was a long time before Coyote came up the river and changed
things, and people were not yet real people. After a time,
Coyote in his travels came to this place. He saw the approach
of conflict . . .*

# CHAPTER 1

THE MOONKEEPER ASHAN TRUDGED ACROSS A WIND-swept plain in the tabu land, with her mate Tor beside her. The Shahala people—eighty men, women, little ones, and grayhairs—followed like a line of ants, carrying packs and pulling travel poles heaped with their belongings and a share of the tribe's. Ashan felt as if she were dragging the whole tribe behind her, instead of just her travel poles.

*Thirty-nine days,* she thought, looking at the notch she'd cut in her staff this morning. *Autumn will soon be winter.*

A howl wavered on the wind, trailing sharp yips, making the hair on her neck stand up. She reached for Tor's arm.

"Listen!"

"It's just a songdog."

Ashan felt foolish: The Shahala chief, startled by a coyote.

"This stupid wind," she grumbled. "It changes the sound of things."

Her mate of six summers laughed.

"It's a good thing your name means Whispering Wind. You can make friends with it; learn its language. The Creator sends more than enough to this place."

"This is not just ordinary wind, Tor. It's so cold we shiver, so dry it drains us, so loud we can't hear each other talk. I wouldn't *want* to make friends with such a beast."

"It's not always like this," he said.

It had been like this for days. But she said, "Don't tell me,

Tor. Tell our people ... tonight, when the wind won't let
them sleep."

"I'll do whatever you say tonight, but now we should go
on before they lay down their burdens. We should put many
steps behind us before the land swallows the sun."

She looked at the late afternoon sky. He was right. The
people were bunching up behind, waiting for their chief to
tell them what to do. Ashan raised her staff and thrust it
forward. She leaned into the horsetail strap across her chest,
into the wind, into the future, and urged herself onward. She
heard grumbling as people fell back into step behind her.

Tor said, "You will see, Ashan. The Great River is near."

"You'd better be right. I don't know how much longer
they'll follow us."

"They have no choice, my love," Tor said, smiling.

"Every creature has a choice—whether they know it or
not is the question."

As she walked, Ashan held a pebble in her mouth to quiet
hunger.

*This prairie,* she thought. *It gives up little water and less
food. Sleep doesn't even refresh us. What am I doing to my
people?*

The Shahala loved and feared Ashan. She healed, punished,
and taught; settled arguments; remembered legends; knew
what needed to be known about animals, plants, seasons,
rituals, and magic. Most important, she spoke with spirits so
people would know what to do. The tribe could not survive
without a Moonkeeper. And so they had obeyed when Ashan
said they must leave their ancestral lands and move to a new
home that only Tor had seen.

No one thought they'd still be wandering after thirty-nine
days. It had been a terrible journey. They'd been lost in mountains. A river had cut them off; Ashan carried the ashes of
two who drowned in the crossing. And now these endless
plains where they'd been forced to stop many times while
the warriors hunted. Ordinary things felt forbidding to weary,
discouraged people. The sun glared without warmth. The
wind—with nothing to slow it but pale, flattened grass—
moaned as if grieving; it searched out every gap in the leathers
and furs they wore.

*Even a coyote,* she thought, *sounds like a lost, lonely spirit.*
Everyone hated the tabu land, but Ashan knew they must cross it to reach their new home: Spirits had shown her in dreams.

A Moonkeeper was the only one strong enough to journey with spirits in the darktime world, and wise enough to understand what they said. Dreaming was forbidden to ordinary people. Babies were most in danger, too often taken by evil spirits who tricked them into the dreamworld before they'd been taught how to stay out of it. Any morning a mother could find a perfect little baby shell—empty and cold. Until little ones were old enough to understand, mothers shook them many times each night.

Ashan's mate, Tor, who obeyed no one, enjoyed how dreaming felt, and lied when asked about his sleep. By dreaming his way to personal and tribal disasters, he proved to people why they shouldn't dream. But when her son, Kai El, kept dreaming no matter what she did, and didn't seem to suffer, others wanted to try. Knowing she couldn't prevent it, she had warned them.

"Dream if you must, but you might not come back. Your dreams are a game you play with yourself. Do not think they are like mine. Spirits speak *only* to the Moonkeeper. Evil speaks to all others."

No matter what others might see in the darktime world, or what use they made of it, the Moonkeeper's dreams must be heeded as spirit messages. Otherwise, why would people obey her?

When Ashan had dreamed about a better life on the shore of a huge river, the Shahala had abandoned their homeland. Most of them had set out in hope, except grayhairs who grieved from the first. But day by day, winter's tightening grip had turned hope sour. Even the breath of the tribe's guardian, Shala the Wind Spirit, had become their enemy— tearing at the tabu land as if to push the intruders back, as if to push the sun and moon back.

Ashan spat out the pebble. *I hate this place.*

She remembered Shahala land and swallowed, for she would never see it again. The summer home on Takoma's forested flank, where Coyote made the First People in the

Misty Time. The winter home in the Valley of Grandmothers, where many horses once roamed, where trees kept the wind from going wild. *Ancestor Cave. Anutash. Never again . . .*

Though many wanted to go home, they could not. All the horses had died. The people would starve without their winter food. The Moonkeeper didn't doubt her vision of the future, but on this late autumn day in this comfortless place, she worried about the strength of the tribe. Hungry, worn-out people, who believed they were lost. How to keep them going? How to keep herself going?

Tears rose behind her eyes, but she knew how to stop them. *Look at the ground, keep moving your feet. Don't let them see what's inside.*

Two little girls ran up to Ashan.

"May we walk with you, Moonkeeper?" Kyli asked.

"You are welcome," Ashan said, smiling. Little ones could raise a weary soul just by being around.

They carried light packs, but were too young to pull travel poles. Only hands and faces peeked out from the warm skins that covered them from head to foot. Matching Ashan's stride, the little girls whispered to each other.

The one named Kyli liked to talk. The other was shy, with a shy name Ashan couldn't think of.

Kyli said, "Wista wants to know if we are going home soon."

Wista—Ashan remembered now—daughter of Keeta and Kowkish. Just five summers. Some people, especially the young, had to be told more than once. Hope died harder in them.

The Moonkeeper's voice was kind, but firm.

"We are not going home, Wista. Not ever. We had no winter food because the horses died out. We were getting hungry, remember?"

"I told you," Kyli said.

"But I'm *still* hungry." Wista's bottom lip stuck out.

Ashan put her hand on the little girl's shoulder.

"You won't be hungry much longer. I dreamed of a new home with plenty of food. Spirits Who Love People showed me the way. Always remember, Wista, the Shahala are Amotkan's favorite tribe."

Kyli said, "My brother says we are the Creator's *forgotten* tribe."

*Hamish,* the Moonkeeper thought. *I must watch him.*

"You know how boys are," she said, giving them a look that showed how much better it was to be a girl.

Ashan remembered last night. Kyli's brother, Hamish, and two of his friends had left the camp, a strange thing to do—on this windswept plain, people liked to stay near the nightfire. With the trained ears of a Moonkeeper, she had followed them into the dark, and heard what they said.

"There's no Great River in this tabu land. No sheltering cliffs, no food forever."

"If it's this bad now, what will we do when it's covered with snow?"

"If I'm going to die, I'd rather starve at home than walk myself to death through this place. At least my ashes would be with the ancestors."

"But the Moonkeeper dreamed the new home. Doesn't that mean anything to you?"

"The Moonkeeper—phhht! All that time, she was fat in the mountains, while we starved. Then she walks out of the woods one day and old Raga tells us to follow her? Tenka should have been chief. What's wrong with her? She wouldn't have made us leave the home of our ancestors."

"And what about Tor? Remember when Moonkeepers were *forbidden* to mate? And that boy of theirs? Where did he come from?"

"All that time, we couldn't even say Tor's name, had to call him the Evil One, and now . . ."

Then the wind had shifted, carrying their words away. Ashan reminded herself that the three almost-warriors were too young to have power in the tribe. But there were others who felt the same. How much longer would she be able to control them?

"Yes," Ashan said absently. "You know how boys are." But Kyli and Wista had fallen back with the tribe.

The wind brought a new scent.

Ashan sucked deep breaths of clean, moist air—

"We made it!" Tor yelled.

"Water!" Ashan yelled, thrusting her hands in the air. "I smell it!"

People threw off their packs and ran toward her.

"Water to drink, and walk in!" Ashan licked her lips. "Water to taste and listen to!"

"Tomorrow you will see the Great River," Tor said in his proudest voice.

Laughing, crying, hugging, people thanked the Moonkeeper for her dream, and her mate for knowing the way. They praised each other for faith and courage.

"Don't forget. Thank the spirits," Ashan told them. "Get this place ready for sleep. Talk in whispers and make no fire. We are the strangers here."

# CHAPTER 2

As THE SHAHALA PEOPLE MADE THEIR CAMP READY for the night, the Moonkeeper went off by herself to offer thanks.

Ashan was twenty-two summers in age, and shorter than most women, but by carrying herself as a chief, she seemed taller, and older. She held a staff with magic powers. She wore a browband with two eagle feathers taken from an old proud bird who'd lived and died in the ancestral homeland. Her black hair separated in back and blew long and thick around her shoulders. She wore a fox cape over a doeskin shirt, pieces of leather as a skirt, and knee-high moccasins.

Standing on a low mound, she dropped her staff and cape, and lifted her slender arms. Her sleeves slid up. The light of the setting sun gave her dark amber skin an unworldly glow.

The Moonkeeper faced Where Day Begins, tipped her face to the sky, and began an ancient song.

"Spirits Who Love People, the Shahala thank you . . ."

The wind whipped at her skirt and stung the backs of her legs.

"Spirits Who Love People," she began again. But her thoughts drifted. She sat on the fox fur cape, and let them go where they would.

*The Great River . . . in dreams I soared above it, but Tor is the only one who has tasted its water. . . .*

Ashan didn't like to think about how he'd found the Great

River—so much bad on the way to something good. She remembered how it began, six winters ago . . .

While she had sat deep in prayers, Tor had kidnapped her— the *only* way he could have the Chosen One. He'd stuffed her in a bearskin sack, and run, and when he'd stopped in snow up to her knees, she hadn't known where she was.

Why had Tor wrenched her from her life like a sapling from the ground? Why not simply ask her to be his mate?

Because Ashan, chosen to lead the tribe after the Old Moon- keeper's last death, was forbidden by ancient law to have a mate.

After a time in the wildplace, Ashan got over hating Tor, because she loved him. She had always loved him. They were soulmates after all. The hardest thing had been to accept that she would never see her people again. She could have found the tribe, but the risk to Tor, and to Kai El, the son she had borne, was too great. There was no way to know what the Shahala would do to them.

Ashan had been happy with her little family, thriving in friendly mountains, living in a cave she herself had found . . . the Home Cave. Then Tor had brought it all crashing down. How like a man to get what he *had to have,* then find out it wasn't what he wanted.

She had known he was dreaming again when he talked about new places and people, about belonging to something larger than just a family. He got all his crazy ideas from dreams. She had tried to make him stop, but in the wildplace, she was nobody's chief.

Tor was unhappy without a tribe. Ashan found out *how* unhappy when he stole away one night—just *left* them—a woman and a baby of only two summers. She had waited at the Home Cave until their food ran out. It broke her heart to leave, but she had to find the Shahala, or she and Kai El would have died.

Maybe she would have found the tribe. But savages stole Kai El, and she broke her leg, and got him back, then they fell in that pit—

Even now, Ashan shuddered to think of that time in her life. One of the things she learned was that a mother would suffer any pain for her child, would even give her life—

indeed she nearly had. "Be strong, be smart, or your child will die." Words that kept a woman going, that taught what she must know. And when her child lived, she believed in herself.

From terror, pain, and the struggle to survive had also come good: the grandfather Ehr, with his love and wisdom. Seasons alone with Kai El in the cave hidden behind the waterfall—to teach, love, and know her son as no Shahala mother ever had.

It all seemed marked with Destiny's handprint.

Still, it was hard to forgive Tor for what he'd done to them. But Ashan loved her soulmate enough to forgive him; he was young, and just a man. Tor had meant to return to the Home Cave by winter. But by autumn, he was a slave. Three summers had passed before she'd seen him again.

*See what dreaming did for him,* Ashan thought.

While they were apart, Tor had found the "Great River" of his dreams. After they were reunited with the tribe, he would praise it to anyone who'd listen:

"Chiawana . . . Mother of Water. Wider than the flat top of Kalish Ridge. Choked with fish. On its shore, a new home for the People of the Wind, Amotkan's favorite tribe, whose old home has died with the dying of horses. A home that does not know hunger, where sunshine and rain are in balance . . ."

If anyone asked about the tribe who already lived there, he would say, "Don't worry. I know these Tlikit. They are simple drylanders. They fear me. I am a god to them."

Ashan pulled a grass stem from a clump beside her and chewed its end. Though it was autumn, there was still a crisp bit of moisture in its fiber. She noticed the wind again.

*Tlikit,* she thought, shaking her head. *What an odd name for a tribe, the sound a tree locust makes. But two bugs caught in the spiderweb of Destiny will share the same future.*

Tor had talked on and on about the Great River, but not much about the Tlikit people. Now Ashan wished she had made him tell her more—maybe she would feel prepared to meet them.

*Raga would know what to do,* she thought. *The Old Moonkeeper had a plan for everything, plans for things that might never happen.*

But Raga died for the last time before this journey began. Her ashes rested in the ancestral burial ground near Anutash. Ashan, the old woman's successor, sometimes felt too young—even at twenty-two summers—to wear the Moonkeeper's robe, and the responsibility that went with it.

*I should be able to talk to Tenka about this. She is the Other Moonkeeper.*

With a sigh, Ashan remembered coming home to Anutash after all that time ... finding Raga near death, and Tor's sister Tenka ready to lead the tribe ... as if Tenka could lead a child.

The Old Moonkeeper had lived long enough to tell the people:

"In the changing world, a tribe needs *two* Moonkeepers, not one. Listen to Tenka. She is the shaman who speaks with spirits. Follow Ashan. She is your chief."

After Raga died, Ashan became "the Moonkeeper," and the tribe followed their new chief. Tenka became "the Other Moonkeeper," but they didn't ask anything of their new shaman. Tenka did her best, but the girl was weak in many ways.

Ashan looked to the darkening sky.

"Raga, we are here at the Great River. What now?"

She waited for an answer. A star appeared, then another. She heard silence, felt cold wind, tasted water in the air. But no answer came. Sometimes, the Old Moonkeeper's spirit would visit her, but on this twilight at the edge of the new beginning, Raga chose to be somewhere else.

The Moonkeeper Ashan returned to the desolate spot on the plains where her people would spend the night, and walked among them to see that all was well. Women were doing the work of evening. Tor sat with a group of men, talking about the end of the journey, the Great River, the tribe called Tlikit—new land, new life, new brothers and sisters—what would it all be like? Ashan heard relief, anticipation, and fear in their voices.

In the center of the camp, where they would sleep together, the little ones played a quiet guessing game with Tenka.

*Yes,* Ashan thought, *there's my boy.*

The best-looking child ever, his mother was sure. Kai El was five summers—hard to believe—little ones grew so fast.

His sturdy body reminded her of a little oak tree. His face was still baby-pudgy, but he could get a determined look in his dark eyes and the set of his mouth. Or he could melt her with baby love eyes and flower bud lips.

Mother and son smiled at each other as she walked by. She would have liked a hug, but he was too old for that in front of his friends.

Tor had put their packs and travel poles a short distance from the others. Ashan took sleeping skins from the packs—a huge grizzled bear from his for the bottom, a smaller black bear from hers for the top. It would be good to nestle between the furs and rest. But the load on her travel poles had come unbalanced. There would be enough to do in the morning without having to repack them.

Travel poles were made from two long, slender trunks of light, flexible alder. Short pieces held them apart. Leather straps spanned the open space. A person's belongings and a share of the tribe's were heaped on the straps and tied down. Once only warriors pulled travel poles, but on this journey, there was so much to carry that all but the youngest and the oldest pulled them.

Ashan's travel poles—lighter than some, more important than any—carried the tribe's sacred things.

She untied the knots in the leather ropes. It felt good to hold familiar treasures in her hands. They gave her strength. The white tail of Kusi, the Horse Spirit, given to the First People in the Misty Time. The ceremonial robe of furs and feathers in its painted horseskin cover. A bear skull with the time balls of long-dead Moonkeepers. Rattles of deer hoof and turtle shell; bird wings, throwing bones, and other pieces of magic. Many kinds of medicine; not knowing what this land would provide, she'd brought all she could. She also had the tools of a woman: baskets, bowls, plates, cups, blades, grinding and scraping stones.

She finished repacking and lay back on the bearskin, snuggling into softness.

It was almost dark when Tor came. He stood over her, hands on hips, smiling like a man who had found a herd of mammoths long after people thought they died out. Here he was, right at the edge of his dream. Had Ashan ever seen him look happier?

"Hello, my love," he said in a lustful voice.

"Hello, Sweetmate," she answered in the same tone. She was tired, but that special energy stirred in her.

"You look like a flameflower to a hummingbird," he said. "I'm the hummingbird, and I'm starving."

"You don't look like a bird to me. You look like a *man*." She said *man* as if there was nothing better. And was there?

Tor slowly untied the laces of his shirt and shrugged it off. After all this time, Ashan still loved looking at his body.

"Mmm," she said. "That broad chest, all curves and shadows and lines. Those shoulders, those muscles. Those arms."

She loved saying these things, and he loved hearing them. Bending over to show his firm rear, he took off his leggings, and flexed his thighs. The wind played with his loinskin.

"Had enough watching, woman?"

"I will never have enough."

He lay beside her, and pulled the bearskin over them so only their heads were showing. She felt his body heat through her leathers. His hands crept over her skirt until they found a way inside. He stroked her thigh. The tingling energy in her lower belly turned to heat. His hand moved up and touched her with the practice of a longtime mate.

"Turn on your side," he whispered.

"It isn't dark yet."

"Close your eyes. Then it's dark."

"People will see us."

"Danger makes it even better."

She turned on her side, pulled up her knees. Tor snuggled close behind, holding her tight, fondling her breasts. He entered her, moving slowly, deeply, until the silent explosion came.

Waves were running through her body and her head was spinning, when she heard a voice.

"Moonkeeper?"

She sat up, cleared her throat.

"Mosscakes, Moonkeeper?" Tashi asked. "There's meat from yesterday's kill, but you said no fire. And these grass stems? I picked them for you."

"Thank you, Tashi," Ashan said. "You are kind."

When the woman left, Ashan said to Tor: "All that water, so close, and my people have to chew grass for their thirst."

"It's almost over, my love. I promise."

He had said those words before. But this time she did smell water in the air.

# CHAPTER 3

BEFORE IT WAS COMPLETELY DARK, ALHAIA THE MOON arose—huge and glowing, dusty golden, in the way of a full autumn moon—soon after Kai, the Sun, descended, taking with him what little warmth he'd given.

Close to Tor under furs, leaning against travel poles, gazing at the wide sky filling up with stars, Ashan didn't mind the cold.

"This Great River," she said. "How far is it?"

"What does your nose say, oh chief who understands the languages of nature?"

"Be serious, Tor. How far?"

"You cross a few more hills. Then there it is, down in a gorge." His voice softened with memory. "A trail takes you down to the place where we'll live. I named it Together Teahra. I wonder if the Tlikit still call it that?"

"Maybe they don't live there anymore," Ashan said, thinking that would be fine with her.

"Teahra has everything. They wouldn't leave."

"Maybe we should wait. Or go up the river, or down the river. Settle somewhere else. Leave the Tlikit alone."

"Ashan, our dreams were different, but they had the same end: people of both tribes living together at the Great River."

"I know, Tor. But how will we get them to *want* to live together?"

"That I don't know."

Ashan shook her head, annoyed. "Where are your promises now? How much help are you going to be? You lived with them. I thought you'd know more."

"I haven't told you everything," he warned.

Without ever speaking of it, both knew there were things Ashan wouldn't want to hear. So she asked questions carefully, learning enough to make a plan, while not learning anything that would hurt her heart.

"How many are there?"

He had to think. "About ten hands."

"What about guards?"

Tor shook his head. "They think they're the only people in the world. Even if they wanted to, the place is impossible to guard. There's more than one way through the cliffs."

*Good for now,* Ashan thought. *Bad for later.* If the Tlikit couldn't guard Teahra, how could the Shahala?

"These Tlikit people . . . are they good, or bad?"

"A hard question. I have seen kindness and savagery."

"What makes the difference?"

Tor shrugged. "There was much about them I never understood. At first they treated me like a god, even called me by the name of one: Wahawkin, the Water Giver, a trickster, like Coyote Spirit. They believe this Wahawkin stole the water from the lake where they lived."

Ashan said, "I always thought it was strange that anyone could look at *you* and see a god."

"I don't think it's so strange," he said. "But later, they turned mean and used me as a slave. I would have died if one of their little ones hadn't helped me escape."

Ashan doubted it. "People might argue and fight, but they don't kill each other . . . except for man-eaters . . ."

"You don't know them."

"I'm trying. But you only told me good things. You never said they were killers."

"I'm telling you now: I would have died at their hands. That's why I took the boy with me when I got away."

"How many did they kill when you were there?"

"None. But I think they would have killed him for letting me go."

She still had trouble believing such a thing.

"I wonder if they still want to kill him?" she said. "It was two summers ago."

"I hope not, but I don't know. Once you make people that angry, it might take more than time to forget. That's why we have to be careful about how we do this."

Ashan nodded. "So. Our new brothers and sisters, with their mix of good and bad—"

Tor interrupted in a firm voice.

"Listen, Ashan: This is what we must do. I know a way down into the canyon, so they won't hear us coming. We'll wait until they're full from eating, then walk right up on them. Can you imagine how shocked they'll be to see the whole Shahala tribe? With our warriors in front, fierce with paint, showing our weapons? We are sixteen hands; they are fewer than ten. They're smart enough to fear us."

"That's a terrible idea. One hand should not be made to fear the other."

"You don't understand how simple they are. How different from us. You never know what they'll do. We must use the strength of how many we are, until they accept our ways."

"But the spirits say we must work together, like bees in a nest, or geese in a flock."

"You may understand this, my love, but no one has told the Tlikit."

"I am the Moonkeeper of Amotkan's favorite tribe. I refuse to lead my people down there like a tribe of man-eaters. What about Elia? He could go first and tell them about us. He'd do anything for you."

Tor sighed. "I know."

Elia was the boy who had helped Tor escape from the Tlikit tribe. The Shahala thought he was just a lost boy who wandered into Anutash one day, but Tor had told Ashan the real story.

The Tlikit called one child the "kicking child," and treated him almost as a slave. His name was Chimnik, their word for "spoiled food." When he and Tor were free, he changed his name to Elia, Shahala word for "friend." He and Tor became close as they searched for Ashan and Kai El. When Tor lost hope, he left Elia near Anutash for the Shahala to find.

Never loved by his own people, Elia was loved by his new people as if he'd been born to them. Most of all by the one who took him to raise: Tor's father, Arth. Elia helped fill the hole in Arth gouged out by the death of his second son Beo at the hands of man-eaters, and deepened when his mate, Luka, had chosen to stop living.

Elia loved Tor and would do anything for him.

"Well," Ashan said, "what about sending the boy?"

"I can't. They still might want to kill him."

"What kind of people would kill children?"

"Tlikit people."

Ashan sighed. "Oh, Tor . . . how will this ever work?"

"I know another way," he said. "I will go alone."

"No."

Ashan would not send her beloved mate into the village of savages with no magic to protect him.

"If this is not work for a Moonkeeper, what will ever be? When the sun rises, you and I will go together."

The round moon crept up the sky and began its descent. The long night was silent, but for the keening wind and the distant cries of a coyote.

Ashan could not sleep. Warm under bearskin, she snuggled against her mate, enjoying the firmness of his muscles, and the way his backside fit the curve of her stomach—feelings to make her forget almost anything.

But not tonight. Worries about tomorrow crawled through her mind like cave bugs through bat dung.

She could tell that Tor was awake by his uneven breathing.

"Sweetmate?" she whispered.

"Mmm?"

"You say it isn't far, this Tlikit village?"

"No, it's not."

"Could you and I walk there tonight?"

"We could."

"Can we see where they live without them seeing us?"

"Yes. Do you want to?"

Tor waited for her answer, but the word "yes" stuck in her throat.

The *Moonkeeper* must protect her tribe, and it might help

if she could see what they faced. But it troubled the *mother* to leave her son ... her baby, she still thought of Kai El, though he was five summers now.

*We were away from people all that time; everything to each other; never apart. I would die without him.*

Ashan knew she shouldn't worry. The Shahala valued and protected little ones above everything, because they were the future. Out here in the tabu land, they slept in a cluster at the center of camp surrounded by their elders. But still ... she would never be comfortable with Kai El out of sight, had come too close to losing him.

Ashan pictured the heap of little ones: tangled arms and legs, some heads showing, some hidden under sleeping skins. *Like the litters of ten coyotes, she thought. No telling which pup is mine.* She took a deep breath and sent a thought to Kai El: *Amah will be back soon.*

"I want to go," she whispered to Tor.

"Make yourself warm," he said.

She looked at the moonbright sky. In autumn and winter, clear nights were the coldest.

"I will," she said.

Under the cover of the bearskin, Ashan pulled on leather moccasins and leggings, and a rabbit pelt robe with the fur inside. She had to get out to lace and fasten, and nearly froze by the time she finished. The wind snatched her hair, so she tied it with a thong and tucked the ends into her robe. She wrapped a fox pelt around her head and neck. Finally, she was warm.

She gazed at the tribe.

"Look at them: Unmoving mounds. How can they sleep with tomorrow's unknown hanging over them?"

"People have a Moonkeeper to do their worrying for them," Tor answered, fastening his bison robe.

The Moonkeeper and her mate left the camp and headed in the direction Warmer. They hadn't gone far when moonlight fell on a path.

"Right where I remembered," Tor said.

"I guess they still live here," Ashan said, looking at trampled grass.

"I never doubted it. Why move? As I told you, everything is here that could ever be needed."

Holding hands, they walked along the path, absorbed in their own thoughts. Aromas of water and fish grew stronger. Ashan sniffed for smoke, was glad not to find it . . . a good sign the Tlikit were sleeping.

The wind died suddenly, as if speared. It had been with them for so long that its absence was eerie, a silence broken only by the occasional barks of a coyote. They crested another hill like the rest—except that Ashan saw no hills beyond. The moon-washed grass of the plateau gave way to flat, rock-strewn ground. They walked on, and suddenly they were standing on a cliff—

*—at the edge of the world!*

Ashan dropped her staff and it went clattering down. She swayed, would have fallen, but Tor had his arm around her.

"Oh Amotkan," she gasped.

"The Great River," Tor whispered. "For so long I've wanted you to see this."

Bands of moonlight shimmered on black water so wide she couldn't see any edges, except one far below, where waves lapped the dark shore. Great herds of fish swam against the current, taking no rest even at night . . . glistening silver specks dipping up and down, breaking the moonlight into splinters that quivered and formed themselves whole again.

"So many!" she said. "They must be huge to be seen from up here. Are they salmon?"

"They are, and they fill the river in all seasons."

She shook her head in wonder.

Tor pointed downriver. A tongue of land pushed into the water. Ashan saw the glow of a used-up fire.

"Teahra," he said in a voice soft as a dream. "See how the cliffs curve round to protect it?"

She wondered where the huts were.

Tor seemed to know what she was thinking. "Someday it will be a great village with many huts. Right now, the people sleep in a cave—see the dark slash? It's long and low, a good cave, except for the smell, and a nose gets used to that. The wind can't—"

A howl ripped his words away.

The hair on Ashan's neck stiffened. She'd heard this coyote before. Closer than ever, it seemed to be stalking them. But why? Coyotes didn't follow people. Known by legend as both trickster and friend, songdogs traveled in families. Why was this one alone?

Tor went on as if he hadn't heard it. "Our people will never know hunger again."

Another howl, closer yet. Then eager yips.

Ashan whirled around. She saw nothing but moonlit ground strewn with rocks too small to hide a coyote. The yipping died away, leaving the night air thick with silence, heavy with power.

Her voice shook. "Why would a coyote stalk us?"

"What are you talking about?"

"That coyote! It's been following us! It's right over there!"

She pointed a shaking finger. The howling started again. It rolled on and on, longer than any coyote ever howled. Noise grew to pain. Ashan covered her ears, but the sound sliced through her hands and pierced her heart like a porcupine quill made of cold stone. A scream rose in her throat. If the beast didn't stop, Ashan would start howling with it.

But it stopped. Thank Amotkan!

The silence roared.

"You didn't hear that?"

"What?"

She shrieked, "What's wrong with you?"

"What's wrong with you, Ashan?"

But she could not answer.

Two lights blinked on in the night, a stone's throw away. Fist-sized, pale green, bright as chunks of sun, the light balls bobbed above the ground, as if thinking—then hurtled, faster than shooting stars—growing huge—coming straight for her face. She saw eyes in the lights—hot, burning eyes—and a black nose, and lips curled back from white, sharp teeth. Coyote Spirit!

Shoving Tor away, she backed up and plunged into empty air. Falling free, she screamed the trickster's name.

"Spilyea!"

The creature of light slipped under her, a sling to cradle a birthing baby, slowing Ashan to float like a leaf above a storm. A point of rock reached out and caught hold of her robe. She began sliding, tried to grab—

Ashan knew no more.

# CHAPTER 4

*THIS CAN'T BE REAL!* TOR THOUGHT. *I MUST BE dreaming!*

A moment ago, Ashan had been here beside him at the edge of Chiawana's high gorge. Then, terrified by—*by what?*—she pushed him away—fell—

Her screams echoed up from the dark canyon.

"Speeel-yea-a-a!"

"No!" Tor cried. "No-o-o!"

Their mingled terror bent the night.

Sounds from below silenced him: a heavy thud, a clatter of rocks . . . then nothing but riversound.

What did she see that sent her backward off a cliff, to her *death.* No, he would not think that word! Moonkeepers did not die like other people.

*Everyone dies!*

"No!" he shouted at the voice inside. "Moonkeepers go to the spirit world many times before they die for the last time!"

Tor went after her. Like a six-legged beetle, he scrabbled down the dark, steep canyonside. He saw nothing but a picture in his mind—*Ashan*—the one he couldn't live without—though Amotkan knew, he had tried.

Down, down, with his hands and feet doing the thinking—

His moccasin nudged something soft—

Flesh—

Tor jerked to one side and stepped onto a ledge, mumbling thanks that it had stopped her fall halfway to the bottom. Still—he swallowed, staring up at the clifftop, black against the starry sky—she had fallen a long way, must be a crumpled heap of broken—there was her robe, he'd have to get it—

He smelled her blood, made himself look.

Ashan lay in deep shadow on a narrow shelf of rock. Her back was bent over the edge, head and arms hanging, long hair adrift. A puff of wind or a bug landing on her chin would snatch her from the ledge and send her flying again.

Tor crept out and pulled her to safety. Blood from the back of her head slicked his hand and oozed through his fingers. She was limp. He couldn't tell, and feared to know, whether she was breathing. He held her to his chest, moaning, "Oh Amotkan, oh Ashan," because he knew his mate was *dead*. No. Terribly hurt. Her skin was so cold. He got her robe and bundled her up. She didn't move.

Tor prayed for spirits to help him, and they did. Carrying her in his arms with his back to the rugged cliff, feet lashing out blind, stumbling and sliding, he reached the riverbank. She never moved. He laid her on moonlit gravel and smoothed her blood-matted hair. His tears splashed her face. He stroked them away, murmuring, like a song or a prayer:

"Ashan, my love, after all we've been through, you cannot leave me now. I need you. Kai El needs you . . . your baby, think of him. And the people . . . with no Moonkeeper, Shahala and Tlikit will fight like black and red ants who live too close. Oh please, Ashan—"

*You're pleading with something that isn't there,* said a pain-sick voice in his mind. *She's dead.* But he refused to believe it, though her eyes were closed, her lips were slack, and she was limp as soaked moss. *She's dead.*

"You're alive, Ashan. You are."

Tor's voice connected them. His voice would keep his love alive. He wouldn't stop until . . .

"I will *never* let you go."

Surrounded by sleeping little ones, Kai El lay awake, gazing at his favorite star group, Soaring Hawk. He was worried. Amah and Adah had gone somewhere. Amah had thought-spoken: They would be back soon. But the boy was young, only five summers, so it was hard not to worry. Why would they leave in the night? What if they never came back? Kai El, who had grown up without a tribe, loved them more than other little ones loved their parents. Especially his mother. What if—

He heard screams far away—Amah! He shook the boy next to him, who was older and smarter.

"Wake up!"

"I heard!" Elia said. "Let's go!"

Wriggling from the pack of sleeping little ones, Kai El and Elia dashed toward the memory of the scream. By the time Kai El realized he should have gotten warriors instead of another boy, it was too late to go back.

They found the path, and ran along it until the ground plunged away. Kai El dug his toes in. He stood at the edge of the world, shaking his head, staring down—*way* down— at what? He squeezed his eyes shut, opened one—but it was still down there—a monster with no end—flat, dark, shiny—

Kai El gulped. "Blood."

Elia chuckled, forgetting the terrible reason they were here.

"Water. Great River. I live here before."

A sorrowful moan rose from below.

"It's Adah!"

"Tor need us!" Elia said, going over the edge.

As Kai El followed in darkness thick as face paint, fear chewed his guts. He hugged smooth stone with the whole front of himself. Fingers jammed into cracks. Toes dug into unseen crevices. He groped around heaps of boulders, clambered down slides of shale—hard going—full of scrapes, bumps, and stubbed toes. At times the older boy had to catch the younger one as he slid by.

Hearts pounding, chests burning, with still a long way to go, they stopped to rest on a narrow ledge. As his ragged breathing slowed, Kai El smelled his mother's blood. She had been here. Where was she now?

He looked down at the moonlit riverbank and saw them: Amah lying still, Adah weeping over her. Kai El's hope crumbled, and his bravery. He heard Shahala voices from the cliff-top above. Thank Amotkan, his people were coming. Kai El was only a little boy—shaking, weak, more scared right now than he'd ever been—just a little boy who needed his mother. And she was dead. He knew it because no thoughts came from her.

His father? Adah's mind must be ruined, for he babbled over and over, "You are alive."

Clearly, Amah was not.

The Moonkeeper's screams jerked many Shahala people awake, one of them Tenka, Rising Star, the supposed-to-be *Other* Moonkeeper.

She sat straight up and clapped her hand over her mouth. *Oh, Amotkan! If anything happens to Ashan, I'm not ready!*

Tenka could heal, and speak with spirits; knew plants, animals, seasons, rituals, and laws. She knew about magic, but it was not her friend. Either it failed when she needed it, humiliating her—or worse, sometimes she couldn't stop it. More than once, she'd nearly killed someone she only meant to frighten.

*The people will never follow someone who can't use magic!*

She covered her ears against Ashan's screams.

"Oh," she moaned. "I'm only thirteen summers—"

*TENKA!*

Dead Raga's voice inside her head stopped panic. Tenka took deep breaths. Ashan stopped screaming. Shock and fear swept the camp on the barren plain as if it were a kicked-over anthill, as people got up and ran around, shaking others awake.

Tenka, the Other Moonkeeper, knew she must take control. One of Amotkan's earliest lessons was that a tribe must have a leader to survive.

Though she had warmer things, she chose the garb of her position—a dress of fox fur sprigged with falcon feathers—and short moccasins that didn't need lacing.

"Warriors! Follow me!" she commanded with a thrust of her staff, as she leaned into the wind and ran off in the direction of the screams.

The warriors took up their weapons and followed—not because they thought she must be obeyed, but because they

were afraid. They'd lost Ashan once before, and the Time of
Sorrows had almost destroyed the tribe.

Tenka stood on the canyon rim gaping at the endless water,
the moonlit riverbank . . . two people . . . Ashan lying on her
back, Tor squatting next to her.

Fear emptied the girl's mind of thought. Loneliness emptied
her heart of courage.

The warriors panicked.

"The Moonkeeper is dead! We are doomed!"

Tenka bit her lip, then spoke to the fastest runner.

"Ashan needs all the people. Go get them."

Deyon disappeared. The rest of the warriors followed the
Other Moonkeeper down the cliff like a hatch of spiderlings.

At the riverbank, Tenka hurried to Ashan. Quiet as death,
she lay face upward to the waning stars; head toward the
river, feet toward the sacred mountain, Pahto—the wrong
way for healing.

Tor was squatting by Ashan—head down, rocking back
and forth, mumbling.

Warriors bunched up around them.

Tenka dropped to her knees. "Ashan!"

Ashan didn't move. Afraid of what she'd feel, Tenka
touched the Moonkeeper's cheek; it was warm. She picked
up a limp hand, found a weak throb in the wrist.

"Our Moonkeeper lives."

"Thank Amotkan!" a warrior said.

*But barely!* Tenka thought. *Unconscious; pale; breathing
so faint her chest doesn't move.*

"Get back," Tenka said. "You're stealing her air."

Tor had not even noticed them.

"Alive, alive . . ." he muttered, like a fool or someone in
a trance.

"What happened, Tor?"

"Alive—"

"Tor!"

Tenka shook him. He swatted her away with no more notice
than he'd give a mosquito, and went on with his stiff rocking.
She slapped him. He looked at her, brows pinched, the pain
of his heart running out his eyes—staring at his own sister

as if he should know her, but didn't; as if he should understand her words, but couldn't.

"Tor, she'll be fine. She journeys in the spirit world as Moonkeepers do."

He went back to rocking and mumbling.

Tenka bit her lip—her big brother—wise, brave—useless as a sixth toe. Useless as Ashan.

As the sky lightened with morning's approach, the Other Moonkeeper spoke to the warriors, hiding her sense of abandonment under her best chiefly voice.

"We must begin the ritual of protection. Find power stones shaped like your love for Ashan."

The Shahala warriors turned to go.


Forty-eight people slept in a cave by the Great River. They called themselves Tlikit, which meant People of the Lake, because there had once been a lake where they used to live—though not in any of their lifetimes.

A Tlikit woman named Tsilka awoke with screams in her ears ... faraway and faint screams, long and awful, like a woman having a hard time dying. Then silence.

*Just a dream,* she told herself.

Others were whispering, getting up, going out of the cave.

*They worry about everything.*

The twins woke up, wanting her breasts.

"No," she said. "Back to sleep." She held them close and tried to sleep herself.

Tsilka was twenty-one summers, the daughter of Chief Timshin and a forgotten woman who died in birthing. The brother she thought of as Wyecat the Weak was twenty summers, with a different mother, also dead. When their father the chief died not long ago, it had been easy to take the power that should have been Wyecat's: he'd always been afraid of his sister, for good reasons.

Tsilka was as much a leader as anyone had ever been, but the Tlikit tribe still did not accept her as a *real* chief. She was only a woman, after all.

*But smarter than anyone,* she thought. *Strong and healthy. And good to look at.* Once a man named Tor, the father of her babies, had told her so. Even though their love had come to a horrible end, she always remembered that.

*You are good to look at, Tsilka, with a body that—*

"Tsilka! Come out here!" someone said.

She would rather have stayed in the cave, safe in the dark, holding her little girls. But if she wanted to be chief—

Tsilka told the twins to stay, and went out.

The People of the Lake stood on the moon-splashed riverbank, peering into the night, listening. Silence—except for Chiawana's low-throated murmur—so ever-present that Tsilka barely noticed it. She did notice the lack of wind—that was unusual.

"It was a woman," someone said.

"Too loud," another said. "It must have been a god."

"Ask Timshin's daughter."

They looked at Tsilka.

"How would I know?" she snapped. Being expected to know everything got tiresome.

Tsilka heard the screaming again—or did she? No—it was in her head. Its memory beckoned. As dawn started to argue with night, she set off in the direction Where Day Begins. The Tlikit people followed the one they secretly called Thinks She's a Man, over boulder heaps and around brush mounds, skulking up the Great River to find whatever had screamed.

Strangers!

Tsilka froze like a rabbit in torchlight, one hand over her mouth, the other over her head in a sign that meant, "don't move, don't breathe."

She and her people were hidden in the leftover shadows of dawn. At least for now.

Strangers—more than all her fingers and toes—large, fierce-looking men, or maybe they only seemed so because of the many skins they wore. Each held a thick spear as tall as himself. They looked down with worry at a woman laid out on the riverbank. The woman appeared dead.

A man huddled on the ground by the body; head down, rocking back and forth, as if grief had made him senseless.

A girl was kneeling over the body. She stood and spoke to the men in a voice of authority. Tsilka thought, *She can't possibly be their leader*. But the men listened as if she were.

The girl's words made no sense, so Tsilka just watched her talk. She had bushy hair, a long, serious face, a lanky frame. She wore a lush fur dress tufted with feathers. Always thinking up clever words, Tsilka named her Many Feathers.

Many Feathers finished speaking to her warriors.

*There was something about her words,* Tsilka thought.

The warriors nodded, turned—

Dawn snatched away the remnants of night, exposing everyone to everyone else.

Startled, the strangers looked back and forth from one to another, to the Tlikit people hiding in shadows, to Many Feathers. Clattering rocks announced more strangers coming down the cliffside. Men, women, and little ones reached the riverbank, saw the others of their kind standing and staring. Stopped and stared themselves.

*Like two bison herds, head to head, waiting to see who will make the first move,* Tsilka thought. *But there are so many of them.*

The girl chief held her arms up, as if asking for help from the sky, then spoke to her people. Tsilka knew some of the words, though she couldn't think how.

The strangers walked off in different directions, leaving their chief alone with the grief-stricken man and the dead woman.

*How can they throw away vigilance like an old piece of meat?* Tsilka wondered.

Without another glance at the Tlikit, the tribe of strangers went about their task—whatever it was. There was no Tlikit word for the way they moved—a slow, floating walk. Each one seemed alone with a spot of ground in front of him, but they also seemed together, since they were all doing exactly the same thing. They made low sounds, between humming and moaning. There was no Tlikit word for such a sound made by people together.

Many Feathers tugged the body; she wanted to move it. She tried to get the huddled man to help, but he didn't respond.

Tsilka had a desire to go to the girl and help—a strange desire that she resisted.

Many Feathers pushed and pulled, and finally the dead woman's feet pointed to the river. Satisfied, the girl settled on the ground, picked up a limp hand, and stared into the face with concentration so strong Tsilka could feel it.

Tsilka named the dead woman Longest Hair.

The sun peeped over distant hills. An old woman picked up a stone and turned it over in her hands. Smiling, nodding like it was something special, the old woman touched it to her forehead, and placed it on the ground near the dead one's feet. Other strangers found rocks and solemnly placed them to make a circle around Longest Hair, like the ring of light around the sun when the seasons are changing.

*What are the rocks for?* Tsilka wondered. *How do they know one from another?*

A child of the strangers found the stone she wanted—a large one, bigger than her head. She made a brave effort, but it was too heavy for such a little girl. She kept dropping it, gave up carrying—dragged, pushed, pulled—then sat down in frustration.

The Tlikit boy named Klee went to the little girl, and together, the two children struggled the stone into place.

These children loosed an invisible power that compelled Tlikit to help Shahala, without knowing what they were doing. As people of both tribes brought stones, the circle around Longest Hair grew to several rows.

And so, at the beginning, the people were together.

# CHAPTER 5

At the edge of the Great River Chiawana, the Moonkeeper breathed, but she did not move, hear, or know anything that happened around her.

In a dream, she was sitting on a high cliff, gazing at a forever view of grass and sky. She was alone, but not afraid, for she sensed an unseen watcher in the rocks behind her. She heard a distant noise. The watcher also heard, and charged by her: a beast with bared teeth, bristling fur, vicious bark. Wolfcoyotedog.

She heard: *Nothing born of earth or sky can harm you.*

The dream faded.

Leaving her body on the riverbank, Ashan rose like heat, unnoticed. Interesting to see the flesh down there, looking so dead, everyone so concerned, all of it becoming smaller as she ascended.

A strand like fine sinew connected her to the shell she'd discarded like a worn-out garment. Tor's voice climbed up the strand, plucked at her.

"You cannot leave me now . . ."

But Ashan was a spiderling caught on a breeze, spinning out an invisible web, carried ever higher, knowing no more than a young spider knew where it was going, nor any more caring. As she drifted through the colors of dawn and into the blackness beyond, the world shrank behind her.

A distant point of brilliance showed her the way.

The Light.

Still Tor reached her, ever so faint: "You are alive."

Ashan's spirit laughed. *Oh, Tor! Of course I'm alive! More than when flesh bound me, more than you ever dreamed of being, more than any creature who ever lived!*

The Old Moonkeeper Raga joined her flight. Ashan knew her Spirit Mother by a new sense—not sight or touch, sound or smell, but all these and more.

*Raven Tongue,* she thought, *I love you.*

*I love you, Whispering Wind.*

Presently Ashan wondered, *Why are we here?*

*We are Moonkeepers,* Raga replied.

Beyond stars the Moonkeepers flew: through light that didn't blind them and heat that didn't scorch them; by clouds of colored dust and swirls of ice specks glittering; past silent voids and rivers of sound. Always toward the Light, whose rays were love.

On her own, Ashan might not have known when to stop, but Raga did.

*The home of Amotkan. We will go no farther.*

There was only light in this part of the sky—no stars, no sounds, no smells. But it was not an empty place. Ashan felt power. Amotkan was everywhere, but would remain invisible to protect the puny visitors.

From the Creator's home far away in the sky, Ashan looked down on a frozen world—a world without people, or any living things—nothing but ice.

*The Beginning of Time,* Raga said.

Ashan blinked, and then she saw people, uncountable as migrating birds.

*The First People,* Raga said. *Our ancestors.*

Had there ever been that many people? If the Shahala were like the seeds in one head of grass, then the ones below were the seeds in all the heads of grass in a meadow. It would take days to walk from the first person to the last.

They snaked along a passage between tall mountains of blue-white ice. They must be freezing, and starving. How could there be any food in that frozen land? Yet the First People seemed happier than people could be.

*Children of the same Father,* Raga said.

Another voice filled Ashan—thunderous, yet soothing—a voice with all the power and knowledge of creation:

*In the Beginning, the people were one.*

Ashan understood. Her destiny was greater than she'd thought, and far from finished. Bringing the two tribes together had been the easy part. Making them into one, in the way of the First People, would demand everything she possessed.

# CHAPTER 6

L IKE A TADPOLE IN ITS BUBBLE, ALONE AMONG MANY, Kai El walked along the Great River searching for a rock with special power. But he felt more like kicking rocks than looking for one.

*She's dead! What will a boy of only five summers do without a mother? Would somebody tell me that?*

*No, no, Kai El,* he said to himself, *she's not really dead. She's the Moonkeeper, who can die and live again, like other people go to sleep and wake up. So they say.*

He didn't understand this rock-finding medicine, but he wanted to do right, and that meant *not* thinking bad thoughts. Too young to have his own song, he walked in silence searching the ground not just with his eyes, but also with the part of his mind above and between his eyes, and with his heart.

He found his stone, gleaming smooth in rough gravel: a blue-lined white agate, as big as his father's fist. Power stretched from the stone—*pick me up.* Kai El obeyed, and found it solid and heavy, though he could see light through it. His hands tingled. Warmth skittered up his arms.

*Yes,* he thought. *This is the stone, the* only *stone that can show my love.*

The Moonkeeper's son walked to the circle, touched the magic stone to his forehead, and placed it on the ground on the side of her heart. He didn't look at her face. He was afraid of what he would see. Looking at the sky, he silently prayed to the spirits he knew best, Sun and River, for whom he was named.

*Warm her. Make her strong. She's not just the Moonkeeper of these people. She is my Amah.*

Kai El thought the spirits heard him. He thought his mother heard him, too. If he had courage enough to look at her face, he believed he might see her smile.

The boy had done all that he could for his mother. He went back to Elia, hiding behind the boulder where he'd darted when they first saw the tribe of strangers.

He nudged his friend.

"Go find a rock. The Other Moonkeeper said Amah needs all of us."

Elia shook his head. Kai El smelled fear.

"How can you be afraid of your own people?"

Elia crossed his arms over his chest, frowning.

Kai El was sorry for his words—his friend had talked about how they had beaten him. But still, Tenka said everyone must help.

He squeezed Elia's arm. "This is important. Amah needs you, or she will die. Your people will see you sometime."

"Not now."

"If you don't go by yourself, I'll push you!"

Not that he could—Elia was much bigger—but he was getting angry enough to try. Kai El made a fist and shook it.

Elia opened his medicine pouch and took out a stone: white with blue lines, like the one Kai El had found, but small as a baby's hand.

"I take when leave here many seasons gone. Look, I carve."

Kai El leaned closer. He could see the rough shape of a bear. Elia touched the fetish to his forehead, put it in Kai El's hand, and closed his fingers over it.

"Courage of bear. Give Moonkeeper."

"I'm sorry I yelled," Kai El said. "We must be spirit brothers. I found the same kind of rock."

Kai El went to the medicine circle and placed the rock near his own.

"The bear's courage," he said. "From Elia."

He took a deep breath, and looked at her. The earth color

of her skin said she was asleep, not dead. Remembering the grandfather, Ehr—and the ash color people turned when they died—Kai El began to believe she would be fine. He wished he could touch her, just to be sure, but he knew Tenka wouldn't let him.

From the hiding place behind the boulder, Kai El watched his people, and these *other* people, all wandering around in a trance.

He was not surprised to find strangers here. Amah and Adah had told the tribe that another tribe lived at the Great River. Kai El even knew their name: Klikit. What surprised him was how different they looked.

They were almost naked. Hanging down in front from a thong around their waists, men and women wore a woven grass mat no larger than a rabbit pelt. A few had something wrapped around their feet—nothing like good Shahala moccasins. That was all—no leggings, shirts, or robes. Warm in his leathers and furs, Kai El thought how cold they must be. Their dirty skin was dull in the early sunlight. Men and boys had chopped-off hair that stuck out stiff. Women and girls had longer, matted hair. They all had well-fleshed bodies. Some of the women were so fat, with hanging breasts and drooping rears, that he couldn't stand to look at them.

Their puny weapons made him shake his head. Some had short, thin spears. Others had blades or hand clubs with stones on the ends. Many had no weapons.

So different from his people. And yet they were walking around looking for healing stones just like his people were. Kai El wondered how they knew what to do. He wondered if they understood what they were doing.

"Look how they work together," he said, shaking his head with disbelief.

"Not like Tlikit," Elia said.

Kai El didn't know if this was like Shahala people or not—he hadn't been with them long enough to know them. Little ones had been warned to expect trouble when the tribes met. But this working together didn't look like trouble.

Kai El explained it the only way he could: "Amah used magic to bring spirits here."

Elia nodded, but his face showed he doubted such a thing.

* * *

The Tlikit woman Tsilka had been watching the strange ritual as if she were dreaming. Now her eyes were drawn down. Sunlight danced on a nearby rock—not big, but important-looking—made of sparkly bits of silver crushed together. She knelt and pried it loose. It was warm in her hand. As she carried the powerful rock that seemed more than a rock, warmth spread up her arm and spilled into her chest.

Tsilka placed her offering with the others. She stepped back to join the people of the two tribes, who stood mingled, gazing at what they had made.

The medicine circle around the Moonkeeper was finished. The chanting fell away. And everything changed. Kai El thought it was as if the invisible bubble enclosing the riverbank had burst, and the friendly magic called by his mother escaped.

People blinked, looked around, found themselves mixed up with others of a different tribe. With suspicion and fear on their faces, they moved away, seeking their own, joining into bigger and bigger clumps, separating—the Shahala on the upriver side of the medicine circle—the strangers on the downriver side.

Whispering, muttering, the strangers looked like they might attack the Shahala.

*Fools!* Kai El thought. *They won't have a chance!*

But what about Amah, lying helpless on the ground? She'd be trampled if people started fighting. What was wrong with Adah? Why didn't he get up and do something?

"Elia," Kai El whined, "they're going to fight."

"I know. I the only one who can stop."

Elia was just thirteen summers, barely old enough to hunt. But he—once Tlikit, now Shahala—was the only connection between the tribes. Kai El understood the older boy's fear, but thought he looked very brave as he stepped from hiding and walked toward his old tribe, arms raised, shouting words Kai El didn't understand because they were in that other language.

The Tlikit people stopped muttering, and gaped at the boy they hadn't seen in three turnings of the seasons.

One came forward, a female with layers of drooping fat.

Kai El wrinkled his nose and stuck out his tongue—why didn't they cover their bodies? He couldn't stop staring at her nakedness, though disgust tried to turn his eyes away.

"Chimnik!" the mean-faced woman spat.

Could *that* be Elia's mother?

Elia-who-used-to-be-Chimnik cowered before the fat, ugly creature. Looming over the boy who suddenly looked much smaller than his age, she yelled—loud, fast, clackety—then struck him.

Kai El could not believe it! Wouldn't a mother be glad to see her missing son?

When the beast started beating his friend with a stick—without thinking of the trouble he was making for himself—Kai El ran at her.

She looked down at him. She was *huge*. She spat on Kai El, and resumed beating Elia.

Kai El grabbed Elia's arm to pull him away, and the woman hit *him*! The Shahala boy had never in his life been struck! He hollered, more from shock than pain.

"Adahhh!"

# CHAPTER 7

TOR BELIEVED THAT ASHAN WOULD USE HIM TO FIND her way back from the world of spirits. He didn't understand how, but he was not going to fail her. Their minds, their very souls, were connected as she journeyed among the stars—so connected that he missed all that had happened since he laid her on the riverbank in the gray light of dawn.

His mind was gone when Tenka brought their people. He was far above the world at sunrise when the tribes saw each other for the first time; missed the ritual of finding stones as morning became day. Even when the spell around the two tribes broke, Tor's mind still did not come back to the riverbank.

It took his son's howls.

"Adah!"

Tor shook off the remains of the trance; glanced around; saw Ashan, sleeping in a circle of stones; Tenka hunched over her—

"Ahhh-dahhh!"

Kai El! Tor looked for his spear, but it wasn't there. He stood, and found himself between two tribes facing each other like bristling cougars.

The Tlikit crone, Euda, was holding two children by the hair, beating them with a stick—Elia—and Kai El!

"Stop!" Tor shouted. Then in Tlikit: "Yah kuut!"

Euda looked up. The two boys broke loose and ran.

Struck silent, the Tlikit people gaped at Tor.

What were they thinking? If they saw Tor, *the man*, their former slave, they might attack him. But if they saw Wahawkin, *the god* they'd once believed him to be . . .

"Wahawkin the Water Giver returns!" he boomed—surprised at how their language came back after so long. "Sahalie the Creator sent me to give you one more chance!"

Euda jabbed her stick in the air. Her ugly flesh shook.

"We know who you are, Tor! You're nothing but a man! Go away! And take these people who hide under animal skins!"

Tor wished he had his spear—he would smash her head. He clenched his fists and took a menacing step forward.

"Stinking woman! I found this place! If anyone leaves, it will be you!"

The crone did not back down. "This is our home, not yours! We will keep what is ours!"

Tor! He'd been there all that time, and Tsilka hadn't known it! It felt like a bird was loose in her chest; her ears buzzed; her head was light. Some old part of her hated the man, but she'd already forgotten that—the greater part had never stopped wanting him.

Tsilka bit her lip—this was no time for passion. The world was coming apart around her like a spiderweb in a windstorm. She had to get control—now. The intruders were too many. If fighting broke out, it would be a massacre.

Tsilka elbowed her way through the snarling mob. She gripped Euda's shoulder, digging her fingernails into fat flesh.

"Do you forget the man-god's power?"

"Man-god!" Euda said, and spat.

Tsilka raised her hand to strike the witch. Euda's chin jutted out and her eyes challenged, but she backed away.

Tsilka looked at Tor again and sighed. Everything else faded from sight but the magnificent creature who stood there looking at her, with long legs spread, hands on hips. A shaggy bison robe made him seem like a powerful, very *male* animal. His flowing black hair gleamed in the sun. His proud face was lean, high-cheeked, and sharp-jawed; with knowing, demanding eyes; long nose with arrogant nostrils; full lips drawn in a faint smile. To see him after so long took her breath away. She imagined his broad chest under the bison robe, his shoulders, his arms; imagined hard flesh under deerskin leggings; her fingernails scratching his back; his arrogance turned to desire.

Forgotten longings shivered inside her. Breathing deep, she went to him. Instead of taking her outstretched hands, Tor held one of his up, palm outward as if to greet a brother. Tsilka bit her lip and lowered her arms. She gazed into his shining black eyes in a way that made men want women. She licked her lips.

"I thought I'd never see you again," she said, and was surprised that her tongue still knew Shahala words.

Frowning, Tor crossed his arms over his chest.

"I told you I would bring my people."

She laughed softly. "We never believed you."

"As you see, I spoke the truth."

"So you did," she said, nodding, then shaking her head. "But I think bringing them was a mistake."

She pointed, first at her tribe, then at his. They were silent now, trying to hear the words of their leaders. But they were stiff and ready to fight.

"Our people don't seem to like each other, Tor. I wonder what you are going to do now?"

Tor looked unsure of himself—a look Tsilka had seldom seen. He took a deep breath, waved his arm toward the ring of stones.

"Ashan . . ." he said, and his voice sounded lost.

*Oh, the look on his face!* Something inside Tsilka broke with awful pain, as the man she loved gazed at another woman in a way she had only dreamed of.

"My Ashan knew what to do, but she's on a journey with spirits. My little sister is the Other Moonkeeper, but I don't think she even knows we're here." He cleared his throat. "It's up to me now."

*Stinking meat!* Tsilka thought, as rage battled searing pain. *It was Tor's other woman, his* Shahala *woman, whose death made him senseless with grief!* Bitterness twisted her as she stared at the body lying in the stone circle.

Something made her wonder if the woman was really dead.

*Longest Hair,* she thought, trying with her focused energy to bore a hole into the enemy's head. *I want this man. If you're not dead already, die now. Do you hear me? Die!*

Tor said, "Tsilka, I need your help."

*Why should I help you,* she thought, but only for a moment. There were many ways to snare a man. A smart woman used them all. Tsilka reached out.

"Take my hand, Tor. You and I must stand together as one, as the leader of all these people."

He just stood there.

"Take my hand," she commanded, "or many will die today."

With his son safe, Tor just wanted to sit by Ashan again, to find her journeying spirit, and be there for her when she was ready to come back.

But Eagle from the Light, Tor's spirit name taken when he was seven summers, also meant Brings Messages. Remembering this, he took Tsilka's hand, not flinching from the sparks it threw into his, and—*no he must not remember when they'd loved like cats*—he thrust their clasped hands high.

"Hear me!" he shouted. "Kah cheat!"

Tor's eyes traveled, striking face after unsmiling face. Suspicion and hostility glared back. Everyone knew him, although in different ways. To the Tlikit, he was a god—or a slave. To the Shahala, he was the Moonkeeper's kidnapper—or the hero who rescued her from man-eaters and returned her to the tribe. *Pride of the Shahala; the Evil One. Water Giver; slave. One woman's mate, another's lover.*

Holding the hand of his greatest mistake, the man who was many spoke in Tlikit.

"Sahalie wants people to spread out in the world and mix their blood, so we do not die out like mammoths and horses. The Creator brought us all here to Mother River to live as one tribe. Reunited—Tlikit and Shahala, children of the same Father, brothers and sisters to each other."

Then he repeated it in his own language, using the name "Amotkan" instead of "Sahalie."

The Tlikit responded with shaking heads, angry looks, grumbles, and snarls; the Shahala with stiff backs, ready spears, the arrogance of greater numbers. Tor saw that many in each tribe did not care what the Creator wanted.

"Listen to him! He speaks the truth!" Tsilka shouted, but it did not stop her people from muttering.

Tor went on in a louder voice, waving his hand—the one not holding Tsilka's—toward Ashan.

"This woman inside these stones—she seems to be dead, but is not. You have reason to fear her. This woman has more power than I. She is the Moonkeeper who speaks with the spirits. She journeys with them now, to talk about this great coming together of tribes. She will be chief when she returns, chief over *everyone*. You will be happy that it is so. You will love her."

At these words, Tsilka stiffened at Tor's side. He released her hand—almost threw it away—glad to be rid of the hot, tight grip of her—and went on about Ashan.

"Like a mother she is to her people, and like a daughter. She is Ashan, Whispering Wind, Song of the People. She is wise, and has enough love for every creature."

Tlikit grumbling brought him to the most important thing they must know about Ashan. At the moment it was the only power Tor had over them.

"You must believe this," he said in a threatening voice. "The Moonkeeper knows magic. *Deadly magic*. She can save your life, or kill you, just by thinking it."

Maybe some believed it, but a tight, angry knot of young Tlikit men stamped away toward their village, hurling words over their shoulders like rocks.

"Go away! You're not welcome here!"

"We're not afraid of a dead woman, or a slave!"

"We will kill you if we see you again!"

Tor said, "Tsilka, stop them."

"Why don't you wake up the dead woman and have her kill one or two?"

Some of the Tlikit were following the angry young men. The Shahala were finding their voices.

"We don't want to live with savages!"

"If we want this place, we will take it!"

"Tsilka, please," Tor implored.

Tsilka squinted up at him. "Oh, all right. For you, I will try."

He didn't trust her, wished he could see what was in her heart as she spoke to those of her people who were still there.

"We are not savages," she said in a loud voice. "We do not have to fight these strangers—not yet. I welcome them."

Holding out her hands, Tsilka went to a Shahala woman standing near her. She smiled warmly.

"People of Tor, I welcome you."

Mani took Tsilka's hands. She hadn't understood the words, but she understood the meaning.

"You are kind," Mani said.

On that bright, cold morning in autumn, the Tlikit who had stayed welcomed the Shahala to the Great River.

Tentative, uncertain, doubtful welcome that it was, Tor felt relieved, even lucky. With Ashan unable to use her powers, he could imagine what might have happened. It bothered him that they'd done it because of Tsilka, not because of him. Had they understood anything of what he'd said about the Creator's plan and Ashan's power? He didn't know, but they seemed to accept each other—*for now*, he realized, seeing the dark thoughts hidden behind some of their smiles.

*At least they won't kill each other today.*

Putting people and their problems out of his mind, Tor went to the medicine circle and stood gazing down.

*Oh, Amotkan . . .*

It took faith to look at Ashan and not choke. She hadn't moved since he found her on the ledge. Her breathing was too faint to see. But her skin was golden with reddish tones, a healthy color. She had never seemed more beautiful to him, or more helpless. He swallowed. *Why now, Amotkan? We have never needed her more.*

Tor sat just outside the ring of stones, with his arms around his knees. He stared at his soulmate, then dropped his head, closed his eyes, and pushed the world away.

*Ashan. Ashan . . .*

Motionless, he tried to recapture the trance between them. But his spirit couldn't find its way out of his body. Even if he could have left himself, only Amotkan knew where to find her now. Fear pricked Tor—she needed him to find her way back—and fear made it even harder to concentrate. He finally gave up, telling himself that a Moonkeeper's death usually lasted three days, and he would have another chance.

It surprised him that the sun had passed the middle of the sky when he opened his eyes again.

He looked at Ashan . . . still the same, except that someone had strung a hide between sticks to give her shade. Standing, stretching, he looked for Kai El, but saw no Shahala little ones. He hoped they had been sent away for safety. The rest of his people and some of the Tlikit were still there. A few were trying to make friends, but most clumped with their own kind—uneasy—hostile.

A voice in his mind whispered, *They need a leader.*

*I don't care. I promised not to leave her.*

He argued with himself. *You must—just long enough to get them settled in the village.*

*But I promised . . .*

*If fighting breaks out, she won't have much to wake up to,* Tor thought, as he lost the argument with himself.

# CHAPTER 8

ENCIRCLED BY THE HEALING STONES, THE TWO MOON-keepers—one hunched over the other—might have looked like one large person. But not to Tor. One was his soulmate; the other, his sister.

*Poor little Tenka,* he thought. As the Other Moonkeeper, Tenka must make sure Ashan had everything she needed on her journey with spirits—a great responsibility for a girl of only thirteen summers—though she'd been trained for it since she was seven or eight.

Tenka was asleep.

"Wake up, Far Away Star," Tor said, using the name he'd called her as a child. He remembered how their mother used to say, "Don't be mean, Tor. Your sister's name is Rising Star." But even Luka had to admit that Far Away Star better described her most of the time.

Tor reached out to touch her. When his hand crossed over the circle of stones, the hairs on his arm stood up. It felt like there was no air inside the circle. The feeling moved up his arm as he reached farther in.

"Tenka, wake up." He shook her, and jerked his hand back into familiar air.

She looked up at him with half-closed eyes.

"Mmm?"

"Where are the little ones?"

"Are they gone? Maybe their mothers hid them."

Tor sighed. How could she lead a tribe when she didn't even know where the little ones were?

"I'm going to take the people to the village now. They need something to do, or they'll start fighting."

"I'll stay here. I'll take care of Ashan. Trust me."

So many refused to take Tenka seriously. With all that had been laid on her young shoulders, she needed her brother's support.

"I do trust you, Other Moonkeeper. Spirits be with you."

*And with you, my love,* he thought, turning away from Ashan.

Tor looked around for Tsilka. He could have used her help, but she wasn't here.

Kai El walked up, pulling Tor's spear along the ground by its point. The boy spoke with pride, holding out the spear that was twice as tall as himself.

"I looked for it. I found it up there."

"Thank you, son. I don't know what I'd do without you."

Tor could not have meant it more. He took the spear and hefted it. Made long ago of oak, hardened by fire, bloodied by many kills, its balanced weight felt good in his hand. It made him more than just a man: With this spear, he was a warrior.

Tor stood tall, bison robe thrown over his shoulder, spear butt in the ground at his side. He spoke in a loud voice.

"It's time for us to go to Teahra Village."

People voiced concerns, but they followed Tor when he walked off. He did not need Tsilka's help after all.

A breeze freshened the bright afternoon. Sheer rocks edged one side of the narrow trail. The water, flowing in the same direction they walked, was close on the other side. People made a long line behind Tor, but he couldn't hear them for the river's voice. How good it was to hear that sound again. He thought of the words "power" and "forever."

The trail widened. The line bunched up behind him, his people eager to see their new home. The trail opened onto flat ground. Cliffs curved back away from the river.

Tor stopped. The view filled his senses. He raised his arms to embrace it.

In the Misty Time, before there were people, River Spirits

could walk if they didn't like where Amotkan put them. Chiawana had done a lot of walking—signs of it were everywhere. Once she had carved a bend from the cliffs, only to abandon it, leaving behind a piece of land shaped like an eye. This was Teahra Village, the place of Tor's dreams and destiny.

*Even better than I remembered,* he thought.

A wall of stone rose at the back—slabs heaped on slabs, looming dark against blue sky, giving refuge from the wind that pushed against the river as if trying to hold it back. The only tree, a huge oak, spread gold-green leaves against the sheltering crags. Bushes of various kinds clumped along the base.

The ancient, fickle river had cut a long, low cave into solid rock. When Tor had come here with Wyecat and Tsilka, they'd slept in the cave. The Tlikit must be sleeping there still. Tor imagined future huts on the flat middle ground of Teahra Village.

At the outer edge, fish-drying racks held their bounty up to wind and sun. Water lapped at a gravel shore. A bit of the shore jutted into the river, like a connected island, ready to catch any driftwood the River Spirit sent.

Back near the cliffs, smoke rose from the village fire. The people sitting around it stood when Tor and his great herd arrived. Others came out of the cave. The seven or eight young men who had stormed off in anger before now approached with raised spears.

*What fools!* Tor thought. He'd done what he had to to keep people from fighting when they were clumped around Ashan. But now, with her safe, he felt strong with his warriors ready behind him. Ashan could worry about making them all into brothers and sisters when she awoke.

"Listen to me!" he said in a menacing voice, and the Tlikit halted their threatening approach.

"This is *my* place," he shouted. "Without me, you would still be living by a lake with no water. I dreamed this place, I found it, and I allowed you to live here. Now it is *ours*. My people will hunt the prairie and fish the Great River, and live on this flat piece of ground. We don't want your cave. The way you live, the way you dress, or don't dress, you need a cave. *This* is what we want." He waved his arm to show the ground just waiting for Shahala huts. "We are here and we will stay. We are many more than you. If you try to fight, you will die. Die!"

He raised his spear to a thrusting position, and felt the tense heat of the Shahala warriors ready behind him.

"We will live *here*," Tor went on, jabbing the butt of his spear in the ground. "And you can live there." He pointed to the cave. "Unless you want to find some other place. Now bring us food. We are hungry."

Tsilka walked up. Tor was glad to see her—which was not a thing he thought he'd ever feel again—even though her face was full of unwanted lust.

"I'm happy to see you, Tor," she said thickly. "I thought you might take your people and fade away."

"No," Tor said. "A man does not fade before destiny."

"Not a man like you," she agreed. She turned to her tribe, and Tor saw the lust in her face change to command.

"Put your spears away! These strangers are hungry, and we are not savages without food!"

Some relieved, others reluctant, Tsilka's people obeyed her. A great variety of food was brought out of the cave. Tor's people ate on and on, washing it down with flavored teas. The Shahala who had eaten mosscakes and chewed grass stems last night kept looking at each other, laughing, saying, "Tor spoke the truth about this place!"

The Tlikit watched the newcomers eat. Some seemed proud of having hunted and gathered it all. Others seemed resentful at being forced to give it away, but they said nothing.

When the Shahala had eaten their fill, Tor spoke in Tlikit.

"We left our belongings on the prairie. You will help my warriors get them. Elia, you go along so they can talk to each other."

After a group of men had gone, Tor and Tsilka talked with the others, putting words in both languages so all could understand. The woman could not hide her lust, but he didn't allow it to distract him. His brain was busy as he tried to keep up with questions in two languages. To Tlikit complaints that they did not have enough food for two tribes, Tor replied that the Shahala were skilled hunters, and soon there would be enough to feed three tribes.

"The Shahala are a people who *like* to share," he said. "Your lives will be better because we have come. We will change this spot by the river where some people live in a cave; we will make it into the fine village that it was meant to be."

Tor knew there would be problems, stresses in learning each other's ways, in understanding each other's thoughts when words weren't understood. Some of the Tlikit would not easily get over resentment that the Shahala had come and chosen to live in the place they thought of as theirs. Many things would have to be worked out in the coming days . . .

Like what to do about the four women who never left a crude shelter against the trunk of the oak tree, unless it was to tend the fire. It took a while, but Tor realized where he had seen them before: They were the forest women he and Elia had spared long ago. They were slaves now. Tor was disgusted, and his people would be too when they realized what slavery meant.

He saw how hard it would be for Ashan to take control without being able to talk to the Tlikit people. Only three knew both languages: Tor, Tsilka, and Elia. The boy would go along with him. As for Tsilka, he would have to keep her wings pinched, like a bug that a man didn't want dead, just flightless.

Night settled on the river village. The slaves made the fire large. Tlikit women offered more food. With full bellies, people settled into quiet talk with others of their own blood— the Tlikit on the downriver side of Teahra Village, the Shahala on the upriver side.

Tor had to return to Ashan. He'd left her for too long with only his little sister and some magic rocks for protection.

But first, he must deal with Tsilka, the she-cat he should have resisted, but to his regret had not—long ago, many times, loving to the rhythm of the river—

Tor told Tsilka to come with him. She eagerly agreed, must think he wanted to make love. He refused the hand she offered. Walking up the riverbank in silence, they came to a flat-topped boulder with its bottom in the water. They had once spent time here, looking at the hills beyond the river, talking about what might be on the other side.

Tor sat down, remembering too late that a rock can hold memories for a man and give them back again, whether he welcomes them or not. This rock offered memories of love-making that should be forgotten. He put all that out of his mind, watching Teahra's fire flicker in the distance, listening to Chiawana's murmur.

Tor spoke in Shahala, the language that Tsilka had once been eager to learn.

"We were lovers, but not in this life."

"What a strange thing to say."

"It's true. The life we had is over. Ashan is my life now. If you ever tell her about us, I will have to kill you."

Tsilka looked straight into his eyes. The firelight made sharp shadows on her face. Her look was one she'd give a stupid child. Her voice wasn't fearful, or desperate—as he'd expected—but sneeringly confident.

"It's not over, Tor. It will never be over."

"Look, woman, I'm telling you—"

"You wait here," she said with a toss of her head. "I will show you."

She got up and headed off toward the village. Tor thought how good her naked bottom looked retreating in the moon-light—all round and firm. He thumped his head, and the unwanted thought fled. Would he never get control of that part of himself?

He drummed his fingers on the rock. Tsilka had better hurry. He was anxious to be with Ashan.

Tsilka strode toward him out of the night, pulling two reluctant children. She stopped before Tor. They hid behind her.

"Girls?" he asked stupidly—in the moonlight, anyone could see that the naked toddlers were female.

Tsilka pulled them out by their arms, and thrust them at him.

"Your daughters, Tor. Our daughters. While our mingled blood flows in their bodies, it will never be over between us."

"But I never knew!"

"That makes them no less real."

Tor's thoughts tripped over themselves.

*Twins. Creatures of heartbreaking beauty no taller than
their mother's knee.*

He blurted, "Do they know who their father is? And your
people, do they?"

Tsilka took her time, then answered with her nose in the
air.

"I say the god Wahawkin is the father of these girls. No
woman ever birthed one baby right after another like that, so
people believe me. People love them to think that their father
is a god. Maybe even fear them."

*Exactly alike,* Tor thought. *Unbelievable.*

He remembered a Misty Time legend about brothers born
to the same mother at the same time. Hoofed animals were
known to have twins. But human twins? Not since any living
person remembered. Powerful feelings surged through him.
They had *his* blood!

The little girls clung to their mother like outgrown leggings.
They peered at Tor with suspicious curiosity, frowns pulling
on round faces. Dark eyes captured and held him.

"What are their names?"

The proud mother patted one on the head, then the other.

"Tsurya. For the graceful water skimmer. Tsagaia. For the
big tan cat. People say they are the finest children ever born."

Tor could not disagree, though he could have picked better
things to name them for than a bug and a cat.

For a long time he said nothing, allowing his eyes to feast
on the twins as people feasted on the sprouts of spring. Tsilka
demanded no talk, as if she knew that her daughters could
most affect their stunned father in silence.

*Tsurya . . .*

*Tsagaia . . .*

Tor rolled the names over in his mind where they made
pleasing sounds. The girls were like shy sunbeams peeking
through clouds, like sweet water quenching thirst. Moving no
closer, they crawled inside him, grabbed on to something
never touched, and held on talon-tight. What was it about
them that could make him feel like this? It must be that he
was male, and they were female. Precious, fragile, lovable.
Girls who would grow up and be women, who carried the
future within their bodies.

Tor was being overwhelmed by something close to worship. But he *must* think without passion, and *now,* or in an eyeblink he could destroy his happiness, and Ashan's and Kai El's. Tor had experience with the power of will, and he was glad: It would take tremendous will to distance himself from these dangerous creatures.

He said, "It's good that people think these are the daughters of a god. They are that special."

A look of triumph stole onto Tsilka's face.

He went on. "But I don't want people thinking I'm the god Wahawkin. It's too much work to be a god. I think I'll tell them I'm Wahawkin's special friend, and they shouldn't make me angry. That will be enough."

Tor took a deep breath, and when he let it out, sent with it lingering feelings of awe about the twins.

"I cannot be their father, or your mate. I can only say they'll never want anything as long as I'm alive. I promise you, Tsilka. Now you must make me a promise: What you and I did long ago must be kept secret. Forever after forever. I belong to Ashan. I will never be yours."

Tsilka's triumph collapsed, Tor saw it, though she tried to hide the misery taking its place. He left no space in his heart for pity.

"I would never harm your daughters, woman, but I could kill you. And I will, if you do anything to harm Ashan or Kai El. I mean it: I will kill you if I must."

Tsilka said she would keep the secret. But her unspoken thoughts were so strong that Tor could feel them: With all her strength, Tsilka wished, hoped, prayed that Ashan would die.

*As if even then,* Tor thought angrily, *she could have me for a mate.*

# CHAPTER 9

The Shahala knew that there were two kinds of death: The first, last, and only death of ordinary people; and a shaman's death, a temporary kind that came several times in her life, so she could learn from spirits what needed to be known.

While the second death of the Moonkeeper, Ashan, continued, the Other Moonkeeper, Tenka, never left the medicine circle.

*Others can do what they want,* she thought. *I'm not leaving Ashan. When we lost her before, the Time of Sorrows almost destroyed us.*

She heard the voice of Raga in her mind: *Rising Star, think only good thoughts when you are with spirits.*

Tenka sent her mind drifting. Inside the stone circle—wrapped in rainbows, flecked with stars—time flowed like the Great River, with nothing to mark its passing. How long had it been since Ashan's screams started the strange events? Tenka opened her eyes. Upriver, in the direction Where Day Begins, gray softened the sky.

*The morning of the fourth day.*

"Oh please, Amotkan, let it end, I'm only thirteen summers, and I'm so tired . . ."

Tenka realized she was whining out loud. But no one heard. Only Tor and his boy were here. It wasn't light enough to see them, but she smelled them sleeping.

From time to time others had come to the stone circle—
people of both tribes. Staring at the Moonkeepers, they talked
quietly, shook their heads. Tenka pretended not to see them,
and after a while they would leave.

Tor had been here the whole time . . . as he should . . . he
was Ashan's mate.

*Except for the first day, when I thought he'd never come
back.*

Tor had solved the immediate problem by taking people
away—Tenka didn't know where he'd taken them, and didn't
care. But he'd stayed away too long. It got dark. Alone with
lifeless Ashan, and the rumbling of the monstrous river, and
a coyote howling somewhere too near, Tenka had been forced
to fight childish fear. That was no way for a Moonkeeper to
behave, even one called the *Other*.

Tenka wondered *why* her brother had left them. Anything
could have happened—wolves coming up the river, or bats
swooping down from the sky—

The Other Moonkeeper put the fearsome thoughts out of
her mind. She had enough to worry about, just taking care of
Ashan. Tenka had gone without sleep, making sure Ashan
was shaded from the sun and warm under the moon and, most
important, never alone. She dripped water and medicine tea
onto Ashan's lips, taking no nourishment for herself: A hungry
shaman focused at her best.

This was the hardest part: With the power of her mind,
Rising Star must keep Whispering Wind part of *this* world,
so she could find her way back. It wasn't easy. There were
many distractions, especially the strangers with their strange
talk. But as always Tenka did her best. It must have been
good enough.

On the fourth morning of her second death, earthly life
stirred in Ashan . . . a miracle witnessed by Tenka, Tor, Kai
El, and a few others who had just come to look.

Amotkan was gone. Raga was gone. The Shahala Moonkeeper Ashan was alone in the endless sky. It was time to go
back. Ashan smiled at her choice of word, for here, "time"
as people understood it did not exist. Still, she began to pull

in her web, returning through air that was rainshower fresh, taking time to enjoy the marvelous creations she passed.

Ashan saw light outside her eyelids ... not spirit light, or exploding stars, but ordinary morning light. She took long breaths of cold air, sharp with juniper smoke. Heard rivernoise, chirping birds. And voices ... unclear, without threat. She didn't strain to understand. Enough to lie here and enjoy living bone, breathing flesh, warm blood pulsing.

Thoughts ... she could catch only fragments, an end or a middle. Thoughts should be a blend of pictures and words. The pictures in her mind were right, but the words for them were wrong ... not even words she knew, just sounds shaped like words. Her mind was speaking but could not understand itself.

*Am I caught between worlds? Is part of me still out there flying with spirits?*

A picture of her son formed against her lids. *Kai El*, she thought, and word matched picture.

Where *was* her son?

Ashan sat up and opened her eyes. Squinting in the brightness, she saw Tenka staring at her, openmouthed.

*As if*, Ashan thought, *she yah ah itchnikai sees a ghost.* She had to smile: that's just what Tenka was seeing. Ashan didn't know how long she'd been away on her spirit journey, but it must have been long enough for people to wonder if she'd return ... even a shaman eventually died for the last time.

Ashan asked, "Kai El tah ah kahnit?"

Tenka tilted her head, wrinkled her brow.

"Tah ah kahnit ... I mean ... *where is* Kai El?"

"He's, he's—"

"E nai ilutya—" Ashan clapped her hand over her mouth to stop the strange sounds.

"Amah!" Kai El shouted, diving on her, almost knocking her over.

"Ashan!" Tor said, grabbing her up in his arms, crushing Kai El between them. It felt so good that she cried.

People talked at once.

"Those sounded like Tlikit words!"

"Itskaya na tucamo!"

"Impossible!"

Ashan's ears buzzed. The people she recognized spoke Shahala. The others—strangers—spoke a language she'd never heard, but suddenly understood.

"Tor must have taught her!"

"No, I didn't."

"What's wrong with me, Tor?" Ashan asked, relieved that the words came out right.

"I don't know. Somehow you're talking in *both* languages, but all mixed up."

"You mean those clacking noises are Tlikit words?"

"Yes."

Ashan looked at a young woman. The only thing the stranger wore was a waist strap with a woven grass mat hanging down to cover her in front to her thighs.

"Enak ahteak?" Ashan asked. It meant, "Do you understand me?"

The wide-eyed woman said, "Chu," which meant, "Yes."

Ashan shook her head. It was all too much. She would figure it out later.

"Bring people to see this talking miracle!" someone said.

Many came. When they heard Ashan speak—first in one language, then in the other—they were amazed.

That night in Teahra Village, no one was more amazed than Ashan herself. The long journey of her people was over. Teahra Village was better than she'd hoped. The Tlikit were so interesting, she couldn't keep from staring at them—any more than they could keep from staring at her and the Shahala.

But the most amazing thing was happening in Ashan's ears, and her mouth. She tried to explain it to Tor.

"I think of something . . . like water falling from the sky. In one ear, I hear 'rain.' In the other, I hear 'uvia.' Both words are right, depending on if you're Shahala or Tlikit."

Tor shook his head in wonder, as he'd been doing since Ashan came back from her second death.

He said, "You aren't the first to use two kinds of talk. I can do it. So can Elia, and one of the Tlikit women—the one named Tsilka. But it was learned. It takes hard work, and time. Ashan, you have never even *heard* Tlikit words."

"And now I know how to say them all, with spaces and

heaviness where they belong. And I know what the strangers
are saying, no matter how fast they talk."

Tor just shook his head.

"It's the most wonderful gift," she said. "I thank the spirits
who gave it to me."

"It's more than just a gift, Ashan. The knowledge of both
languages is a needle you can use to stitch the tribes together."

Ashan agreed.

Tor said, "Do you know what I like even more? It's *proof*
of what I promised when I didn't know if you would live:
'Forget what your eyes see,' I told them. 'This woman who
is dead will one day be your chief.'"

"Well, I have a better chance at it now." She took his face
and turned it so their eyes touched. "Thank you for your part
in this, Sweetmate. It must have been like walking on a vine
stretched across a canyon."

"Oh, it was," Tor said, smiling.

She kissed him, then said, "Tell me all about it."

A woman who could learn another language without being
taught . . . people much in need of leading accepted it as an
omen of spirit approval, a sign of good times to come. A
relief.

# CHAPTER 10

Several days had passed since the Shahala Moonkeeper awoke from her second death.

"Tor, take me away," Ashan said in a rare moment when she was not the center of a crowd. "These people are like spiders sucking prey. I'm dry, and they still want more."

"Come with me."

Leaving Teahra Village, they walked a trail that followed the river. Chiawana's low-throated rumble took the buzz of human voices from her ears. Tor strode tall beside her, a powerful warrior to protect her from everything. Ashan was a small woman; her head reached the middle of his chest. At times the weight of her duties made her feel even smaller. His arm around her shoulder reminded her that she didn't have to be strong every moment of her life—not as long as she had Tor.

*Raga, you were wrong*, she thought. *The law was wrong. A Moonkeeper can have a mate and still do her work—maybe even do it better.*

Tor turned from the trail, and led her to the water's edge. He spread his deerskin shirt on a flat-topped boulder. They sat close together.

Ashan could still see Teahra. And its people. Two tribes of them. Young and old; alone and in groups; standing, sitting, walking, talking, working. So *many* people.

She had a vision of a bee tree—with something wrong—

the bees swarming around like the mother had forgotten to tell them what to do.

She looked away, and let herself be amazed by Chiawana's tremendous size. Ashan had never seen a river that couldn't be crossed. It shone blue under the autumn sky. Its ancient voice seemed to say, *What is a day in the space of forever?* A breeze lifted her hair. The low sun warmed her skin. She breathed deep.

"Mmmm . . . it's nice here."

Tor said, quite seriously, "I don't think winter comes to this place."

Ashan smiled. "Winter comes to every place."

"Well, autumn was never this warm at home. It's probably already snowing in the Valley of Grandmothers."

She pictured Anutash, with snow covering any sign that people had ever lived there.

"We were right, Tor. If we can't live in our homeland, this looks like a good place."

"We?" he said, smirking. "I'm the one who found it."

"But I'm the one who got our people to come."

"Well I'm the one who kept them from killing each other while you had your nap."

They laughed. Besting each other was a familiar game, with no winner or loser.

It felt wonderful to be alone with Tor. Ashan had been surrounded by people since she woke up—*speaking that language*, she thought, still not used to it. The Shahala wanted to talk to their Moonkeeper about all kinds of things. Some were nervous and wanted reassurance; they didn't know how to act around these *strange* new people. Others shared their excitement—what a good place this was, all the food, the *interesting* new people.

Tor had been kept just as busy by the Tlikit.

"Oh, Ashan," he said suddenly, enfolding her in his arms. He whispered into her hair, "It's so good to be with you. So good." The depth of feeling in his voice said how terrified he'd been of losing her.

"I love you," she said. "I pray we never have to be apart again."

Eyes closed, lips pressed to his muscled chest, nostrils filled with the man-scent that was his alone, she gave herself to his embrace. If she lived to an age of ten women, she would never stop loving this feeling. So warm, so safe, to hide in the cave he made of his body, to be at the center of a warrior's strength and protection.

She murmured, "The longer I love you, the more I love you."

"Not as much as I love you. Everything about me is bigger."

Another familiar game ... arguing about who loved the most. Little memories known only to the two of them ...

It took a long embrace to satisfy them. Releasing her, he put his arm behind her back for her to lean against.

Ashan gazed at the village.

"So many people," she said, shaking her head. "I tried to count them. I sat where I could see the whole place, and spread out a piece of leather. I started with the women. I'd pick one, and put a pebble on the leather—two if she had a cradleboard; then again for each one I saw. But then they'd move, and I'd forget who got counted and who didn't. There are too many, unless I could get them to sit down at the same time."

"What does it matter how many?" he said happily. "There are plenty. Amotkan's plan is for people to spread out in the world. It will take many to do that."

Tor wasn't seeing this the same way she was—not at all.

She said, "A tribe of people may look like a nest of bees, but they aren't. One bee is the same as every other. They all want the same things—enough honey for winter, to protect the nest—"

"Quit talking of pebbles and bees, and say what you mean."

She cleared her throat. "I'm getting to it."

As Moonkeeper, Ashan had been trained to keep worries to herself. There was no reason for secrets between mates, but sometimes the early training got in the way of talking openly to Tor.

She said, "Each person has things they love and hate, and ideas and beliefs all their own. Our people have been learning to live with each other since the Misty Time. Now there's this whole new tribe, each with things they love and hate. All these people, with so much to learn about each other, and they can't talk about it."

"I see what you mean." He laughed like it wasn't important. "You'll just have to sit them down to learn words, the way you tell stories. Then you can even count them if you like. But don't worry yet, my love. The stomach speaks a language everyone understands. The Tlikit have enough to feed both tribes until spring."

"I know. I couldn't believe it," she said, remembering when she'd seen the cache of food for the first time.

The day after she awoke, some Tlikit women had come to her.

"Munkeppa?"

"You may use your own words. I understand them."

Clicking and clacking, they had taken Ashan to their cave. When her eyes adjusted, she saw that it spread out long and low. Only the middle was tall enough for standing. Tor had warned her about the smell, but he hadn't come close. Sharp sweat; dirt and mold; and the stink of body waste, like the tunnel inside Ehr's cave that she'd had to clean long ago.

*How can anyone live with this?* she wondered. *Maybe their noses are just for breathing.*

She forgot the stench when they showed her their stock of dried food, filling a corner that could only be reached on the knees: stacks of slabbed fish in layers separated by woven mats; mat-covered holes in the dirt floor, lined with fish skins, filled with pouches of fish meal; holes with berries and roots and leathermeat.

"It goes all the way back," a woman said proudly.

"Enough for all. We want to share."

"How kind," Ashan said. "These people who have traveled far are hungry. Sahalie is proud of you."

It felt strange to use the name "Sahalie." She hoped Amot-kan wouldn't be offended.

*The Creator has many names,* she heard in her mind. After that, she didn't worry.

Later, as the Shahala people sat around in a haze of well-fed bliss, the Moonkeeper had spoken:

"Hunger has chewed our bellies for the last time. Our old enemy would not dare come to this place. We would beat him with clubs of salmon, bury him under a sturgeon longer than a man. We would deafen him with laughter . . .''

A splash of water brought Ashan back. Tor dabbed at her face. A herd of fish passed in front of them, leaping, showing their silvery rainbow sides, as if they couldn't contain the joy of living. Tor tried to cover her from the splashing, but she pushed his hands away. What was a little water, to see something so great? She laughed and couldn't stop.

After the rainbow fish had gone, Ashan said, ''It's so good to eat all you want. Even if it *is* fish, full of sand from being wind-dried. But who with a full stomach would complain?''

Tor laughed. ''Not our people, not after all those hungry days.''

She watched the quiet water for a while.

''The Tlikit people seem nice. They share. But you know, Tor, they *are* different, and language is just part of it. I may understand their words, but I don't understand *them*.''

''Like what?''

''Like why do they go almost naked, with only those grass things hanging from their waists? Grass is fine for a basket— and the Tlikit do make excellent baskets—but to cover the body, well—it doesn't fit like leather. It doesn't move when they move. It's strange to look at a man's power staff flopping around, or to see a woman's secret when she bends over. And don't they get cold? Or is their skin different from ours? Will they wear leather when winter comes?''

She realized she was babbling, but these questions really bothered her. ''Those things they wear on their feet . . . at first I thought they were made of bark, but it's really thick leather tied on with grass cords. Why don't they have real moccasins? And when I was in their cave, I didn't see any sleeping skins.''

''They don't know how to cure hides.''

''What?'' she said in disbelief.

''That's right. I was going to teach them, but after they made me a slave, I refused.''

''What do they do with hides?''

''Once in a while they cut off pieces and leave them in the sun. They get hard and curl up, and that's what they put on

their feet. Mostly, they throw hides in a stinkpile with guts
and bones, and let them rot."

"How wasteful! How stupid!"

"It's not their fault. Coyote Spirit never taught them. You'll
be surprised at what they don't know, from roasting food in
the ground, to washing smells from their bodies."

"It's a good thing we have a lifetime to do this," Ashan
said. "We will need at least that long."


Against the cliffs, in flat places and on ledges, the Shahala
made temporary shelters with wood from the Great River and
hides brought from the ancestral land.

On a fog-shrouded day—the coldest so far—the Tlikit
people stayed inside their cave.

Ashan approached a group of Shahala women. They sat
with their backs to the cliff, bundled up in furs, passing a
wooden bowl, dipping purple mush into their mouths.

Ashan joined them, and tasted some.

"Mmm. I wonder what these are? They're almost as good
as huckleberries."

"I wouldn't say that," Tenka said. "But they're very good."

Ashan took another bite and passed the bowl.

"We're lucky," she said. "I don't know how much longer
we could have lasted. Little ones and old ones were getting
weak. But with all this food, they're getting fat now."

The women nodded, smiles on stained faces.

Ashan said, "Our new sisters are kind to share their food
with us. I didn't even have to ask them." She paused. "We
came to Teahra Village poor in food, but rich in cured hides."
She hoped someone would get her meaning, but no one did.

"Did you notice that they stayed in their cave today? Do
you know why?"

The women shook their heads.

"It's too cold out here. They don't have anything to wear
except those grass mats."

"Why?"

"Coyote Spirit forgot to teach Tlikit women to cure hides
as he taught Shakana, the First Woman." Ashan didn't mention
the other things Spilyea forgot to teach them.

The Shahala women felt sorry for their new sisters. How could something so *ordinary* as curing hides be unknown?

"It doesn't matter," Ashan said. "What matters is that Coyote taught *us*. We have plenty of hides. They have shared with us. Now we should share with them. When hunting begins in spring, we'll teach them how to make leather for themselves."

"Oh," they said. "We see."

Over her deerskin dress, Ashan wore a robe made from two goat hides. She stroked the long gray fur.

"I'm going to give this to one of them, I think maybe the woman who acts like their chief."

"It's a fine robe, Moonkeeper," Karna said. "Anyone would want it. I have some old moccasins. I will look for a woman whose feet are like mine."

"That would be kind of you, Karna."

Ashan left them discussing things they could give away.

Next she talked to some warriors, who were not so agreeable.

"So," she said after telling them the same things. "The Tlikit have food, and we have hides. They share. We will too."

The men frowned.

She said, "People can live with nothing to wear, but they die with nothing to eat."

"We wouldn't starve here," Lar said, waving his hand at a fresh-killed orak that had come to the Great River to drink.

"Then you'll just have to do it because I say."

The warriors grumbled as the Moonkeeper walked away.

"Coyote forgot to teach them!"

"How much more proof do you want that the *Shahala* are Amotkan's favored tribe?"

Ashan understood why they felt as they did, but she thought this sense of being better might cause future problems.

She turned. "We are the *Teahra* tribe now. In some ways, they will be like our little brothers, but in other ways, we will be like theirs. We are children of the same Father. That is what Amotkan told me, and I am telling you."

Ashan's people gave away furs, leathers, and sleeping skins. Whether they wanted to or not, they did it smiling.

The Tlikit were happy with their new things. Women urged men to go hunting, so they could learn how to cure hides for themselves. Some had their own ideas about wearing skins—people laughed to see a man with leggings on his arms.

A few refused them. "Bad smell," they said. "If it gets *that* cold, we stay in the cave."

Ashan changed her mind about who should have her robe. She cut the goat hides apart and gave them to two of the women who lived out in the open by the oak tree. Her friend Mani cut up a similar robe and gave it to the other two.

To the woman named Tsilka, Ashan offered an old skirt. At first Tsilka acted as if she might refuse it, then she took it—with hard, narrow eyes—as if she were entitled to it.

Ashan thought, *This woman who thinks herself some kind of chief will have to learn that a tribe can have only one chief. Someday . . .*

# CHAPTER 11

In fury, Tsilka climbed to the clifftop, tore off Ashan's leather skirt, threw it to the ground, and stamped on it. Standing near-naked in the Tlikit way, proud and cold in a lonely wind, chin up, feathered hair blowing out behind, dark gold skin oiled and glistening, arms crossed defiantly over breasts, she watched the village below.

The woman who thought she didn't need a friend could have used one today. A friend would have known she was upset and come up here with her, would have asked how all this came about.

"I feel stupid," Tsilka hissed. "Ugly. Gouged, raw and shrieking inside with rage. I feel sick, like I'm being dragged through dung. How am I hiding it? Why don't I vomit from swallowing lies? Why isn't my skin red with the hatred burning me up?

"I was happy before they came. I had my daughters. I had people coming to me, treating me like the chief I was born to be. I didn't have Tor, and I didn't care. But now that I see him every day, how I care!"

She snuffled and blinked away hot tears. It wasn't smart to lose control, not even up here by herself. Tsilka indulged her hatred of Ashan to battle self-pity.

"She has everything I've worked for all my life. I'm the daughter of Chief Timshin, but people listen to her as if she spoke the gods' exact words. She's not even tall, yet she gets respect. It makes me so mad I could scream!''

That was why Tsilka had stormed out of the village. Ashan was telling the proud, ancient Tlikit how humans were created from mud and smoke and other stuff, not pulled from deep water as everyone knew. And they were accepting this foolishness!

Tsilka stamped her foot.

''Worst of all, she has Tor. She could have everything else, if I could have him. Is that so much? For people who claim to be *fair*?''

Tsilka swallowed bitterness.

''He's the father of my children. He belongs to me!''

Not having Tor was like a hand around her throat, squeezing; like a punch in the chest every time she breathed. Standing in the lonely wind above Teahra Village, she thought about ways to get her man.

Could she do something to make the Shahala and their chief leave, while making Tor štay? Then it would be just like before. Tsilka, the twins, the Tlikit people, and Tor—a free man this time—living by the Great River. Tsilka laughed at herself. After all Ashan had done to get here, she wasn't going to leave.

Just as wild: the idea of getting Tor to take Tsilka and the twins away to live by themselves. Ashan had Tor under a spell that made him forget he'd ever loved Tsilka. Someday, after seasons of seducing, he might leave Ashan for the better woman. But no time soon. And would he ever leave his son? Of course, he'd left them before, long ago—that's how Tsilka had come to have him.

What would happen if Ashan found out that Tor had been Tsilka's mate for a time, and was the father of her children? Ashan might banish him. Or forgive him. Or kill him. But Tor had promised he would kill Tsilka if she ever told, and she believed him.

Maybe she should kill Ashan. That would solve everything.

Danger pricked her skin. A Moonkeeper's magic was deadly, if Tor could be believed. Tsilka had doubts about this magic that no one had yet seen, but there must be some reason the Shahala did what Ashan said. It was unwise to think of killing her rival until she understood her powers.

Tsilka would do anything to possess Tor . . . but what? She felt as if she were trapped inside a tunnel with a flapping, shrieking condor, as if there were a weapon on the ground, but she couldn't find it in the dark, and she had to fight an overwhelming urge to roll up in a ball and cry.

If she didn't *do something,* she'd go crazy. But nothing she could do would make Tor hers; any move against Ashan would be the cause of her own death. She would have to hold all this inside, and wait. Oh, how she hated to wait! But while she waited . . .

"I promise myself," she said, making it true with a blow of her fist to her chest. "I will do all I can to make her life as miserable as mine. Somehow, without putting myself in danger. And always, I will be thinking, watching, waiting for the moment when I can explode like a tree struck by lightning, and take her down."

Focused rage was better than scattered rage. Tsilka felt better as she thought about how to make Ashan unhappy by getting in the way of what she wanted.

Ashan spent most of her time among people, telling stories, teaching words, talking about whatever they wanted to talk about.

*Poor Tor,* Tsilka thought. *How neglected he must feel.*

It seemed that Ashan wanted more than anything for people to get along, to like each other, to be friends.

"I will be the horse thistle spreading my seeds over new grassland," Tsilka vowed. "No—I will be the *wind,* blowing the thistle seeds—invisible. Ashan will never know from where the enemy comes, and will not look too hard. With luck, she won't know there *is* an enemy.

"Because I have already found her weakness. The great chief of the Shahala tribe sees only what she wants to see. She lies to herself and does not know it. So great is her arrogance, she believes things are true just because she wants them to be. That is how I will bring her down."

Tsilka went along with the rest of her people, as they went along with the Creator's Plan—as Tor called it. Meaning that everyone went along with Ashan. Tsilka pretended to accept it. She hated the leather skirt Ashan had given her, but she wore it—with the split front where the back should be, so her naked bottom still showed when she bent over. Except for that, she did nothing to make Ashan or Tor notice her.

Tsilka dug through her tribe like a mole through soft ground, coming up here and there in places secret from Shahala ears, talking to one or several. She scattered her thistle seeds as questions, knowing it would take time for them to grow.

"Why must we share our home and our food just because Tor—who used to be our slave—speaks words about some Creator's Plan?" she asked. "Why are we being so generous? What do we get from it?"

"It's not so bad," they said. "We have enough to share."

"These Shahala think they are better than us," she said. "Doesn't that insult you? What's wrong with our ways, our language, our gods? Where is our Tlikit pride?"

"We still know our gods. What does it hurt to hear about theirs?"

"You're afraid of them," she taunted.

They grumbled, and said they were not afraid, but it was obvious that they were. And why shouldn't they be? Of the Moonkeeper, and whatever magic she might have. Of Tor— who might be the god Wahawkin. Of the number of intruders who had claimed their home—there were nearly two Shahala for each Tlikit.

Tsilka said, "I'm not saying we should raise weapons against the intruders—at least not yet. I'm saying we should stand up for ourselves like men and women, and not lie down like slaves."

Tsilka found little support. Most people didn't mind—and some enjoyed—having the Shahala here. Even Tsilka had to admit that it was good to have so many children of new blood.

A few agreed with her. Two men, Tlok and Chalan, seemed to hate the Shahala almost as much as she did. She asked them to meet her away from the village.

"This is our home," Tsilka said. "Life was good before these strangers came. What do we need them for?"

Chalan said, "They are noisy. They fill the place up. You can't even walk without stumbling over one of them."

Tlok said, "They eat our food."

CHILDREN OF THE DAWN 73

"They think we are stupid and dirty."

"They insult us. They think they're better than we are."

"We must rid ourselves of them," Tsilka said.

Chalan said, "Have you forgotten how many there are?"

Tlok said, "How would you get rid of them, woman? We can't throw rocks and see them run like a herd of animals."

"I know. We'll have to be more clever than that. I think we must work on our own people first. The three of us will find times to talk to them alone. We'll show them that this isn't right. The Tlikit are a proud people, and there's nothing wrong with the way we are. We don't need new gods, new laws, new *chiefs*."

They agreed.

"Now go convince our people," Tsilka said.

# CHAPTER 12

WINTER . . . IN SPITE OF TOR'S HOPE, IT CAME. THE SUN deserted Teahra Village. The clouded sky varied from gray to grayer. The nights were moonless, starless black. Wind whipped the rivertop to froth, and slanted the rain, which never stopped.

Drip. Drip.

Splash. Ashan awoke with wet hair stuck to her face. One corner of their rough shelter had come loose. She shook Tor awake. He put on his leathers, and tied the flapping hide up again.

"On, no!" she said. "My medicine pouch!" She picked it up. Water dripped from the fringe. She looked inside.

"My herbs are all wet! They'll get moldy, and make people sick instead of well. What am I going to do? If I had a hut, I'd just hang them up by the fire."

She couldn't help sounding like a little girl with a broken doll.

"I'm sorry, love," her mate said. "I'll make you a fire, and you can heat rocks to dry your herbs on."

"You're sweet, Tor."

He headed off to get coals.

As she always did when she had that lost little girl feeling, Ashan thought of Kai El and wished she could hug him. But Shahala little ones had been sleeping in the Tlikit cave since winter got serious. And besides, she was the Moonkeeper, not a little girl.

Hunched under the stretched hide with water dripping from its edges, she separated wet clumps of herbs. *Winter in Teahra,* she thought, *is as different from winter in Anutash as a cougar is from a rabbit.* She remembered gently falling snow, slowly piling up; bright days, starry nights. Rain, certainly, but it came and then it went, and people saw blue sky for a while before it returned. Cold, yes, but not like this. In this wet cold, it hardly mattered what people wore. They froze anyway, unless they stayed by a fire.

At least there was plenty of wood here. From branches to whole trees, it washed up where the land jutted into the water. The Shahala had never had wood just *come* to them like this.

"What a wonderful gift from the River Spirit who already gives so much," some said.

Others said, "It's a good thing the river brings us wood, since this barren place doesn't grow any trees."

That wasn't quite true. Trees grew here and there along the Great River and up on the plateau—junipers, spruces, others the Shahala had never seen—but compared to the lofty giants of their homeland, these were hardly worth mentioning.

"That big oak," Ashan once heard a man say of the single large tree in Teahra Village, "would make many huts."

"Leave it alone," she'd said. "How can you think of killing something that has lived so long? Even the Tlikit, whom some of you consider savages, have saved that tree."

Though a village fire was tended day and night by the women who lived under the oak, the Shahala used riverwood to keep a fire of their own blazing against an overhanging cliff where they liked to gather.

They saved the best pieces of riverwood for huts. On days like today, when it drizzled instead of poured, they worked on them—one for each family.

A family included a warrior, his mate, and their little ones. Girls moved out when they grew up. Boys brought mates home, and added little ones. If a hut became too crowded, a young man might have to make one of his own. Eventually, parents moved to the old people's hut. With repairs by each generation, Shahala huts lasted forever.

Tor returned to their crude shelter against the cliff wall. He carried two flat stones in his leather-wrapped hands.

"Here," he said, dropping them.

Ashan spread her herbs on the hot stones. She set a loose-woven basket upside down over them, to keep the heat in while letting the water out as fog. Tor made a fire with coals from his clamshell carrier. She placed stones around it, to take the place of the ones he had brought when they cooled. They chatted in the easy way of mates.

"This will take all day," she said. "But I have to save these medicines. We may never see some of these plants again."

"Spring will surprise you," Tor said. "I think you'll find more than you expect."

From a goat bladder, Ashan poured water into a bowl-shaped basket given to her by a Tlikit woman named Skacha.

"I'm so impressed with these baskets that don't leak," she said. "I think this one is made of spruce roots and nettles."

She added dried, ground fish, mashed juniper berries, and small hot rocks, and kept it moving with a stirring stick, changing the rocks several times until the mush was hot.

"This is different," Tor said as he ate. "I like it."

She said, "I thought juniper berries might help the taste. Fish, fish, fish. I think I'm turning into one."

"It's not just *fish*, Ashan. It's *salmon*, and I could never tire of it."

When they finished, Tor said, "It's nice by this fire, but there's a lot of dirt between me and our hut."

He removed his shirt and leggings. She looked at him, wearing only loinskin and moccasins.

"It's cold today. Aren't you wearing anything but that?"

"There's no reason to get my leathers soaked. It takes forever to dry anything. Besides, digging keeps me warm."

"I think you're turning into a Tlikit," she said. They laughed, and Tor headed off to work.

As she tended the fire and dried her herbs, Ashan watched her man. The woman of twenty-two summers loved looking at him as much as the girl of fifteen summers had. Muscles bulging, working together or against each other; straining face; rain-sleek skin and hair. What a perfect thing, the body

of a man and the way it moved—as he broke the hard ground
with a stick, gouged, scooped, piled, tamped. Other men did
the same work, but Tor was the only one worth watching.

The Shahala were making their huts on the flat middle
ground of Teahra Village, with the Moonkeeper's hut in the
center.

Knowing Tor, their hut would be the largest and finest.
For days he'd been working on the floor—a flat-bottomed,
straight-sided hole; knee deep; round in shape; wide as three
men. He piled the dirt around the outside. When the floor was
finished, he would bury pieces of wood in the earth wall, and
weave them with others to form sides and a roof with a round
shape. Then he'd stretch hides over the frame—the same hides
that had covered their hut in Anutash—leaving an opening for
smoke in the top and a door in the side.

Ashan closed her eyes, imagined what it would be like
inside, and sighed . . . dry, warm, and private . . . wonderful.

When Tor came for midday food, Ashan patted his wet hair
and cold, red skin with fur, wrapped him in a bearskin, gave
him hot stew, and rubbed the muscles in his shoulders as he
ate.

"Look at that hut," she said, though it was nothing yet but
a half-dug hole with a pile of wood pieces next to it. "Good
floor—smooth, flat, easy to sweep. Deep hole, high sides—
it'll be warm and dry—better in every way than sleeping
under the sky. And Kai El will sleep with us instead of in the
Tlikit cave, and we'll have dry leathers, and—" She sighed.
"Oh, Tor, it will be wonderful."

"Mmmm," he said, savoring the food, the shoulder rub,
the praise. Ashan knew the value of appreciation to someone
working so hard.

"Have you decided where to put our sleeping shelf?" she
asked in a voice that suggested what—besides sleeping—
happened there.

"Anywhere you want, my love. I'm doing this all for you.
I do everything for you."

# CHAPTER 13

THE WORD "SISTER" HAD SEVERAL MEANINGS. A
Shahala woman called all the women in the tribe "sisters."
There were blood sisters, who had the same mother; time
sisters, born of different mothers during the same summer.
And spirit sisters, closest friends from one lifetime to the
next, like soulmates were lovers over and over.

Ashan—lucky enough to have a spirit sister—valued the
seasoned relationship with Mani that was like no other. Also
time sisters, born twenty-two summers ago, Ashan and Mani
had discovered their *spirit* relationship as little girls. Tor was
the best friend that a man could be, but Mani was a woman,
and there were some things that could only be spoken of
between women.

Mani and her mate, Lar, had two little ones: Tahm, a boy
Kai El's age; and Yayla, a baby girl. A good woman with a
strong sense of right and wrong, and a healthy fear of the
spirits, she was not afraid to speak freely to Ashan, as most
people were. Moonkeeper or not, Mani knew Ashan would
never harm her.

On a mild winter morning soon after the Moonkeeper's hut
was finished, Mani came to visit. Her long black hair, pulled
back and tied, was damp from river washing. Her open,
friendly face had a shiny, scrubbed look. She wore bison fur
around her shoulders, a loose dress of two doeskins, and low
elkhide moccasins.

The baby Yayla, snug in the cradleboard carried by her mother, moved only her curious eyes.

"Let's sit outside," Mani said. "The sunshine is good for the little one." She propped the cradleboard against the hut wall, turning it so the arched hood shaded Yayla's eyes.

The women talked about how this was as good a winter as either tribe could remember . . . lots of food, not much work, new things to be learned. Even the weather hadn't been bad, except for some rainy times.

Ashan said, "I'm surprised by how well this has gone. It helps that the Tlikit have no chief to stand in my way."

"Well, there's one who'd *like* to be their chief, but they call her names when she's not there . . . like Thinks She's a Man."

"And Ram with no Horns."

They laughed at Tsilka, and made up a few names of their own. Ashan didn't like her, without knowing why.

She said, "I haven't had to do much in the way of being chief. People are getting along on their own. I know they disagree on many things, but each tribe seems content to let the other behave as it wishes. So far, wishes have not collided."

"This is like living with a mate at the beginning, when everything seems wonderful just because it's new. Wait till they learn to talk to each other."

Ashan looked at her friend. "Do you think time will change tolerance into a struggle for power?"

Mani answered slowly: "You must make sure they know that to struggle with a Moonkeeper is to die."

Ashan thought about that . . . Shahala people were born knowing it. They were also born knowing they would be led by *women*.

"Tlikit chiefs have always been men. I'm going to have a problem with that. They believe women are *less*. Even the women believe it."

Mani made a sound of disgust. "You may need to kill a man or two to prove them wrong."

"Only if everything else fails."

Ashan, like Raga before her, had managed to lead without

having to kill. She hoped she'd never have to, but if the good of the tribe required it, she wouldn't hesitate.

After a pause, Mani said, "You know what's going to be your biggest problem, Ashan? Those four women who live under the oak tree."

"The Forest Women bother me too."

"Forest Women," Mani said. "That may be what Tor calls them, but they are slaves, and they bother everyone of Shahala blood."

Ashan's deep sigh blew strands of hair off her forehead.

"Women afraid to say 'no.' Others who want to keep it that way. I don't understand it, Mani."

After they'd been in Teahra Village for a few days, Ashan had questioned Tor.

"Are those women being punished for wrongdoing?"

"No."

"Why do they have to sleep on bare ground out in the open, when the rest sleep inside the cave? They do the work of others. They are the only ones who tend the fire. I've seen Tlikit women yell at them, and even hit them, yet they don't fight back."

Tor had explained what it meant to be a slave. Even though he'd told her before, to actually *see* it shocked Ashan. It had never occurred to her to make people work, to beat them, force them . . . well, as Moonkeeper, yes, but that would only be for the good of the tribe. Ashan thought the Tlikit acted out of laziness and meanness.

Tor had been surprised to find the Forest Women living in Teahra Village. Long ago, while searching for Ashan and Kai El, he had come upon them, questioned them, then left them unharmed. Their home was far away in the mountains near the Hidden Cave of Ehr. But now, somehow, the Tlikit people had the women, and forced them to work. They ground food for everyone; made plant parts ready for weaving; hauled water; kept the village fire day and night, so the Tlikit never had to wait, or start it themselves, which wasn't easy, since they used firesticks instead of sparkstones. The Forest Women worked wood and stone into whatever was needed, and did anything else they were told to do.

"They aren't tied up," Ashan had blurted. "Why don't they just go home?"

But even as she'd said it, she knew they couldn't, unless they were willing to leave their little ones. The slavewomen would forever be tormented outsiders, but the Tlikit had accepted their little ones as their own. Five of them, from two to eight summers in age, slept in the cave, were mothered by Tlikit women, and played with Tlikit little ones as equals.

"It makes no sense," Ashan had said. "Why do they not make the little ones slaves too? They could work. Look at what they did to Elia, and he was one of their own."

"It makes perfect sense, if you're a Tlikit," Tor had said. "The Forest Children will grow up to be mates of new blood for Tlikit children. That's more important to them than a few more slaves."

"These drylanders seem to be very selfish creatures."

"It's because of where they came from. Their homeland was a cruel place. Think of it this way: The Shahala are like a mountain lion who kills an elk, eats all it wants, and is happy to leave the scraps for whatever hungry creature comes along. The mountain lion has no reason to be selfish. Now think of the vultures who gather for the meager remains. Those vultures squawk and beat each other with their wings."

"I see what you mean, Tor, but these are *people* we're talking about, not some old piece of meat."

"I know. The problem of the Tlikit tribe was far more important than you understand. Until we came, they needed new blood more than anything. They couldn't mate among themselves without horrible consequences. They were a dying tribe that could not save itself."

When he made her look at it this way, she understood— there was *nothing* Ashan wouldn't do to save the Shahala tribe. But understanding didn't mean she could allow it to continue.

When her people asked about the slaves, Ashan told them to be patient. She would deal with it when she was ready. She wanted to understand everything before deciding what to do. So far, one thing she knew was that the Tlikit had *always* kept slaves, if they could get them. They said it was a right given by their gods.

Mani adjusted Yayla's cradleboard for the path of the sun.

"Have you seen the sadness on their faces when they look at their little ones?" she asked.

Ashan nodded. "It grabs my heart. Losing their children must be the worst. They're not really *lost*, like drowned in the river, or stolen by savages. But they might as well be. The mothers have no time for them in the day, and they can't even hold them at night."

"These Tlikit are so different," Mani said. "I'll never get used to them. Remember when Deyon brought his Outsider to Anutash? We washed and dressed her? Named her Kalatash, New Woman? We made her our sister. And so the Tlikit are with us, like they want to be our sisters. Then how can they be so cruel to those poor women?"

"I don't know. But it's wrong. I must stop it, somehow."

"I'm glad it's you who are Moonkeeper," Mani said, not for the first time. "Spirits will show you what to do, Ashan. They always do."

The women were quiet for a while.

Mani said, "This day is too nice to waste worrying about other people. You should go to that special place of yours and let the sun work magic on you."

It sounded wonderful to Ashan. She took leather-working tools and the hide that Mani had given to her last moon, and climbed the cliffs behind the village. She reached the sitting stone that she thought of as her friend with a view, and settled into the curve that fit her backside.

*Takoma*, she thought in Shahala, meaning "where spirit lines cross." *Lu It*, she thought in Tlikit, meaning "sacred place." It no longer surprised her when thoughts came with two names.

From her sitting rock on the high cliff, the Moonkeeper looked down on Teahra Village. She smiled, remembering the first time she'd seen it. She had thought, *That can't be a village—there are no huts*. With the work of strong Shahala warriors, Teahra looked like a *real* village now, with several huts finished, and others on the way.

The Moonkeeper's hut sat in the center. Sleeping warm and dry and having privacy made Ashan happy. When she lived under the crude shelter against the cliffs, people could see if she was busy or not, and come to her anytime they wanted. Now they had to ask permission to enter. And if she made some small lovemaking noise, people wouldn't hear and think she was speaking with spirits in the dark.

Today, Teahra Village was alive with people enjoying the mild midwinter air. Women were doing their work. Men rested or talked. Boys and girls played a rough but friendly game, kicking a pouch full of pebbles, and keeping it out of the water. Faint shouts of fun in two languages reached Ashan.

*Little ones,* she thought. *I love them. The first to learn each other's words. Even before they learned words, they understood play. A good sign for the future.*

A faint greenish yellow color in the air—the color of discontent—drew Ashan's eyes to the far end of the village, where a small group sat far enough away not to be heard by others. The Tlikit woman who'd like to be chief was talking earnestly, gesturing with a finger pointed at the village, pounding her palm with her fist. The others were nodding their heads at whatever she was saying.

Ashan had a feeling that they were plotting against the Shahala. But what could they hope to do? Most of their people were accepting, or at least going along with, Shahala ways—except for the matter of the slaves, and Ashan hadn't yet confronted them about that.

Was Tsilka just a joke to be laughed at, as she and Mani had done? Or was she like a sickness left untreated by a busy shaman that grew ever more virulent until it was out of control and the victim died?

Ashan wanted to lead without fear or force. She wanted to leave magic in the past. *Still,* she thought, *magic might prove to be the only way to control the woman.*

The Moonkeeper turned her gaze to the Great River of Tor's dreams. Chiawana, who could wear many colors, had today chosen deep blue flashed with silver. Ashan admired the magnificent river, then looked to the sere hills on the other side, up to the pale sky, to the low white sun.

Half closing her eyelids, she let sunrays creep under her lashes. She tilted her head back, ran her hands through her long hair, down over her stretched throat. Crossing them over her breast, she inhaled, opened the pores of her skin to sunshine, filled herself with it, became it. Joy slipped out as praise.

"Spirit of the Sun! I love your light and warmth, most of all in winter!"

Then she became herself again, a woman sitting on a rock.

Ashan took the piece of cured hide from her medicine pouch and stretched it in her lap, leather side down, fur side up. She stroked the fur: soft; red-brown, white and gray; long and thick around the ears, short on the nose. Once it had shaped itself around the top of a coyote's head.

A coyote skin was a strange thing for Ashan to have—her people did not kill sacred animals.

Tor hated the songdog's hide. He wanted her to get rid of it. She had thought he'd get used to it, but he never had.

Mani had found it when she and some Tlikit women were away from the village gathering nettles for cording. They came upon an argument of vultures, and drove them away to see if there was anything people could eat. The coyote they found was not long dead—the vultures had just begun their work. The meat was still good, and the Tlikit women thought they should take it home.

They didn't know about sacred animals, so Mani had explained, doing her best to use the proper Tlikit words.

"The coyote, the eagle, and the beetle are the Creator's favorites. People do not kill these sacred ones, even other animals do not. You see," Mani had said, showing them its gray-furred chin, "this songdog died because of too many seasons. To honor it, we will burn it and bury the ashes."

Mani was learning the new language faster than anyone else—except Ashan, who'd awakened knowing it. The Tlikit women liked Mani, so they gathered dry brush and helped her cover the carcass.

Before she sparked a fire, Mani had cut away the coyote's headskin and put it in her waist pouch. She'd given it to Ashan, telling her she didn't know why. It was one of those times when she just *knew*: She was supposed to bring it to the Moonkeeper.

Neither did Ashan know why, but she had accepted it, and was making it into something that had no name because such a thing had never been made before.

Following an inner voice, she scraped it clean; trimmed it, cutting carefully around the eyes, then sewing them shut; cut away the nose, lips, and whiskers, until what remained was a shape with three even sides. She burned the remains in a sacred fire. She left the ears on, split so they would dry straight; worked in brainflesh to cure it, fat to soften it, and wood ants to sweeten it.

The headskin of the songdog was a fine thing now.

This day Ashan planned to sew a piece of bison skin to the back. She had cut it in the same shape, and changed its color from golden to brown with root tea, an idea that came from watching a Tlikit woman color grass to weave into a basket.

Twisting and pushing a bone awl, she began making sewing holes.

The hairs on her neck stiffened; her eyes darted; her ears opened.

*Here it comes,* she thought, gritting her teeth.

Whenever she worked on the songdog's hide, fear crept in and overshadowed respect and gratitude. Fear was not a good feeling for a Moonkeeper.

"But it was so bad," she said. The memory choked her, filled her with tears. "To see those lights rushing at me. To fall and fall."

The bone awl pierced the other side. She backed it out and started another hole, trying to keep them evenly spaced.

"Why would Coyote Spirit throw me from a cliff? Why did I have to suffer that? How can I trust anything?"

She heard only the whine of her own voice.

Because of his twin natures, Spilyea was the hardest of the Animal Spirits to understand. What could not be understood could not be predicted, and predicting was a Moonkeeper's work. She had to keep trying, in spite of fear. The headskin in her lap forgotten, she concentrated on what she knew:

From the Misty Time, Coyote Spirit was a friend to people. He had a quick, stubborn mind. Coyote was the one who suffered many failures making the First Man and First Woman, but did not give up. Coyote begged Amotkan to give his mud dolls breath—and speech, which he himself did not have. Through time, he stayed interested in people, teaching them survival skills, as if he wanted to keep improving what he had made.

"I understand that," Ashan said. "Coyote made us. So he loves us. Like we love our children."

She looked at a nearby rock where a spirit would sit if one were here.

"Or do you?" she asked.

No answer.

Ashan would not give up—not this time.

"Spilyea: We know you as Friend, and also as Trickster. You are the Playful Spirit. But what is play to you can be death to others. How can you play deadly tricks on your friends? People would not indulge in such mean fun."

Today, because she had been strong and patient, Spilyea spoke in her mind.

*You know me as two, Trickster and Friend, but I am many. I am Destiny's hand. Destiny needs your sacrifices, but you are weak. Would you have jumped from the cliff?*

"Of course not."

*So I pushed you. As a Friend.*

"Why would Destiny need me to bear such terror? To be so badly hurt? Is Destiny an unkind spirit?"

*No. But only shared crisis kept the meeting of the tribes peaceful.*

"I see."

People *had* come together over Ashan's almost-death.

After that day, she no longer feared Spilyea. She had a better understanding of him than anyone ever had. No one, not even a Moonkeeper, could ever know, or trust, Coyote Spirit. But if he harmed her again, Ashan believed that it would be for a reason more important than one woman's terror and pain.

# CHAPTER 14

T SILKA SAID TO THE WOMEN, "BOTH OF YOU WILL
pretend to get sick."

Elia's mother, Euda, had a sister named Yak. One was as
fat in body and sour in spirit as the other. Neither had a mate.
Before the Shahala intruders came to the Great River, they'd
spent much of their time arguing with each other. More than
once, Tsilka had had to get between them, and send one up
the river and the other down to cool their anger.

Now, with Tsilka's help, Euda and Yak had turned their
sourness against the intruders instead of each other. Today
they were making a plan to ruin belief in Ashan's power to
heal.

Tsilka said, "You'll pretend to be *very* sick ... maybe
something in the belly ... something with lots of howling,
so everyone will know. One will go to the Shalala Moonkeeper
to be cured. The other will refuse."

The fat sisters looked baffled. They were not the smartest
women in the tribe.

Tsilka continued. "The one who goes to the Moonkeeper
will pretend to get *sicker*. The other will pretend to get *better*,
without any help from the Shahala medicine woman."

The sisters looked at each other, smiling as they understood.

Euda sneered, "I want to be the one to go to her. I want
to be there when she sees that her medicine isn't working."

"Fine," Yak said. "I will be the one who is smart enough to refuse."

Tsilka smiled. She couldn't help thinking how smart she was to have these two agreeing with each other.

"You will come to *me* for help, Yak. *I* will be the one who makes you well. Our people will see that Tlikit ways are good enough for Tlikit people."

"But Tsilka, you don't know anything about medicine."

"What does that matter? You won't really be sick."

Awakening, Ashan touched the empty place next to her, and remembered that Tor had gone hunting. Kai El and Tenka still slept in the gray light of early morning. Ashan knelt by the fire ring and struck her sparkstones. As she blew into a glowing wad of dry grass, she heard scratching on the doorskin.

"Moonkeeper?" Elia said.

"Shh . . . I'll come out."

She blew again and the smoldering grass flamed. She used a stick to poke it under the waiting kindling, then stepped out into a drizzle.

Elia looked worried. "Mother very sick. And mother sister. They cry. Moonkeeper fix?"

The Tlikit tribe had no medicine woman. Over time, they had stumbled over a few helpful plants, but they possessed nothing close to Shahala knowledge, taught to First Woman by plants themselves, handed down from Moonkeeper to Moonkeeper since the Misty Time. Tor had told Ashan that the Tlikit seldom got sick; if they did, they either got better by good luck, or died. As she followed the boy, Ashan thought this would be a good chance to show the Tlikit people the value of a chief who was also a medicine woman. That is, unless the sickness was something over which she had no control. No shaman could heal every person who came to her. The Shahala understood this. Would the Tlikit?

*Let it be something easy,* she prayed, but loud groans as she approached told her to expect the worst.

Entering the cave, Elia said in Tlikit, "I brought the Moonkeeper. She knows everything. She will fix what is wrong."

Stepping into darkness, Ashan wrinkled her nose, then told herself to ignore the stale, unpleasant smell. An oil lamp glowed in the depths of the cave. A knot of Tlikit people parted to let her through. She saw two moaning women, side by side, doubled up, writhing under sleeping skins. Tsilka was kneeling at one side. Ashan knelt at the other.

Euda grabbed her hand.

"We're sick!" she cried.

"We're dying!" cried the other, whose name Ashan didn't know.

"Easy," she said in their language. "Let me look at you."

The Moonkeeper felt their tear-streaked faces: sweaty and warm with excitement, but not hot with fever. She pushed the sleeping skins down.

*They should eat less,* she thought. *All this fat isn't good. It's like carrying a heavy pack around all the time.*

The weeping women clutched their bellies. Prying Euda's fingers loose, Ashan pressed on her belly, feeling for hardness, but couldn't feel anything through all that flesh. She thumped with her fingertips. The sound was solid, not hollow as it would be if the woman were filled with stinking air.

Euda howled and pushed her hand away.

Ashan thought it odd that the same thing happened at the same time to sisters. They must have eaten something harmful. If so, she would have them eat ashes to soak up the poison.

"Did you eat something different?" she asked.

"No," Euda moaned.

"Think," Ashan said. "You were out gathering yesterday. Maybe you found something new and tasted it?"

"No," the other one said. "We did not."

"Did you eat food that was spoiled?"

"Do you think we are stupid?"

"Of course not . . . what is your name?"

"Yak," the woman said, then scrunched her face, let out a long, painful "ooowww," doubled up tight, and rolled onto her side.

Maybe they were bound up inside from eating too much meat and not enough plants. For that she would give cascara bark she had brought from the homeland.

"Do you make waste every day?"

"Yes," they groaned.

"Are the wastes runny or strange-colored?"

"No," Euda said.

"Who looks at their own waste?" Yak said.

"Do you feel like vomiting?"

"No. It's pain I feel." Euda howled. "Owwww ... the pain!"

"Aiyeee!" Yak cried.

Ashan thought of little worms that could get in the belly, but they usually took their time to make a person sick, and these two had been fine yesterday. Kia leaf, the poison to kill worms, was strong. She didn't want to chance making them sicker than they already were.

Ashan didn't need to look at the people around her to feel their fear—not so much for the sick women, but for themselves, that it might happen to them.

She wished she knew what was causing the pain, so she'd know exactly how to treat it. Sweet spear was the only thing she could think of to use. At least it was safe. Tenka had found a patch in a tree-sheltered place up the river, dug some roots and brought them home. If only Ashan could be sure that it really *was* sweet spear.

Sweet spear and blue spear—named for the shape of their leaves—both had healing power in finger-thick roots that ran just beneath the ground. They liked damp, shady places, and sometimes grew together. Sweet spear made stems with fleshy thumbs on the end instead of flowers. Its roots were good for stomach pains. Blue spear had beautiful, large three-part flowers. The ground-up root was used as a poultice for wounds, but must never be eaten, for it was poisonous.

Because the plants could easily be mistaken, they were only gathered in the spring when the blue was in flower. It was autumn now, but ...

"Rest," the Moonkeeper said to the groaning women. "Try to be calm. I'll bring medicine to ease your pain."

In the Moonkeeper's hut, Ashan questioned Tenka about the roots.

"The leaves were withered," Tenka said. "It's lucky I even saw them. Maybe it was their voice I heard."

"Did the leaves smell tart, like sorrel?"

"Umm, I think so."

Ashan scraped a root with her thumbnail and smelled. She tasted. She couldn't be certain.

Tenka said, "It was very wet there, more than blue spear likes. I'm sure it's sweet spear."

Euda ate the ground-up roots.

But Yak refused.

"Shahala medicine is for Shahala people," she said loudly. "Tsilka will cure me with Tlikit medicine."

As the cave full of people watched, Tsilka gave something to Yak. She swallowed it before Ashan saw what it was.

Soon Euda was howling, then screaming.

But Yak was better.

"Look, people," she said, getting up. "Tsilka's medicine has cured me. My foolish sister should have listened."

"Aiyee! Aiyeee!" Euda cried, rolling from side to side, clutching her gut. "Somebody help me!"

Ashan tried to comfort her, to no avail.

"She's dying!" people said. "The Moonkeeper has killed her!"

Ashan turned to them. "Trust me. Euda is not dying. She needs another medicine, that's all."

"Show me where you dug the roots, Tenka," she said, and they hurried off.

The autumn-yellow spears lay withered on the ground. Ashan crushed one in her fingers, and her heart sank. It smelled bland, like grass—even dead, a sweet spear leaf should have a faint tart smell.

"We've made a mistake, Tenka. It's blue spear. I gave her blue spear."

"Oh, no. Will she die?"

"Maybe not. If we hurry."

The Moonkeepers ran all the way.

After the Moonkeeper left the cave, Yak went around telling people how good she felt from Tsilka's medicine.

Tsilka whispered to Euda, who was still crying loudly.

"How convincing. You sound like you're dying."

"Ohhh," Euda moaned. "I *am* dying. Ohhh . . ."

"You don't have to pretend for me."

"I'm not pretending. I'm *dying*, I tell you. She gave me

poison. She knew our plan, and she poisoned me. Ohhh . . .
I should never have listened to you."

Tsilka actually saw Euda's gut tighten in a cramp. The
woman wrapped her arms around herself, weeping from the
pain.

What was happening?

Tsilka's plan had fallen apart, but she liked where the pieces
were landing. If Euda died—and Tsilka thought she just
might—no one would ever trust Ashan's medicine again. If
they didn't trust her medicine, they would not trust *her*.

*One step closer,* Tsilka thought, *to pushing my enemy out
of power, to taking her place as chief of this village.*

Ashan brought a bowl of wood ashes to the sick woman, but
she screamed in pain and fear.

"You poisoned me! You poisoned me!" she cried, refusing
to eat any.

Ignoring the people around her, Ashan—who was truly
afraid for Euda's life—chanted a song about courage in the
face of evil, shaking an old turtle-shell rattle. She called on
pain-soothing spirits. Euda began to calm, then slipped into
Ashan's control. She ate some ashes, and in a while she felt
a little better.

Ashan stayed until Euda was well. It took three days.

Only she and Tenka knew about the mistake. Tenka would
not forgive herself. Ashan told her over and over that everyone—even a Moonkeeper—makes mistakes.

"In this whole world, Rising Star, only Amotkan is perfect."

Tsilka's plot had mixed results. Euda called her an evil witch,
blaming her for all her pain, for almost dying, even though
she herself had thought it a fine idea at the beginning. Euda
believed in the Moonkeeper now, partly from fear of what
she could do to someone who plotted against her. But there
was more to it than just fear. She also believed the Moonkeeper
had saved her life. Ashan had somehow won her over in the
three days she sat by her side. Tsilka had lost a weapon.

But others announced they wouldn't let the Shahala Moonkeeper touch them, no matter how sick they might get. Tlikit

medicine was good enough for Tlikit people, as Yak's experience proved.

Had the enemy really known what they were up to? Had Ashan poisoned Euda? Tsilka didn't know. She felt a small, cold knife of fear in her heart. She blunted it by turning her mind to what she could do next.

"There's something strange about what happened, Tor. I wish you had been here," Ashan told her mate.

"What's so strange about you curing a sick person?"

"Euda almost died before I cured her. But I did nothing to help Yak, who seemed just as sick at first. She said she didn't want Shahala medicine. Tsilka gave her something, and she got well long before Euda did."

"Maybe Tsilka gave her the same thing."

"No. I don't know what it was, but it was not wood ashes. I just don't see how it's possible, Tor ... unless Yak was never sick in the first place."

"What do you mean?"

"I think they were pretending."

"Why would they do that?"

"I don't know, but I think Tsilka had something to do with it," Ashan told him.

# CHAPTER 15

THE MOONKEEPER SMILED: ANOTHER COLD, SUNNY day. It was good in the middle of winter for people to see blue sky instead of gray.

She spoke in Tlikit, her second language.

"This should be the worst season. Instead, spirits give us one fine day after another, strung like beads on a time ball, so many it's becoming hard to think of them as rare. It's a sign that spirits approve the joining of our tribes."

Most of the faces around her were Tlikit. Ashan doubted they knew what a time ball was. But they nodded agreeably. The winter sun had them smiling, too. Warm in their furs, with the cliffs at their backs to keep the wind up high, they sucked in sharp air, puffed out mist, and waited for her to say more.

Ashan's ability to use both languages fascinated the people of Teahra, especially the Tlikit. She had no trouble getting listeners, and gathered them often. There was so much they needed to learn.

She said, "But fine as it is right now, the Darkest Day is coming soon. It's a dangerous time. We almost lose the Balance."

"What do you mean?"

Knowing Tlikit words did not make communicating easy. Besides not knowing Shahala words, these people knew little of Shahala ideas, especially those about what spirits wanted from people. So she could say "the Balance," and they might think of one rock sitting on another, not *"the Balance,"* as *That Upon Which All Life Depends.*

"I have told you about the war between the Spirit of Light and the Spirit of Dark, and how people are keepers of the Balance. Soon a day will come that is the shortest. Then that night will be the longest."

"We know of winter's long darks."

Ashan nodded. "It's the hardest time, for animals, plants, even for the sun and the moon. They become weak. The Spirit of Dark is about to win the ancient war, and that would be terrible: Night forever. Do you understand? *Night forever.* People must help the Spirit of Light. We sing, dance, and offer sacred smoke. It's medicine for the sun, and we do it all day. Then I stay up with the moon while the rest of you sleep. After that, the days will grow at both ends. Green grass will come. What are your questions?"

"Are they sick, the sun and the moon?"

"More like tired."

"We don't know songs for things in the sky."

"Listen to your Shahala sisters and brothers," she said.

"Will there be a feast?" The Tlikit had heard about feasts, but had not yet enjoyed one.

Ashan shook her head. "In summer when we celebrate the longest day, then we will feast. But winter is not a time of plenty."

"It is in Teahra."

"That doesn't matter. These things are always done the same."

"So people are Keepers of the Balance?" asked a woman named Chianli.

"Yes," Ashan said, thinking, *I love it when understanding breaks into a person's head.*

"Then we have the power to make it light all the time?"

*Oh! Just when I thought they understood!*

"Think, Chianli. What if night never came? The sun would burn holes in our eyelids. How would we sleep? What about the night creatures? It is the Balance that matters. Everyone say it with me."

"It is the Balance that matters."

Ashan thought some understood. Most were just being agreeable, and that was enough for now.

A man named Tlok, who never smiled, said, "The Tlikit are an old tribe. We have never done this. Why haven't we lost the Balance before?"

Ashan answered with pride. "Though you did not know it, since the Misty Time there have been Moonkeepers in the world taking care of these things."

Someone asked when the Darkest Day would come. Ashan knew the answer by her shadow stick, and held up seven fingers.

She ended the teaching with a request: "Will you join us in the ceremony? Will you tell others it is a good thing?"

"We will."

*That went well,* the Moonkeeper thought.

Ashan and Mani sat by a small fire in the Moonkeeper's hut— alone, except for the sleeping baby. In the comfortable silence of long friendship, they made sage bundles for the Darkest Day ceremony, one for each person past the age of seven summers. She pulled twigs of sage with fragrant gray leaves from branches that had been drying. When she had a bundle the size of Tor's excited staff, she wrapped it with green grass string, tied it off at the top, put it on the stack growing between them, and started another.

Ashan had invited Mani for more than help with the sage. Mani was allowed in places where Ashan was not. People liked the Shahala woman who thought it was fun to learn Tlikit speech. Though Mani's name meant Earth Sister, some now called her Talks to All. She knew much of what went on in Teahra that Ashan would never hear about, and she knew the importance of sharing it.

Ashan asked, "What are they saying about me?"

"I heard a woman say that you are more like Yaculta— the mountain on the other side of the river, too remote to be reached—than you are like a *real* person."

"I'll have to work on that."

It was important to her to be *liked*, even though—as Raga had told her over and over—it was not necessary for people to *like* their chief.

Mani said, "Some of them are afraid of your magic."

"I haven't used any magic, except a bit of medicine for Euda."

"Tor has warned them about your powers."

"That's good. I may need that fear someday."

"You may. I've also heard it said that you are like Lu It, the mountain who rumbles and threatens, but never does any harm."

The sharp aroma of sage cut Ashan's senses like tiny blades. She knotted the grass string, bit off the end, and put a finished bundle on the stack.

"What do people say about the Darkest Day ceremony?"

"Our people are glad Nah Ah Kahidi is near. They look forward to the coming of spring."

"What about the Tlikit people?"

Mani sighed. "That woman named Tsilka—I don't like her, she tries to hide her meanness, but she doesn't fool me—Tsilka says you are only doing it because you like how power feels."

"Really?"

"Yes. My own ears heard it. Some say they'd feel like fools if they sang at the sun. But everyone knows you want this. Most of them want your ways to be true. So I think they will join in the ceremony. For you."

"Good. It doesn't matter why, as long as they do it."

The spirit sisters worked in silence for a while.

Mani said, "Do you know the one called Akli? Her name means Remember the Lake."

Ashan pictured the pleasant, curious face of a woman in the middle of life, the mother of Klee, no one's mate.

"I think I know who you mean, though we haven't talked."

"You'd like this one. I've been sharing Shahala ways with her. She wanted to show me something I didn't know about, so she brought some roots to my hut."

Ashan smiled. "Sharing is what we need to bring our tribes together."

Mani put down the sage bundle and described the roots with her hands.

"There were four of them—long, fat at the top, coming down to a point. Brown skin, with little scratched trails, as if groundbugs tried burrowing and gave up. Akli called the roots 'pahto.'"

Ashan said, "It's odd that they use the name of the sacred mountain for a food."

"That's what I thought," Mani said. "Akli used a rock to scrape the skin from one, broke it open, took a bite of the yellow flesh, and handed it to me. I bit off a piece. It was dry and hard to chew. It tasted a little like sweetroot, but not sweet. I said the pahto was very good, and she'd have to show me where it grows. She gave me what was left—for my family, I think she said.

"After she left, I thought how much better it would be roasted in the ground like we cook sweetroot—well, like we did in the homeland. I also thought how nice it is that such a thing grows here. I don't think we'll find real sweetroot in this place."

Mani went on. "Some people would think Akli stupid for not knowing how to cook roots. Some might even tease her. But you know I'm not like that. I roasted and mashed the rest, and took it to her on my nicest wood plate. Well, she *loved* it . . . and my plate! I didn't know she'd keep my plate! But I let her have it as if I'd meant to all along. Now she's been showing her sisters about roasting. They say it's too much work, but I think we'll see more of it on the Tlikit side of the village. Cooked food tastes so much better, their mates will demand it."

"I'm proud of you, Mani. I wish there were more like you."

The baby fussed for Mani's breast. Soon Kai El and Tahm, the women's sons, and Tor and Lar, their mates, would be showing up for midday food.

"I'll finish the sage, Mani. You go home and get ready for the attack of the hungry ones."

When Ashan awoke on the Darkest Day, her mate was not beside her.

*If I didn't sleep so late, this wouldn't happen!* she thought, chilled by the memory of another morning long ago when she'd awakened to find Tor gone, and had not seen him again for three lonely summers—

*But that was then.*

Ashan heard faraway thunder—just the kind of day she expected Nah Ah Kahidi to be. She rubbed night dirt from her face, fingered tangles from her hair, put on a white leather dress and high moccasins. She crossed the hut and sniffed her son: Healthy. Light as a butterfly landing on a finger, she kissed his cheek.

From behind the sleeping place she shared with Tor, Ashan took the painted leather pouch that held garments from the Misty Time. She breathed a blend of familiar aromas as she unfolded the Moonkeeper's robe.

Ashan had brought the sacred robe from the homeland on her own travel poles. Made of sewn-together pieces of fur and hide, tufted with feather clusters, strewn with teeth and claws, it represented every animal and bird known to the Shahala people. Many times old Raga allowed young Ashan to hold the robe . . . how long ago it seemed. As she listened to stories of the Animal People, the Chosen One would stroke the soft furs, breathing the fragrances her fingers loosened.

The good memory made Ashan smile. She draped the ancient robe over her shoulders, and stepped outside. Under thick, dark-bottomed clouds, in a bitter, howling wind, the Moonkeeper offered the song of morning to the Four Directions, and a song of respect to the Spirit of Thunder. She went to a tongue of land that stuck out into the river. Bushes and rocks had been removed, the earth smoothed. Teahra's new ceremonial ground was ready.

Tor had a good fire burning. He smiled and held out his arms for her. The heat of his embrace was better than the heat of the fire. How bleak, Ashan remembered, were mornings without being held by Tor, even for a moment.

Two men brought an ancient drum from the Moonkeeper's hut. It was made of thin wood forced into a circle three arm lengths across and one tall. A skin stretched over the top, tightened by thongs that went down the sides and across the open bottom. The One Drum. It had been with the Shahala for so long that they no longer knew what kind of skin it was, or who had painted the faded picture of a flying owl. Its voices were many and rich.

Ashan had the men place the One Drum on the new ceremonial ground near the fire. Around it, they arranged pieces of flat wood padded with thick sheep fur, for the bony old rears of the drummers.

Not so long ago, the Shahala had four drums, from old to ancient, each pounded by a grayhair during rituals. The joined voices of the drums made sounds the spirits could not ignore. But when hunger drove them from their homeland, the People of the Wind couldn't take everything. One of many sad decisions had been made: Only the One Drum—the oldest, given to First Man by the Spirit of Thunder—would be taken to the new home. The Two Drum, Three Drum, and Four Drum had been burned with other tribal treasures that could not be moved.

The drummers came from the old people's hut, settled around the One Drum, and rapped together with padded sticks. In one of its many voices—slow, deep, and hollow—the One Drum called the people of Teahra Village—the Shahala from their huts, the Tlikit from their cave.

"Tun TUN, Tun TUN, Tun TUN!"

As they came to the ceremonial ground, the Moonkeeper gave them sage. She showed the ones who didn't know how to use the sacred plant, holding a bundle by the cut, bare stems at one end. Leaning away from the wind-snapped flames while she stretched her arm toward them, she touched sage to fire and pulled it back, sparking and smoking.

"Fan the smoke with your hand, like this. Offer it up to the sun. Then put it out." She stubbed the bundle on the ground. "Dance for a while or sing. Then light the sage again. And again later . . . so you still have some left when night comes."

Ashan smiled, watching the first ceremony in the new home, the first shared with their new sisters and brothers, nearly everyone taking part. . . . Her eyes went to the four women watching from their lonely place by the tree.

Except for Tsilka and a few others, the Tlikit had joined the Shahala in the rituals of the Darkest Day.

"We're not savages," they had said. "We have rituals of our own. But of course, the slaves will not join us. The gods would be offended."

Still looking for a peaceful way to solve the problem, Ashan hadn't mentioned it again. Besides, she knew the poor women wouldn't do anything to bring trouble on themselves.

*One thing at a time,* warned a voice in her mind. *At least their children are accepted, and that means there is hope.*

Looking away from the slaves, Ashan went back to watching what was *good*.

Nah Ah Kahidi, the Darkest Day, was not a lively celebration like Kamiulka, the Autumn Feast. Guided by the somber beat of the One Drum, people offered song, dance, and smoke—medicine to help the sun, so the Spirit of Dark would not win the ancient war, and the world would not suffer endless night.

Morning turned into day. Smoke rose. Feet danced. The songs of drum and people told the sun to be strong.

"Tun tun TUN tun tun tun . . ."

"Aya ne ki yi yi, aya ne kay yay . . ."

Thunder joined them, rumbling ever closer, as Nah Ah Kahidi went on under the lowering sky. Ashan saw Tlikit smirks, frowns and sighs of boredom. It was more work than fun. In the cold gloom, people couldn't see the sun they were doing all this for.

Ashan wasn't worried about the sky-war. Keeping the Balance didn't depend on whether everyone helped—the prayers of one Moonkeeper would have been enough. But it was good for these people to work together and celebrate together. It gave them reasons to like each other.

The Moonkeeper went among them. "What a good song," she told one. "Save some of your sage for later," she told another.

Her words were swallowed by thunder. The sky broke and dumped a torrent on the people. The fire sizzled out in a cloud of steam.

The Tlikit ran for their cave.

The Shahala knew the sun still needed help. They danced and sang in the pouring rain, leaving out the smoke part of the ceremony.

"Tun tun TUN tun tun," said the wet drum. "Aya ne ki yi," sang the wet people, their dancing feet making splashes as the new ceremonial ground turned to mud. When night came, the Shahala went to their huts, glad to leave the keeping of the moon to the Moonkeeper.

The days began to grow at both ends, and green grass softened the hillsides . . . as the Moonkeeper had said. Some of the Tlikit were amazed. Others said it would have happened anyway. Hadn't spring always come before, all by itself?

# CHAPTER 16

TENKA HAD JUMPED AT THE CHANCE TO MOVE INTO THE Moonkeeper's hut with Ashan and Tor, her only brother since Beo died in the massacre six autumns ago. She loved Ashan. Living with her gave them more time together, and Tenka knew this was good. It took one's whole lifetime to learn the ways of a Moonkeeper, and she had had a late start.

Tenka was coming to think of Kai El as her little brother. He was the sweetest thing, though sometimes his energy irritated her.

She was glad to get out of her father's hut, with his three mates, five little ones, and Elia. It was terribly crowded, but it was more than that. Tenka had never forgiven her father. After her mother, Luka, died from grief over losing her sons—everyone thought Tor had died too—Arth had taken another mate, and then two more. Tenka had only been seven summers, and she needed a mother's love, but she wouldn't allow those women to give it to her. Their little ones were her friends, but *not* her brothers and sisters.

Arth's *real* daughter could never stop thinking that what he had done was wrong—though he was not the only one. By ancient tradition, Shahala people took only one mate, but the massacre left more than half the women without mates and their little ones without fathers. Raga had allowed the old law to be broken—one time only—for the good of the tribe, and now there were several of these strange families.

The Moonkeeper's hut was better than Arth's hut, but what Tenka really wanted was a place of her own. She kept the wish secret. People would think it odd for someone her age, and no one would want to help. She couldn't make a hut by herself. She might be the Other Moonkeeper, but she was only thirteen summers.

*Someday* . . . Time moved slower than a forest slug. Tenka wished she could get behind it and push. She had wonderful dreams of walking out of a forest one morning to find that summers and winters had passed like a storm, and she had grown older, taller, and fiercer. But every morning brought the realization that she was still a small, timid girl that even the wind could blow around.

One morning in early spring, Tenka and Ashan were alone in the Moonkeeper's hut, smudging sage, shaking deer-hoof rattles, and praying for a sick man named Snomish. In less than one moon, he had changed from a strong hunter into a creature too weak to stand alone.

His daughter, Mani, came to tell them that Snomish had gotten worse in the night. The Moonkeeper, Ashan, tied on her medicine pouch. The Other Moonkeeper, Tenka, checked hers, and added things they might need. They hurried across the fog-shrouded village.

Snomish's mate, four sons, and Mani waited inside the sour-smelling hut. They clustered around Ashan, twisting their hands, shaking their heads, whispering.

The sick man lay on a raised earth shelf across from the door. Drowning from within, his chest rattled with liquid that took up space where air should go, making breathing hard. He coughed, snorted, and spat. He choked, gasping, and the hut seemed to hold its breath. When choking quieted to gurgling, the whole placed sighed in relief.

His head protruded from furs. Framed in black hair, his skin was so pale that Tenka wondered if it would bleed. His half-open eyes stared at nothing.

His mate, Kish, whispered, ''Snomish believes he's going to die. This morning he told me who should have his favorite things.''

''Everyone dies,'' the Moonkeeper said.

"I know, but Snomish is not an old man. This is no way for a warrior to die."

"Is there nothing more you can do for my father?" Mani asked with tears in her eyes.

*There should be,* Tenka thought. *But there isn't.*

Amotkan had given people medicine for this sickness: the inner bark of pine, made into steam with water and hot rocks. Inhaling the steam made breathing easier, and sometimes the person got better. But pine—so common in Shahala land—had not been found here.

The Moonkeeper cleared her throat. "I haven't tried passinowik. Did you bring it, Tenka?"

From her medicine pouch, Tenka took powdered orange-brown leaves—meant to be mixed with fat into salve for itching—a pinch for Ashan, one for herself. Tenka was proud. She always liked to have medicine for whatever might happen. But she wondered how Ashan would use passinowik. If Snomish itched, that was the least of his problems.

Ashan said, "Get our rattles, Mani, the ones we were shaking when you came." Mani nodded and left.

"Wake up this fire," Ashan said to the oldest son.

With a wedge of sharpened oak and a pounding stone, he split thin strips of soft riverwood, laid them across the resting coals, and blew on them. A flame awoke, then another. He stood more splits with their tops together, and the dancing flames reached higher.

Tenka noticed that the family had calmed down the moment Ashan began speaking with a shaman's authority.

Ashan and Tenka chanted, and danced around the eager fire. Mani brought their rattles. They stood over Snomish, and shook the rattles like snakes about to strike. They shouted at the spirits making him sick. Ashan opened her hand, blew, and passinowik puffed over him.

The powder in Tenka's sweaty hand had turned to mush. She flicked it on the sick man with her finger.

"Thank you, Moonkeepers," Kish said, holding out wooden beads.

*Pretty,* Tenka thought.

Ashan said, "Keep them, Kish. I can't promise this will work."

Tenka pulled her hand back. The Moonkeepers walked out into the crisp, clean fog.

"What was that all about?" Tenka asked. "I thought passinowik was for itching."

"It is. But those people needed medicine for their feelings. Just seeing us do *something* made them feel better."

"I noticed that, too. When you demanded the use of your rattles, everyone changed."

"Add that to your knowledge of healing. I have seen made-up things like that help someone get better. Hope and belief are powerful medicines."

Tenka nodded.

"But Snomish needs more," Ashan said in a worried voice. "He must have pine steam to breathe."

"We've spent days looking."

"We have to try one more time. I don't know if it will save him, but without it, he will die."

The Moonkeepers dressed in warmer clothes.

"Walk fast to cover the most ground," Ashan said. "Check rocky places and canyons. Look all day, and come back a different way. Be home by dark. I don't want to worry about you, too."

They set off into the fog, Ashan going downriver, Tenka upriver.

It was another gloomy day in early spring when Tenka could throw a rock farther than she could see. This was not ordinary gray fog. Tlikit people called it *ty ash*, silver mist, because it turned into frost that stuck to every leaf, rock, and piece of grass. The air stayed too cold for the frost to melt. Every day it got a little thicker. At first she thought it was pretty, but . . . it had been like this for more than the days on two hands, and people, especially Shahala people, wanted some sunshine, or at least a nice, warm rain.

Hoping to leave the freezing mist, Tenka climbed up to the prairie, but it was just as foggy, and even colder because of wind.

*The seeds of the morning bear the fruit of the day.* The Shahala saying proved true: Beginning the day in the presence of a dying man, Tenka thought about death, even as she searched for a lifesaving plant. Her mother, Luka. Her brother,

Beo. Too soon dead. A long time dead. Her chest still ached when she thought of them. Death might be good for the dead person, but it hurt the ones who were left—more if the dead one hadn't lived long enough.

Like Snomish. Tenka thought about him. He was different things to different people, as everyone was ... mate, father, grandfather, friend, maybe even someone's secret enemy. But too young to die.

Ashan had made a mistake that many might die from—though Tenka would never say those words out loud, especially since her own mistake with the blue spear. Certain that there must be pine everywhere, Ashan hadn't brought much to the new land. A medicine for many things, the supply of pine was quickly used up. And now a man faced death with no help from plant spirits.

Tenka came to a fold in the land and headed down it, stopping here and there to sing to the Pine Spirit, and listen for an answer, which never came. When she heard the Great River, she thought of warmth and food. Lingering thoughts of Snomish almost made her go back and search some more. But how could she find anything in this fog? She was lucky to have found her way home.

If Ashan's luck had been no better, Snomish would be dead soon. Too bad, but there was only so much that Moonkeepers could do. Not every life could be saved. Tenka was coming to understand and accept this.

As she came into the village, she heard Mani and the Tlikit woman, Akli, shouting at each other. Surprised, she hurried toward them. *It's not like Mani to yell,* she thought.

The women stood too close together, leaned inward, looked like they were going to tear into each other.

People gathered to watch—not too close—they didn't want to get hurt if the argument exploded into a slapping, hair-pulling tumble on the ground.

*Some of them would love to see that,* Tenka noticed with disgust.

Where was Ashan? Still hunting pine? Sitting up on that rock of hers? It didn't matter ... she wasn't *here.* Tenka would have to do something.

Akli yelled: "I not be going to your women's hut any-more!"

"Good! You make it stink!"

"Stop it!" Tenka shouted. But they didn't listen.

"I rub your face in dirt!"

"Then it will look like yours!"

Tenka strode to the women, both a head taller than she, and stepped between them—just enough space so the hot bodies didn't touch her. She shoved on their chests, and they moved a bit.

"What's wrong?" she said. "I thought you were friends."

Akli looked down on Tenka. She spoke in the Shahala that Mani had been teaching her, which was good since Tenka had a hard time understanding Tlikit.

"We not friend! I hate how Mani treat me!" Akli looked over Tenka's head to the watching people, and said, "What wrong if we eat on mat? I threw away Mani wood plate. Anyone find, can have."

Mani shouted. "You are lucky, and you don't even know it! I take my time to be your friend, teach you things, try and make your life better ... and ... and ... you turn into a screech bat and fly in my hair!"

They were closing again. Tenka felt their heavy auras squishing her, felt their heat. But she would not move. They'd have to fight with her in the middle.

Akli screeched. "You not understand pride! *You* right. *Your* way better, *you*, *you*, *you*! Why? Who say you can treat me like little one?"

"I never treated you—"

"You too stupid to understand. We not friend. I not visit you again. You not visit me."

The Tlikit woman turned and stamped away.

The Shahala woman yelled after her. "I hate that stinking cave anyway!"

Mani stalked to her hut and jerked the doorskin closed after her. The people seemed to melt into the fog.

Tenka sagged, letting out a huge breath.

For a Moonkeeper, it was just as important to keep peace within the people as to keep the moon healthy. Tenka asked herself how she had done. Bad would have been a physical fight that might have spread to others. Good would have been to get the women talking to each other again. The confrontation had ended somewhere between.

Could Ashan have done better? Maybe, but Tenka decided that she had done well enough. She was proud of herself. It had taken courage to put her body between theirs.

Ashan returned to the village after the fight was all over. She had found a low, creeping shrub with a piney smell. She told Snomish it was called ground pine, and his eyes glimmered with hope.

*Better than nothing,* Tenka thought, *if only for the effect on his mind.*

But she was wrong. Nothing would have been better. The steam of the ground pine blistered the inside of the sick man's nose, mouth, and throat. He died.

# CHAPTER 17

ASHAN BROODED OVER THE DEATH OF SNOMISH.

"Men die," Tor said, wishing he could help her get past this feeling of failure. "There's only so much a Moonkeeper can do."

"I should have saved that one, Tor."

"It's not your fault Amotkan didn't tell the Pine Spirit about this place."

"I should have brought more pine from the homeland." She shook her head; her voice was dull. "How many are going to die because of my mistake?"

If Ashan would just cry like other women, Tor would act like other men, hold her in his arms, comfort her, and she would get over whatever bothered her. Fathers taught their sons that women needed comforting. But Tor's mate, chief of a great tribe, believed she must always appear strong, even with him.

To see her like this gave him a helpless feeling that made him want even more to do *something*.

"My love," he said, "I'm going to find you some pine. Then you'll never have to feel like this again. Those hazy blue mountains where the sun goes down remind me of the sacred mountains of our homeland. Pine must grow there."

Hope shimmered in her eyes.

"How lucky I am to have you, Tor. What a good mate you are," she said, and all those other things he loved to hear.

Tor headed out in the direction Where Day Ends. The prairie rose and fell in gentle slopes. Bright green grass pushed through last summer's bent, gray stalks. Tribes of birds heading for Colder filled the wide blue sky with loud, sharp barks.

Half a day away from the village, Tor saw two antelope herds, and decided to have a hunt as soon as he returned. After a long winter, the people were hungry for fresh meat.

The sight of a third herd made him ask questions. Spring had barely arrived—why did antelope come to this part of the land so much earlier? Did they live here all the time? If men could hunt all winter, people wouldn't have to live on dried fish. Tor thought fish tasted fine, but Ashan didn't. "Don't tell anyone, but I *hate* fish mush," she'd said more than once.

The prairie was mostly barren, but he did find trees: scattered groves of leafless oaks, and others with leaves just starting to show, whose names he didn't know. Trees with thick, prickly leaves. Trees with bare branches that draped down. Different kinds of bushes and shrubs.

In Shahala land, there were many different kinds of pine. Here he couldn't find one. He wondered if he might have to go back to the homeland, so Ashan wouldn't think she was killing people because she made a mistake.

*Are you crazy?* said a voice in his mind. *Do you know how far it is?*

Returning to the home of the ancestors was a staggering thought. How long would it take? Could he find the way? Would he go alone or take someone? How much pine bark could a man carry? Would they have to do it forever, every autumn, like they used to get huckleberries? Was pine really worth that much trouble?

*Do you see why the ancestors called this the tabu land?* asked the voice in his head.

Tor said, "I've known for a long time."

As his shadow lengthened behind him, he realized that the blue mountains were much farther than they had seemed. He stopped at dark by a tiny spring-fed pool. Willows garbed in new leaves made the place smell fresh and alive. He drank woody-tasting water, ate leathermeat, rolled up in a carrying skin, and stretched out under the stars with his head on a sweet grass clump. Chewing a manroot, he saw the star group Hunter and Bear low in the sky toward Colder.

"Well," he said, "I haven't found what I'm looking for, but I did find another water place. A hunter can never know too many. Isn't that right?" he asked the star man with his spear raised to the star bear.

He was glad that the tabu land had the same sky. What if people had to learn new stars and their stories, along with everything else?

Tor thought of Shahala land and its bounty of useful trees.

Mountaintop pine, gnarled and tough, clinging to Takoma's flank higher than anything else—too rare to be touched by men.

Grandfather pine, in forests that reached the sky, giving people many things they needed.

Ridge pine, short and round, with excellent nuts if you could stand the sharp needles. Of course, women had to worry about that, he thought as he fell asleep.

In the morning, Tor noticed an unmoving heap on the ground nearby, and went to look.

It was an eagle, with black wings spread, white tail flared, head thrust to one side, dead eye fixed on the sky.

He fell to his knees. His stomach lurched. Shahala people revered eagles, sacred to Amotkan, not to be killed. No one loved eagles more than Tor. They were sons and daughters of his guardian, Takeena, the Eagle Spirit.

Filled with sadness, he stroked the feathers on its back. For a moment he thought he would weep. But however sacred, it was only an animal. And as he'd told Ashan, everything dies.

He turned the stiff bird over. One taloned foot was tangled in a cord weighted with stones—a Tlikit sling.

Tor ripped the sling off and threw it to the sky.

"I warned them!" he cried. "I'll kill whoever did this!"

Tlikit men were good at sling-hunting, and took many ducks, geese, swans, and other fat low-flyers. To bring down an eagle would take impossible skill. Tor never imagined they would try. Then one day some proud fool had brought a dead eagle to the village.

Tor was shaking the man by the throat when Ashan came

running and tore them apart. She called the Tlikit together and told them about sacred animals.

"Wear what you want, eat what you want. But you must not kill sacred animals, or terrible things will happen."

Tor had said, "I will kill you, that's what will happen."

He'd thought they understood. Until now.

"Kree-e-e!"

Tor looked up. The eagle's mate circled above the desolate plain. He felt her sorrow like cold, invisible rain. She spoke in his mind.

*Sky Dancer should not be wasted. Use him to make people learn.*

Closing his eyes, Tor saw a deadly predator: A winged man ... Eagle from the Light and Sky Dancer become one. He opened his eyes and searched the sky. He wanted to tell her that he understood. But the eagle's mate was gone. Tor made a promise to the sky where she had been.

"When I finish with them, the men of Teahra will never kill another eagle."

As if they knew he would need them, a flock of geese landed at the spring. Tor lobbed a flurry of rocks. They squawked away, except for five. He killed and gutted them and tied their feet.

He headed out for Teahra Village with geese slung over his shoulders, an eagle in his arms, and fury in his heart. Stopping in a grove of oaks, he made a fire and kept it going as he worked, pulling out coals before they turned to ash.

Tor plucked the geese, thanking them for their feathers, and the yellow fat he would use later. He took the eagle apart, cutting the wings off as one piece, connected by the muscle and bone of the back. Straightening the long flight feathers, he wondered how it felt to glide. He plucked the remaining feathers, cut off talons and beak, and put what was left on the fire.

"Sky Dancer," he said to the rising smoke. "Go to Takeena. Say hello to your mate on the way."

From the white feathers of the eagle and the geese, Tor made a tailpiece that covered him from his rear to below his knees. The remaining goose feathers were brown. Rubbing them with coals made them black like the eagle. He tied them in bunches with strands of his hair.

He blackened the soft leather of his loinskin, and stripped thongs from the long side, keeping one piece just wide enough to fit between his legs and hide what made him unmistakably a man.

The eagle's wings had to be separated after all; to work right, the joints must line up with the ones in his arms. He cut a legging to fit across his back, and lashed the shoulder bones of the eagle to it.

Covered with feathers, Tor became one with the eagle.

, He made paint of ground-up coals and goose fat, and wrapped it in leather, to be used just before he swooped down on the village. He packed white goose fluff for his face, and the beak and talons.

Tor had used up the whole morning. He'd have to run all the way to get back in time. Maybe if he ran fast enough, he'd lift off into the sky. . . .

Most of the strangers—as Tsilka still called the Shahala— had huts now, and said it was too cold to be outside at night. That was fine with her. She saw more than enough of them in the day.

It was dark, except for firelight; quiet, except for rivernoise and whispered Tlikit words. Tsilka liked this time, after eating, before sleeping, when warmer weather let her people sit outside by a slave-tended fire. The twins had fallen asleep across her lap. Stroking their soft hair, she gazed into the waning flames. Her head nodded. She got up and helped her little ones to their feet. Others stood, yawning and stretching, and headed for the cave.

A cry shattered the night.

"Kree-e-e!"

Whirling around, Tsilka saw a winged monster sweeping down from the rocks. Big enough to carry off babies. She grabbed one under each arm and ran.

"Kree-e-e! Ree-e-e!" it screamed, coming at them.

People fell to the ground, arms over heads. Tsilka stumbled into them, going down.

"Look at me!" it screeched in Tlikit.

Tsilka looked up. *A bird? Too big. A man? A god?*

The monster strode back and forth on the other side of the fire, menacing wings stretched. Chest and legs were shiny black and sprigged with feathers. A yellow beak gaped in a white feathered face. The beast had no eyes.

"I am Sahalie, god over all!"

Tsilka thought, *We're dead.*

"You sicken me! I sent Tor to teach you about sacred animals. But what did you do?"

The god threw something across the fire that hit the ground near Tsilka. It was an eagle's foot, with talons spread for striking.

"Who?" Sahalie demanded. "Who killed my son!"

No one was fool enough to answer.

"Speak, or I will tear you to pieces, one by one, first the young so parents may watch!"

*Not my babies,* Tsilka thought. But her people just lay there.

Standing on legs that felt like water, she tried to keep her eyes down, but she glimpsed the god, who seemed to be growing larger. She shook like the last leaf in a windstorm.

"I did it. I'm sorry. Spare us. Please."

The god had nothing to say. Did he see through her lie? When he spoke again, his voice was not so fierce.

"Obey my laws and live. Disobey, and die as the eagle you have killed. I will not give you another warning. Now get out of my sight."

Tsilka and her people ran for the cave. She didn't see Sahalie fly away, but she would never forget the sound of his rushing wings.

Later, Tsilka was astonished at herself: She had stood face-to-face with the god over all, ready to take another's punishment—even if it meant dying. She'd done it for her daughters.

As for the guilty one who had killed the eagle, she'd find out who he was and punish him herself for causing Sahalie's rage.

On the second night that Tor was gone, Ashan let Kai El sleep in their bed—as much for herself as for him. They snuggled like coyote pups, warm in memory of the time in Ehr's cave.

"Kree-e-e! Ree-e-e!"

It sounded like the Eagle Spirit himself, diving for a kill. Ashan's first thought was to pull the skins over their heads.

"Amah! What was that?"

"Stay here."

As any chief would whose tribe was in danger, Ashan got up, threw on her moccasins and robe, and peered out the doorway of the hut. She saw an enraged man striding behind the fire, flapping huge wings, shrieking—and knew in an instant that it was Tor who had brought the Tlikit to the ground and trapped them with his disguise and words. It was Tor, but she had to keep reminding herself—he seemed to have *become* an eagle, and as she watched he became something worse.

He claimed to be Sahalie, their Creator, and said he would eat their little ones.

Moans came from the pile of Tlikit people, and a sharp smell—there would be wet stains under some of them.

*What are you doing, Tor? Why?*

It was awful to see people in such terror—even if they were Tlikit and not Shahala. The Moonkeeper realized that she had come to consider them her own. She was seized by an urge to run out and stop him, but ... she trusted Tor.

Ashan was amazed when Tsilka took the blame. She couldn't have killed the eagle Tor was raving about—Tlikit women weren't allowed to touch weapons.

As the terrified Tlikit fled for their cave, and Tor went flapping away, Ashan wondered what the Shahala people thought ... she wasn't the only one who'd watched from a hut.

Ashan awoke when Tor came home in the night. A strange energy followed him in. He moved their sleeping son to his own bed.

"That was quite a scare you put into them," Ashan said. "Maybe *you* should be the Moonkeeper."

"Wasn't I magnificent?"

"More than magnificent."

Ashan couldn't see Tor in the dark, but she smelled him.

"Goose fat and firecoals?" she asked.

"Yes. How did I look?"

"Scary or exciting, depending on who was doing the looking."

"How about you? Were you scared, or excited?"

"Neither. I knew it was just Tor wearing some feathers. Now come here and let me clean you. I don't want the sleeping skins all greasy."

"I already did, but maybe I missed some."

She went to light the oil lamp, but he said not to: He didn't want anyone knowing that he'd come home. In the dark, she rubbed his naked body with a soft piece of doeskin, starting with his face.

"Take your time. I don't want them to see any black on me."

"I have the rest of the night."

She made slow swirls on his shoulders, back, and chest.

"How did you know it was me?"

She laughed. "I've known you for many lifetimes."

He told her of his day on the endless prairie, and the mountains that seemed to move ahead of him as he walked; the antelope; the spring; the eagles—both the dead one, and its mate who told him what to do.

She said, "I don't think there'll be any more eagle-killing around here."

"Good! I won't allow it!"

Kneeling, she rubbed his tight belly, thighs, legs, and rear. He must be clean everywhere by now, but she didn't want to stop. She dropped the doeskin and stroked with bare hands. His body answered.

"Soaring bird," she whispered. "Take me down and wrap me in your wings."

"Ashan," he said, between ragged, heavy breaths.

He crushed her to his chest, taking her mouth in a kiss, reaching in her robe for her breast.

Pressed to him, she drank his kiss like a woman dying for water, but it only made her thirstier. She slipped out of her dress and under the furs.

"Come, magic bird," she whispered, holding the furs open.

# CHAPTER 18

THE TLIKIT PEOPLE DIDN'T LEAVE THEIR CAVE THE NEXT day.

Tsilka kept her daughters within reach of her arm. Thoughts of what almost happened to them swept through her mind. Between rushes of fear, she listened to her people.

Was the thing a god, or not? That's what they talked about all day . . .

"Of course it was a god. What else could look and sound like that?"

"Maybe it was *some* god. But Sahalie? Our Creator is like a wind, not an eagle."

"Don't you think the god over all can be anything it wishes?"

"Sahalie has never appeared to people."

"Maybe they didn't live to tell anyone."

"Maybe we're lucky."

Most decided to believe what they'd seen and heard: the god over all commanding them not to kill sacred animals, or they'd be torn to pieces, starting with the little ones.

"We can get along without eagles, coyotes, and beetles," they said, relieved that Sahalie demanded so little.

Venturing out the next day, Tsilka found the eagle's foot thrown by the god, and put it in the fire. She found prints in the gray firedust where the thing had stamped about—prints the size and shape of a man's feet. She found a tuft of feathers, tied at the top with long black hairs. If it was a real god, or even a real bird, its feathers wouldn't fall off, would they?

She wasn't so sure that the monster had been their god. She kept thinking of how it looked and moved and sounded.

And Tor was gone, wasn't he?

Tsilka felt like a fool to think of Tor watching her shake in terror. She was furious.

Out in the dark away from the village, with her legs gripping his hips and thighs, her fingers digging into his chest, Tsilka rode Chopunik like a fish on a wave. She loved to have a man grunting and thrusting beneath her. Power swelled inside. He reached for her bouncing breasts and squeezed, and the power exploded. She threw her head back and cried out as spasms shook her body.

In lightning flashes behind her eyes, she saw the face of Tor.

Tsilka slumped and rolled away from the gasping man.

Chopunik was Tlikit. He had a mate. What he did with Tsilka had to be kept secret, which made it more exciting. If only it was so easy to get Tor away from his mate . . .

Tor . . . fury swept her again. Tor had made fools of her and the proud Tlikit people.

"I hate him!"

"Who?"

Chopunik's question made her realize she'd spoken out loud.

"The one who made fools of us. Tor."

Chopunik was angry. "You make a fool of me, Tsilka, to talk of another when I am with you. I know you and Tor were lovers."

"Well I hate him now," she said, "for making us scratch in the dirt begging for our lives."

"You're crazy. What are you talking about?"

"And you are stupid. Don't you know who that feathered creature was?"

He looked at her, stupidly.

"It was Tor, you fool. Tor."

"You are the fool, woman. You see Tor in everything."

His face was an ugly scowl. Tsilka had hurt his pride, and

as any woman knew, there was nothing a man hated more. For now it was good to have Chopunik whenever she wanted him. Her body needed a man.

"No, Chopunik," she said in a soft voice, stroking his sweaty cheek. "It is *you* I see in everything, the shape of your face in a cloud, your power staff in an upthrust rock . . ."

Her fingertips trailed down his chest, lingering at his nipples, down his belly, to the roots of his limp staff. She took him in her hand, moving the way she'd seen her brother move his hand one time when he'd thought he was alone.

"Roll over," he said in a broken voice. "This time I will be on top."

Tsilka lay on her back and opened her legs. Maybe this time she wouldn't see Tor when her explosion came.

As Chopunik ground away at her, she thought, *I hate you, Tor. I don't need you, Tor. If you saw me now, you would be so jealous that this man gets what you should have.*

*I hate you, Tor . . . I don't need you, Tor . . .*

Was it any wonder that Tor's image kept dancing in her mind, exploding in a shower of sparks?

# CHAPTER 19

THE MOONKEEPER'S SHADOW STICK SHOWED THAT it was mid-spring. Warm air, fresh food, smells and colors of growth and life kept the people of Teahra Village smiling.

Ashan walked along the river one morning, seeking quiet before her day filled with people. Chiawana had grown, as rivers did in springtime, covering up a beach where she liked to sit. She found a rock on higher ground, settled in the sunshine, and took in the magic she'd come for. Adorned with green grass, willow leaves, and flowers in many colors, the world seemed happy. Birdsong filled the air. Herds of salmon swam against the rushing current. The river sounded like it was laughing because the fish tickled it.

The Tlikit man named Chopunik came onto the trail below, gripping a woman's arm, propelling her toward the village.

*Ugly man,* Ashan thought. No man—especially a Tlikit—could come close to Tor's good looks, but some were worse than others. Chopunik was tall, fat, and naked. He greased his skin and hair, and stank as if he never washed it off, just kept adding more as it wore off.

He swaggered with the unmistakable look of a man who had just flung his juices.

The woman was a slave. Ashan didn't know her name. She had tried talking to them, but they wouldn't speak. The defeated creature stumbled along, head down, keeping pace

the best she could. But he jerked her arm anyway. Near the
village, he pushed her.

"Get back to your place."

Swelled up like a rutting elk, he watched the woman slink
away.

*Of all the things I've handled, why have I let this go on so
long?* Ashan asked herself.

*Worry about that later. Are you going to do something
now?*

Ashan strode up to him.

He greeted her with a grin. "It's a fine day."

She did not smile back. "Do you know who I am?"

"Everyone knows who you are."

"Then you know I have magic."

"I have never seen it."

"I think you know. It would *please* me if you never do
that again."

"What? Her?" He gave a deep, curt laugh. "She belongs
to us, not you."

"She doesn't belong to anyone but herself."

Anger replaced amusement on his face. "You do not understand Tlikit ways," he growled.

"I don't care about Tlikit ways. It will *displease* me if you
ever force yourself on a slave again. Believe me, you will
wish that you had not."

He came toward her, fists clenched at his sides, hulking,
menacing. She didn't back up, though he was like a wall of
hot rock right in her face. He could crush her. His size made
her shake inside, but she stood her ground, making herself as
large as possible—shoulders straight, chin up, eyes on his.

He hissed, "What if I take my pleasure with you next time,
instead of the slave?"

When he said the word "pleasure," a drop of spit hit
Ashan's face. Her blood boiled.

"You will die for *thinking* it! But not until you have watched
your children die!"

Ashan sizzled with a Moonkeeper's heat—the kind that
explodes with deadly force. Chopunik felt it. His eyes darted.
He backed away, still puffed up, but much less sure of himself.

"This time I will forgive your ignorance," Ashan said.

"But never again. You have a mate for your pleasures. Leave others alone, or you will regret it."

"Warriors do not need women to tell them what to do," Chopunik said as he swaggered off.

*What savages,* Ashan thought, stamping her foot. *How could a man find pleasure in forcing himself on an unwilling woman? Maybe my threats will stop him from doing it again, and if not—I think I'd enjoy boiling his insides to mush.*

As she cooled off, the Moonkeeper realized that Chopunik was just the pus oozing from a sore. A person who was owned by another . . . a person who had no rights . . . that was the festering sore that oozed many evils. Slavery could poison her people. It could destroy all she was working for.

She forgave herself for not stopping it sooner. The idea was so strange to a Shahala mind . . . it took time to see all that slave-keeping meant, to understand that it was worse than it looked.

Ashan shook her head. She thought people were born knowing how to treat other people.

*That's always been one of your problems, Windpuff,* said Raga's voice in her mind. *You want to believe in the goodness of everyone.*

Confronting Chopunik had made Ashan realize that it wasn't a matter of *if* something must be done about the slaves, but *what and when.*

Ashan spoke to three of the Tlikit who seemed to have influence with the others.

"We must talk. Come to the Moonkeeper's hut," she said, knowing they were uncomfortable in the closeness of huts. She told them to sit, then remained standing herself.

Tlok was a grumpy old man; Chalan a rash young warrior. Tsilka was . . . Ashan was still trying to figure out just *what* the woman was, but she had to admit that people listened to her. There was much in Tsilka's eyes, Ashan thought, if only she knew the language they spoke.

The Moonkeeper began, "We are all children of the Creator, Sahalie-Amotkan."

Looking at her hands, cleaning her fingernails with a twig, Tsilka said in a bored voice, "So Tor tells us every day."

Chalan said, "If I complain that a Shahala sneezed on my

food, Tor says, 'Love your brother. You are children of the same Father.'"

"Tor is right," Ashan said. "That's why slavery is wrong. It's wrong to use people that way."

Tsilka shook her head. "You are the wrong one. The slaves are the Lost People. Our gods gave them to us in the long ago. They need us, and we need them."

Tlok said, "People are nicer when they can yell at a slave and not each other."

"These people make life better for everyone by doing the worst work," Tsilka said, her eyes challenging slits. "We wonder why you do not know these things."

Ashan bristled. "How would you like to be a slave? Have you ever thought how it feels to be treated like that?"

Tsilka snorted. "What does it matter? I am not. But if I were, I'd be proud. Slaves keep peace in the tribe."

That was one of the most ridiculous things Ashan had ever heard. *Savages,* she thought. *They are hopeless savages.*

Chalan said, "Those women would die if we ran them off. Would you want us to kill them?"

"No," Ashan said. "I want you to take them back to the forest. They had a life there."

They laughed with derision.

Tlok said, "Do you know how far it is, woman?"

Chalan said, "Do you think they'd stay without their little ones? They'd be back before we were."

Ashan said, "You must let them have their little ones. You cannot take little ones from their mothers."

"Phhht!" the men responded.

Tsilka stood, her body tense, her voice dangerous.

"The little ones are ours now—new blood for the tribe. Before you people came, that's what we needed more than anything. The gods answered by giving us those little ones."

"I don't care," Ashan said. "Your gods speak to me now. They say—"

Tsilka cut her off. "We have listened to you about foolish things that no one cared about because we are a peaceful tribe. But this is between us and our Tlikit gods. Stay out of it, Ashan. You will not win."

"How dare you challenge me! This is not a game to speak

of winning. The gods have told me that keeping slaves is against the Balance. How long do you think they will allow it before they destroy us all?"

"Tlikit gods are not afraid of Shahala gods."

Ashan took a threatening step toward her.

"*You* should be afraid of a Moonkeeper's magic."

Tsilka didn't move. Her voice was an icy sneer.

"But I'm not. To me, you are just another woman. We may sing your songs and dance your dances and quit stepping on beetles, but I am telling you to leave us alone about the Lost People. They are *ours,* and we're not going to give them up."

"Oh, yes," Ashan said. "You are."

"And if we do not, will you make the sky fall upon our heads?"

"No, Tsilka, I'll just start making people die one by one. And I will start with you."

"Huh!" Tsilka said without a glimmer of fear in her eyes. "Come on," she said to the men. "The air in this place stinks."

They left Ashan standing there, impotently fuming.

"I warned you!" she yelled after them.

Reason hadn't worked, nor threats of magic. That left real magic. People could be terrorized into almost anything. But terror was more Raga's way than Ashan's. She was glad she had not yet needed the old way in the new land. Also, she suspected that people had to believe in magic for it to work. Shahala people believed in a Moonkeeper's magic, and feared it enough not to provoke it. But at least some of the Tlikit did not. For the first time, Ashan doubted her power. What if she tried magic and it failed?

The only thing left was to *remove* the problem. For that, the Moonkeeper needed her mate.

They relaxed in their hut that night, side by side on the floor, leaning back against the earth shelf bed, embers at their feet. Tor smoked kinnikinnick leaves in a stone pipe. He and Wyecat had found a patch of the creeping shrub. He'd picked some leaves, knowing Ashan brewed a tonic from them. Wyecat had shown him how to make a pipe and smoke kinnikinnick, and now he liked some every night. Ashan had tried it once. It burned her throat and made her cough. But she liked the smell when he smoked it.

She heard a slight quickening of breath—the first sign of Tor's desire. His hand, which had been resting on her knee, caressed its way up her inner thigh. Ashan had no desire for lovemaking, not with the disgusting image of Chopunik still swaggering through her mind.

"The slaves, Tor. We have to talk about them."

He sighed. "Please, my love. Leave it alone."

"What . . . pretend it isn't there? Pretend it isn't wrong? I can't. I'm the Moonkeeper."

Tor's hand dropped from her thigh as she went on.

"It's up to me to keep the Balance, and there can be no Balance where there are slaves."

"For us that may be true, but it seems to work for the Tlikit."

"Oh, it works all right. Those poor women work—the hard work, the filthy work, the lonely work."

"Maybe it's part of *their* Balance, Ashan, and without it— well, I don't know what might happen. But I can tell you this: The Tlikit will not free the Forest Women, no matter what you do."

"I know. I tried talking to them." She didn't want him to know how badly that had gone.

"You see? Waiting is what you should do."

"I have wasted the whole winter waiting."

"I know, but in time they'll see that ours is the right way. It worked with the eagle. They haven't killed one since. It's always better when people see things on their own."

"But Tor, before that happens, our people might start thinking that having slaves is *good*. I mean, having your dungwork done by someone else? How nice. I think I've seen the desire to use others in *you*. Sometimes I think you wouldn't mind—"

"Sometimes I wouldn't," he admitted. "But I never will, because I am Shahala, and I know right from wrong. They are Tlikit, and it will take a long time to make them into Shahala. You have to let them keep some of their ways for a while."

"Not this one. I can't. Not after what I saw this morning."

She told him about Chopunik and the slave.

Tor said, "Well, that is bad, but it's not like he beat her. They almost never beat them anymore, because we give them ugly looks when they do."

Ashan was infuriated.

"You don't think forcing yourself on a woman is so bad? Then let me tell you what else Chopunik did. He got right in my face and—"

Tor sprang to his feet.

"Did he touch you? I'll kill the stinking savage!"

Ashan shook her head, holding her hands up. "No, Tor. No." She was glad he'd cut her off. She'd nearly blurted the man's words about taking his pleasure with her. That would have been a mistake.

"He didn't touch me. But he challenged me. I almost had to hurt him. If we don't do something, I'm going to have to kill one of them. You know I don't want to do that."

"I'll be glad to kill as many as you wish, beginning with Chopunik."

"Well, that's not what I need. If you'll sit back down, I'll tell you what we're going to do."

He settled beside her again. She took his hands and looked into his eyes.

"Tor, the Forest Women and their little ones must be taken back where they belong."

The way she said it did not allow argument. Whatever else they were, Tor was a Shahala warrior, and Ashan was his chief.

# CHAPTER 20

Seven Shahala men, chosen by each other for hunting ability and bravery, were known as the First Warriors. They would lead the defense if the people were attacked, but that hadn't happened in living memory. Their purpose had become to hunt ceremonial animals. Now that was in question, since no one knew yet—in the six moons they'd been here—what kinds of animals the new land would provide.

As a young man, Tor had worked hard to become a First Warrior, as his father and grandfather had been in their time. After other tests, he was given his chance at sixteen summers to kill Mahto, the bear. Spirits sent a grizzled male so huge it took many trips to carry it all home—meat for the tribe, the hide for his mother, the claws to wear around his neck. Tor became the youngest First Warrior ever, to his family's great pride. And Ashan . . . he remembered the desire in her young eyes as she'd watched him dance, firelight gleaming from the polished claws around his neck. But all of that was long ago.

The morning after Ashan told Tor what must be done about the slaves, he gathered the First Warriors at one of the ledges where the Shahala had lived when they'd arrived. No one could come up behind them.

Tor, Lar, Lyo, Deyon, Takluit the Outsider, Kowich, and Hamish, between the ages of seventeen and twenty-four summers, were the best that men could be in strength, endurance, and cunning. They had reason to be proud of who and what they were.

Tor said, "How long has it been since we've been out, just the seven of us?"

"Too long," Hamish grumbled, rattling his necklace with his fingers. "I finally get to wear these claws, and now we're not needed anymore."

"The tribe may not seem to need us," Tor said, "but our mates would appreciate what I found yesterday."

"What?" they asked.

"A rainwater pond not far from here. It will dry up by summer, but now it's covered in blue-winged ducks."

"You want First Warriors to hunt *ducks*?" Lar said, stiff and proud as he'd been when they were boys.

"The ducks don't matter. I was just thinking of having a day with each other, like old times, for the fun. Am I the only one who is tired of women and strangers?"

The men smiled at each other. The spring day was lush, and being together did seem like a good idea. They thrust their hands toward each other and slapped them, the sign of First Warriors agreeing.

"Get your bird-hunting weapons," Tor said. "And be quiet about leaving. Shahala men know better than to ask to come with First Warriors, but who knows about Tlikit men?"

Hamish, the newest, said, "I'll bring one of those Tlikit slings."

"Fine," Tor said, stiff-lipped.

In the Moonkeeper's hut, he nodded to Ashan, and she nodded in return. They had said all there was to say last night. She had his things ready: A leather pouch that held several spears, thin as a finger and long as an arm, and the notched stick for throwing them; and a waist pouch with dried food. That's all he would need besides his heavy Shahala spear, which he took everywhere.

He embraced his mate.

"Here," she said, opening her hand. Seven white stones lay in her palm.

"One for each of you. They're magic. They'll protect you."

"It's only a day of hunting ducks," he said, taking the stones and putting them in the waist pouch.

Ashan shook her head. "It's the beginning of far more than that."

Tor left the village, followed by the others. They walked along, talking the talk of longtime friends, laughing and slapping each other's backs. If they'd known Tor's real purpose, they might not have been so happy.

He stopped on the wind-free side of some boulders.

"The ducks are on the other side of that hill. But that's not the real reason I wanted you here. I have something to say."

They looked at each other, then settled on the grass in a half circle with their backs to the boulders. Tor squatted in front of them.

"We have to take the slave people back to their own home."

"You're crazy," Lar said.

"I know that's how it sounds, but I'm here to tell you that we must. You know it's wrong to keep people."

"They're not tied," Kowich said. "They could run away if they wanted to."

Tor shook his head. "Four women with seven little children? I've been where they live. It is far."

Takluit, who had once been a slave, said, "It's not as easy to run away as you might think. I had to leave my mother and my sister behind."

Lar said, "But you became one of us. You lived."

"I lived, but I wake up every morning wondering what happened to them."

"This is a Tlikit problem," Hamish said. "Why should we get into it?"

It was time for Tor to bring the discussion to an end.

"Because the Moonkeeper commands it. We are not here to decide yes or no. We are here to plan how to do it."

There was no reason to argue about a Moonkeeper's command. They nodded and touched hands in agreement.

Tor took the stones from his pouch. They were all alike—smooth, ice white, the size of flattened acorns.

"The Moonkeeper made these for us. They are magic. They will protect us."

He handed them out. Awe settled on the men as they fingered polished surfaces. Shahala people loved the Moonkeeper. Her life was busy, yet she had made these stones and filled them with magic. The men knew they were loved in return. And protected.

The stones also said how much it meant to their chief that they do this for her.

"We'll do it at night," Tor said, "while the Tlikit sleep in their cave. As loud as the snoring gets, they shouldn't hear a thing."

Lyo said, "The slaves don't seem to understand either language. How will we explain what we're doing?"

"We'll have to sneak up on them," Tor said. "Kidnap them."

Hamish laughed. "You have practice, Tor! You're the only man who ever had to *kidnap* a mate!"

They all laughed, but Tor ignored it.

"So," he said. "We will kidnap the slaves and their little ones—"

"Little ones?" Lar said with alarm.

"The little ones aren't slaves," Kowich said. "They treat them as well as their own."

"I don't see any problem with the little ones," Hamish said.

Tor let them go on. Then he cleared his throat loudly.

"The Moonkeeper says mothers must have their little ones."

The men grunted. The sound meant, *Women—what can you do?*

Tor continued. "When we're far enough away from the village, we'll let them loose. We'll make them understand that we're taking them home. The rest should be easy. They'll be happy to follow. We'll be back in little more than a moon. By then—"

"A moon? What about our families?"

"They'll be fine, Lar. By the time we get back, the Moonkeeper will have everyone's fur smoothed. The Tlikit will think the slaves ran away, at the same time as we left on a long hunt."

"Even the Tlikit aren't that stupid, Tor," Hamish said. He talked too much and lacked respect for his elders.

"Maybe they're not, but Shahala First Warriors have no reason to fear them."

The warriors grunted in agreement.

Lar said, "Seven against four—I can see us kidnapping the slavewomen—they sleep out by the fire. But who's going to fight off the Tlikit when they wake to find us stealing little ones from their cave in the middle of the night?"

"Have you ever been in their cave?" Tor asked.

Wrinkling their noses, the men said no.

"I've looked in there," he said. "The children of the slaves don't sleep with the Tlikit children. They sleep near the front, where it's colder. Look tonight."

The men nodded.

He continued. "We'll creep in. Each of us will pick a little one. We'll cover their mouths with our hands—maybe stuff them with leather—get them out of the cave, leave them tied, and come back for the women."

"I help," said a child's voice.

The men jumped to their feet as Elia stepped from behind the boulders.

*He was listening,* Tor thought, *and we didn't even know it! The Shahala First Warriors have turned into sleepy old men!*

"Get out of here!" he shouted.

"You need me," Elia said.

The men sat back down, laughing at the boy of thirteen summers acting like a full-grown warrior. Except for Tor, angrier than he should be without knowing why.

"We do not need a boy," he said.

"You do. Your plan about the little ones." Elia shook his head. "Not work. They think bears got them. They kick, they bite, they scream whole village awake."

The others laughed, but Tor yelled. "Warriors can handle little ones! Now get out of here before I beat you!"

"Show them your plan, Tor," Elia challenged. "Carry me off."

He dropped to the ground, curled up, and pretended snoring sleep. Tor *would* beat the little dungball.

"Get him, Tor!" the warriors said.

Tor picked Elia up by his head and slammed him against his chest, where he dangled, kicking and squirming. Neck clamped in the crook of Tor's arm, he squalled like a stuck deer. Tor squeezed until he stopped gurgling, took him to the others and dropped him. Elia lay on the ground gulping air. The warriors rolled over laughing.

"We heard him!"

"Try again, but be careful you don't kill him by squeezing!"

Tor didn't think it was funny.

"See what I mean?" Elia said, coughing.

They looked at each other. They did see what he meant.

"Tell us your idea, boy," Lar said.

"I go with you?"

"No!" Tor yelled.

He remembered his brother: Beo with dancing black agate eyes; Beo dying in his arms, because Tor persuaded their father to allow a child of only eleven summers to go on the hunt for the last mammoth, the hunt that found man-eaters instead of mammoth, bringing the Time of Sorrows that tried to destroy the tribe.

Like Beo, Elia had black agate eyes that danced.

But the others said, "Listen to him, Tor. At least listen."

Elia said, "You not steal little slaves. Too noisy. But I know slave talk. I say they going on hunt with great Shahala warriors. Little slaves be ready when you want."

"We need him, Tor," the First Warriors said.

Tor sighed. They did. He prayed he would not regret it. The place in his heart that held sorrows was already full.

Several nights later, the half-round moon lit a cloudless sky. The First Warriors agreed that the time was right.

Though Tor had been against it at first, the heat in his blood, the tingle on his skin, the challenge in his head—any man thrived on these. He made rousing love to Ashan before he went out into the night.

Seven men and a boy did as they had planned. The slave-women and their children might have been carried away by spirits, or turned into mist to float away in the first rays of the sun.

Ashan didn't sleep after Tor left that night. She thought of the ways tomorrow might unfold, and how she would handle each.

*Whatever happens, I will prevent violence.*

There had been many arguments between Tlikit and Shahala, but none had yet come to blows. Ashan had a terrible, perhaps unreasonable, fear of that. Once violence was loose among them, the tribes could become like a stampeding herd of bison that throws itself off a cliff, trampling anything that gets in the way.

At first light she emptied her mind of her own thoughts, and invited spirits to enter. She waited in the Moonkeeper's hut.

"The fire is dead!" someone shouted. "Where are those stinking slavewomen?"

"Gone! The new-blood children, too!"

"How can they be gone?"

"Well they are! Look around!"

The loudest, angriest voice was Tsilka's.

"Tor! Where are our slaves?"

The doorskin flew open.

"Come out, Tor!" Tsilka shrilled.

"Tor went hunting."

"Our slaves are gone! You are the big chief! You tell us what happened!"

Ashan stalked toward her.

"Get away from my door."

Tsilka didn't move. Ugliness twisted her face. Ashan had to push by her, getting invisible poison on her hands.

"Rattlesnake's daughter," Ashan hissed.

By now, all the Tlikit were outside, milling around, angry and upset. Women cried. Men threatened agonizing death to whoever had taken the slaves. As soon as they saw the Moonkeeper, they started talking at once.

"The Lost People! Someone stole them! And the new-blood children! All of them—gone!"

Tsilka shouted, "Look in Shahala huts!"

"Don't be ridiculous!" Ashan said. "Why would we take them? We think keeping slaves is horrible."

But some of the Tlikit started toward huts. Shahala men bristled, ready to stop them. The Tlikit might be happy sleeping together in one place, but no one entered a Shahala home unless invited.

The Tlikit hesitated.

"What's the matter? Are you afraid of them?" Tsilka screeched, right behind Ashan's ear.

Ashan whirled around.

Tsilka screamed in her face. "The Lost People don't even belong to you, and you turned them loose!"

"Your slaves ran away, or the spirits took them. Now get out of my space, or I will boil your insides to mush!"

Tsilka didn't move. Power rose in Ashan as she glared at her. She gathered it as heat and sent it shooting from her eyes.

Tsilka said, "I do not fear you, Ashan. You could not boil water for soup." Then she shouted, "Look people! Look who else is missing! Tor and those bear-claws-around-the-neck, better-than-us Shahala First Warriors! That's who took our slaves and our new-blood children!"

A man came running, yelling that he had found tracks. The stew Tsilka had been stirring came to a boil.

"Well?" she yelled. "Go get them!"

"I forbid you!" Ashan commanded.

But the Tlikit men stormed to their cave, came out with weapons, and headed down the river after the one who'd found the tracks.

Ashan could have had her people stop them . . . yes, they could have had a war right there at Teahra Village. And maybe that's just what she should have done. But she let them go, hoping Tor and the slaves were far enough away that the Tlikit would never catch up with them. She hoped Tor would be looking behind as well as ahead.

After the Tlikit warriors left, Tsilka had no more words for Ashan, but plenty of evil, gloating looks.

"What are you standing around for?" the Moonkeeper said to her people. "If they want to chase the wind, let them, but we have work to do."

Ashan went in her hut, hanging feathers by the door to tell people to leave her alone.

"Failure" was a word that did not apply to the Moonkeeper, but there was no other word that would work. Ashan had failed to stop the Tlikit from going after the Shahala. What would happen now?

*All because of Rattlesnake Woman. I should have struck her dead the first time I saw her.*

*Indeed,* Raga's voice said in her mind.

Ashan answered out loud. "Do I hear your disapproval, Old Moonkeeper? Where were you and your spirit friends when I needed you out there?"

Raga said, *Why did I bother teaching you magic if you are never going to use it?*

"I tried, and it failed. I tried to boil her, but she did not feel the heat. Because she did not believe."

*Because you did not believe, Ashan. That's why your magic failed.*

# CHAPTER 21

"Faster! Hurry!" Tor kept yelling, as the band of slaves and rescuers traveled through the night and the next day.

The setting of Kai, the Sun, wouldn't have stopped Shahala warriors: Alhaia, the Moon, would be bright again this night, and Haslo, the Star, would keep them going in the direction Colder. But Tor had more than just warriors to think about. Looking at the Forest Women didn't tell him much; they had practice at hiding how they felt. But the little ones, so eager at the start, were visibly exhausted. At a marshy place edged with scattered alder trees, he decided to stop for the night, in spite of a prickling he'd felt at the back of his neck all day.

"How does this look?" he asked the warriors with a wave of his arm.

"Anything looks good now," one answered.

Picking their spots on the ground, they put down their spears and their packs, which were heavier than usual because of the many things they'd brought for the women, who'd have nothing at their home in the forest.

The women stood in a tight cluster around their little ones. Tor gave one of them a pack he'd been carrying.

"Food. You carry it. Make it last the whole trip."

He repeated it in Tlikit, but he could never tell if they understood, because they never looked in his eyes. He handed another woman a water bladder and pointed to a shimmery orange spot out in the tall reedy grass—the reflection of the setting sun upon water. She walked off toward it.

The warriors took extra sleeping skins from their packs and tossed them on the ground, making signs to show that they were gifts. At first the women seemed afraid to touch the skins, but then they pulled them together at the base of a large tree and sat down.

*Just like Teahra,* Tor thought. *They want to sleep by a tree, clumped together like mushrooms. Except now they have their little ones to huddle with.*

Tor pawed through his food pouch and took out a piece of stringy, dry elk. *At least in Teahra, they had better food to eat,* he thought.

*And what will they eat when you leave them in the forest?* asked a voice in his mind.

Tor had thought about it, but he hadn't told the First Warriors: They would have to stay for a while and hunt for the women.

The voice pestered him. *And what will they eat when that is gone?*

Tor was tired of the talking in his head.

*Spirits said we must take them back, and that is what we're doing,* he said to himself. *Spirits can take care of them after that.*

As soon as the sun was gone, the twilight air got cold. Fingers of fog lifted from the marsh and crept toward the trees. Tor heard scattered croaks—frogs whose deep-sounding voices said their legs were large enough to be eaten.

The woman returned with water, and everyone drank. Tor didn't mind the mossy taste, glad to get the crust of dry meat washed out of his mouth.

In spite of how tired they must be, the woman took her sisters into the misty marsh. Tor thought they were going to catch frogs, but they pulled broad-leafed plants, stripped off roots, and brought them back.

A woman gave him a handful of knuckle-sized knobs.

"What are they?" he asked.

She stared at her bare feet.

"Keachak?" he asked in Tlikit. But she was silent. He

shook his head, knowing why Ashan had been so frustrated by her attempts to talk with the Forest Women.

"Go and get your rest," he muttered.

She must have understood that. She went back over to the others of her kind.

Tor ate the reddish brown roots, which were crunchy, and bland.

Higher-voiced frogs gave themselves to the song rising from the marsh, as if the oncoming dark were morning to them and they were glad they had lived to see it.

Lar said, "I don't understand these women. They must know they're going home, but they look as pathetic as ever."

Kowich said, "I know. Doing what they're told. Afraid to make someone mad. Tor, you told us the Moonkeeper said they'd be happy."

"I guess you don't get over being a slave in one day."

"Believe me, you do not," said Takluit the Outsider, who'd been born one.

"Maybe they don't understand that we are rescuing them. Maybe they think they belong to *us* now, instead of the Tlikit." Deyon didn't talk much, but what he said was usually worth hearing.

"By the looks on their faces, I think they liked the savages better," Hamish said, insulted.

Tor was more disappointed than insulted. The Forest Women understood what was happening—he knew they did. He had thought they'd thank him for it and was hurt that they did not.

"Oh well," he said, "at least they're not trying to escape."

The men could barely hear each other. There must be vast herds of frogs out there. The marsh throbbed with rhythmic sounds, from deep rumbles to high chirps.

The treetops were black against the dark gray sky.

"Enough talk," Tor said. "Get rested. I'll take first watch, then I'll wake you, Deyon."

The men rolled up in their sleeping skins, grunting and sighing.

A short distance away, the scattering of alders thinned into grassland. Leaning back against a trunk, holding his spear in both hands with its butt on the ground, Tor stood facing the way they had come. He could see open prairie on one side. On the other, he could see his sleeping friends and the marsh. It was a difficult time for guarding: almost dark, except for the fog, which held on to a trace of light as it drifted just above the ground. Since his eyes were almost useless, Tor told his ears to listen hard, but frog noise was all he heard. He asked Alhaia, the Moon, to hurry. After Alhaia arose, watching was easier, until sleepiness sat on his eyelids, and the thought of lying down became irresistible.

Tor was about to go and wake Deyon, when he saw movement in the trees along the edge of the marsh. He blinked.

A line of men, coming right toward his sleeping people! Two for every Shahala!

"Get up!" he yelled, racing to his men. "It's the Tlikit!"

The First Warriors sprang to their feet and stood with Tor, spears held across their chests in both hands.

The Tlikit stopped, just as surprised.

"Don't do it!" Tor warned, with a menacing thrust of his weapon.

For a moment the Tlikit seemed confused. But their greater numbers made them bold.

"Get them!" one yelled.

Screaming like savages, they ran at the Shahala with spears and branches from the ground.

As they came, Tor gripped the end of his spear in both hands and swung it back and forth in front of him. Wood cracked against wood and flesh and bone. Hollering, grunting, men went down and came back up. Wielding his spear like a club, Tor stayed on his feet, while all around him, men punched, kicked, and scuffled, tearing up the ground and each other, feeling no pain in the heat of battle.

Cra-a-a-ck!

Tor's head filled with stars. He pitched forward, his shoulder digging into the ground. He pushed himself up, and felt warm blood running down his arm.

"Now you've made me mad!" he yelled. He struggled to his feet, swinging his spear wildly in the night air.

Thump!

Kicked in the back, Tor whirled around. Wyecat went down

under the butt of his spear. Wyecat! A thought flashed in Tor's mind to help his old friend get up. But he kept swinging, bringing down another one coming at him with a blade.

He heard someone yell, "The slaves are getting away!"

Tlikit men went after them.

A scream rose over the clamor—a scream of mortal injury. Tor's blood froze.

"Elia!" he cried, running.

Tlikit men knelt around the boy. Tor shoved them away.

Chest to the ground, butt in the air, Elia thrashed, shrieking loud enough to deafen the Spirit of Thunder.

"Hold him down!" Tor said.

A thin spear protruded from his back below the shoulder. Tor pulled it out. Elia wouldn't die from such a wound, but that wasn't how he sounded.

Filled with rage, Tor broke the spear over his knee and flung the pieces away.

"Look what we've done!" he said, first in Tlikit, then in Shahala, for all were to blame. "We have killed a boy because we cannot agree!"

Elia's cries had ruined the fighting mood. Such a thing wouldn't have stopped a battle of strangers, but these men had lived together for six moons. Perhaps they were becoming brothers.

The slavewomen and the little ones had vanished.

Tor spoke to Wyecat, who was holding his head.

"We need sleep. How about you?"

Wyecat nodded. "We'll decide what to do in the morning."

Tor carried Elia, who had finally stopped screaming, back to the place where they had been attacked, to find some skins and get some sleep.

He whispered, "That was a good show, Elia."

"Best ever. But shoulder *does* hurt.

"I'm just glad it only tore up flesh," Tor said. Elia could never know *how* glad he was.

"What were you doing?" Tor asked.

"Crazy men scare little ones. I take them away. Women want come too. We running, I get hit, go down screaming." The boy smiled. "Slaves know what I doing. They get away."

"The Moonkeeper will be proud of you."

"She who I do it for." Elia's voice was full of love. "She beautiful. I grow up, take away from you."

Tor cuffed him lightly on the head.

Just before Tor drifted off to sleep, he noticed the frogs starting up again. He hadn't realized that the battle of men had silenced them.

In the morning, groaning from pain they hadn't felt the night before, the bloody, grimy men staggered to the water to clean their wounds. When they returned to the place where they'd fought as enemies, then slept together as brothers, Tor thought they looked ashamed.

Gashes and scrapes; swellings and bruises; missing teeth; a nose or two that seemed to have moved; an arm that needed a sling—the injuries were more ugly than serious.

Elia, who had taken no part in the battle, had received its worst. The flesh below his shoulder had been pierced all the way through. But he hadn't bled much; the wounds in his back and chest must have closed as soon as Tor pulled out the spear. He had good color, was alert and showing off the first battle wounds he'd received to any who would look.

Elia said to Tor, "Want spear. Where is?"

Tor shook his head. "It's an evil thing that brought you down. Not something you want to save."

Elia nodded. "Want *kill* spear. Where is?"

"I killed it and threw it away."

"Mine to kill."

Tor shrugged. "Too late."

The men of Teahra were sorry the boy got hurt, but glad that his howls had brought them to their senses.

Tor said to them, "Men get angry because they are men. But there must be a better way to fix it than by killing each other. Think about it. Say I killed you, Tlok—"

"You almost did," Tlok said, rubbing an ugly red smash on his forehead.

"What if I had? Who would feed your mate and little ones? I'd have to. I'm sure I'd come to wish I had found another way."

They laughed. Tlok was cursed with a demanding mate who liked to keep herself and four little ones fat.

Tor continued: "Forget about ancient laws. Forget about what Moonkeepers say. See if you agree with this: It *doesn't make sense* for men of the same tribe to kill each other, no matter how angry we are—because the tribe needs *all* its men. The death of one hurts the tribe and everyone in it, including the man who killed him."

They nodded. It made sense.

"This is how Shahala warriors agree," Tor said, thrusting out his hand. It was met by six others.

Tor looked at the Tlikit. "Join us."

Twenty hands slapped. The loud noise said that no Teahra warrior would kill another, no matter what kind of blood flowed in him.

"Let's go home," Tor said.

"What about the slaves?" Wyecat asked.

"They're gone."

"But we know where they live. There's more to this than agreeing not to kill each other, Tor. Are you going to leave our slaves alone?"

The answer was no. Ashan would not give up. Tor knew that, but he couldn't say it.

"I don't know, Wyecat. For now I'm asking: Do you want to die over them?"

"Not really."

"Neither do I. I think we should go home and let our mates fuss over our wounds. And then we should talk about it. Everyone in both tribes—I mean—"

"I know what you mean, Tor. Slapping hands doesn't make our blood the same."

"I'm trying, Wyecat. I'm not a god."

"Not since you found out how much work it was."

The men from Teahra Village went home.


For now, there was no problem to be solved. The slaves had run while they were being fought over. But not toward the faraway forest—the home Ashan was so certain they must crave. No. They ran back to Teahra Village.

Like the Shahala, like the Tlikit . . . their old home wasn't home anymore.

Ashan said, "Finally, Tor, one of them talked to me, in a mix of Shahala and Tlikit. Her name is Weechul. I asked why they came back here when they could have gone anywhere. Do you know what she said?"

"What?"

"Being a slave is not the worst thing. Not being able to feed your little ones is. I realized she's right. I would have done the same thing they did." Ashan shook her head. "I can be so stupid, Tor. I'm a mother. Why didn't I look at it through a mother's eyes?"

"You may be a Moonkeeper, my love, but you *are* human."

Ashan didn't like excuses, especially for herself.

"But I caused all that trouble for nothing. Everything is the same as it was. No matter what *people* say, I have to listen to *spirits,* and I've never known one to change its mind. Having slaves is against the Balance."

"Ashan, you need to relax a little . . . be easier on yourself and others."

Tor knelt behind her and massaged her shoulders, speaking in a soothing voice.

"What happened out there was *not* for nothing. Something *very* important happened—a man-thing, but I'll do my best to explain it . . ."

Ashan sat with Tor on a ledge by the cliffs, watching the village. After all that had happened in the last three days, people were subdued as they went about their work.

An argument by the oak tree got everyone's attention.

"No!" Weechul shouted. The other slaves stood behind her. She threw something down in front of Tsilka.

"I won't do it! Neither will my sisters!"

People stopped what they were doing and listened.

Fists clenched, Tsilka shook with anger.

Weechul spoke loudly in a mix of two languages.

"All you people, I have something to say. We will not do the dungwork of these women anymore. We will keep the village fire. That is more than most women do. We want to do it, for our tribe."

Tsilka sputtered, "You already keep the fire, or we beat you!"

"Come on, Tor," Ashan said.

As Ashan and Tor hurried toward them, Tsilka picked up the hide thrown down by Weechul and thrust it at her.

Weechul didn't take it, and didn't back up.

"If you don't chew this hide, I will—"

"You will do nothing!" Ashan said.

Tsilka whirled around.

Ashan spoke loud enough for everyone to hear.

"Keeping the fire is the work of four women. They will be known as Firekeepers. They will be no one's slaves, and their little ones will be their own."

Tor said, "Brothers, we don't want to fight. We already know why. Why should men care? It is only women's work the slaves do. Let the women do their own work."

People agreed.

Except for the Tlikit women. They lost their workers, and the little ones they'd been mothering. But there was nothing they could do.

That night, the Firekeepers and their little ones slept together by the oak tree.

Ashan said, "Someday, Tor, they should have a hut."

A few nights later, Elia died in his sleep.

Shocked, Ashan found no cause. She told people there must have been something bad on the spear.

Tor suffered terribly.

So did Ashan.

She'd made magic stones to protect the First Warriors. When Tor told her Elia would be going, she had planned to make him one too, but . . .

*A boy died because I didn't find time to make him a rock. A brave, loyal boy . . . clever, funny, loved and loving . . .*

People mourned him. Elia had belonged to both tribes—the Tlikit by birth, the Shahala who had taken him in. They grieved as a whole village, not blaming, not asking what kind of spear killed him.

Elia's death had meaning. People always remembered the boy whose name meant Friend as the one who gave up life

so his tribe could see that they must never do that again. It
came to be told that he jumped in front of the spear.

Because of Elia, no Teahra warrior would ever again raise
a weapon against another. They were all one now: the People
of Teahra Village.

# CHAPTER 22

Aꜱʜᴀɴ ꜱᴀᴛ ᴡɪᴛʜ Tᴏʀ ᴏɴ ᴛʜᴇ ꜱʟᴇᴇᴘɪɴɢ ꜱᴋɪɴꜱ. Sʜᴇ pretended not to watch Kai El on the other side of the hut as he made himself ready for his power quest.

"Oh, Tor," she whispered. "How can my baby be seven summers already?"

Her mate shook his head. "I don't know, but my stomach is still full from yesterday's feast. And there are the gifts-people gave him." He waved his hand toward Kai El's side of the hut.

"It's hard to believe," she said wistfully. "We've been here for almost three turnings of the seasons. Elia's been gone more than two." She still thought of him often.

Tor sighed. "Yes."

"In the homeland," she said, "time flowed like winter honey. Here it rushes like the water in the Great River."

"Mmm," he said, lost in his own thoughts.

"I think it's because I'm so busy. Even with Tenka, I'm so busy."

The Other Moonkeeper had her own hut now, and took some of the work from Ashan's shoulders. People liked to talk to her about their problems. Instead of giving good advice, Tenka told them what they wanted to hear, but it seemed to make them feel better. She was good at storytelling, talking to girls when they made their first blood, and other work like that. It helped, but Ashan was busy all the time with spirit speaking, decisions, rituals, healing, magic rocks, and all the other demands of a tribe so large she couldn't keep count. And her family, too.

Ashan watched Kai El lacing his new moccasins. She swallowed hard. Yesterday a feast marked the day of his birth. Today he would begin his power quest.

A power quest was like a door Shahala boys and girls passed through to get from one part of life to the next. With no food and only a little water, Kai El would go alone to a special place and wait, perhaps for several days and nights, for a spirit to reveal itself as his guardian. It would give him his own song, and his new name.

He would be different when he returned, ready to join in the things of older boys. He would call her Mother instead of Amah, and she wouldn't dare call him "her baby" again.

Like every mother, Ashan had different feelings about it. She was proud of his strength and courage. She was sad, because after this he wouldn't need her in the same way as before. And like any mother, she was afraid. Some did not return from a power quest. No one knew what happened to them. It was a sad thing for the tribe, worse than a baby lost in birthing—but it happened. It was a natural part of life. Easy to say, unless you were one of those unfortunate mothers.

Ashan gazed at the little boy she loved so much. Her throat tightened. Tears filled her eyes.

Kai El was tall for his age, with just enough baby fat to make him look squeezable. Thick black hair reached his shoulders. His soft skin was the color of sunset amber; an ochre glow touched his high cheeks. His black eyes sparkled with eagerness. Ashan was certain that her son was the best-looking child of Teahra Village.

He loved laughing, but today he was serious.

*So grown up,* she thought. *It seems like only yesterday he was a baby, and we lived in the mountains, and . . .*

Her tears spilled over. To hide them, she got up, crossed the hut, and knelt by him. She had made him all new things: tough elkhide moccasins; lightweight deerhide cape, loinskin, and leggings. She fussed with his moccasins.

"Ah-mahh," he said, squirming.

"Hold still. I want to make sure these stitches are tight."

Tor said, "He's fine, Ashan. Spirits will be impressed by what they see."

She stepped away, sniffling behind her hand.

Tor had something hidden behind him, and brought it out with a flourish ... a traditional Shahala headpiece.

Sucking in his breath, the boy looked at his father with wide eyes.

"You made it from your horsetail rope," he said in a voice filled with awe.

Once common among Shahala men, horsetail ropes were becoming rare as they wore out and couldn't be replaced. Ropes could be made of leather strips or plant fibers, but nothing matched the long strands of a horse's tail.

"Adah, you love that rope."

"I love you more."

Once white, now gray with age, made from the tail of the first horse he'd ever killed and lengthened with others over time, Tor *did* love the rope, so much that Ashan had once risked her life to save it from a river when he lay unconscious.

But now his boy needed the protection it would give. Little ones didn't take weapons on their power quests. To carry a weapon they didn't yet know how to use might be seen as a challenge by an animal or a spirit who would otherwise leave them alone.

To make the headpiece, Tor had straightened the twisted strands on a heated rock, and woven a strip for a base. One by one he tied lengths as long as his hand to the base, so thick he couldn't get another one in. The stiff strands stood up on top, and trailed down in back.

With thongs and porcupine quills, Tor secured the headpiece in Kai El's hair.

"I give you the power of Kusi, the Horse Spirit, so you can outrun anything that tries to get you, or catch anything you want."

Kai El looked up and around, trying to see the headpiece, but he couldn't. He ran his hands over the strands, his round face split by a smile.

"Thank you, Adah."

Tor nodded. "You are lucky. Once every Shahala boy wore

such a headpiece for his power quest, but you will be one of the last, now that all the horses are gone."

Ashan said, "You will save it for your first son." She was serious, but it made Kai El giggle. A boy of seven summers couldn't imagine having a son someday.

She held out her open hand.

"I have something for you, too. It's a magic stone. Wear it all the time."

The Moonkeeper made a stone for every child's power quest, to be worn on a thong around the neck. Spirits helped her pick the right one for each. As she shaped and smoothed, thinking about the child, the stone absorbed the power of Moonkeepers from the Misty Time. She scratched the name sign given at birth on one side. When the boy or girl returned, she would scratch the new name sign on the other. This showed that people changed their names, but were still the same people.

The stone the Moonkeeper had made for her son was a flat circle, light blue because he said his eyes liked the sky when it was that color. Ashan had never worked so hard on a magic stone. She had *pushed* her power into it, gathering it up, sending it to her arms, her hands, and into the stone until the stone became hot, squeezing herself until she felt drained.

Kai El took it from her, turning it over, fingering the lines of his name. He looked up, and love flowed between their eyes.

"I like it more than anything!" He put the thong over his head. The blue stone lay against his chest.

"How do you get magic into stones?" he asked.

"I'm the Moonkeeper—I just do it. The magic works, especially for you."

Teary-eyed again, Ashan embraced him. He allowed it for a moment, then wriggled out of her grip.

"I'm ready to go."

Ashan looked at Tor. He nodded. They went with their son to the edge of the village. She pointed in the direction Colder, toward the lands of their ancestors.

"Walk into the hills. You'll be drawn to a sacred place, and you will know when you have reached it. It will be higher than the places around. That's all I can tell you."

In the ancestral homeland, seekers had gone to the top of Kalish Ridge to meet their guardian spirits. In the new land, the Moonkeeper had not been shown such a spot, so she let seekers find their own.

"When you get there, pray for your guardian spirit to come. Then wait. It may take time, but your guardian won't let you die."

Well . . . there *had* been the occasional little one . . . but why remind Kai El?

Tor said, "Stay awake. You don't want to miss the spirit if it comes in the dark. And don't leave just because you get hungry. Hunger helps."

"I wouldn't do that," Kai El said. "You have raised a brave son."

"I know," Tor said. "You make me proud."

"You make your people proud," Ashan said, speaking as the Moonkeeper.

Kai El left them. The sunshine gleamed on his hair. Watching him climb up through the cliffs, Ashan's chest hurt; it was hard to breathe. Tears ran down her cheeks.

Tor said, "I wonder what his new name will be?"

"Oh, Tor, how can you think about that? No food, no weapon, just enough water to keep him alive. That's all I can think about. It's hard."

"You did it. I did it. Everyone does. It *is* hard. It's *supposed* to be hard. Little ones have to learn courage if they are to survive and grow up and become useful to the tribe."

"I meant hard for *me*. I never realized how much harder a power quest is for the mother than it is for the child."

"Oh," Tor said, understanding. "Just remember how smart he is. Remember all the things you taught him when you two were alone in the old man's cave. I know he won't forget."

# CHAPTER 23

Kai El's power quest was the most exciting thing that had ever happened in his life. They said *something* would happen out here, but what? They said he'd be different when he returned, but who would he be?

Soon he would know!

Proud, brave, feeling very grown-up, the son of Ashan and Tor strode across the prairie on a summer morning so fine that he sometimes forgot the seriousness of his quest.

He felt a bit of fear following him like a shadow, though he wouldn't have admitted it. He could never catch it when he whirled around, so he just laughed at it. But he wished they had let him bring a weapon. Maybe *most* little ones didn't know how to use weapons yet, but *he* did. He felt better after he picked up a hefty stick. Now he could bash any bad animal that tried to get in his way. And it was a good walking stick, too.

Flat prairie gave way to low hills. The sun was high in the hot blue sky. After yesterday's feast to celebrate the seven summers of his life, Kai El still wasn't hungry. But he was thirsty, and a bit tired, so he stopped for a drink and a rest.

Amah said he'd feel something to tell him which way to go. He hadn't felt anything yet. What would it be?

"Be alert, and you will know," was all she would say.

Kai El knew that some little ones never returned. Maybe

they *never* felt the thing that told them which way to go, so they just kept walking until they fell over and died.

*If little ones are so important to the tribe, why aren't we given more help for our power quests?* he wondered.

After more aimless walking, he worried about what he should do if he never felt the thing that would tell him where to go. Then he thought he heard something. Standing still, he emptied his mind. An invisible whisper tugged from the direction Where Day Begins. He went that way, and the pull strengthened. He climbed up a long slope that ended in a steep decline.

The little boy sat at the edge of the drop-off, the late sun warm on his back. A breeze feathered the strands of the magnificent horsetail headpiece. Higher than the surrounding lands, he could see forever in all directions: hills behind hills, then distant mountains.

He noticed a slight heat rising into his bottom. He closed his eyes and put his hands flat on the ground. Yes, it was really there. The air around him had a mild sting. And a smell like after a thunderstorm, though the sky had been blue for days.

Kai El knew that he had found sacred ground. He stood, crossed his hands on his chest, and announced himself to the spirits of the place.

"I am Kai El, Sun River. I have come to meet my guardian."

Sensing approval, he claimed the spot by kicking a circle in the tall yellow grass all the way down to dirt. He got inside the circle to wait.

Kai El said prayers as the sun went down, speaking in a loud voice—if bad animals were waiting for dark to attack him, they would hear the voice of a large man and leave him alone. After thanking the Four Directions for another day, and for guiding him here, he prayed to his unknown guardian.

"I don't know you, but you know me. You have waited since I was born. Now I am ready to meet you."

Ignoring his powerful hunger, he drank water. Night came. In moonless black Kai El tried to keep his mind empty, open and ready for his guardian spirit. He should stay awake, they said—that was easy. Scary sounds filled the star-pricked night: birds, bugs, coyotes, wolves, and who knew what else. The skinny moon rose just before morning. He drank, stood, stretched, walked around inside his circle. Stood at the edge aiming a yellow stream out. Prayed again. Sat back down. Fell asleep in the sun for a while. Night again. Harder to stay awake, even with the noises. Another day. Hunger had stopped bothering him. Strange thoughts wandered through his mind. His eyes and ears played tricks on him, seeing and hearing things that weren't there. But none of the real or the unreal was his guardian spirit.

Night came for the third time. Lying on his back, arms crossed behind his head, one leg straight out on the ground, the other knee cocked up, Kai El stared at the sky. Instead of standing still, the stars swirled and swooped, trailing sparks. He tried to use his gaze to stop them, but it didn't work—his eyes watered with the effort. He squeezed them shut. Blinked. Opened them—

In the center of a golden glow, a red-tail hawk perched on Kai El's raised knee. Wings folded, shoulders hunched, the bird stared at him with fierce eyes and stern beak. Kai El didn't feel its weight, or the talons digging into his legging, but its stare bored into his forehead. He did not move.

"Skaina, Hawk Spirit," he said. "It is you."

He heard wind as the hawk must hear when it flew. The bird cocked its head and spoke in his mind.

*I have always been your guardian. Now you know.*

"I am honored."

The red-tail hawk was a magnificent animal. Kai El had felt like a hawk sometimes, his heart and thoughts soaring free, as if nothing could hold him back.

Beyond the wide glow cast by his guardian spirit, the stars were crazier than before, twirling, sweeping across the sky, as if they were birds. Kai El couldn't feel his body.

*Listen . . .*

He heard drums and singing; saw a shadow-boy dancing in the glow; and it was he. He listened to his other self. The song became part of him.

"With the eyes of the hawk, I see what others can't. With the heart of the hawk, I have the courage of ten men. With the wings of the hawk, my spirit soars."

*That is your power song. There is no other like it. Spirits will know who you are when you sing it, and all creatures will be warned of your power.*

Hot tingles passed between the spirit and the boy, rushing through him, filling him up. In that moment, he knew Skaina's love, and love was born in him.

"What name have you chosen for me?"

*What name do you wish?*

Kai El didn't know that it mattered.

"Any name you give me, Skaina . . . that is what I wish."

*You are free to name yourself.*

"But I thought you would give it to me. That's what they said."

*Amotkan wants people to listen to themselves. You are the first.*

Kai El said, "But . . . but . . ."

This was too strange. For a moment he thought he was dreaming, instead of talking to an actual spirit. And then fear rushed in.

"You mean I won't have a guardian spirit?"

*No. I mean that you may choose your own name.*

He had no idea what to say. Before he could think of anything, the Hawk Spirit disappeared between eyeblinks.

The people of Teahra Village cheered when Kai El returned. They gave him special things to eat, knowing how hungry he'd be after four days. His friends had many questions, though no one asked who his guardian spirit was, or what his new name would be. They would have to wait to find out, until the Naming Ceremony at the Autumn Feast, three moons away. Even parents had to wait. Only the Moonkeeper would know between now and then.

That night, Ashan sent away Tor from the Moonkeeper's hut so she could talk to their son. She and Kai El settled together.

"Tell me all about it."

She listened to a story much like others. The same story was different, though, coming from her own son. She *heard* the sounds, *felt* the fear, *tasted* the hunger, *knew* the courage.

"I opened my eyes," Kai El said. "There was a red-tail hawk on my knee."

"Hawk Spirit!" She hugged him. "I knew you were special! Will you be called Skaina, then, or did he give you some other name?"

He didn't answer.

"I'm the Moonkeeper. You are supposed to tell me."

Kai El cleared his throat.

"Skaina said that I am to choose my own name."

"What?"

He nodded.

"No! You must be mistaken!"

"That's what he said. I am the first."

"I'm not in the mood for your tricks. What name did Skaina give you?"

Kai El heaved a big sigh.

"I told you what he said, Mother. On the way back I decided—since it is up to me—that I'm not going to have a new name. I will still be Kai El, Sun River. I like my name."

The child wasn't playing. He believed himself. Her mind raced. What was she going to do about this?

Tor burst through the doorskin. Mother and son jumped to their feet. She instinctively put her arms around the boy.

"How dare you listen to the Moonkeeper speaking to one of the tribe!" she said.

"He's my son! Of course I listened, you fool of a woman! What are you talking about, boy?"

Kai El was shaking. Ashan thought he couldn't talk, but he did.

"Father, I found my guardian spirit."

"So I heard. What name did he give you?"

"Skaina said Amotkan said that we—"

"The name. Just tell me the name."

Ashan said, "Give him time, and maybe he will. Go on, son. What did Amotkan say?"

"That people should . . . I don't know . . . stop asking spirits for everything . . . they are tired of doing everything for people . . . something like that. All I know for sure is that Skaina said I am the first. I asked and asked, and he would not tell me a name. So I decided to stay Kai El."

Shaking his head violently, Tor said, "Well—I don't—it just can't—that's not the way it's going to be. Not *my* son."

"Father, all my life, you talked of guardian spirits, and said we should trust them to guide us. I'm not going to say no to the first thing Skaina asks me to do."

"You made a mistake. Or maybe something worse. I don't think you met your guardian spirit. Maybe you just hid in the cliffs like that boy Nubish."

Kai El jerked away from Ashan. He strode to his father, fists clenched at his sides, and shouted up at him.

"How can you say that? You know Tor's son is no coward!"

The rage went out of Tor. He sat down, head in his hands.

"A man's name ... next to his family, it's the most important thing he has. Our son doesn't want a name. What are we going to do, Ashan?"

Kai El said, "There is nothing you *can* do, Father."

Over the next three moons, his parents tried to change his mind. They suggested names, made him think about them. Especially his father, who thought a name meant much more than Kai El did. But he would not be swayed and could not be forced.

At the Naming Ceremony, he stood with other little ones before the gathered tribes. The Moonkeeper commanded him to step forward.

"I am Kai El, Sun River. Skaina, the Hawk Spirit, is my guardian. My new name is my old name because my guardian said it should be."

Shahala people were shocked, offended, angry.

Ashan defended Kai El, speaking as the Moonkeeper.

"I told you things are different now. Why do you keep being surprised? What happens between a person and his guardian spirit is not the concern of other people. This boy is Kai El, and I suggest you call him that."

So they did, and a few other things.

# CHAPTER 24

ONE MORNING IN KAI EL'S TENTH SUMMER, HE WOKE up from a dream—such a crazy dream he couldn't tell anyone.

It was about Tsilka's daughters. He dreamed he had seen them naked, and they had boy-parts growing between their legs. The dream bothered him all day. Though most Tlikit little ones went around naked, Kai El realized he'd never seen those two, not that he could remember. He tried to tell himself it was crazy; it couldn't be true. But . . . being daughters of a god, the twins *were* different from other little ones. Could they be different in *that* way? Part-girl and part-boy? He had to find out.

Kai El thought he was lucky when the twins left the village walking to the Great River. If they were going to bathe, he could see them naked—and prove the dream right or wrong. Of course he could be *killed* if women caught him peeking— but he had to know.

He followed them. But the twins didn't go to the women's washing place. They turned away from the trail and joined some other girls in splashing, laughing play. Kai El thought of going back to the village, but now that he was this close to water on a hot day, he might as well cool off. And maybe he'd see something yet.

Hidden by tall bushes, he stood up to his thighs in cold swirling water, leaning forward on his spear, peeking through a bare spot. The girls splashed and pushed each other, shriek-ing with laughter.

He wondered what was so funny about getting shoved under water? *Girls,* he thought, shaking his head. *They're so silly.*

Something large brushed against his leg. He looked down and saw a fish the size of a grown man! A sturgeon! The biggest he'd ever seen!

His spear came up without being told, thrust out, and stabbed the monster, in one side of the flesh behind its head, and out the other.

*Perfect!*

With a hand on each side of the head, Kai El gripped the spear—*huge—Amotkan, it's huge!*—throwing his weight back to haul it up on the rocks.

The fish leapt straight up out of the water, shook in the air, slammed back down. Kai El hung on in shock. He and the fish headed for the bottom. He couldn't see anything in the blood-colored bubbles rushing by, except that it was getting darker fast. The thing-that-should-have-been-dead thrashed, bucked, and rolled, but Kai El was not about to let go.

*What a warrior I'll be! They'll talk around fires forever of the boy who caught a fish longer than a man when he was only ten summers!*

Kai El had never held his breath this long.

*I have to have this fish. I will not let it go.*

With incredible strength, it swam *up* the river.

The current helped one of its own, trying to sweep the boy off. Rocks scraped him. But he would not let go. The fish plunged in a twisting spiral. Kai El thought he saw many red eyes on the bottom of the river . . . he didn't know what kind of eyes, just eyes.

Out of air, he thought, *Maybe I will let go.*

That was the moment when the mighty sturgeon died. It went limp, turned belly-up, flipped Kai El under, and floated downriver, grinding him on the bottom. Kai El kicked with all his strength, rose through lighter-colored water, and burst through the water's skin into air. Gasping, coughing and spit-ting, the current swept him downriver, slammed him into a mass of boulders and wedged him. Water roiled and splashed. Somehow, he still had the speared sturgeon.

He heard yelling. Hauled upriver, then down, he had ended up almost where he started, only farther out in the water than anyone had ever been.

"Kai El! Kai El!"

The riverbank crawled with blurred people, screaming, crying, shouting his name.

He heard his father's voice. "Stay there! We'll come out to you!"

Men waded in up to their chests. Tor and a few others hurled themselves out to farther rocks, but they couldn't reach Kai El. Men could swim if they had to, but not here: The current was too swift; it would sweep them away.

"Stay there!" his father yelled again—as if Kai El could go anywhere. "We'll get a rope to you!"

He saw his mother pacing back and forth.

"Hurry, Tor! Hurry!"

Kai El yelled. "I'm fine! I could stay here all day!" But still she paced.

They tied strong grass fiber ropes together to make one long one, and attached a rock to its end for weight. After several throws, it caught in the boulders. Kai El took the rock off and lashed his spear and his fish to the end of the rope.

"Let the fish go," Tor yelled.

Kai El laughed. "You won't say that when you see it. I'm not letting it go now."

Holding on to his treasure, Kai El was dragged through water one more time.

Oh, the ground felt good.

People were amazed by his bravery and strength. No boy had ever tried to catch a sturgeon. This was the largest one ever caught, heavier than three boys. What Kai El had done seemed impossible.

Women carried the slippery monster back to the village, cut it into steaks, and cooked them over hot fires. Everyone ate at the same time.

People went on and on with their praise.

"Best sturgeon I ever tasted, Kai El."

"Probably because it was so old."

"It must have been smart and strong to grow so old."

"Believe me," Kai El said. "It was all of that, and more."

Girls fussed over his wounds. It was a strange feeling. He didn't know what to make of it, but he thought he liked it. It made him feel proud to say, "It doesn't hurt." Although it did—every single part of him felt what he'd been through.

That night the warriors around the village fire asked him to tell his story again. He didn't just tell them, he showed them, becoming both the sturgeon—twisting, turning, thrashing—and himself—scraped on rocks, dragged on the bottom, holding his breath, hanging on.

Kai El had watched warriors tell stories of their great hunts. Now he knew why they loved it so much.

Later Tor took him aside.

"You know, son, when you came back from your power quest, and I thought . . . I said . . . well, I was . . ."

His father made a gulping sound. He just couldn't say he was wrong.

Kai El said, "I know. You were angry. You didn't understand. I forgave you a long time ago."

"I'm proud of you, son. What you did today was brave. What you did three summers ago was maybe even braver."

"It was," Kai El agreed.

# CHAPTER 25

Little ones of different ages sat on a knoll above Teahra Village, listening to Kai El's story again. He couldn't tell it enough for some of them, especially boys. He spoke in the new way: mostly Shahala words, some Tlikit, a few from the Firekeepers. The mixed language of Teahra had come about naturally, though there were people in both tribes who refused to use any words but their own.

"And then," Kai El said, "they told me to let go of it! After all I'd gone through for that fish!"

Tsagaia—a Tlikit girl of seven summers, Tsilka's daughter, Tsurya's twin sister—listened with a drifting mind. She wondered if people would get tired of hearing the story of Kai El's big fish before he got tired of telling it.

A girl named Nissa said, "Tsagaia, tell your part again."

Startled, she jumped.

Others had been at the Great River that day, but Tsagaia was the only one who'd been looking when the sturgeon flew out of the water like a bird. The shy twin, she'd talked more in the last few days than she had in her whole life. She was beginning to enjoy it.

"My sister shoved me under, and I came back up. Just as I went to push her, I saw a monster leap high in the air, with Kai El hanging on. It seemed like they were up there for a day, but they hit the water before anyone could turn their head to see what I was screaming about. I ran for the village, yelling all the way, 'A fish got Kai El! A fish got Kai El!' People heard me and came running. They almost knocked me down."

Her sister, Tsurya, said, "When they got there we pointed to the water. It was still red. We said, 'A monster fish! It got Kai El! Save him!'"

Kai El said, "Quiet, Tsurya. You didn't see anything. Tsagaia, what did I look like, hanging on up there in the air?"

She could tell that he wanted to hear handsome or strong.

"You looked like a boy who was going to die," she said. Everyone laughed.

"Kai El is too brave to die," said a boy named Bot, who was seven summers, and about to go on his power quest. "Kai El is so brave that he told his guardian spirit that he was going to keep his old name."

"I am brave, but that's not what happened. My guardian spirit told me he wanted me to choose my own name."

"What's a power quest like?" Bot asked.

"You'll see," Kai El said, "if you don't get lost, and wolves don't eat you."

"Kai El!" Bot's older brother, Elkin, shouted.

"Just joking. It's nothing to be scared of, Bot."

Tsagaia couldn't think of anything scarier than being all alone in the wilderness for days and nights. Even the Breath Ogre who sometimes choked her couldn't be scarier than that. She liked Shahala people and their ways, but they could keep their power quests.

"You twins," Kai El said. "You're seven summers, aren't you? Are you going on a power quest?"

"We are seven summers," Tsurya said. "But Tlikit people don't make their little ones do stupid things."

Nissa said, "How boring to keep the same name all your life. I loved it when I got my new name . . . Sunrise with No Clouds."

"Sure you did," Tsurya said. "Your old name was ugly."

Tsagaia wished her twin would learn to be nicer.

"It was not ugly!" Nissa said with her nose in the air. "Tsurya—now there's an ugly name."

Elkin said, "They're just afraid to go out and meet their guardian spirits."

Tsurya stood, hands on hips, and glared at him.

"I'm not afraid of *anything*. I just think it's a stupid thing to do. Come, Tsagaia. Let's go."

"You go."

Maybe the others would want to know what the fish looked like. They were interested in what Tsagaia had to say, and it felt good. So what if they thought she was afraid?

Her twin stamped off, with boys yelling after her.

"Water bug! Water bug!"

The taunts made Tsurya want to run, but that would show weakness. Shoulders straight, head up, she strode away. When the dung piles were out of sight, she ran for the place where she hid when things made her *so mad!*

No one knew about her secret place—not even her twin. The river trail left the water's edge to skirt a rock outcrop. A path led down to a brush-sheltered finger of land called the women's washing place. Tsurya crawled along an animal track that left the path. Her secret place was just a hole in thick brush at the edge of the river. Boulders forced the current around a little pool.

Lying on a low rock, staring at the water, thinking about her twin sister—who stayed with *them* instead of coming with her—Tsurya grumbled to no one.

"Always the lucky one, from birth. Our mother gave her the name Tsagaia—Big Tan Cat. People love cougars. I get named *Tsurya*—Graceful Water Skimmer. A fancy name for a bug! I hate it!"

Tsurya watched water skimmers stride across the pool, from one side to the other and back again. Spring through autumn, they would stride and stride, going nowhere, until winter swept them away. They didn't seem to have mates or families, or any purpose for living other than being fish food.

She caught one by its skinny body, held it up, watched it struggle between her thumb and finger. It wasn't even a pretty bug—just a black stick with four spidery legs, and tiny flat feet that never broke the water's skin. She pulled off a leg, and threw the crippled bug back in. It thrashed on its side. A water spider shot out from under the rock and took it.

"I am nothing like you! Nothing!"

But Tlikit people died with the same name they were born with. Tsurya would always be the bug.

She thought of going on a power quest and getting a new name, like Shahala little ones did. Her mother would fight the idea, but the Moonkeeper, Ashan, would stand up for her. The Moonkeeper liked her, and she had backed Kai El when he changed old ways.

But . . . to go out and be hungry, and maybe be killed, just to get a new name . . . she wasn't afraid to do it, it was just *stupid*.

On another day, in a better mood, Tsurya went to her secret place to eat some red berries she'd found—very sweet, too few to share, with juice that didn't stain, so no one would know.

She was sitting there, making up sounds and saying them out loud just to hear herself, when it came to her . . .

"Tahna."

She loved the strong sound with a soft edge. It had no meaning in either language.

"Tahna, tahna, tahna . . ."

It was the sound of herself. She wanted it for her name. How could she have it?

Thinking up a story, she asked to speak with the Moonkeeper.

"I want to be like a Shahala and take a new name."

The Moonkeeper looked surprised. "It's more than just standing up in the Naming Ceremony and getting a new name. Have you thought of all it means? To go on a power quest? To have a guardian spirit? Have you thought of what people will say? Tlikit people?"

"I have thought of all that."

"What does your mother say?"

"I have not told her yet."

"She may be afraid for you to go on a power quest. Tlikit little ones have never done it."

"I don't want to go on a power quest."

The Moonkeeper stared at her. Tsurya thought it must take a lot to silence a chief, but she had done it.

"I don't need a power quest," she said. "I met my guardian

spirit at the Great River. He is the Water Giver, Wahawkin.
My father.''

The Moonkeeper's mouth fell open.

"He told me my new name. Tahna. My name is Tahna.''

The Moonkeeper found her voice.

"But that doesn't mean anything. People are named for
things."

"Wahawkin told me it means Daughter of a God.''

"But you are Tlikit, little one," Ashan said, shaking her
head. "I don't think you know what this means."

Tsurya stood firm. "Why am I any different from Kai El?
You said that just because things have always been done one
way doesn't mean they can't be done another."

The Moonkeeper cleared her throat.

"You're right. That's what I said . . . Tahna.''

The little girl smiled and sighed in pleasure at hearing her
name spoken by another. She realized just how beautiful it
was. But her pleasure didn't last long.

The Moonkeeper said, "You are going to need my help.
Shall we go and see your mother?''

Tsurya—who would be Tahna if she lived through this—
bit her lip, swallowed, and nodded.

Kneeling by the fire in the Moonkeeper's hut, Ashan stirred
with a stick in each hand: herbs, water and hot rocks in one
basket—medicine for a man with fever—and in another, fish
mush for Tor. She had just come from Tsilka's hut, and her
blood still boiled. They had shouted, but just being with the
woman would have been enough. Ashan couldn't stand Tsilka.
She stayed away from her—until a child with a wild idea had
forced her to do otherwise.

The Tlikit woman had been in Ashan's way from the beginning. At first Tsilka was a real danger, encouraging her people
to resist everything Shahala, including the Moonkeeper. Ashan
knew how close she'd been to losing control. But Elia's death
had helped to heal the rifts between the tribes. No matter how
Tsilka tried to keep people stirred up, they blamed her for the
events that led to the boy's death, and eventually stopped
listening to her.

Tsilka was no longer a spear about to be thrust. She was

more like a sharp stone in Ashan's moccasin. She hated Ashan, showing it in moments gone in a flash, by a narrowing of her eyes, a twist of her lips, a color that rose in her cheeks. There was no reason for it.

And then there was the way Tsilka acted around Tor . . . giving him sly, hungry looks. She did not have a mate, but she had lovers to satisfy her. She had no right to look at Tor that way.

Or did she?

Ashan stirred angrily, flipping out bits and splashes. She'd heard it said that Tor had once been Tsilka's lover. But Tor said it wasn't true, and Ashan chose to believe him.

What could she do about the woman?

*Guard your mate,* answered a voice inside.

While she stirred, Ashan told Tor about Tsurya wanting a new name.

"Little ones," he said. "What a lot of trouble they are. It almost makes me glad Alhaia the Moon never sent us another."

"I know," she said. "Stamping on the ways of their elders, making up their own. And what can we do? The spirits are behind them."

Well, she wasn't sure spirits had anything to do with the latest request, but there was no reason to say so.

He shook his head. "I don't know, Ashan."

She said, "First a Shahala, our own Kai El. Now this one, a Tlikit, daughter of that—that—"

"Rattlesnake Woman?"

"That name isn't mean enough for her anymore. She loves those twins, but she also beats them. I know she does. I'm really worried for little Tsurya. Tor, there are times when I'd just like to vanish that woman!"

"I don't think she beats the twins."

"How would you know?"

"Well, I've never seen it."

"I'm telling you, she beats them. She's just that kind of person."

"Ashan, I wonder why you *really* hate her so much. What has Tsilka done to you? She's been meek as a mouse since Elia died."

"Don't be stupid," she said, annoyed that Tor defended the woman. "Moonkeepers don't hate people." She heaped mush on a wood plate and thrust it at him, then went back to stirring the fever medicine.

The Moonkeeper didn't *hate* anyone; Ashan *disliked* Tsilka. Beating her little ones was just part of it—she wasn't the only Tlikit who did that. It was true that Tsilka never said or did anything wrong to Ashan—nothing that could be proved. But how can you like someone who hates you?

"Aren't you eating?" he asked.

She shook her head. Arguing with Tsilka had destroyed her appetite.

"What name was given to the little girl?" he asked.

"You know I can't tell you that," she said. If the girl *had* a guardian spirit, it was their secret until the Naming Ceremony. "But I will tell you it's a very interesting name."

Ashan sniffed the steam rising from the fever medicine, and the smell told her it was finished. She took some extra sniffs, letting it calm her, then removed the rocks from the cooking basket.

"You know, Tor, I do admire the bravery of these children—one Shahala, one Tlikit—standing up for what they alone believe. Maybe someday they'll grow up and fall in love."

"No!" Tor said, with a violent shake of his head. "They're not right for each other."

"How can you say that? They're just little ones."

"I can tell. I know my son. Believe me, Ashan, they are not right for each other."

She was about to ask if he'd seen the path that rabbit drew for Kai El and Tsurya to walk, but the look in his eyes— determined, almost fierce—stopped her. Whether the little ones were meant for each other was not important at this time in their lives; she had only been musing.

She wondered why Tor seemed so upset.

Kamiulka, the Autumn Feast, arrived. On the morning of the second day, the One Drum called the spirits and the people of Teahra Village. It was time again for the Naming Ceremony, one of life's important rituals. Except for Ashan, who was preparing herself in the Moonkeeper's hut, everyone gathered around the ceremonial ground.

*Almost everyone,* Tor thought, noticing Tsilka's absence. *How can she not want to hear our daughter's new name?*

The drum thumped. A circle of mothers danced with waving arms, singing in high, thin voices about a bird's first flight.

Tor gazed at the twins. His mind wasn't sure what made one child prettier than another, but his eyes knew. And these two were beautiful. They had a sparkle, an intelligence that he didn't see in other little ones—well, except Kai El. It was hard to keep his pride hidden. He saw himself in their matching faces and wondered that no one else did.

*Which one is Tsurya, who wants a new name? Which is Tsagaia, who thinks her old name is fine?*

They looked so much alike that Tor couldn't tell them apart. But were they alike? One wanted to be Shahala—*like her father,* he couldn't help thinking. The other was happy to be Tlikit. Yet they both had his blood.

He looked at the other child who had his blood. *And then there's Kai El. He went a way all his own, but he took the name I gave with him . . .*

But this was his daughter's day, not his son's. Tor looked back at his girls. He felt love, and pity. They wore old dresses, though he had given Tsilka deerhides to make new ones.

*A girl should have a new dress for her Naming Ceremony, whether her mother believes in it or not—*

Tor heard Ashan shriek. The drum stopped in mid-beat. He bolted for their hut. Just as he was about to burst in, Ashan stepped out, looking regal in her Moonkeeper's garb: the ancient robe of fur and feathers; the long tail of Kusi, the Horse Spirit, in her hair; high boots of black bear fur on her feet. But he saw the shaken look on her face.

"What happened?" he said.

"There was a bisonsnake in my boot," she whispered angrily. "I will thank Tsilka for the addition to our stew."

"Oh, Ashan, I don't think she'd do that."

She gave him a narrow look. "All you know about women, Tor, would fit in the shell of a beetle."

Well, he could not deny that. He wondered if Tsilka would

do such a thing? Maybe it was time for him to have a talk with her.

*At least,* he thought, *it was a bisonsnake, not a rattlesnake . . . this time.*

The ceremonial ground was silent but for sounds of water and wind. The Moonkeeper walked to the center and faced Where Day Begins. The One Drum spoke four knocking beats. She raised her arms to the sky and shook deer-hoof rattles, then did the same for the other directions.

It filled Tor with awe to see his mate like this. He thought how much he loved her.

Having summoned the spirits, the Moonkeeper spoke to the people.

"Some of our little ones have reached seven summers. They went on power quests to meet their Spirit Guardians, and they are ready for a new part of life. Come, little ones, and tell us what you learned."

Tsurya, Bot, and Aknit stepped onto the ceremonial ground. When her turn came, Tor's secret child spoke with dignity beyond her age.

"I am Tahna, Daughter of a God. Wahawkin the Water Giver is my Spirit Guardian."

If anyone had looked at Tor, they would have seen the unmistakable pride of fatherhood beaming from him. But everyone was looking at the little ones.

From her secret spot near the women's washing place, Tahna could hear talking on the other side of the bushes. One day she heard some of her Tlikit friends.

"Not only don't we change our names, but the name itself! Tahna, just a sound, like the first babbles out of a baby's mouth."

"She says it means Daughter of a God. She couldn't pick something like Dove Song or Sage Flower," said Wenot, whose name meant Summer Night.

"And to claim the god Wahawkin as her Spirit Guardian— it's like her mother claiming that Wahawkin is their father."

"Shh," said another. "Do you have to say 'Wahawkin' all the time?"

Tahna tossed a stone into the brush behind the girls, and

they flew up like a bunch of quail. She had to cover her mouth to keep giggles from getting out. Some people, especially those of Tlikit blood, didn't even like to *think* about Wahawkin. It might make him come back, and they knew what that god could do.

The Moonkeeper came up on them.

"I heard you," she said. "No one lies about their Spirit Guardian. If Tahna says it, then it is so."

Tahna knew that taking a new name had been the right thing to do. She loved being called Tahna, a word all her own. She believed she had become another person. What she didn't like about herself, she gave to Tsurya to bury in the past. What she did like, she gave to Tahna to carry into the future.

# CHAPTER 26

Stripped to his loinskin, Tor sat at the Great River's edge with his feet in the water. Heat lay on the land like an unwelcome fur robe. A good strong wind—so much a part of life along the river—might have blown it away, but the wind had deserted. Tor watched little ones play in the water. They knew what to do about heat. Grown men were too dignified—especially tribal elders, as Tor was regarded, though he was just twenty-seven summers.

*A man can only wet his feet and wait for dark,* he thought. *Or he could escape for a while.* That's what Tor decided to do. Others wanted to go with him.

Two summers ago, Tor and a band of Teahra hunters had ventured to the mountains where the sun went down. Days later they had returned to the village, each with a deer over his shoulders. They could have killed more, but one was easy to carry. Prairie deer came to the Great River often enough to satisfy hunger, but the Shahala thought the meat of mountain deer was richer because of what they ate. The Tlikit had never tasted mountain deer, but after chunks of seared meat and portions of savory stew, they agreed.

Even more important, the Teahra hunters had found pine trees and brought back pungent bark. No one would die for lack of pine medicine again.

The next day before it got hot, Tor and ten good friends headed out from the village. Under a high blue sky, they were no cooler than they'd been before, but they were happy to be away. They walked down the Great River for two days, then up a smaller river that emptied into it.

The land rose. The air was hot, but not so heavy. The place reminded Tor of Takoma's lower slopes in the land of his ancestors. The trees changed from ash and maple to pine and oak. Underbrush opened onto grassy meadows where skittish deer grazed.

The men hunted with weapons like the one Tor had taken from the man-eater who killed his brother Beo long ago. The notched stick that threw a thin spear was a good way to kill some animals—but not bears, as Tor had learned the hard way.

The hunters killed eleven deer in one day. That night they feasted on the hearts. Eating a bite or two raw captured the animal's power; deer gave the ability to be constantly alert. They cooked the rest of the heart meat on sticks over a fire. The smell of dripping juice, the sight of beads of fat sizzling on crisp meat—Tor's stomach growled. When he ate, the taste was even better than the smell had promised.

Afterward, the hunters sat with their backs against trees, belching and smiling.

"Eleven," Lar said. "We head for home tomorrow."

"Why hurry?" Tor asked.

"I don't want to carry more than one."

"We don't have to hunt. We could hang the meat in trees, and come back for it. It will taste even better in a few days."

"I suppose we could," Lar agreed.

Tor said, "This is the farthest we've ever come. I'd like to see what's higher up."

Takluit said, "It's hot here in the mountains, but it will be hotter at the Great River."

Lyo said, "It's good to get away from women and little ones. The older I get, the more I enjoy it."

No one was ready to go home. They hung the deer carcasses in trees. After a good sleep, they walked higher into the mountains, to find what might be found.

Two days later, Tor stood at the top of a ridge, gazing toward Colder. A field of huckleberry bushes spread down the slope in front of him, stopping at the edge of a dark forest of lofty cedars that stretched away for days. In the far distance, the snowy peak of a great mountain climbed out of the forest and reached for the sky.

Tor turned the mountain's shape around in his mind as if he were seeing it from his ancestral homeland.

*Yes, it was Pahto!* The Shahala hadn't seen the sacred mountain since they'd left the Valley of Grandmothers for the last time, six autumns ago.

Tor pointed. "Look. What do you see?"

"Huckleberries!" Hamish said, stuffing his mouth. "I haven't had one since I was a boy!"—an exaggeration, but it *had* been a long time.

"No, not just huckleberries. What more do you see?"

"Forest that runs on for days."

"Snow-covered mountains."

"Are you blind?" Tor said. "It's Pahto!"

"It *is*!"

Cheering Shahala men punched the air, danced around, slapped each other's backs. Though the mountain was turned backwards, and very far away, she let them know where they were, in a way they hadn't known since they'd left their homeland.

The two Tlikit men in the hunting party didn't understand why anyone would get so excited about a mountain.

"Is that where you used to live?" Wyecat asked.

"No, but we could see her."

"So?"

"When we can see Pahto, we know where we are."

"Oh."

"We honor Pahto. She brings the waters of life to the land of our ancestors. Coyote made the First People up there."

Tor could have told the Tlikit men more about the sacred mountain, but he had lost them to the huckleberries—sweet, juicy morsels the size of a fingertip—heavy on the waist-high bushes.

Women would pick the fruits gently, one at a time, but there were no women here to tell the hunters what to do. They stripped handfuls and stuffed themselves, moaning with delight, laughing at how they looked with purple hands and faces.

When they couldn't eat one more berry, they threw them at each other ... eleven grown men, acting like little ones, but there was no one to see. Finally they lay down in an open spot and rested.

Tor wanted to see Pahto again. He walked to the top of the ridge. Behind him, the deep forest they had come through stopped, opening in front of him to the scattered leafy trees and huckleberry bushes. The way the berry field swept down the mountain made Tor wonder if a long-ago wildfire had taken the forest, leaving a place where sunlight could reach lower plants. Wildfire, like all the powers of nature, could be a friend to one thing and an enemy to another.

He sat on a downed tree. With the sun at his back, he feasted his eyes on the distant mountain. The broad base of She Who Brought the Waters of Life rested in forest. Her snow-covered peak was bright white in the late sun, except for a strip of cloud near the top. He watched the shadow of night creep up the slopes until the tip of the mountain was a shining light in the darkening sky. Then he joined his tribesmen to sleep in the mountain air so crisp it crackled.

In the morning they picked berries to take home, using more care than before. As the piles on their sleeping skins grew, juice squished out, making dark purple stains.

Hamish said, "Look at these skins. My mate will yell at me. She just finished this one." But he laughed to show that he wasn't serious.

As they worked, the men of Shahala blood talked about berrying in the land of their ancestors. Telling the Tlikit gave them an excuse to relive good memories.

It took a long time to get enough berries to impress anyone. The hunters told each other they were glad that berry-picking was the work of women. When their stooped-over backs told them they'd had enough, they tied their bulging, dripping skins into packs, and headed for home.

The people of Teahra Village were so excited by the berries, they gave little attention to the deer. The hunters laid their skins out, and people ate the squashed fruit right where it lay.

*All that work,* Tor thought, *devoured in a heartbeat. No wonder women sometimes hoard what they pick.*

Ashan made plans for a trek to the huckleberry fields ...

a lost strand from the past picked up once more and woven into the future. In the good mountain air, men would hunt while women picked and dried berries. Little ones would play more than they helped, young people fall in love, old ones tell stories and enjoy the cool after the heat of summer on the river. Nights of talking around a fire; sleeping under stars . . . the autumn trek for huckleberries was a wonderful time. Once, the whole tribe would have gone . . .

The Shahala people had thought they'd never go berrying again. Some couldn't wait for the trek to begin. But others thought it sounded like work; they didn't miss huckleberries.

The Firekeepers, once silent slaves, now talked as much as anyone. Born in a forest, they chattered happily about being among tall trees again.

Most of the Tlikit wanted nothing to do with mountains. Their legends said evil spirits lived in high places.

Long after his mate slept, Tor lay awake. He had another thing to do. He'd saved the biggest huckleberries, putting them in an extra moccasin he carried, being careful they didn't get squashed on the way home. At eight summers, his secret daughters had never tasted huckleberries; he thought they should have the best.

Tor sneaked away without waking Ashan. It was a moonless night, but he didn't need light to find his way to Tsilka.

Most of the Tlikit people still lived in the cave. At their old home by the dried-up lake, they'd had mud-covered brush huts that leaked and sometimes blew over. Shahala huts were better, and Shahala people would have helped them with the work. But except for a few, the Tlikit said no, they liked their cave.

Tsilka had made herself a hut of wood and hides.

"Like a Shahala hut, but better," she'd told Tor, showing him pictures she was carving in the wood.

Occasionally Tor went to Tsilka's hut while the village slept—not to see the woman, but to leave things for the twins. It made him feel better about not being able to act as their father, even if they didn't know where the gifts came from.

Tsilka could be cold and distant when he came, or warm and tempting. Tor knew she would give anything to have him for her mate. It might *seem* better to stay away from her, but he knew what she was capable of . . . the scar on his leg reminded him of being stabbed in his sleep with his own fishing spear. Tor told himself that coming here once in a while kept Rattlesnake Woman under control.

Tsilka's hut sat by itself outside the cluster of Shahala huts, with the door facing away. Tor scratched on the skin.

"Yes," she whispered.

He entered. Hanging mats closed off the space where the twins slept. The air smelled pleasant—she had learned from Shahala women to keep herself and her little ones clean.

An oil lamp cast a soft glow over Tsilka, lying on her side on a fur spread out on the floor, wearing a short sleeping robe—obviously waiting for him. She preened, pulling strands of hair through her fingers, looking up at him from under lowered eyelids, full lips smiling. The soft leather robe slipped from her shoulder, showing her breast before she pulled it up again. A beautiful woman, she knew how to use her body to make men think of taking their pleasure with her. Tor wondered how many did.

He had to admit that he sometimes liked it when Tsilka behaved this way. But tonight it annoyed him. They were twenty-seven summers, not young people. Ashan didn't do things like that anymore.

"Sit," the she-cat whispered, patting the fur.

He sat, but not where she wanted him. He brushed a spot on the floor, put down a mat he'd brought, and emptied his extra moccasin onto it.

"I saved the best huckleberries for the girls."

"Oh," she said, rolling her eyes, sounding bored.

He preferred it when Tsilka appreciated what he did for the twins. Keeping such a secret was difficult. He could just stop bringing things.

"It wasn't easy to keep them from getting squashed."

She shrugged.

He pointed to the pile of berries.

"You can have some."

"Already tried them. Not much taste. Made my tongue purple." She stuck out her tongue—pink in the lampglow.

She made Tor laugh—one reason he liked coming here.

Tonight he felt full of himself, proud to have found the berry field, excited about Ashan's plans for a trek.

"Going to the mountains to pick berries," he said. "A tradition as old as the Misty Time. You'll love it, Tsilka. All women do. So do little ones. I'm glad these girls will have some good Shahala fun."

"We won't be going."

"What?"

"Flatland people like to see in all directions without forest in the way. Once some men went to a mountain and never came back."

"Everyone goes, Tsilka, even grayhairs. There's a ritual for berry spirits. You people need to start learning these things."

"My people know what they need."

"Fine," he said. "You do what you want. But my girls are going on the berry trek. You don't need to worry. I'll look out for them."

She shook her head. "I'm not going to a mountain, Tor, and neither are *my* girls."

"We will see about that."

Tsilka had ruined his mood. As he left her hut, Tor thought, *Soon enough, woman: I'll see your backside stooped over a berry bush while my daughters play in the mountains.*

Tor had assumed that Ashan would make everyone go. He was wrong. She let people decide for themselves.

Would he ever understand women?

# CHAPTER 27

T HE MOONKEEPER WALKED ACROSS A HILLSIDE OF autumn-gold grass, followed by sixty chattering, laughing people. A fresh-smelling breeze came up the Great River, blowing her hair back from her face, making the osprey feathers on her new walking stick dance. She wore low moccasins, a skirt of grass woven in the Tlikit way, and a deerskin cape with squirrel tails swinging from the bottom. The cape was hot, but it looked good.

"Ahh!" she said to Tor. "It feels right to be at the head of a great tribe again!"

"It is!" he agreed with a big smile.

There were little ones right behind them: Kai El, the twins, and three or four others. Little ones always liked to be at the front of fun. Ashan turned and spoke to them.

"Treks to hunt and gather, to move from the winter home to the summer home—these have been Shahala tradition since the Misty Time when Coyote Spirit took the First People on a walk just like this one to show them what to eat. We love these treks. Are you having fun?"

"Yes, yes, yes!" a little one said. "How can we *not* be having fun? We've never been this far from the village. All that we see is new."

Before Tor found the berry field, Ashan had heard people say, "If there's one thing missing from life at the Great River, it's the need to make treks. We liked the changes they brought."

At least that's what they *said*—when they believed that huckleberries were as lost to them as horses.

Ashan did not expect that the Tlikit would want to come; their fear of mountains was an ancient spiritual belief. What surprised her was how many Shahala didn't want to come. It saddened her Moonkeeper's heart, but she didn't force anyone. In the six summers they'd been here, she had never used magic against people.

Still, Ashan was pleased. At least half the tribe had come on the trek—plenty to do the work that needed doing, plenty to create fun. The laughter she heard said they were already having fun.

The people stopped at sunset, and talked late into the night before they slept. After walking two more days, they left the Great River and followed a smaller river coming down from the mountains. The higher air was nearly as hot, but it was crackly dry—not like the heavy, late summer heat at the Great River that clung to the skin. Afternoon thunderstorms rumbled across the sky, but they brought no rain.

The people from Teahra arrived at the ridge with its view of the sacred mountain, dropped their packs, and ran cheering into the huckleberry field, eating like starved creatures. Ashan couldn't remember when she'd last seen her people so happy—or when she had been so happy herself. The sweet, juicy berries were the best she had ever tasted, but it was more than that. The joy came from finding a connection with their ancestors they believed to be forever lost.

Tor said, "I'll show you where we should make camp."

Ashan walked with him down the slope between clumps of waist-high berry bushes.

"Not so fast," she said, plucking and eating as she walked. "I can't get enough."

A small creek meandered along the lower edge of the slope. Ashan crossed ankle-deep water with her moccasins on, cooling her feet. There was a meadow on the other side, backed with cedar trees that climbed up another slope. From the meadow, Ashan could see the beloved sacred mountain.

"This is perfect, Tor!"

The people from Teahra Village settled in for a stay of more than half a moon. Families chose places to keep their things and sleep. A firepit was dug, and surrounded with downed wood to sit on. A place for women's work was prepared with tools and mats.

The traditional autumn berrying was under way. Work filled the days. Song and dance filled the evenings. The nights were cool and breezy, sweet with pine smoke, noisy with cricketsong to lull people to sleep under stars seen through swaying treetops.

Spreading out in twos, threes, and fours, women filled their baskets with berries while they filled the air with talk about men, little ones, who was in love and who wasn't. They returned to the camp many times each day, spread berries on mats to sun-dry, and went out to pick again. Old women waved leafy branches over the drying fruit to keep bugs away. Little ones could help if they wanted to, but mostly they played—part of the reason for being here was to have a good time.

The men left the camp at dawn and returned at sunset, weighted with deer and beaver. After eating what the women cooked, they drummed, danced, and told stories around the fire. Women skinned the kill and cut the meat into strips for drying. Men were asleep when they finished their work. Tired as they were, most awoke their mates for quiet lovemaking under the stars. The people who had come from Teahra Village were having a great time.

The Moonkeeper Ashan went out to gather medicine, sending the Other Moonkeeper Tenka in another direction so they could search the most land. Ashan was thrilled to find pine, alpine fir, yew, red mountain berries, and others she thought she'd never see again. These medicines would make life easier and healthier for her people.

On the second morning, a little one approached Ashan as she left the camp: one of Tsilka's twins, now eight summers . . . Tahna, the one who'd pushed aside the old ways and made up new ones for herself.

"Moonkeeper, could I come with you? I could help gather plants."

Ashan enjoyed time by herself, and didn't get enough of

it. She almost said no, but changed her mind. She had admired Tahna since the Naming Ceremony. It had taken great courage for the child to make up her own name and force everyone to accept it. Ashan would like to know such a person better.

"Gathering medicine is serious," she said. "Not like playing games or picking berries. You will have to do exactly what I say."

"Oh, I will!" Tahna said. "You will see!"

When Ashan had first come to the Great River, she couldn't tell the twins apart. Six autumns later, it was easy.

Their pretty, little-girl faces were shaped alike, hinting at the dawn of womanhood: upturned noses a bit longer, slimming of cheek and jaw, wider smiles with bigger teeth. But their distinct personalities gave them different looks. Tahna's look was bold, eager, wild. Ashan had seen flashes like fire in her dark brown eyes. Black, shoulder-length hair separated into twisty strands that looked windblown even on a calm day; she didn't seem to mind when it fell across her face. Some part of her clothing was often hanging loose or missing. Tahna never walked where she could run.

Ashan was glad she'd brought her. The little one knew when to ask questions and when to be quiet. She was smart for eight summers, and eager to learn. Her energy made Ashan remember her own childhood. Her funny way of seeing things made Ashan laugh.

She thought, *There are things about this child that remind me of myself.*

Ashan found a big patch of starflowers in a meadow.

"These make tea for babies with hurting stomachs. Pinch off the flowertops carefully, so you don't pull the stems out of the ground. That way they'll come back, and we'll gather them next autumn."

The woman and the little one crept along on their knees, picking white blossoms and talking.

Ashan said, "I know you're a brave girl, Tahna, but I'm surprised that you weren't afraid to come on the trek. Many Tlikit people believe evil spirits live in mountains."

"But you said it isn't true. I believe *you*, Moonkeeper."

That pleased Ashan. She might never change the way adults thought, but little ones held the future in their hands.

"I'm surprised that your mother allowed you and your sister to come."

"It wasn't easy." Tahna hesitated. "I had to be mean to her."

"Oh?"

"I told her that the God Wahawkin was coming on the trek, and wanted us to come."

"Really? Did your Spirit Guardian tell you that?"

"Well, no—but don't tell my mother."

"I won't. What did your mother say?"

"She didn't believe me at first. So I told her Wahawkin said we *must* come, or he would burn our hut."

Stunned, Ashan stopped picking and stared at Tahna as she continued.

"I took a stick from the cooking fire. I gave my mother a look with my eyes—like *this*." Tahna glared; her voice took on a fierce sound. "I pretended I was going to touch the burning end of the stick to the floor mats. Then I made my eyes plain again, and put the stick back in the fire." Tahna's voice changed back to a little-girl lilt. "And so my mother said we could come."

*What kind of child is this?* Ashan wondered.

One morning the Moonkeeper and the girl left the camp, following the creek. Red alders grew here. Ashan wanted to take back a supply of inner bark.

"Look," Tahna said as they walked along. She pointed to a high ridge. "See where the rock is painted white? What is that?"

"I think it's an owl cave. They drop their waste over the side, and that's why it looks painted. Do you know what owls are?"

"Of course. Night-flying hooting birds. But I've never seen one. You mean they live up there?"

Ashan nodded.

"Let's go see!" Tahna said.

"No. Sit down, and I'll tell you a story."

The girl was disappointed, but she sat down. Ashan sat next to her.

"These are owl feathers," she said, showing Tahna the

pledge band on her upper arm—the arm not on the side of the heart; the heart-side arm was for Tor's pledge band.

"When I was a girl of fifteen summers, I got them from a cave like that."

"They're beautiful," Tahna said, though the feathers were ragged with age. "I'm only eight summers, but I'm strong. Why can't I go up there and get some? I would love to have an armpiece like that."

"It's not just an armpiece, Tahna. It's a pledge band, the sign of a Moonkeeper's courage, and no one else may wear one like this."

"The Other Moonkeeper Tenka doesn't wear owl feathers. Will you bring her here to get some?"

"No."

Removing her headband, Ashan pushed the hair from her forehead.

"These are owl scars."

Tahna sucked in her breath when she saw the faint old talon slashes.

Ashan said, "See? They go up into my hair."

She pulled the hair back around her face and tied her headband on.

"It may look like an easy thing to get owl feathers, but I almost died doing it. I was afraid. I didn't want to go. But Raga, the Old Moonkeeper, forced me. The owls attacked me, grabbed me with their talons, and threw me from the cliff into a raging river. I was sucked through a whirlpool. I didn't wake up for three days."

Tahna listened with wide eyes.

"Fear was the old way, Raga's way. Fear is not my way. That is why I will not bring Tenka here. Feathers are just feathers, not something worth dying for."

Ashan stood. "Let's get some red alder."

Choosing one whose trunk was about the thickness of her thigh, Ashan showed Tahna how to remove pieces of the smooth bark in a way that wouldn't harm the tree. With a stone blade, she sliced two up-and-down lines, as long as a child's arm, three fingers wide, deep into the soft bark. Cutting a point at top and bottom, she pried the strip out with the blade.

She handed the blade to Tahna. "Be careful. It's sharp."

The first piece Tahna cut looked as good as Ashan's. When they had enough, they sat down to peel the inner bark, the only part they would take back.

"What will you use this for?" Tahna asked, holding up a thin, slippery strip.

"When someone gets hair bugs, I boil red alder bark with wood sorrel leaves. They put the tea on their heads. The bugs die."

"Really? We just pick them off each other's heads and squash them."

"I know. Without red alder and sorrel—which I found growing by the creek where we're camped—there isn't anything else to do."

"How do you know all these things?"

"The Old Moonkeeper Raga taught me. The Moonkeeper before taught her, all the way back to First Woman. Coyote Spirit took First Woman on a trek to show her the plants that help people."

Tahna said, "Plants *want* to help people? Now I know why I've always liked them."

"Not all plants want to help. Some will kill. It is part of the Balance."

"Oh. Well, I still like them. Learning about them makes me like them more. It's like having a secret."

"That's the way it is for me," Ashan said.

"Did you teach the Other Moonkeeper Tenka about medicine plants?"

"Yes. If something happens to me, the people must still have a medicine woman."

"Oh," Tahna said with a sigh.

As they headed back to the camp, Tahna said, "Moonkeeper, did you know the God Wahawkin brings my sister and me gifts in the night?"

This child was always surprising her . . . the God Wahawkin was just something Tor made up when he needed to control the Tlikit people. Ashan was quite sure that there was no such creature.

"What kinds of gifts?" she asked.

"Sometimes a fur, or a special piece of leather. Or good

things to eat, like crystal honey. Wahawkin brought us some huge huckleberries just before this trek.''

*Huckleberries . . .*

''How do you know who brings these things? Have you ever seen him?''

Tahna shook her head.

''I've tried to stay awake, but I never can. But I know it's Wahawkin. Who else could it be? The god is our father, you know.''

Ashan cleared her throat. She couldn't think of what to say.

''Well, you are lucky girls.''

*Ashan, Ashan . . . how can you be so blind?* Tor, who claims to be Wahawkin when it suits him? These twins who claim Wahawkin as their father? If she allowed herself to think that Tor might have fathered Tsilka's daughters—no!—it was much too painful to consider for even one heartbeat.

*You know how little ones are. They lie. There are no gifts brought by Wahawkin, or Tor, or anyone else,* she told herself until she believed it.

Tor had chosen a spot for himself and Ashan at the back of the meadow on a low rise. She lay there that night, snuggled against her sleeping mate. With the sweet warmth of lovemaking still pulsing through her, she gazed at Alhaia, the Moon . . . Alhaia who had sent no more babies to her and Tor. Kai El was enough for any mother—and Ashan was Moonkeeper as well. But she had always thought there'd be others. Her son was eleven summers now. Ashan was twenty-eight. She'd known for a long time that there would be no other little ones. She accepted it, never forgetting how lucky she was to have Kai El.

As she drifted between waking and sleep, her thoughts wandered.

*Tahna . . . while I've been teaching her, I have learned.*

Tahna was no ordinary child. She would use terror to get what she wanted. She loved medicine plants. She told lies for no reason. These things did not go together. It was as if Tahna were more than one person.

*Yet we get along,* Ashan thought. *We enjoy each other's company. I like her . . . more than like her.*

It was that time of night when thoughts go where they will, even bad, bad thoughts. . . .

*I wouldn't mind having those twins. Maybe I'll put a spell on their mother. I wouldn't want to kill her, but Alhaia sends us no more little ones, and Tsilka's not a good mother, and they don't have a father. They'd be better off here, with us. They're special. They deserve . . .*

She drifted off to sleep filled with thoughts she would never allow in the day, and a desire too wrongful to act upon . . . asleep or awake, Ashan honored above all others the relationship between mother and child.

# CHAPTER 28

In the afternoon of the fifth day, a cloudmass strode out of Warmer, covering the sun. Bursts of lightning lit it from the inside, turning the sky underneath dark orange-gray. A smell that was other smells missing came before it. The Moonkeeper knew that thunderstorms of the greatest power sucked smells from the land. This storm would be different from the dry storms of other afternoons. It was coming straight for them, and fast.

Ashan and Tahna ran all the way back to the camp.

As the cloudmass marched toward them, women and little ones hurried to cover the drying berries with skins and mats. They layered cedar branches for a rough shelter, and crouched together inside, laughing at the men who'd be caught unprotected. Wind tore at the shelter. They had to hold on to the branches to keep them from blowing away. Thunder booms came one on top of the other, shaking the ground. Through the cedar needles, they saw lightning flashing.

How frightened the little ones must be! Ashan shouted encouragement, but only the closest ones heard her above the noise.

Rain slashed through the cedar branch shelter, drenching them in the short time it lasted. When the rain passed, the women threw off the branches. The wet air was cleaned of late summer dust, charged with power from the lightning. The sun made steam rise from the ground. They laughed without knowing why.

Kai El and several other little ones were missing, but Ashan didn't worry. It was only a storm. No one died from being wet.

The storm caught seven little ones away from the camp playing Find Me. When Kai El—at eleven summers the oldest in the group—saw how fierce it would be, he yelled for the others. They huddled together with skins over their heads, shrieking and laughing to hide fear of thunder and lightning, until the pounding rain decided they were wet enough.

Terrible hot wind followed the rain. Strong enough to knock a small child down, it whipped branches, swirled, changed directions, like a thing mad and confused. It howled coming through the thick fir trees. Behind the howling, Kai El heard a muffled roar.

Life along the Great River came with many kinds of winds, but he had never known one like this. He didn't know why, but it scared him.

The sky was wrong, too—low, heavy with fast-moving clouds, and darker than any daytime sky should be. Above the tall, pointed treetops, it looked thick and orange-brown.

Kai El smelled smoke.

His friends were afraid.

"What it it? What is it?"

"I don't know," he shouted over the wind, "but it's bad! Run!"

They ran for the camp. Undergrowth tripped them; wild dashes across open spots made the slower ones fall.

"Stay together!" Kai El yelled.

They helped each other, jerking up a downed one, dragging a slow one.

"Faster! It's coming!"

The sky got darker, the wind fiercer, the strange roaring louder. Thickening smoke burned their eyes and throats and made them cough. Something evil was after them. They didn't know what it was. They were terrified it would catch them before they reached the parents who would save them.

The little ones slid down a dirt bank, splashed through

a creek, scrabbled up the other side, and out into a small clearing—

Kai El froze.

Wildfire—coming too fast to outrun, chasing tumbling clouds of orange sparks along the ground in front of it. Bushes burst into flame before the fire reached them. Behind the sparkclouds, the sky—which had been getting darker—was now becoming brighter. The trees were black shapes against pulsing red-yellow-orange. One by one their tops exploded, turning them into torches that burned from the top down.

With every heartbeat, the fire became bigger and brighter. Kai El's eyes cried. His skin burned. He coughed. He could barely breathe for the smoke and heat.

He wanted to run! Run for his life! He pawed at small hands clinging to his leg—

The voice of Tsagaia jerked him to his senses.

"Get in the creek!" she yelled. "Get your clothes and hair wet!"

Nissa cried, "There's not enough water! The fire will boil it away! Boil us like roots in a stew!" Screaming, "Run!" she took off across the open ground.

"Get her, Kai El!" Tsagaia shouted, as she shoved the others toward the creek.

Tackling Nissa, he dragged her—shrieking and fighting— to the edge of the small ravine, and tumbled her over. She landed on her rear—babbling—crazed eyes darting. Tsagaia took her hand, and she hushed. They lay down and squirmed among the others.

The water fell over a heap of rocks and splashed into a little pool. Kai El looked through smoky air at his friends— stretched out on their stomachs; arms around each other; heads in the waterfall; coughing and gasping. Some cried; some were terrified beyond tears—except Tsagaia, comforting the others. Shoulders and rears stuck out of the water. Kai El thought of digging at the rocky bottom to deepen the pool, but there wasn't time. The heat was unbearable; the fire would be on them in moments.

"Come on, Kai El!" Tsagaia yelled.

Kai El slid down the bank and got in the water.

"Breathe through this," she said, giving him a wet piece

of her woven grass skirt. She was very close, but he barely heard her voice above the roar.

"We're going to die!" a little one cried.

"No, we're not," Tsagaia said. Her soothing voice was sure of itself.

"Keep your heads in the waterfall. Listen to the splashing. Focus on the sound. The water will save us. Think of nothing else. Listen to the splashing. Breathe the wet air . . ."

As she talked, Kai El found himself pulled into watersound, lifesound, foreversound . . .

Wildfire swept over the gully. Kai El did not look up. Heat seared his back through wet deerskin. He thought he heard animal screams in the deafening roar.

"Listen to the water," she kept saying, and he did, and the awful sounds faded.

"The water's getting hot!" a little one cried.

She had answers for everything.

"As long as you can hear the waterfall, the fire hasn't boiled it all away."

But the stench, the choking smoke. Kai El tasted ash in the splashing water. He thought he smelled cooked meat. He prayed to Amotkan and Skaina and all the spirits who love people: *I don't want to die!* His back must be blazing! He rolled over to get it wet.

Looking up at the yellow bottom of the wildfire, Kai El thought no one who had seen such a thing could live. It was so hot! Flames raced overhead, dropping burning twigs. As fast as the flames moved, more were right behind.

He realized that the wildfire—in its hurry for bigger prey— was jumping back and forth across the gully with its puny willows. Thank Amotkan for the creek that had carved this gully. Maybe they would survive, after all.

*But how long can we stand this?* he thought.

His friends cried in pain, but Tsagaia's voice controlled their panic. Kai El wet them down, put his head in the waterfall, and gave himself to her voice.

Everything changed so fast!

Surrounded by frightened women and little ones, Ashan

stared at the pulsing orange-brown sky. Wind whipped and howled. Burning things flew through the hot air.

*Kai El! Where are you?*

The men who had been out hunting burst from the trees.

"Wildfire! It's coming fast!"

"We know! We see it!"

Voices rose to a clamor.

"We have to run!"

"No!" Tor yelled. "We have to get in the creek!"

"It's too small! It's in the path of the fire!"

"We have no choice."

But some of them—Tlikit and Firekeepers—took off up the slope.

"You can't outrun it!" Tor yelled. "You'll die!"

Ashan grabbed his arm. "Kai El is missing!"

"What?" he said in shocked disbelief.

"Kai El is missing, and some others! We have to find them! I think they went down the creek."

Those who had listened to Tor were in the water, scrabbling at the bottom, making deeper places to hide.

"Little ones are lost!" he said. "Who will save them?"

More than enough men stood.

"I'll take the fathers and a few more. The rest of you stay with your families."

Ashan said, "I'm coming."

"No. The people need you here."

Tor shouted to the men as they rushed away from the camp, into the wind and smoke.

"The Moonkeeper saw the little ones go down the creek. Stay by the water. That's where they'll be. If you find them, throw yourself over them. If the fire gets too close before you find them, get in the water and save yourself."

Ashan ran with the men. Nothing had ever kept her from Kai El, and nothing ever would. They searched in fear—fear of what they would find, and fear for themselves—shouting their little ones' names, even though they knew the children could not hear them.

They saw the wildfire's face.

"Get in the water!" Tor yelled.

"No!" Ashan screamed and kept running. Kai El might be just ahead. She could save him with magic.

Tor slammed into her. She pitched to the ground. He picked her up and carried her. She fought him, screaming.

"Let me go! My baby! I can save him!"

Tor slid down a bank, dropped Ashan on her back with a splash, and threw himself on top of her. The water was deep enough to cover her body, but not his. He held her face out with his hand. She struggled against him, but she couldn't move. Her screams became sobs, and then coughs and gasps as she fought for air in the smoke. She smelled burning hair, saw Tor slap his head.

"We're going to die," she screamed. "All of us. Even Kai El."

But the wildfire did not bother burning out little gullies.

After it had gone, Ashan and Tor crawled up the bank and looked at a gray, smoking world, with black leafless trees still burning, and death everywhere.

She stood in dazed horror. What could have survived—

"Amah! Adah!"

Oh Amotkan! Kai El and the little ones were running toward her!

"Kai El!" she cried, and beat Tor getting to him. She swept him in her arms, covering him with weeping kisses.


No one died in the wildfire. It seemed as if the spirits came together to tell them what to do. The creek saved the little ones and those at the camp who trusted its wet shelter, though many had blisters and painful red skin.

The Tlikit and Firekeepers who had run were even luckier. Fire swept up the huckleberry field after them, but with little to burn, it lost power. They made it over the top of the ridge. That's where the wildfire died.

The people from Teahra spent a few more days in the gray-and-black place. A few swelled up and had fever. The Moonkeepers treated burns with beaver fat and herbs to soften skin and ease pain.

People needed rest. They needed to talk about what they'd been through.

Good friends Kai El and Jud were usually together. But on

that terrible day, when Kai El had taken the little ones for a walk, Jud had decided to stay in camp. He was interested in Yohee, who would be picking berries.

Jud had said, "I will get her to sneak away, for some—you know—kissing."

"Blah," Kai El said, sticking out his tongue. "Why would you want to do that?"

Jud shook his head. "Are you ever going to grow up?"

"Not if it means kissing girls."

So Jud had stayed in the camp, surviving the fire in a hole he dug in the creek bottom to share with Yohee, her sister, and her mother.

Kai El told Jud what it had been like for him, leaving out the moments when he'd felt like deserting his friends and running for his life.

"Of course *I* was brave," Kai El said. "But Tsagaia surprised me. I thought I knew her, but she changed into someone different."

"What do you mean?" Jud said. "She looks the same to me. Same old Tsagaia, too shy to look in anyone's eyes, too scared to speak."

"She was different out there. She took over and told us what to do, talking all the time in this soft voice almost like magic. It was like she sucked fear out of us and turned it into a blanket to protect us from the fire."

"You don't make sense."

"I know, but that's what happened. Tsagaia saved our lives."

"Maybe you should think of kissing her."

"Blah! Don't make me throw up."

Kai El told his mother what Tsagaia had done. His mother thought everyone should know about her bravery. But the girl was her old, scared self again. She said she hadn't done anything but save her own life. And that's what she would tell anyone who tried to make a heroine of her.

# CHAPTER 29

A MEAN SICKNESS STRUCK TEAHRA VILLAGE THAT autumn, forcing many people to their beds. They ached in every part of their bodies; guts cramped and they threw up food; waste came in uncontrollable rushes of stinking brown water. Weak as newborns, feeling horrible, some thought they were dying.

The Moonkeeper danced, sang, and shook rattles over the sick, gave them some kind of tea, and comforted with promises of recovery. No one refused the shaman's medicine—even the few Tlikit whom Tsilka could always count on to stir up trouble begged Ashan to help them.

Tsilka, who didn't get sick, prayed that some would die. Then maybe people would see that the Moonkeeper's medicine was useless, that the woman herself was a fake. Tsilka never stopped hoping to destroy Ashan by destroying people's belief in her.

But after a few days the sick began to get better. Today some had come out to sit under the pale autumn sun. Watching them heap their gratitude on Ashan, watching her accept it as her due—Tsilka couldn't stand it. Boiling with rage, she stamped away from the village.

*I hate my life! I hate my fate!* she thought, tramping along with her head down, not knowing or caring where she was going. *I hate the way everything works against me! All I want and cannot have, all my misery—it's all Ashan's fault!*

Tsilka's poisoned thoughts were not unusual. Hatred filled her all the time, spilling onto everything she did or thought about. Almost equal to her hatred for Ashan was disgust with herself: In five turnings of the seasons, Tsilka had not been able to harm her enemy in any serious way.

*I have failed to turn my people against her. Maybe I will never get her position or power, but I can try harder to get Tor. Without him she'd be nothing.*

*Oh, Tor . . .*

Pain stabbed Tsilka like a twisting knife. Hot tears ran down her face. She fell to the ground, pounded her fists, and howled.

"Oh, Tor! It's so unfair! You are mine, not hers! Mine!"

When her weeping was done, Tsilka saw that she was in a meadow sheltered from the wind by a rocky ridge. The grass was nipped short. All around were piles of bison dung, unnoticed in her blind approach. She wondered that she hadn't plopped down in one.

Little mushrooms grew from the edge of a nearby dung heap. She picked one. Holding the thin stem, she stroked the light brown pointed top. The flared underside was dusted with black. Rubbing black powder between her finger and thumb, she inhaled an odor like fresh-dug dirt.

*Shimnawa mushrooms?*

Shivering with excitement, she scratched the top with her fingernail. The wounded place turned blue.

*Yes!* These were powerful mushrooms that caused strange, overwhelming feelings—mostly wonderful, occasionally horrible—visions of the impossible for eyes and ears and mind. Though very rare, they had grown in the Tlikit homeland. When someone found shimnawa mushrooms, the whole tribe would eat them, and for a day and a night abandon itself to whatever might happen.

Tsilka loved these journeys of the mushroom trail. Real colors were never so bright, or smells so sharp, or touches so intense. She loved, too, the thrill of risk, for mushrooms could turn against you, creating ugliness and fear not to be matched by real life, and not to be escaped until the mushrooms were finished with you.

She sighed as she remembered making love . . . pleasure

almost too fierce to be survived . . . explosions that stopped her heart and made her wonder if it would start beating again.

Shimnawa mushrooms had not been found in the new land. Tsilka doubted the Shahala even knew about them.

It came to her suddenly: The gods had brought her here.

She yelled, "These mushrooms will help me get Tor!"

Tsilka put a handful in her waist pouch and headed back for the village, bubbling with triumph instead of hate. As she walked, the mushrooms tempted her. Not wanting to wait, she found a friendly place and marked it with a circle of rocks. The afternoon shadows were long; she would not be herself again until morning. She thought of the twins; they were alone, but used to spending occasional nights by themselves.

Tsilka chewed and swallowed nine little mushrooms one at a time. They tasted the same as they smelled, like dirt—not dry, dusty prairie dirt, but moist, mossy dirt found by a spring. Leaning back against a rock slab, she waited for the mushrooms to possess her.

Puffy clouds wandered across the pale blue sky. She stared at them as they drifted along, wondering if she should eat a few more, wondering if maybe they weren't shimnawas after all—

She smiled as the sky became bright sunflower yellow. The clouds transformed from white fluff to roiling amber liquid. The sky went murky orange, the clouds blood red. Darkening red splotched with dirty orange, pulsing greenish yellow spots—swirls and globs—merging, separating, dripping, running—the colors made her sick. They were the colors of her hatred for Ashan. She forced her eyes away from the sky, but the sickening colors followed wherever she looked. Her head spun. Her stomach twisted. Gagging, she fought to keep from throwing up.

Tsilka saw someone coming—Ashan! Struck by terror, she pushed herself back against the rock.

No, it wasn't Ashan, wasn't anyone at all—just churning mist in the shape of a person. Tsilka shivered, and willed herself to stop, but it intensified to violent shaking. The vapor person solidified, growing and shrinking, growing and shrink-

ing as it came toward her. Tsilka tried to push herself inside
the rock. *It is not real, is not real, is—*

Another shape approached the first—a man who looked
like Tor. The ghosts embraced, fell to the ground, and made
wild love. She heard them gasping and moaning and crying
each other's names.

Tor and Ashan ... they followed Tsilka everywhere,
flaunting her failure in her face.

*I hate you, Ashan!* she tried to scream, but made no sound.
She seethed with rage. Her stomach cramped. She vomited
violently.

Lying back, everything was black behind her closed eyes.
The sick feeling passed.

She saw Tor in her mind, opened her eyes, and he was still
there before her. Naked. Bathing in the grass that turned into
a river. Head thrown back, wet strands of long hair sticking
to skin that glistened with sun-gold droplets, he stroked his
muscled thighs with his large hands.

Tsilka's body—the *woman* part of it—came alive. On hands
and knees she crept toward him, a cougar stalking a fawn,
aware that she had left the protection of her stone circle,
wanting him too much to let fear stop her, telling herself that
there was enough power in her lust to overcome anything.

Sensing a heaviness lurking behind her, she turned and saw
Ashan. With the strength of her passion for Tor, she forced
Ashan inside the stone circle, and thought a misty, yellow-
green cloud around it. Believing she had trapped her enemy
made it so. Ashan could watch, but was powerless to interfere.

Tsilka leapt and brought Tor down. They made love, doing
things to drive each other wild—rising, exploding, collaps-
ing—again and again. The mushrooms coursing through her
body made it seem perfectly real. Their savage passion went
on and on into the night. The stars swirled and exploded.
Night birds cried with Tor and Tsilka, who could not get
enough of each other.

If it ever *really* happened like that, Tor would never again
be satisfied with his pale mate.

Exhausted, drained, gray as the early dawn, Tsilka returned
to her hut and slept the day away. She dried and crumbled
the rest of the mushrooms, and mixed them with powdered

elderberries and water. Storing the magic brew in a goat bladder, she waited for her chance. Several nights later it came.

The twins were asleep. Tsilka was ready to snuff the oil lamp when Tor flung the doorskin open and stamped in, fists clenched, face slashed by angry lines.

"We have to talk, woman!"

This was not exactly the chance she had hoped for, but it would have to do. *Be careful,* she told herself. *Stay calm.*

"Shh ... you'll wake the girls. Sit down while I make tea."

"I won't be here that long."

"My mouth is dry. I can't talk till I have something to drink. Now sit, or you can just leave."

With a snarl, Tor squatted. Tsilka poured the magic brew from the goat bladder into a basket and dropped in several rocks that were still hot from her cooking fire.

"This has got to stop," he growled.

Did he mean his coming to see her? She shivered at the thought.

"What?" she asked, keeping fear from her voice.

"Your vicious tricks. If Ashan doesn't kill you, I will."

Tsilka hadn't done anything to Ashan lately—except for taking her man in the mushroom dream.

She huffed. "I don't know what you're talking about."

The tea was hot enough. She filled two ram-horn cups and handed one to Tor.

"I'm talking about her dress."

*Oh that,* she thought.

A moon ago, she had stolen a buckskin dress from the Moonkeeper's hut—not to wear, but to have fun with. Working all night in mean delight, she took it apart and cut strips from the pieces, then sewed them together again. The dress didn't look any different, but it was smaller. Secretly returning it, imagining Ashan's frustration when she tried to put it on, Tsilka waited. But nothing ever came of it.

With an innocent shrug, she drank from her cup.

Tor glared, shaking his head. He took a drink.

"What is this?" he said with a look of disgust. "It tastes like dirt."

"Elderberries. I dropped my basket and they rolled on the ground."

"You might have thought of washing them. I don't want it." He handed her the cup. "Now what about Ashan's dress?"

Dipping her fingers in a pouch of honey and stirring them in the warm liquid, Tsilka sweetened the tea.

"Mmm . . . better. Try this." Giving Tor the cup, she sat next to him.

"What would I know about Ashan's dress?" she asked, her voice sweet and innocent.

He took a long drink, looking at her as if she were a stupid child.

"She knows it was you who took her dress and made it smaller."

Tsilka laughed. "Ashan is just getting fat in her old age."

"It isn't funny, woman. If you don't leave my mate alone, I will stop bringing gifts for the twins."

"That would be cruel, Tor. It's not their fault you refuse to be their father."

He drank as they talked. All she needed now was time.

"I promised to take care of the twins," he said. "You promised to leave Ashan alone."

"No, Tor. I promised to keep our secret. And I have . . . so far."

"Don't threaten me, Tsilka. I could snap your neck like a twig."

His slurred words lost their menace. The centers of his eyes grew larger and blacker as the mushrooms began the work of making him hers. Tsilka smiled.

"I would not threaten you, Tor. I'm not so bad, you know."

"You're worse than bad. You are . . . you . . ." He dropped his head in his hands. "I feel . . . strange."

In the lampglow, each hair on his head stood alone, long thin strands of shimmering light, blue-green and purple. Tsilka blinked. The mushrooms were working fast. She had to get him out of here. The twins must not hear them making love.

"I feel strange, too," she said. "It's hot in here. Come outside, and I'll tell you all about Ashan's little dress."

Tsilka led Tor away from the village. Nothing moved but swaying shadows that walked before them on ground washed white by the full moon. The mushrooms danced in her body and in her head. She floated along, the touch of her feet on the dry grass too light to be felt. She wanted to throw her clothes off and run, run naked under the moon.

"It's so bright I have to squint," Tor said, shading his eyes.

It was not *that* bright: Tsilka knew the mushrooms had him, too. He staggered.

"Why . . . what . . . where are you taking me?"

"The dress, remember? I'm going to show you what happened."

"Oh . . ."

He slumped to the ground.

"What's wrong with me? Everything's so . . ."

She sat beside the one she loved, put her arm around his wavering shoulders. His skin was soft as new velvet on the horns of an autumn buck. Man-scent filled her nostrils; she could taste him in his leathery smell.

"What did you give me, woman?"

"It's magic, Tor, my own special magic that Ashan, with all her power, knows nothing about."

"Magic," he murmured, lying back on his elbows. Moonshine poured down like silver honey. Tsilka wanted to lick it from his long, lean body.

But he said, "Tell me."

"I wanted her dress, so I took it."

"I knew it! Why?"

"I don't know. Maybe because you hunted the buck. Maybe because I pictured you slipping it from her body before you made love, and I wanted it to be me you undressed."

"Me," she repeated, tasting her lips. "Like this . . ."

Tsilka rose, hips and shoulders undulating to a song in her head. Tor watched with helpless eyes as she slowly pushed her fur cape from one shoulder and then the other, exposing her breasts. With a shrug, the fur slid to the ground. She untied her skirt and it fell away from her rocking hips. Her body moved like wind-teased grass; she ran her hands up her stomach and cupped her breasts, full and tingling, ready for Tor's mouth. Arching her back, she felt the moonshine bathe her naked skin.

"Tor," she breathed. "I am yours."

His helpless gaze turned hungry.

"Tsilka," he groaned. "Oh, Tsilka . . ."

# CHAPTER 30

Ashan awoke and found Tor gone. It had happened before. Sometimes he stayed away for several days. She didn't like it, couldn't help thinking about when he'd left and she hadn't seen him again for three autumns. But the fear was her problem, not his. She had to accept his need for time alone.

She remembered watching Kai El and Ehr feed animals by the Hidden Cave.

"I love these squirrels," the little boy had said. "Let's make a trap and catch one. I'll tie a thong around its neck and take it everywhere. I'll always be happy with a friend beside me."

Shaking his head, the wise old man had thought-spoken: *You must not keep one who needs to be free. Its misery would poison your happiness.*

Ashan tried to go back to sleep.

*This is different,* whispered a voice inside. *Your mate is in danger.*

She trusted that voice. As she left the Moonkeeper's hut, Kai El stirred, and for a moment she felt afraid to leave her son alone. But Tor was in danger.

Under the last full moon of autumn, the night was almost as bright as day. Moonlight stripped the colors away, leaving only black and white. The wind whooed. Crickets—soon to be silenced by winter—chirped frantically.

Ashan left the village, following the voice inside saying, *this way*. Hurrying along the river trail, she saw movement. Naked in the white moonglow, a woman writhed in a dance that reminded Ashan of rattlesnakes mating in one of their secret caves—twirling, dipping, swaying, oozing raw passion.

It was Tsilka. What was she doing out here alone in the night? Dancing for one of her strange Tlikit gods?

The woman's hands stroked her flesh as if she were going to make love to herself. Ashan had never seen anything like this. Fascinated, she crept closer.

A voice groaned at Tsilka's feet.

"Oh, Tsilka, please . . ."

Tor!

Hot light exploded in Ashan's head.

"I'll kill you!" she screeched, crazed with rage.

Ashan hurtled at Tsilka, knocked her down, straddled her. Like a pack of coyotes ripping into carrion, she clawed naked flesh to bloody shreds, slapped the ugly face, jerked the evil head by the hair, smashed it again and again on the ground.

"I'll kill you! I'll kill you!"

Tsilka's puny struggles meant nothing to the enraged beast tearing her apart.

"Help me!" Tsilka screamed.

"Ashan! No!"

Barely hearing Tor's voice, Ashan ignored it. She pulled her stone knife from the sheath at her waist. Shoulders pinned under Ashan's knees, Tsilka begged for her life. Ashan jerked her head back, thumped it hard on the ground. The throat shone white in the moonlight. The blade glinted. Holding it crosswise, she raised it—

"Mother!"

Ashan froze.

"Mother, stop!"

Kai El's horrified voice brought her back. She couldn't kill in front of her son.

Tsilka gurgled. Giving her head a last hard thump on the ground, Ashan climbed off the quivering lump. Her heart pounded; her head pulsed; her breath tore through her. The feel of Tsilka's blood on her skin, the flesh under her finger-nails—it was sickening. Ashan had never known she could feel such rage, couldn't believe she had nearly torn another human to pieces.

"Go home, Kai El."

Looking uncertain, her little boy backed away.

Tor lay there on the ground.

"Get up, Tor! What's wrong with you?"

"I'm sick. She gave me something bad to drink."

His words slurred. Ashan stared at his slack face and unfocused eyes—he did look sick.

"You made the choice to drink it," she hissed. "You're the one I should kill."

"I'm sorry," he moaned.

"You're disgusting!"

Tsilka cowered on the ground, crying like a baby. Ashan kicked her.

"Listen, you snake! You'd be dead if Kai El hadn't come!" She kicked again. Tsilka screamed in pain and rolled away. Ashan followed. "If you ever"—kick—"do anything like this again"—kick—"I *will* kill you. I know you don't believe in magic, but there are other ways. This knife"—she slashed the air above the terrified face—"this knife would have killed you if my son hadn't come. There is poison. There is fire—"

People must have heard the screams. Several were approaching. Ashan, about to rip into Tsilka again, looked inside for dignity. *I'm the Moonkeeper,* she told herself. She smoothed her hair, straightened her clothes, wiped blood from her hands.

"Moonkeeper, what happened?"

"Tsilka tried to take my mate. I convinced her not to try again."

The Moonkeeper sent them away. Leaving Tsilka lying there, she jerked Tor up by his arm and shoved him stumbling in front of her all the way back to the village, filled with anger, suspicion, hurt, and disbelief.

"You would have made love to her."

"No, Ashan. She gave me something to make me crazy, but I would not have made love to her. You are the only woman I could ever love."

"Then why were you with her?"

"I went to talk about your dress, to tell her to leave you alone."

"I don't need help from you. From now on leave Rattle-snake Woman to me."

"You're right, my love. I'm sorry. I never should have gone there."

Ashan couldn't help wondering if this was the first time Tor had gone to Tsilka in the night, but she pushed the question aside, buried it without asking him. How could she stand it if it were true?

To the Shahala, attempting to take another's mate was intolerable. The Moonkeeper had every right to banish Tsilka for what she had done to her personally. But looking at it as a chief . . . this was Tsilka's home, her children were here. Ashan told herself she had done all that needed doing. Surely Tsilka did not think Tor was worth dying for.

# CHAPTER 31

THE PEOPLE OF TEAHRA VILLAGE LOST ANY RESPECT they might have had for the woman who tried to steal the Moonkeeper's mate. Tsilka was shunned, even by men who had once sought her favors. The whispering, the ugly stares— she'd even had rotten wapato thrown at her by little ones. Tsilka couldn't stand it. She took to staying in her hut, feeling sorry for herself.

Poor, poor Tsilka. Life was so unfair. Ashan now had everything *she* wanted and deserved. People obeyed the Moonkeeper, even loved her. Tor was her faithful mate. Tsilka's own daughter, Tahna, spent more and more time in the Moonkeeper's hut learning medicine. All Tsilka had left was her beauty—which men no longer cared about—and a shy daughter, Tsagaia, who would someday lose her fight with the Breath Ogre, as the Moonkeeper called the invisible creature who stalked the girl and choked her.

What could Tsilka do? She hated Ashan, but everything she had done to destroy her enemy had failed. Now, in addition to humiliation, she lived in fear that Ashan might go crazy again someday and kill her.

And then, on a chilly autumn afternoon, she saw a way out of her intolerable life.

"Hayah!"

Hearing the shout, neither Tlikit nor Shahala, Tsilka peered through the door of her hut.

At the downriver end of the village, five strange men stood on a rise of ground. They looked massive in furs that covered them from shoulders to feet.

Sitting around the village fire, waiting for food the women were preparing, the men of Teahra jumped to their feet and scurried for their weapons.

"Hayah! Ee cha!" one of the strangers yelled. They threw down their spears and held out their arms in peace.

"Ee cha! Ee cha!" they said.

Nothing like this had happened before. Women and little ones scattered in noisy confusion, hiding in the huts. Brandishing spears, blades, and sticks, Teahra men charged at the strangers. But they didn't run.

"No!" the Moonkeeper yelled, putting herself in front of her men.

"Who are you?" she said. "What do you want?"

The strangers looked at each other. One pointed at the Moonkeeper, shook his head, touched his ears. She repeated the words in Tlikit. It was obvious they did not understand.

"Masat," one said. "Chi chi ah nee." Which meant nothing. But from the looks on their faces and the way they held their bodies, Tsilka knew they meant no harm. Besides, what could five men do against a whole tribe?

"Ee cha," said the one who spoke for the others. Stepping forward, he took off his fur robe and held it out, offering it to Ashan.

"Get away from her!" Tor yelled. With a thrust of his spear, he knocked the robe out of the man's hands.

"Tor!" she said. "There's no reason for that. I don't think they came to hurt us."

The Moonkeeper picked up the fur and draped it over her shoulders. The size of it made her look very small.

"Thank you," she said. "You are kind."

Behind the Moonkeeper, the men of Teahra grumbled.

"We should kill them," Tor said, "or at least chase them away. What if they have a tribe behind them?"

"If they do, it could be much larger than ours. We will welcome them. That is my command."

The Moonkeeper motioned for the strangers to come into the village. Teahra warriors opened a path for them. Women cautiously came from the huts bringing food. Even Tsilka came out. This was too exciting to miss.

The night passed uneasily around the fire. With hand-signs and marks on the ground, the strangers told about their tribe, the Masat, and about their home, far away in the direction Where Day Ends. There, they said, the dirt-world stopped and the water-world began. Compared to the water-world, the Great River was just a trickle flowing into it. The Masat men patted their well-fed stomachs to show that life was good there.

As Tsilka watched, an idea was born: She saw herself in a new home, with a new tribe, living a new life that had to be better than this miserable existence. Here was a chance to start over with people not poisoned by Ashan, people who would value Tsilka for the beautiful and powerful woman she was. She bubbled with excitement to think of going away with the strangers, of leaving forever this hateful place and its memories of humiliation, pain, and loss.

When it was time to sleep, the strangers chose a spot by the riverbank. Tsilka followed. She dropped her dress and stood naked before them, becoming the animal that drove men wild. She gave herself to the one who seemed strongest. The others watched—strange, though not unpleasant. Afterward she let them know that she wanted to go away with them. Eagerly agreeing, they headed down the river trail in the dark.

Tsilka wished she could have said good-bye to her daughters, but she wasn't worried. Tor would take care of them. The twins would be better off without her. She wondered what people would think when they found her *and* the strangers gone. Would they think she'd been stolen, or would they realize that she'd run away? Tsilka didn't care what they thought. In her mind, the people of Teahra Village already belonged to the past. A whole new life awaited her. She would be happy at last.

Filled with dreams, thriving on everything new and different, feeling like a girl again, she traveled with the five men for many days. She turned the dried food they carried into tasty meals, adding things she gathered along the way. Every night she made love to the leader, Lacanya. Not understanding each other's words didn't matter. The sounds they made would not be mistaken for anything but lust.

Hills turned into mountains, prairie into forest, as they followed the Great River along low banks and high, gouged canyons. They crossed rivers that flowed into it, making it ever wider, until she could barely see the gray-green trees on the other side. At a place where the water began to flow backward, they turned away from the Great River and headed in the direction Colder. After walking for several more days, they arrived at the home of the Masat tribe.

Dense forest marched down to a beach at the edge of a gently sloshing bay. A line of rocks separated the bay from the water beyond that went on until it joined the sky. It was raining, but Tsilka thought it was a wonderful place. She saw many huts, each large enough for several families to live in. There were people everywhere, many more than lived at Teahra. They stopped what they were doing and rushed to greet the returning men.

Standing tall and proud, Tsilka readied herself to meet her new tribe. They would see from the beginning that she was someone to be reckoned with.

Suddenly Lacanya grabbed her arm, threw her to the ground, and put his foot on her back.

Face down in the mud, Tsilka was too shocked to move. All the way here, he'd treated her like she was something special. Now this? Why?

"Let me up!" she cried, struggling.

The pressure of his foot increased. He sneered down at her, then said something to his people in a proud voice. Everyone jabbered at once. She couldn't understand their words, but they were happy and excited.

Lacanya jerked Tsilka to her feet. She was wet, muddy, humiliated, infuriated, and, most of all, scared. People surrounded her, pinching, poking, laughing. They shoved her into the village, pushed her down at the base of a tree, and tied her arms to it. As if she were some fine piece of meat, they sang and danced around her in the rain.

"No!" she cried. "This isn't how it's supposed to be!"

Tsilka was just what the five Masat brothers had gone

hunting for: a gift for their father to give away at their sister's mating ceremony.

*A slave.*

Her new life was nothing like she had hoped for. The family who received her forced her to work from morning till night. They watched her all the time, and beat her if she did anything wrong or moved too slowly.

She and another slave lived with three men, four women, and six little ones, in a large hut made from stacked cedar slabs split with sharpened blades of yew. Long, thin pieces lapped over each other on top, and the hut didn't leak. On rare sunny days, pieces were removed. It always smelled fresh inside.

Masat huts were much better than the hide-covered brush huts of her own people. Everything about her new home was different. It rained when it wasn't foggy, but the air was usually warm, except when storms blew in from the great ocean beyond the line of rocks.

The Masat floated in carved-out cedar trees that held twenty men. Far out in the endless water, they speared black-and-white fish—monstrous creatures larger than tree trunks—layers of fat over mountains of meat that fed the village for days. Animals with shells lived in the salty water, and strange-looking fish. People were fat from so much food. They had skins of beaver and otter, furs of bear, cougar, and sheep, hides of elk and deer—more than they needed. And plenty of time to enjoy it all, since slaves did most of the work. When they weren't out hunting or fishing, the men sat around smoking dried plants in carved wood pipes. They threw bone pieces and guessed how they would land, and the wrong one gave something to right one. They carved the walls of their huts, and made totems of people and animals that stood up in the ground. Women made baskets of spruce roots with woven grass designs. They made beads of shell, wood, and seed, and wooden holders to keep them in. Little ones didn't do anything but play.

They gave feasts for any reason, with lavish gifts to each other. Sometimes at a feast a slave would be killed, just to show how rich a family was. Of course, Tsilka was much too smart to let that happen to her.

Each morning some half-grown boys took Tsilka and other slaves into the forest. They lashed wood to a carrier on her back until it was so heavy she could barely stand, roping large pieces to her waist to be dragged. To stumble or fall brought scornful laughter or a beating. Morning after rainy morning, one exhausting trip after another, autumn turned to winter. There were huge woodpiles stacked all around the village, covered with leather to keep them dry, but no matter how much wood the slaves hauled in, the Masat never had enough.

Afternoons were spent with the four women of the family she belonged to. Tsilka and their other slave, a girl named Eenoway, worked hides, prepared food, twisted ropes, made baskets. Though the women expected their slaves to work without stopping, they were kinder than the men.

Winter passed in a dull haze. Tsilka, at first too shocked, was now too tired to fight back or try to escape. For a Masat slave, the only escape was death.

Though at first it had seemed impossible, Tsilka began to adjust. She realized that sullen or angry slaves were treated with the greatest cruelty. Those who were pleasant had better lives. If she had to live here, she would make the best of it. Forcing herself to be pleasant, she learned the Masat language. Gradually the women demanded less work of her and gave her more freedom.

She became a friend to Twe We, the young woman she'd been given to. One morning Twe We confided in her.

"I don't enjoy making love with my mate," she said, rubbing her bruised eye. "I think that's why he hit me."

"Lovemaking is not for enjoyment," Tsilka told her. Of course that wasn't true, but Twe We needed to learn the most important thing first. "Lovemaking is power, the only power a woman can have over a man. You are wasting it. I can teach you how to use it."

The grunts and groans she heard in the night as Twe We used her new skills made Tsilka long for a man. It had been a long time. Lacanya had wanted her on the journey, but once she was a slave, no man wanted anything to do with her.

She turned her attention to the youngest son of the Masat chief. Squill was little more than a boy, but Tsilka knew there was a man growing inside that hard, muscular body, a man who hadn't yet known a woman, but who must surely be dreaming of it. She could tell by the way he looked at her. She returned looks that would encourage him.

One day she found him alone.

"Haven't you dreamed of being with a woman, Squill? Of making love?"

"You are a slave. I would not make love with an animal."

"I'm a woman, just as human as you are. See?"

Tsilka shrugged the robe from her shoulders. He stared openmouthed at her breasts.

"Touch me."

She guided his hand. It lay hot on her breast, without moving.

"I am more than just a woman. I am a Tlikit, and we know things about making love that Masat women have never thought of."

Pulling him down on the soft forest floor, Tsilka showed him. It was wonderful—*wonderful*—to have a man again, even a half-grown one. In fact it was better to have one so young, so eager, so grateful. Tsilka never forgot that the boy was the best-loved son of the chief. If she used him well, maybe she could someday become an important woman who would have the best of everything.

At times being a Masat slave seemed better than being a free woman of Teahra. Tsilka didn't love Tor anymore; she didn't hate him; she didn't care. She missed her daughters, but not enough to return.

# CHAPTER 32

WHEN THE PEOPLE OF TEAHRA VILLAGE DISCOVERED Tsilka and the strangers missing, a few thought she'd been stolen, but most thought she had left because she wanted to. People knew of her unhappiness. They had seen her looking at the strangers in a hungry way. Warriors were not sent in pursuit. Tsilka's hut was taken by a family who'd outgrown theirs.

The twins came to live with Ashan and Tor.

Ashan knew that she hated Tsilka, but she hadn't realized how *pleasant* life would be without her. The strange tricks stopped. A snake in a boot, a dress somehow made too small during the night, being startled by tossed pebbles—Ashan had thought Tsilka was responsible. Now she knew for sure.

She loved being with the twins. They unfolded like trilliums who'd been waiting for snow-melt.

Tsagaia had always kept to herself because the Breath Ogre could attack her at any time. She didn't want anyone to see the helpless gasping, and no one but her mother, sister, and Ashan ever had. But the demon must have gone away with her mother. Cautiously, Tsagaia joined other little ones in play.

It pleased Ashan to see Tsagaia and Kai El becoming friends. Friendship might someday become love. The sweet girl would make a good mate for her son.

And Tahna . . . after her mother left, Ashan saw no more

dangerous flashes in her eyes. Tahna wanted to learn. Ashan loved to teach. Someone so eager and smart would learn fast. The growing tribe could use three women who knew the ways.

Tor surprised Ashan. She expected complaints about the crowded hut, but he seemed to love having the twins as much as she did.

For Tor, life without Tsilka was beyond wonderful. He'd been her slave—bound by the secret Ashan must never know—and now he was free. No more sneaking to her hut and resisting temptation so he could give his daughters gifts; no more gazing at them with longing.

All his little ones with him . . . his secret safe forever . . . it was so good that it scared him.

The friendship between his son and his daughter *should have* scared him. What if it did turn to love? He told himself that it wouldn't, that being raised together would make them feel like brother and sister.

But what if Tor was wrong? Maybe there *was* no such thing as a "safe" secret.

Tahna loved the Moonkeeper's hut. Its muted light calmed her eyes. The air, smelling of smoke and herbs, seemed to wrap around her. She delighted in learning new things from the Moonkeeper, in being smart, and doing important work. She liked medicine plants, and thought they had a language not made of sounds. Holding them, staring until her eyes blurred, she tried to understand.

One morning after everyone else had gone, Tahna said,

"I think plants want to talk to me, but I'm too stupid to understand."

Ashan smiled and placed her hand on Tahna's shoulder.

"You're not stupid. It seems you have the gift."

"What do you mean?"

Ashan didn't answer.

"Let's sit and work. I have herbs for Mitawi. She's been bleeding since her baby was born."

They sat on the mat-covered floor. Ashan unfolded a medicine pouch, and put pinches of dried leaves on a flat grinding stone.

"Watchwater, goldengrass, and stick-to-moccasin."

She crushed them with the stone's worn mate, grinding slowly, round and round, pulling Tahna's eyes into her hand.

When she spoke again, the Moonkeeper's voice was different, as if some other creature used her, a deep, sure voice, in no hurry with its ancient words.

"In the Misty Time, Amotkan gave the work of healing to Plant Spirits. They divided human sickness among themselves, making sure every sickness had a cure. But how would people know which plant to use for what? The plants decided that Coyote should teach First Woman their language."

Tahna blurted, "They do have a language!"

"Yes," Ashan said in her own voice. "That is the gift of medicine . . . to understand the language of plants. It takes patience. And you will have to learn not to blurt."

The Moonkeeper ground the herbs in silence, then spoke in the strange voice.

"The people were glad First Woman could heal them, but they weren't interested in how. So she taught her daughter, who taught hers, and hers, until the knowledge reached me."

The Moonkeeper picked up a pinch of the pungent powder she had made, rubbed it between her fingers, let it drift down.

"Take some. Feel it. Smell it. Taste it. Say: Watchwater, goldengrass, stick-to-moccasin. Stop the bleeding that is no longer needed."

When Tahna had done this, Ashan smiled and spoke in her own voice.

"If you have the gift—and I think you do—plants will share their secrets with you. You'll know what's wrong with people when they don't know themselves. But there's a lot of work between now and the day we can call you Medicine Woman."

"Medicine Woman!"

"Someday, perhaps. Would you like to be my helper for now? Amotkan knows I need one."

"Oh yes!" Tahna said, clapping her hands and trying not to jump up and down. "This is the happiest time of my life!"

After many moons, a bedraggled Tsilka returned to Teahra Village. Everyone gathered to hear her story.

"Those men," she said. "I don't know why they wanted *me*, but they did. They came in my hut and took me away, and kept me tied for days while we walked down the Great River. When we got to their village, I was a slave. They were cruel. They made me work from morning till night. I cried all the time, missing my daughters. I thought I would never escape, that I'd die and they'd throw my body in the water that reaches to the sky—that's what they do with the bodies of slaves.

"Then I heard something that scared me, and at the same time gave me courage: They were planning to raid our home."

Shocked sounds rose.

"Yes. Teahra Village. To get more slaves. I thought of my daughters. I thought of all of you. I saw slaves killed, just to show how rich their owners were."

The people of Teahra couldn't believe it. Even the Tlikit, who had once kept slaves, had never *killed* one.

Tsilka said, "How could I let that happen to my own people? I stole food and leathers, and slipped away from their village in the night. It wasn't enough just to warn you. I had to stop them from coming here. So I did what Tor did that time . . . remember how he tried to scare us by dressing in feathers and yelling?"

People laughed. What had seemed so terrifying then was now seen as a joke—no one would admit they had ever believed Tor was a god.

Tsilka continued. "Raven is the trickster of the Masat, like Wahawkin is to the Tlikit, and Coyote to the Shahala. Hiding in the forest, I carved a raven's head out of cedar wood to fit on top of my head, and painted it black, with a huge yellow beak and orange eyes. I painted the stolen leather black, cut feather shapes, and made a cape that looked like wings."

She pointed at Tor. "You who looked like a half-dead crow would have been impressed. I looked like a huge, fierce raven—a god with no mercy, and power to kill. I stood on a tall rock at the end of the village. Flapping my arms, I yelled at them in a voice of wind and thunder. Of course I knew their language by then.

"I said, 'You stole Tsilka, one of my people from up the river, but I came and flew her home. Now I hear you talk of stealing more. I say you must not. Take people who live in the forests, and ones who live by the endless water, but you must leave my river people alone, or I will tear you to pieces, starting with the chief.' "

"They believed you?" someone asked.

"Oh, yes. What happened next terrified them. The chief clutched his chest, gave a loud groan, and fell to the sand. I disappeared behind the rock, and made my way home as fast as I could."

"Are they coming?" people asked.

"I don't think so, but we must be careful from now on."

Tsilka had not been kidnapped, but the rest was true. Her tolerable life with the Masat ended when she heard about the slave raid they were planning. It wasn't the people of Teahra she cared about—many of them deserved to be slaves. But her daughters! Her beautiful twins! Leaving them with Tor was one thing, but they were not born to be slaves. Tsilka had to stop it. There was a good chance that she had: The Masat would believe that Raven struck down their chief for stealing river people.

On the long way home, Tsilka let herself dream of being called a heroine, but it didn't turn out that way. Teahra people knew her too well to believe her—though for a time they guarded the village.

They had not liked Tsilka before, and still didn't.

Being back in her own hut with her daughters was enough to make up for the rest. Tsilka felt better than she had before she left. She tried being nice, as she'd been forced to do to survive with the Masat. People responded by being nicer to her.

Within herself, she made peace with Ashan. No more tricks. Let Ashan have Tor. There were better lovers somewhere else. One would someday come her way. And she would leave again.

This was not her home anymore, nor were these her people.

# CHAPTER 33

Ashan's son grew to an almost-man of sixteen summers. Her mate enjoyed long hunts with old friends. With Tenka and Tahna sharing Moonkeeper work, Ashan now had time for herself. She liked to spend it at her place in the cliffs above Teahra Village—her takoma, where trails that spirits traveled crossed in the sky.

In the Summer of Little Deaths, the lives lost were minor compared to human life. But the deaths were odd.

A gray bird came to Ashan's takoma. The next day, she brought oily sunseeds and dry worms. The bird ate the sunseeds and stayed. Ashan began to look forward to their perfect visits: She talked, the bird listened. Soon it would sit on her knee and eat from her hand.

She saw the bird as she approached one day, sitting at the edge of a rock. It fell over when she touched it. She made a small fire and burned it. Because it was her friend, she didn't keep its feathers.

Peeping guided her to two nestlings—half–yellow fuzz, half–gray feathers. Ashan brought mashed seeds and water to the ugly things until they grew beautiful and flew away. She admired the gray bird, who had lived long enough for her babies to be safe.

A cougar came to the women's washing place at the Great River's edge, lay down on the flat rock, and died. The women with babies in their futures shared the beautiful, unmarked fur to line cradleboards.

Teahra Village had one tree, an ancient oak back near the cliffs. It gave the people summer shade, and dropped its leaves in autumn so the sun would warm them in winter. Its dried leaves made comfortable stuffing under sleeping skins. Its acorns—ground up, soaked, and rinsed to get the bitterness out—made a bland, white meal.

Long before people came to live here, the oak had split into the shape of a man with his arms out. The arms were monstrous branches, like two trees growing out of a trunk that took four or five children linking hands to encircle it. The deep grooves in the tree's bark were like an old person's wrinkles . . . a proud thing.

When the Tlikit warriors captured slaves, the oak gave them a place to tie them. Mats were attached to the trunk to shelter the prisoners from rain. After the slaves had been given their freedom, and their new name, Firekeepers, they built a real hut for themselves and their little ones against the trunk of the ancient oak.

Ashan used it to teach about Balance.

"When you look at that tree, its arms growing straight out instead of up, each with a huge top, you wonder why it doesn't split in the middle and come crashing down. Can you think how heavy those branches must be? They have to grow together, stay the same weight. They depend on each other. That is Balance."

The previous autumn, one side of the oak tree had lost its leaves as usual. The other side browned, but the dead leaves clung all through winter. They drifted down in spring, while the other side greened. That summer there was only half as much shade. People noticed that the side still living had covered itself with acorns—more than the whole tree used to give them. They worried.

"What will happen when the dead side falls? What will hold the living side up?"

"It will be many winters before the dead side falls. Look how healthy the living side is."

What could they do but wait? And stay out from under it, once it started giving occasional creaks.

Many were there when the dead branch gave up, warning them with groans from deep inside. Out of reach of its arms, people watched in fascination.

With a loud crack, the huge branch slowly peeled from the trunk, seemed to hang in the air, then fell with an echoing boom. The ground shook. A dust cloud filled the silence.

Alone against the sky, the living branch was too heavy to hold itself without the other for balance. It crashed down. The butt smashed the Firekeepers' hut to splinters. A mound of green leaves covered it.

They saw that the tree's heart was dark and hollow where there should have been living wood.

It took days to haul the wood out of the middle of the village. When the debris was all gone, the ground underneath was thick with acorns.

The newborn showed its glistening head.

The Moonkeeper urged, "Again, Shavon! Push!"

The Shahala almost-mother bore down. The grunting and gnashing of tenacity over pain stirred Ashan's memory of her own triumph long ago: Kai El's birth, the purest joy she had ever known.

The tiny warrior slid into the Moonkeeper's hands. She wiped his mouth and nose. He howled before she had to slap him, a sign he'd been here before.

"A boy!" she said, holding him up. "Eager for life!"

The baby's cries were lost in the cheer that arose in the women's hut at Teahra Village, echoed by the men waiting outside at a safe distance.

Ashan put the baby in his mother's arms.

"You did well, Shavon. He's beautiful."

Exhaustion and pain, forgotten in the wonder of birth, washed over Ashan.

"Tenka, you finish."

She handed Tenka the sacred blade for cutting the cord, left the women's hut, and made her slow, painful way downriver.

After her recent fall, Ashan had given up medicine work. Tenka, the Other Moonkeeper, could have managed a birth by herself, but this baby was so special that Ashan would not have missed the privilege of welcoming him.

The one just born was the *first* of mixed Shahala-Tlikit blood. Who would have thought he would be eleven summers coming? Or was it twelve since she had seen the Great River for the first time? It was becoming harder for Ashan to remember things like that without looking at her time ball.

Twice before, a mixed-blood baby had been lost in birthing—one took its Tlikit mother with it to the otherworld. Ashan had prayed nothing would go wrong this time. Some people would take another failed birth as a sign that the tribes should separate. There had always been a small, unhappy minority who felt that way. After Tsilka, their leader, was subdued by her life as a slave, they had caused less and less trouble in Teahra Village. The Moonkeeper wanted to keep it that way.

Ashan reached the Great River. Tall bushes hid large, flat rocks at the water's edge . . . the women's washing place. Early morning was the best time to be here. Sunlight floated on the water. Ashan cleaned herself, her robe, and a spot on her moccasin. She spread her robe in the sun to dry, and pulled her long skirt around her shoulders as a cape. Sitting with her head on her knees, the Moonkeeper listened to the Medicine Drum, muffled by the lapping water, welcoming the newborn. The sun gave her energy. Wind blew up the Great River, taking exhaustion away.

Because of a trick of the wind, she heard the Medicine Drum as if it came from the cliffs instead of the village. Her takoma called to her, or maybe it was the wind-whipped drumsong, or her own longing.

Ashan hadn't been to her place in the cliffs for more than a moon. Not since the day she'd slipped coming down. Her feet had flown out, and she'd landed on her back. Not much of a fall—she'd had worse—but that one moment ruined life.

Crippling had come on suddenly. Life had been hard on Ashan's body. She didn't know anyone whose bones had taken more abuse—anyone still living. The old wounds had healed without lingering pain. But since that little slip, pain and stiffness in her back grew worse by the day. She'd seen the same thing happen to old people. Ashan wasn't old, but thirty-three summers was way past the middle of life. Before the fall, she had found it hard to believe her advancing age. This pain made it easier to believe. Fearful of moving the wrong way, of even being touched, she felt *old*.

She put her head underwater—a good, cold shock—then shook out her hair, long and black as in her youth. She filled her chest with air. This morning she felt good. But crippling never got better with time.

The Moonkeeper longed for her place in the cliffs, where invisible lines of beauty, peace, and harmony crossed overhead. She had to accept that she wouldn't see the world from her takoma many more times—not through human eyes.

With the Medicine Drum giving a bounce to her steps, climbing was easier than walking had been lately. Ashan noticed everything with pure clarity, touched a rock, smelled a plant, looked at the sky. Clouds trekked in from Where Day Ends. Far-off thunder rumbled. The people of Teahra had enjoyed a long dry summer, but it couldn't last forever. The first clouds arrived, furiously scattering a few raindrops—for some reason making Ashan laugh. The sun came out again. The needy earth smelled happy to be wet. The Medicine Drum sang for it.

At last her takoma welcomed her. Pain denied while climbing enfolded her. She settled on the stone seat, knees pulled up, back against familiar rock. Each breath made her moan.

Through tears of pain she gazed across the Great River, wondering if people lived on the other side.

Below, Teahra Village lay under shifting shadows of cloud and sun. Ashan felt the joy of her people all the way up here. With the birth of this morning's child, the tribes finally had shared blood to bind them together.

How the Moonkeeper loved her people, wanted life to be good for them. She hoped this birth would help them see that life would be good for one only if it was good for all ... Shahala, Tlikit, and Firekeeper.

She took her time ball from her medicine pouch. Hers was different from those made by other women, marking not only her own life, but the life of the tribe during her time as Moonkeeper. The tribe had the time ball of every Moonkeeper,

from Shakana the First Woman, to Ashan. Of the fourteen,
Ashan's was the largest. Not surprising . . . she was chief of
two tribes.

She held her time ball to her cheek, breathing old odors,
then unwound the beaded string, going back to the beginning.

Remember . . . she touched a fragment of polished antler.

*Tor, our youth, our passion for living and each other. How
lucky I've been. I have you to this day. The flame between us
still burns fierce, with love enough to feed it forever.*

Remember . . . she touched a clear crystal from Ehr's cave.

*Kai El, my baby who's grown into a warrior. Remember when
we were alone together, just me and my little boy. Such a
beautiful time. No other comes close.*

Memories dried tears. Sleep took Ashan. The time ball
slipped from her fingers.

Rattling like the wind in the autumn oaks of Anutash, a Dust
Ogre came up the Great River. The whirling cloud of sand
danced above the water, touching down here and there. The
Dust Ogre paused over Teahra Village, then twirled up the
cliffside and came to a spinning rest before the Moonkeeper.

Inside she saw an old man, who changed into an old woman,
who changed into Coyote. The sand spinning around Coyote
changed to sparks of light. Ashan had no fear of yellow eyes
and bright teeth as the creature wearing a whirlwind settled
nearby.

*Wolf Friend,* she thought, gazing into sparkling eyes.

Coyote asked: "Do you treat these people well, or are you
one of those evil women?"

She considered. Hunger was only a memory. People were
healthy. Most lived in huts. Only a few still clung to the Tlikit
cave.

"They live well. And I'm teaching them to build good
huts."

But Coyote's eyes said that he wanted more.

Ashan said, "I'm teaching them to live in Balance."

The creature nodded. Glittery eyes softened.

"Soon the world will change," he said. "Women will no
longer be chiefs. You have been a good chief, Whispering

Wind. I reward you: You shall stay here and watch over the people who live here forever."

Thunder cracked, with Ashan inside. Her blood stopped. Pain squeezed across her shoulders, down her arms. A moment's panic, then used-up, pain-racked flesh went limp.

Ashan soared.

*I have hurtled through this darkness splashed with sunset colors; seen the Light, brighter than the sun, beckoning. This time my loved ones are here.*

Her mother, Kira, and father, Kahn. The Old Moonkeeper, Raga. The grandfather, Ehr. Others she did not know. They carried her on wings of love.

"All of creation," they sang. "Into our world has come a new life. Make her path smooth, so she may live among the stars, or at the Creator's side, or in the minds of people."

Most of the men, including the Moonkeeper's mate and son, were away hunting when the tempest exploded over Teahra Village. With thunder shattering their ears, and lightning so near they smelled it, everyone hid in the cave.

As frightened as anyone else, Tenka was more frightened to think of Ashan out there all alone, too weak and crippled to get to shelter. Taking Mani, she went to find the Moonkeeper.

When they stopped to rest halfway up the trail that led to their chief's special place, they saw her, stretched out on her stone seat, surrounded by coyotes. One stood over her, nose to nose, sucking out her life. Tenka thought she heard it speak.

Screaming at the animals, they ran toward her.

When they got there . . . No Moonkeeper. No coyotes. Nothing but her unwound time ball on the stone seat.

Above and behind, rain beat on the strangest thing they had ever seen: A slab of stone, wide as a woman's reach, tall as her chest, reddened with ochre, incised with a beautiful image . . . a face with soulful eyes, arched brows, owlish horns, mouth open to speak the wisdom of ages, silent as only stone can be.

The rock picture was too high to reach from the stone seat. It had not been there before, would have taken moons to make, yet there was no work debris.

It was just *there* in the pounding rain. And the Moonkeeper wasn't.

Tenka and Mani held each other and wept . . . Mani for the loss of her best friend . . . Tenka for that, and for the knowledge that *all* was now upon her small shoulders.

# CHAPTER 34

KEENING ROSE FROM THE CANYON TO MEET THE MEN returning from the hunt. Dread seized Tor's heart. He broke into a run, crested the last hill, and looked down. Teahra Village reeled in panic as if it were a hive of bees whose mother had been lost. In the confusion of wails and shouts he heard, "The Moonkeeper!"

"What happened?" he yelled, running down the trail.

Followed by a jabbering swarm, his sister Tenka reached him.

"Oh, Tor!" she cried. "Ashan is dead!"

He grabbed her shoulders.

"What do you mean?"

Tenka collapsed in his arms. "I can't take her place," she sobbed. "What am I going to do?"

Tor shook her. "Where is Ashan?"

"Coyotes killed her! Up in the cliffs!"

"Dead!" people cried. "The Moonkeeper's dead!"

"No!" Pushing Tenka away, Tor shoved his way through the mob. "You're lying! All of you!"

He dashed into their hut. Ashan wasn't there. He ran to her place in the cliffs, barely aware of his son and others behind him. She wasn't there. Tor could not understand the picture of a woman's face carved into the stone.

"Ashan!" he cried. "Where are you?"

The story Tenka and Mani told was crazy. Coyotes could

not kill a human. And if they had, where were the signs of struggle? Where was the body? No. Whatever the foolish women saw and heard was a trick of wind and rain, and Tor refused to believe it. Ashan was alive, because Tor couldn't live without her. If ever he believed she was dead, grief would kill him.

He searched in wild desperation. His son and others came along, but Tor didn't talk to them, barely noticed them. Every moment of every day and night was a hideous mix of emotions, uncontrollable, inescapable, unbearable.

Guilt: He was a terrible, worthless mate, had not been there when she needed him. By neglect, he had allowed this to happen.

Rage: He was angry to the point of hatred. At the spirits, the tribe, himself, even at Ashan. How could she do this to him?

Worst of all was wrenching sorrow: She *wasn't* dead, no, but she was gone, and he needed her, ached for her.

He grew haggard from lack of food and rest, but he kept on as if he were a man running in front of stampeding bison. If he stopped, he'd be trampled to death. He didn't care if people thought he was crazy. Nothing mattered but finding Ashan.

The people struggled to accept the disappearance of the Moon-keeper. No one would ever know what happened in the cliffs that day, but they believed their beloved chief was dead. They deeply mourned her loss. For some it was especially hard. Mani desperately missed her closest friend. Tenka, who wasn't ready to lead the people, had no choice; they gave her no time for her own sorrow.

And Kai El . . . All alone one day, Kai El wept.

"Oh Mother, you are gone, and it hurts so much . . . help me . . . I can't stand it . . ."

Through tears he saw a white hawk fly up out of the canyon and soar over him in peaceful circles. He knew it was his mother. She was dead, but she was not gone. They would be together again. After that he could close his eyes and see the white hawk again. His own soul would rise up as a red-tail hawk and fly with her, love flowing between their touching wing tips.

Death had not broken the bond between mother and son. When he understood this, Kai El began to heal.

But Tor was destroyed by the loss of Ashan.

# CHAPTER 35

F<small>AR AWAY FROM THE VILLAGE OF HER PEOPLE</small>, THE Spirit of Ashan was over, under, part of a world of water, witnessing the live birth of a whale that her people—except for Tsilka—had never imagined. They'd never seen fish larger than sturgeon, didn't know about this ocean with its strange creatures. Though they lived in a world of water, these whales were more like humans than like fish. They spoke a language of whistles; they loved each other.

Ashan's spirit would have followed the mother and baby on their migration, but she wanted to be at Teahra Village for the Ritual of Giving for the last baby she had brought into the world—named Chanok, Blood of Two Tribes.

*. . . His birth day, my birth day . . .*

*. . . Or as humans understand it, my death day . . .*

When they began their second summer, little ones were given gifts to honor their courage. People knew how hard it was to survive the first part of life.

All little ones were special, Chanok more than most.

*. . . The first of mixed Shahala-Tlikit blood . . .*

*. . . As far as the people know . . .*

After her last death, the Spirit of Ashan had been thrilled to discover that she could move around in time and space. She had always wondered about the time when Kai El was a baby and Tor had left them. He would never tell her much, and part of her had been instinctively afraid to push too hard.

But, believing that spirits would be immune to the pain of their human counterparts, now she sought answers to all the mysteries of her life.

Traveling to that long-ago time, the Spirit of Ashan had found her beloved mate . . . making love to another woman. Tor had been Tsilka's lover. He was the father of the twins. His youthful betrayal was bad enough, but to know that he had lied to her for the rest of her life—Ashan was devastated. She learned that—whether joy or pain—spirits feel much more deeply than humans.

Why, she wondered, had she discovered this now, and not when she'd traveled in the otherworld after falling from the cliff when she first reached Teahra? It was because that death, her second but not her last, was to learn what she needed to fulfill her destiny of uniting the tribes. Now, in the death that would last forever, she had freedom to travel and learn anything and everything. In death as in life, though, there was danger in the search for knowledge. One should be prepared for whatever truth might be discovered.

Ashan was not prepared for this truth, in life or in death. She was tossed about in an ocean of pain, felt she might drown in it. She struggled for a way to save herself, and found it.

. . . I forgive you, Tor . . . I forgive you . . .

Forgiveness healed her pain, but the Spirit of Ashan would always have a fear of traveling in time.

When she desired it, Ashan was at Teahra Village. Still perfecting wingless flight, she sped toward her rock in the cliffs for a high, wide view of the celebration for the child Chanok.

The sight of Tor made her lose focus. She came down almost on top of him. A living person would have landed with a thump and a cloud of dust, but the spirit was silent as mist in motion, invisible in the way of wind. Whether she wanted to be or not.

Time was different for the spirit, but in any measure of time, she'd been too long away from her beloved mate.

The warrior Deyon stood by Tor.

"When I think of her, I miss her," Deyon said.

. . . Tor, I love you . . . If only I could hold you . . .

Ashan became strandlike and wrapped around Tor, but she couldn't feel him, any more than he felt her. She had no fingers, no skin, no body.

"I miss her, too," Tor said.

Ashan saw past the brave voice, saw emotions as plain as bones and blood. Tor was overwhelmed with anger and pain, but he refused to scream, refused to weep.

Ashan longed to comfort her soulmate. She'd always thought they'd be able to feel each other after one of them died—their love was that special. But she could not make Tor aware of her existence. He didn't want to know of her existence. It might light the way out of his black pit of grief, and he wasn't ready for that. He clung to his grief, believing it was all he had left of Ashan, that letting it go would mean letting go of her.

At least Kai El knew the spirit his mother had become. She could enter his dreams and comfort him. He was journeying through grief on a straight path.

His father was not. Like a star when too much heat builds up, Tor could explode, flying apart with such force that he'd never pull himself together again.

"I'm going upriver," Tor said.

"Say hello to her for me," Deyon said.

"I wish I could."

Tsilka stepped out of her hut as Tor passed.

As always, it surprised the Spirit of Ashan to feel a flash of hatred for the woman.

. . . *I would have thought spirits would be more understanding of humans* . . .

If not for Tor, Tsilka would be a different person. If not for Tor, there would be no fatherless twins.

. . . *I should be more generous toward her* . . .

Tsilka ran after Tor and stopped him. She held out a piece of dried red meat.

"I made saltfish, the way you like it."

"I'm not hungry."

"Try it, and tell me what you think. Does it have too much white rock?"

He tasted, and spat. "Too much."

"That's what I thought," she said. "Drink this to clean your mouth."

Tsilka held out a ram-horn cup. Ashan became the liquid in it: A tea of mushrooms sweetened with honey, shimnawa mushrooms that could put a man's better senses to sleep. She remembered finding the two of them on a moonlit night— Tor stupid with mushrooms, Tsilka dancing naked.

*. . . With all these men, why can't you leave Tor alone . . .*

Tsilka did not hear the Spirit of Ashan.

"It will make you feel better," she said in a voice sweet as the honey in the poisoned cup.

*. . . No, Tor, don't take it . . .*

He said, "I feel fine, Tsilka."

"I know you better than that, my warrior god." It was a name Tsilka used to call out when they made love.

Tor reached for the cup. Ashan heard him thinking, *What would I give to feel better for a while?*

The spirit put all her effort into making a sound, any sound. She'd tried before, but maybe this time . . .

It was hard to get used to being nothing.

*. . . Why do I care if Tsilka makes him drunk . . . Doesn't he deserve some relief from his misery . . .*

Tor drank the mushroom tea.

*. . . Stop it, Tor . . . She's bad for you . . .*

The spirit wasn't jealous, as she might have been in life, but she had to stop Tor from hurting himself. She liked to believe he'd grown past that, but she knew better. If he drank enough mushroom tea, he'd give in to the part of his mind that lived between his legs. Taking pleasure with Tsilka would be bad for him anytime, especially now. Tor was capable of desperate acts; he might regret it enough to end his life. As much as the spirit longed to feel her mate's embrace, it wasn't time for him to join her in the otherworld.

Tor drained the cup. Tsilka took it, and refilled it from a shoulder pouch.

*. . . What am I going to do . . . Tor can't hear me . . . A bodiless creature can't slap the cup from Tsilka's hand . . .*

The Spirit of Ashan might have left. She could be anywhere faster than an eyeblink, didn't have to know what happened in this village. Part of her wanted to leave. It might be said that Tor deserved whatever he got at Tsilka's hands.

Or . . . she could go further than a spirit should, and interfere in the affairs of humans. Ashan believed she had powers not yet discovered. The spirit also knew the gravity of harming people. Just because she *could* do something did not mean that she *should*.

*. . . I can't let Tor hurt himself . . .*

Without knowing how it would end, the Spirit of Ashan pulled herself into a ball and exploded in Tsilka's face.

"Fire!" Tsilka shrieked.

She dropped the ram-horn cup and fled.

*. . . I can get her attention . . .*

"Fire?" someone said. "What's she talking about?"

"I don't know," Tor said. He hadn't seen the flash, though he'd been looking at Tsilka, reaching for the cup.

"Maybe she had too much of the mushroom."

Now that the father was safe, the spirit should have looked in on the son. And she should have left a gift, a prayer perhaps, for the mixed-blood child. That's why she'd come to Teahra Village instead of following the migrating whales. But Ashan had had enough of people. She desired to return to the ocean, and she was there.

# CHAPTER 36

K AI EL WAS SEVENTEEN SUMMERS, THE AGE OF UNEX-pected stiffening under his loinskin, of watching girls and imagining the unknown.

He was tall like his father, wide of shoulder, long of arm and leg; with well-shaped muscles under brown skin dusted with gold; thin Shahala nose and high cheeks. Girls called him handsome. He saw in himself his Spirit Guardian, Skaina the Hawk—wings folded in a dive, keen eyes focused, power-ful legs thrust out to kill—but once a girl said he reminded her of a stalking cougar. He tied his hair back with thongs, keeping it long for the night he'd loose it to brush across a woman's breasts. He loved the feel and smell of animal skin. Because people brought gifts to the Moonkeeper's family, even now that she was dead, he had many leathers and furs for different seasons. On this summer day, he wore only a fringed loinskin and moccasins that came to his knees.

Kai El's spirit brother, Jud, would never be mistaken for his birth brother. Except for their age, they were different in every way. Who knew what made best friends?

Jud was short like most men of Tlikit blood, with muscles so large they threatened to burst through shiny, dark gold skin. He could make his bearlike body do almost anything. When hair got in his face, he cut it off. He wore a loinskin because it was expected, but it took an ice storm to make Jud cover the rest of himself.

The two stood watching the tribe's young, unmated women. Kai El felt the throb of the great One Drum in his blood.

"TUN TUN TUN, tun tun tun, tuntuntun. TUN TUN TUN . . ."

The fascinating creatures danced in a loose circle around the drum. Of different shapes and sizes, each dancer wore what she liked best. Hair was tied up, or let loose to bounce and sway. Feathers swung across faces, fringed skirts opened for glimpses of legs, breasts moved in pleasing ways. The young women were supposed to be dancing for the little one, Chanok, but the dance was really for the unmated men—like Kai El and Jud.

Kai El stood tall, flexing his arms and shoulders. He snapped his head so his heavy black hair went behind, leaving the feather of a red-tail hawk and some thin leather strips to brush his bare chest. He kept a disinterested look, as if he were only watching them dance because there was nothing better to do.

Tsilka's daughters of fourteen summers danced side by side with matching movements.

"Those twins," Jud said. "It's hard to tell them apart. If a man took his pleasure with one, it'd be like having both."

Kai El elbowed him. "Where do you get your ideas?"

"I get them at night while lazier men sleep."

Kai El laughed. Jud always made him laugh, one thing he liked about his friend.

Kai El said, "I have no trouble telling them apart. Have you ever looked in their eyes?"

Jud said, "I don't waste my time looking at eyes when there are bodies to be looked at."

Kai El watched the twins, thinking about when his feelings had changed.

One day last summer, he had looked at Tsagaia, and there was something different about the way she looked back. Maybe it was that she *did* look back. She was so shy that Kai El and his friends laughed about it.

"Tsagaia must know every crease in her moccasins," they said, "as much as she stares at them."

Of all the girls of Teahra Village, Kai El knew Tsagaia the least. Long ago, when the twins lived with his family for a

time, Kai El and Tsagaia had started becoming friends, but
that all changed when Rattlesnake Woman returned. Tsagaia
changed back to the way she was before: timid; afraid to play,
or talk, or look in anyone's eyes.

And then one day last summer, Tsagaia had looked at Kai El.
From under thick lashes, soft eyes reached across a blackberry
bramble. Her eyes seemed to say: "No one has ever been
inside me before, because no one has ever been trusted, and
I am waiting."

Then Kai El's mother Ashan had disappeared, shaking his
life to pieces, casting the pieces everywhere. He'd taken part
in the hopeless searching, though his heart knew that the one
who loved him more than anything was dead. Some people
still searched for Ashan, as if she could be alive after all this
time. But they said, "She's been gone before," and, "You
know how Moonkeepers are," and refused to give up hope.

When Kai El had stopped looking for the shell of his mother,
and instead welcomed her spirit to his dreams, healing had
begun.

Lately he'd been thinking of Tsagaia again . . . *Gaia*, the
voice in his mind called her.

The unmated women finished their gift of dancing.

"They'll be going to bathe. Maybe we can get a look."

"Grow up, Jud. That's for boys."

"You grow up, Kai El. It's for men."

"Men need to eat. Let's go see what the women put out."

A group of girls headed down the river trail.

"I can eat anytime," Jud said, going after them.

"Don't let Tahna catch you again," Kai El said, shaking
his head.

The gray-haired drummers stood, stretched, walked around,
then took up their sticks again and began a lively song. Little
ones danced next—some playful, others serious, small adults.
They made Kai El smile.

He saw Tsagaia off by herself, unlacing her knee-high
moccasins, special ones for dancing. He swallowed, licked
his lips, and went to her. She looked up long enough to see
who he was, and went back to her laces. Inside the tan leather
painted with flowers, her feet were small.

"Have you seen the world from my mother's place?" he asked.

"Up in the cliffs? Where She Who Watches lives?"

He smiled. "She doesn't live there."

The girl shook her head. Loosed from the dance feathers, her shiny black hair swayed back and forth.

"People are afraid of the Moonkeeper's place," she said.

Kai El smiled. "There's nothing up there but wonderful sights. I'd like to show you."

"I shouldn't . . . the celebration . . ."

"We won't be missed. Rattlesnake Wo—I mean—your mother is hiding in her hut. After her screaming fit, I doubt we'll see her till tomorrow."

Tsagaia looked down. A wing of hair fell over her face.

Kai El thought it must be embarrassing to have Tsilka for a mother. He didn't like the woman who gave him strange looks that he didn't understand. He couldn't think of anyone who *did* like Tsilka. Especially since she'd left the tribe to go with the strangers who came up the river. Even though she'd returned, with wild stories about being kidnapped and killing a chief, people never trusted her again.

Tsagaia brushed her hair back and looked at him with a shy smile on her pretty face.

"I would like to see the world from up there."

The girl stayed close behind Kai El as they climbed. She said nothing, but he felt her there. His chest swelled. He would show her things she'd never see if not for him, give her gifts for her eyes.

She reminded him of the lynx kitten left behind when his family abandoned Ehr's cave—Ayah was its name. Tsagaia would be soft like that kitten, he could tell, though he'd never touched her . . . except once, when they'd huddled together in a creek while wildfire swept over them. He liked her scent. He liked the way her long hair hung down her back, how it swayed when she walked—a graceful walk that made her seem smaller, and somehow vulnerable. Tsagaia was a quiet girl, but Kai El knew that didn't mean she wasn't thinking. She was comfortable to be with, like being with the grandfather Ehr, who'd had no tongue and couldn't talk.

Ehr had taught Kai El and his mother to speak with their

thoughts. Kai El missed thought-speaking, now that Ashan was dead.

*I should teach Gaia. We could have secrets, laugh at people without their knowing why, tell each other things that would get us in trouble if we spoke them out loud.*

The long climb brought them near the top of the cliffs. A level stretch of trail opened onto the place Ashan had loved—and disappeared from: the Moonkeeper's takoma, overlooking Teahra Village and the Great River beyond.

Kai El and Tsagaia sat on the stone seat, leaning back, not quite touching. The mysterious carving called She Who Watches was above and behind them.

Hearing the cry of a hawk, Kai El looked up. A pair of red-tails soared above the Great River. He wondered if they were fishing, or just enjoying being here, being with each other. As he was.

"Skaina, the Hawk, is your Spirit Guardian," Tsagaia said. "I think hawks are beautiful."

Kai El was surprised, and flattered, that she knew it.

"Why didn't you take your guardian's name?" she asked. "Why did you keep your birth name?"

"You Tlikit people think one name is enough. I like my name. How it sounds. What it means."

"Sun River." Her voice was easy in his ears. "That makes a nice picture. I like it, too."

Kai El felt *wonderful.*

"Were your parents angry?" she asked.

He snorted. "Tor has never forgiven me, though he's the one who named me Kai El. He has names of his own to call me when he's angry."

"Ohh," she said with sympathy, her lips forming a shape that should be kissed. Kai El took a deep breath, and talked instead.

"But my mother . . . she's the one who taught me to follow the voice inside. She let me do it."

"You were young to be so bold."

He shrugged, but Tsagaia's words made him proud.

"Now it's every child's choice," she said.

"Why did you keep your name?" he asked.

She hesitated, as if deciding whether to tell him.

"I like Shahala ways, but I was afraid to go on a spirit quest."

Kai El caught himself just before he laughed. A spirit quest was nothing to fear.

She continued. "So I decided to keep the name Tsagaia. Big Tan Cat. I admire the cougar."

"Yes," he said. "The most magnificent, beautiful animal. There is nothing more wonderful than a cougar."

But praise that would make Kai El puff up made her pull inside herself. He let some quiet time go by in the pleasant, sun-drenched place, until he felt a little melting from her.

"Would you mind if I called you Gaia?"

"Kitten? I suppose you may. But why?"

She gazed at him. Her beautiful eyes invited him to share himself.

He began, "Once my mother and I lived with an old man named Ehr. He taught me how to make animal friends. You just feed them at the same place and same time, every day. There was a lynxcat, and some kittens—"

Kai El was so focused on Gaia's eyes that he did not hear his father coming.

"What do you think you're doing!" Tor yelled.

Kai El stammered. "I—we—"

"This is a sacred place, not a place for children to make trouble!"

Kai El felt Gaia shrink beside him. Tor was scaring her.

The young man stood—tall as his father, defiant. On the small piece of flat ground, they were closer than angry men should be.

"It's my mother's place. I have the right to be here. What kind of trouble could we make sitting here looking at the river?"

Tor's face was red. A vein in his jaw throbbed.

"You don't know anything!" he shouted in his son's face.

The argument of loved ones brought the Spirit of Ashan. The colors swirling around and between them were awful— hot muddy reds and oranges, sucking and pulling at each other.

They had to stay close. They needed each other's strength. She hovered over them.

*. . . Please don't hurt each other . . .*

Tor's shoulders slumped, as if a heavy weight had settled on them.

Kai El looked up, feeling something in the air, not knowing what.

Tsilka's daughter, Tsagaia, sat on Ashan's stone seat: tight, small, trying to be invisible. Ashan sensed Kai El's fierce passion to protect the girl, a passion growing under Tor's attack.

*. . . Oh Amotkan . . .*

It dismayed her that spirits did not know everything.

*. . . My boy is falling in love . . . with his sister . . .*

"Just go, Kai El," Tor said in a voice choked with anguish. "Don't bring anyone here again."

Kai El led the way. Gaia followed with downcast eyes. Ashan knew her son's thoughts: The girl would never look into his eyes again, shy as she was. Tor came right behind them, as if they couldn't be trusted. Humiliation burned around Kai El, fire flashes leaping from the sun.

The angry young man thought, *And I felt sorry for Gaia because of her crazy mother*.

Tsilka came running up the narrow trail.

"Daughter! Why didn't you tell me you were leaving?"

The girl said, "I thought you were asleep. I didn't want to bother you."

"Why would I sleep in the day? You should have let me know. I worried."

Tor shouted, "I told them to never go up there again! They shouldn't even be together!"

Tsilka said, "Tor, don't be an old bear. There's nothing wrong with two young people going walking. Remember when we—"

The Spirit of Ashan swirled around Tsilka so fast that it chilled the air. Tsilka shivered, not finishing her words.

Tor said, "Tsilka, you know as well as I that these two must never—" He stopped himself.

"What are you talking about?" Kai El said, getting angry at all these half-spoken allusions. "Why shouldn't Gaia and I—"

Tor raised his hand as if to strike his son.

"When I want to hear from you, I will ask you to speak!"

Tsilka did not give up. "Tor, remember when you and I—"

Ashan wrapped the chill around her tighter.

"Oh, forget it!" Shivering violently, Tsilka grabbed her daughter's hand and hurried toward the village.

"My son," Tor said.

The young man turned burning eyes on his father.

"What right do you have to humiliate me before a woman?"

Fourteen summers hardly made a woman, but Tor didn't want to humiliate Kai El any more than he already had.

*... Tell him, Tor, tell our son what he must know ...*

Tor wanted to speak. He tried to speak.

*... TELL HIM ...*

"What?" Kai El demanded.

"Nothing! Just don't ever do that again."

"We weren't *doing* anything."

"Stay away from her. Those two are strange, born at the same time, with no father, or any father, who knows. They're bad luck. They'll bring you nothing but trouble."

"I'm not a little one. You can't tell me what to do."

"Your mother would want a better mate for you than the daughter of crazy Tsilka."

All his life, Kai El had done what his mother wanted.

Fathers knew the weapons to use against their sons.

# CHAPTER 37

Curses and groans awakened Kai El, sounds of angry pain: Tor thrashing under his sleeping skins.

*Worse than an old man,* the young man thought.

It was bad enough before as father and son struggled with the loss of the woman in their lives. Now they could not move beyond what had happened in the cliffs. Days went by with few words. Kai El left early in the morning and didn't return until night. Some mother or daughter was always happy to feed him. Tor spent more and more time alone in the hut. Kai El didn't know what, or if, he ate.

"Smells bad in here," Kai El said, shoving the skins from his naked body and getting up.

"Dung!" his father said. "This hurts!"

What was it today? Kai El wondered. Ankle? Shoulder?

"This elbow is swelled like a condor egg. Your mother would have made me something to put on it."

*It's your mind hurting your body,* Kai El thought. But he didn't say it . . . he didn't know what it meant to lose your mate.

He knew what it meant to lose your mother. If only he did not. Amotkan, how he missed her. Needed her. She knew how to soothe his father. Most important, she would answer Kai El's questions about Gaia.

Beautiful Gaia filled his thoughts.

As young men do, Kai El wanted many things at once. He

would like to think about his dead mother ten times a day
instead of twenty. He'd like to feel comfortable with his father
again.

But most of all, his young body demanded a new kind of
satisfaction, never before experienced, except in his mind
uncountable times each day. He wanted to know Gaia's mind,
but more, he wanted to be naked with her, roam her body
with his eyes and hands. He couldn't stop thinking about it.

Kai El wanted her even more because his father said he
could not have her.

He'd tried talking to Jud, but his friend was only interested
in whether he had "buried his love-spear."

Tor's unfairness bothered Kai El the most. Once, he would
have avoided the argument brewing in the hut. But this morning he couldn't leave it alone.

"How could you treat me like that in front of a girl?"

"How many times are you going to ask the same question?"

"Until I hear an answer I believe."

Tor's voice was weary. "If you never in your life do another
thing I say, just leave the twins alone."

"Why?"

"I'm your father and I say it. That's reason enough."

Kai El clenched his jaw, shook his head. A little one might
have to accept such an answer, but he was seventeen summers.

There was reason to stay away from the few girls with
whom he shared blood. But he would never have such thoughts
about them; they were like sisters; it was disgusting. Of course,
they were Shahala girls. Sharing blood with a Tlikit, like Gaia,
was impossible. He hadn't met the Tlikit people until he was
five summers.

"I don't understand your problem, Father."

"Craziness comes from the mother," Tor said. "Look at
Tsilka. Do you want your little ones to be crazy?"

Kai El laughed. Tor must have stayed awake late to think
of that.

"I'm not talking about little ones. I just want to be her
friend," he lied. "And their mother—she's different, but she's
not really crazy."

Tor shouted, "You don't know anything!"

Kai El hated those words. He wrestled clothes on, and stamped out of the hut.

The sky was blue, and it would be warm after the chill of early morning—another late summer day to push the rainy season back. These were some of the best days, because they were unexpected.

Kai El put his father out of his thoughts. He would enjoy this day. He'd found a cluster of rock pictures yesterday worth looking at again.

Rock pictures had been found before. The largest and best was the one called She Who Watches, which had appeared in the cliffs above the village at the same time his mother the Moonkeeper disappeared. People had different ideas about rock pictures. The Tlikit thought their ancient ancestors created them. Others believed they were spirit-made.

The ones Kai El found showed long-bodied people standing straight, arms at sides, short legs, small feet. They had round heads with no faces, so it must have been their stance that said pride, grace, and wisdom. Whether made by man or spirit, Kai El thought they showed a gift for creating beauty. And an ability to make a rock say something that a man can understand.

Gaia would like them.

Kai El heard arguing as he approached the hut where Tsilka and her daughters lived.

"Why would you steal my neckband, Tahna? You could never wear it!"

"I don't know how it got there! I've never stolen a thing in all our life!"

"Ohhh!"

"Get out!" their mother yelled. "I'm sleeping!"

The doorskin flew open, the twins came out and stamped off in different directions.

Kai El acted as if he were just walking by.

"Gaia," he called, then thought maybe it was a bad time. She looked angry enough to challenge a bear. But she stopped and waited.

"I found some rock pictures you'd really like. Want to see?"

"I'd love to get away from this place."

With Gaia behind, Kai El walked up the river trail, too fast for conversation. Much as he loved to talk, glad as he was that she'd come with him, now he couldn't think of what to say. He would talk when they got to the picture place, using between here and there to decide what to talk about. There were apologies to be made for his father, strange new feelings to understand.

Maybe unimportant talk would be better at first . . . *what's your favorite season? . . . do you like yellow?*

The young man sprinted along, not looking back. He stopped at the mouth of a flood-scarred canyon to let the girl catch up, turned and looked at her—

Something was wrong with her. She plodded toward him, every step an effort.

*Look what you've done!* he thought, then answered himself: *I was walking fast—well, almost running—but we haven't come that far.*

He rushed to Gaia and put his cape on the ground. She sank on it, head down, arms around her knees, wheezing, trying to breathe. Desperate gasping, noisy struggling— against what? This was more than being tired from walking too fast. Scared, Kai El touched her heaving shoulder.

"Is something in your throat?"

She shook her head. She gasped. She pulled on the air, getting some, but not enough. He could almost see her snatching at the invisible stuff that no one ever thought about.

"Tell me what to do!"

"She can breathe if she wants. She does that to get out of work."

Kai El went for the spear he'd dropped.

It was only Tahna—a good thing. A warrior should never forget his back like that.

"Give some warning, girl! I almost put a spear in you!"

"Sorry," Tahna said sweetly, with eyes that looked bitter.

Gaia began coughing, and in between, her breathing eased. Kai El wondered if what Tahna said was true, then felt a stab of guilt. Gaia wasn't that kind of person.

"What happened?" he asked.

"I just"—cough—"got too tired," Gaia said.

"It looked like more than that," he said. It had looked like she was *dying*.

"I know it's scary, but it isn't dangerous. It always stops."

"What is *it*?"

"I—it used to come when I was little. It's like something inside closes up and won't let air come in. But I thought I'd grown out of it, like my rabbit-fur boots." Cough, cough, cough. "I don't know why it happened now."

"You should have told me. I would have gone slower."

"Tsagaia makes her own trouble," her twin, Tahna, said.

"Let's go back to the village," Kai El said.

"I am fine now. I want to go ahead."

"Where were you two sneaking off to?" Tahna asked.

Gaia gave her twin a sour look.

Kai El told Tahna about the rock pictures.

"I'm coming," she said.

Gaia was furiously silent. The twins usually got along, but sometimes were known to butt heads like autumn elk. Kai El thought Gaia wanted him to say something to make Tahna leave, but he'd been taught to avoid rudeness. He had no reason to be rude to Tahna.

He thought . . . two pretty girls at his heels. That was a picture worth sharing with Jud.

"Are you sure we should go on, Gaia?" he asked.

"Yes, I'm sure."

"Gaia . . ." said her twin. "What a pretty little name."

Kai El felt Gaia's heat, a different kind of heat than he'd felt when they had climbed to the Moonkeeper's takoma. She was furious at her sister—more than she needed to be, he thought. But he didn't know what it was like to have a sister or brother. It seemed you would love such a person, but he supposed you could hate them, too. A mate you could choose, a friend you could get away from, but a brother or sister lived in your hut.

He led the way into the canyon—going slower this time. It was like walking the bottom of a wild, narrow river whose water had been sucked out—a twisting, turning channel, scarred by long-ago floods rushing to join the Great River. Dry now, it would be a bad place to go in the rainy season.

They turned into a side gully that ended on a slope of loose scree. The remains of an old trail cut up and across the scree, heading toward smooth outcroppings near the canyon top.

"The rock pictures are up there. You girls go first. I'll be behind if you slip," Kai El said, thinking he'd get plenty of looks at legs in motion.

Tahna took off with the speed and agility of the cat for which her sister was named, throwing challenging glances back at Kai El. Gaia needed a slower pace, and he didn't mind staying with her. The distance increased between them, then Tahna was out of sight. In places there was no trail, but Gaia knew about keeping hands, feet, and sometimes belly, touching the ground.

Like the shaking of a shaman's rattle, Kai El heard the warning of the snake coiled across the trail, within distance, ready to strike. The rattler shot out. Kai El threw his spear, shoving Gaia with his other hand. The spear ruined the snake's aim. Kai El caught it slithering away, and killed it with a blow from his spear butt.

He heard those awful, desperate gasps again, the sound of dying for breath.

*Oh Amotkan . . .*

To save her from the snake, Kai El had almost thrown Gaia down the canyonside. She was on her knees below him, clinging to the steep ground, shoulders heaving.

He scrabbled to her, knelt, tried to hold her.

She pushed him. "Go away. I'll come later."

At least he thought that's what she said, between those terrifying noises of pulling, reaching, grasping—sounds of a fish snatched out of water, drowning in a river of air. He admired the courage that kept her struggling. He couldn't imagine what it must be like. Never in his life had anything kept him from breathing.

What would happen if Gaia gave up? Why didn't Tahna come back?

He had to get her to Tenka, the Other Moonkeeper, who was now the only Moonkeeper.

"I'm taking you home. You'll have to hold on to my back going down this scree."

To his surprise, she agreed.

When they reached lower ground, Kai El carried Gaia in

his arms. New desires filled him. He wanted much more than to make love to her. He wanted to protect her, to spend every moment with her, to hear her laughter and wipe away her tears. He thought the name for these feelings was "love."

The attack on Gaia ended with a coughing fit. But it— whatever *it* was—had done something to her this time. Her heaviness in his arms was a sign of her weakness.

"Put me down," she said as they approached Teahra Village. "Please don't tell anyone what happened."

"But—"

"I promise I will talk to your Moonkeeper."

Kai El didn't believe her, but he didn't know what to do.

Gaia might think this was the end of it, but she was wrong. He had to know more about the thing that attacked her. If she was just *any* girl . . . but she was not. That had changed when he held her in his arms carrying her home.

# CHAPTER 38

ASHAN'S DISAPPEARANCE UNSETTLED TEAHRA Village. Even after a turning of the seasons, people still thought of Tenka as the "Other Moonkeeper," of her hut as "Tenka's hut," and Kai El and Tor's as the "Moonkeeper's hut."

Compared to Kai El's mother, Tenka was an oil lamp next to the sun. She would not have been his choice for chief, but no one cared what an almost-man thought.

On the way to see Tenka, Kai El told himself that she was doing her best, and she was the only one who knew medicine.

Tenka welcomed him to her hut. The warm air was heavy with sweet grass smoke. She bent over a small fire, spreading it with a stick.

Kai El caught his breath. In the Moonkeeper's cape of black condor feathers, it was like—

"How are you?" she asked, smiling up at him—Tenka, after all—his aunt, not his mother.

"I did not come about myself."

"It's Tsagaia, then?"

"How did you know? Did she talk to you?"

"I'm the Moonkeeper. I'm supposed to know. How may I help you, Kai El?"

Of course she wouldn't say whether she and Gaia had talked—visits with the Moonkeeper were secret.

Kai El settled cross-legged on a woven mat. The firecoals glowed between them. Tenka looked like an ordinary woman, except for the shining condor feathers. Whatever power she had wasn't obvious in her long-boned, pleasant face, an open face that invited trust.

"Tsagaia is my friend," Kai El said. "I took her to see some rock pictures. But I walked too fast, and a rattlesnake scared her, and . . ." He didn't know how to describe the rest.

"She couldn't breathe?"

Surprised, Kai El nodded.

"I thought she was dying," he said. "I didn't know what to do. I was carrying her home, but her breath came back, and she made me put her down. She made me promise not to tell."

Telling took a weight from Kai El. Of course he hadn't told Tor—his father was the last person who should know about a flaw in Gaia.

"I'm glad you told me," Tenka said. "I didn't think she could keep her secret forever. Though I did hope so, for that would mean she was over it."

"You mean it's happened before?"

"Many times.

Kai El was astonished.

"How could I miss it?"

"She didn't want people to see. She thought it made her look weak, and you know, Kai El, among animals, sometimes the weak do not survive."

Tenka looked at Kai El to make sure he understood. He swallowed.

"Her mother brought her to your mother when she was about knee-tall. I was young and still learning medicine. I thought she looked perfect, but Tsilka told us it was sometimes hard for the child to breathe. Your mother gave her sage to carry. When the Breath Ogre wanted to steal Tsagaia's air, she could drive him away by smelling rubbed sage. It helped, but it didn't stop the attacks."

Something called a Breath Ogre did not like sage . . . the mysteries of plants amazed Kai El. None of his mother's healing skills had been passed on to him.

Tenka continued. "Tsagaia learned things no other child had to learn. Hard things. How not to be terrified when you feel like you are dying. How to hide such a thing from others. Her shyness comes from it. So does her courage."

"Courage? No one thinks of Tsagaia as having courage. They think she's afraid of everything."

"What about the wildfire, when she stayed calm while the rest of you panicked? Wasn't that courage?"

"Of course. It was so long ago, I guess I'd forgotten." Kai El shook his head. "How stupid I am. I thought she had the heart of a mouse, but she has the heart of the cougar she is named for."

"Yes, she does. But it's not your fault you didn't understand that. She works hard to keep people from knowing her."

*She won't keep* me *from knowing her,* Kai El thought.

The Moonkeeper said, "When she was ten summers, the Breath Ogre left her. Season after season, he didn't come back. I think Tsagaia had begun to believe she was safe. I'm sorry to hear that her old enemy has returned."

It was hard to ask this question, but Kai El had to.

"Could the Breath Ogre kill her?"

Tenka hesitated. "I don't know."

He frowned. His mother would have known.

"What should I do?" he asked.

"Don't tire her. Don't frighten her. Get her to carry sage."

"Would birthing tire her too much?" he blurted.

"I don't think so. Nor would lovemaking."

Tenka's look said she understood what was in Kai El's heart.

Heat rose in his face. He didn't want anyone to know how he felt about Gaia. He himself did not really understand how he felt.

# CHAPTER 39

PEOPLE SAID THAT IT WAS HOTTER ON THE GREAT River that summer than it had ever been in Shahala land. Those who thought Ashan was the last *real* Moonkeeper didn't trust Tenka to change the seasons, though she had done so several times.

"It might not work this time," they said, and talked about what would happen if summer went on and on, agreeing it would be better to get stuck in summer than in winter.

Ridiculous. Kai El respected his mother, but seasons changed themselves. It was one of the things Ehr had taught him.

Yesterday Kai El had taken refuge from the heat at his mother's takoma in the cliffs, where there was always a breeze. He had slept here last night and might again. The night would be warm and full of bugsongs, whose rhythm heightened as autumn approached, until they were silenced by the first frost.

He wished he knew what to do. Gaia was hiding. He hadn't been able to talk to her, not once, since he'd carried her home the day the Breath Ogre had attacked her. The only time he'd seen her alone, she hurried away as he approached.

What had he done to make her act this way?

*Why do you care?* asked the part of his mind annoyed by the summer heat. *Why would you want someone like that?*

*But I do. And she needs me. All I have to do is convince her.*

Kai El opened his waist pouch and took out a bundle of strands—long black hairs pulled from all over his head, gathered and tied like a horse's tail, and ready for braiding—the beginning of a pledge band.

Pledge bands were an old Shahala tradition that few men bothered to make anymore. He thought few even remembered what they meant. Kai El remembered. His mother had worn his father's pledge band until she died. And afterward, for all he knew, since only her time ball was found.

When horses still roamed the earth, pledge bands were made from their tails. The work told of a man's love for a special woman. More colors meant more horses killed, and that meant the man would be a good mate. Horses were only a memory now . . . sad, they must have been beautiful, the way people talked of them.

Kai El decided to use his own hair to make his pledge band. It was shiny and coarse, and his head had more than it needed. He would line it with soft leather, so it wouldn't make Gaia's arm itch.

He smoothed the hair bundle, combing the strands with his fingers. Gaia liked Shahala ways. Gaia made beautiful things. She might appreciate a pledge band.

She might use it to choke him.

That gave him an idea. He took sage from his medicine pouch and rubbed it between his fingers. The sharp fragrance reminded him of rain on the prairie. One at a time he pulled the strands of hair through his scented fingers—like women used beeswax for sinew—making the strands stronger, wrapping them with the sacred plant's protection.

Kai El separated the magic strands into hanks, brought one over, another under, beginning a band for Gaia's arm that he hoped would bind their hearts.

Through a gap in the hut's cover of woven tule reeds that needed patching before the autumn rains, a girl of fourteen summers watched stars fade from the dawn sky. Her name was Tsagaia, Big Tan Cat; but since a warrior had called her the name that meant Kitten, she thought of herself as Gaia.

She'd been elated by his attention. All a girl could want in a mate, Kai El was wellborn, son of the lost Moonkeeper and

Tor. He was kind, funny, and smart. She pictured his muscled body—the strength and grace of his movements; a face for dreaming about; eyes that spoke a secret language she understood; voice that stroked her ears.

Sun River—she loved the meaning of his name—could have anyone. How could he be interested in her?

This and other worries had kept Gaia awake most of the night.

She'd been afraid her sister would take Kai El from her, when the real worry was herself . . . and the Breath Ogre. After what he had seen, Kai El must think her unfit for mating.

Tears blurred the patch of morning sky. More than anything, Gaia wanted to be a mother. But what if the Breath Ogre attacked while a baby was being born? She had watched birthing; she knew how hard it was for the mother. What if she became too tired to fight? What if she died? Who would care for her baby? Once she would have trusted her twin, but no longer.

What if the Breath Ogre attacked the helpless baby?

*I'll burst if I don't talk to someone,* Gaia thought.

She'd always felt comfortable with the Moonkeeper Ashan, but Ashan was gone. Anyway, how could she have talked to a mother about her son . . . about these kinds of feelings . . .

Why not talk to Tenka, the Other Moonkeeper, who had taken Ashan's place? Tenka was said to be wise and kind. Gaia would trust her about medicine, but what could a mateless woman know about love? She had promised Kai El she would talk to Tenka, but she just couldn't. *You have to know someone to trust them,* she thought.

Gaia was nearly miserable enough to talk to her twin. They used to be closer than bark and tree. Tahna knew how to help fight the Breath Ogre. Gaia never needed another friend. But womanhood changed Tahna's mind along with her body: She became selfish, sneaky, and mean. Gaia didn't hate her, though she sometimes felt like choking her almost to death. When Tahna stole her neckband, Gaia knew she'd never trust her sister again.

*If she knew how much I want Kai El . . .* Gaia pictured the tongue of a lizard shooting out for a sleepy fly. *How easily she could get him . . . with her boldness and her health.*

In desperation, Gaia decided to talk to her mother. Should she forget about Kai El? Or try to make him love her?

When dawn lit the hut, Gaia found that her mother hadn't come home. She didn't bother to wonder what man Tsilka had shared the night with.

No one to trust. Her sister would steal Kai El. Her mother had her own complicated life. Kai El's father Tor was too unhappy to help anyone. His mother Ashan was dead. The Other Moonkeeper a stranger . . .

*Spirit quest.*

The words just came to her mind. It was a custom of the Shahala part of the tribe. She'd been afraid to go on one when she was small. Maybe a spirit quest could help her now.

No one saw Gaia leave Teahra Village. She carried a water pouch and wore two light skins. She might stay away for a day *and* a night . . . that's how much thinking she needed to do.

*You wouldn't!* said a voice that came from inside, and reminded her of her sister's voice. *Our mother would have the whole village searching before the nightfire is lit.*

With the village barely out of sight, Gaia's courage was already failing. She told herself it wasn't how long she stayed gone that was important, but what she learned.

She took the trail that led to the rock picture called She Who Watches—the special place of the lost Moonkeeper. Ashan's trail was an uphill slope for a long way—straight up through a series of clefts—then level, but narrow and dangerous, near the top. It wasn't the hardest trail to climb, nor the easiest. Maybe Gaia just wanted to test her body. Maybe she was angry at her body.

There was another reason to take Ashan's trail: Since no one she knew could help her, Gaia might as well be alone. No one would bother her up here. People were afraid of the Moonkeeper's takoma.

She thought of Kai El . . . *Most people* . . .

Gaia had been afraid of it herself, until she'd gone there with Kai El. It was a wonderful place. There was a feeling of—she couldn't think of a word—of everything as it should be.

*Maybe he will be there,* she thought.

Gaia kept a pace to tempt the Breath Ogre.

*What Breath Ogre?* her clear chest asked. *Now that there's no one here to see, I have the strength of a cougar.*

"Gaia!"

She looked up to see a dark shape against blue sky—Kai El, waving and calling.

"It's me!" he shouted, running toward her.

She'd been avoiding him so carefully. Now what? She looked back at the trail, but she couldn't run. It was too steep. She waited for him.

"I shouldn't have come," she said.

"No, I'm glad you did. I was wanting someone to talk to. Give me your water pouch. And your hand."

Gaia allowed him to help her. But she wanted to get away. What must he think of her? She couldn't stand it.

When they got to the Moonkeeper's takoma, she saw that Kai El had slept there. He smoothed the skins on the stone seat, inviting her to rest.

"I don't need to rest," she said. "I was going to see what's over the top, so—so good-bye."

"I'll come with you. If a big animal or something attacks, a man should be there."

She knew what he meant. If the *Breath Ogre* attacks. Gaia hated people feeling sorry for her, thinking they had to help her.

"I want to be by myself. Give me my water pouch."

Holding it out, he gripped her wrist as she reached for it—not hurting her, just stopping her. Confused pain filled his eyes.

"Why are you angry, Gaia?"

"I'm not. I just want to be alone."

"Please," he begged. "Tell me what I did wrong."

"Let go."

Releasing her, he took some pungent gray sprigs from his waist pouch.

"Look, I've got sage. If I'd known it could help, I would have had it before."

For a moment, she softened. *How sweet of him.* Then she wondered.

"How do you know about sage?"

"Tenka told me."

Devastated, Gaia said, "You told her? I asked you not to. Now everyone will know."

"Tenka won't tell anyone. Even if they knew, they'd want to help."

Gaia shook her head, blinking back tears.

"Now I know how much I can trust you."

She slung her water pouch over her shoulder, made her way past him, and got on with her spirit quest.

"Well," Kai El said after Gaia left. "I finally get to talk to her, and I ruin it completely."

He closed his eyes and pictured his mother's face.

"I wish I knew if you could hear me," he said to her spirit. He waited, but nothing happened, so he just kept talking.

"Something happened when I carried her, something much greater than lust. I want to take care of her. I think I love her. But she won't even look at me. What did I do wrong? Go too fast? Too slow?"

He hit his palm with his fist. "The more things get in our way, the more I know she must be my mate."

To make his frustration go away, Kai El made up the conversation he and Gaia *should* have had.

"The Autumn Feast is coming," he should have said.

"It's a custom of your people I truly enjoy."

"It's a time of great changes."

Kai El realized the made-up Gaia knew this, but he went on. Even in a pretended conversation, it was hard to keep from saying, "Oh, Gaia, be my mate."

"Changes in people's lives. Little ones taking their spirit names. Men taking their mates."

"And the feasting," she would say, "and the dancing."

He pictured her dancing. His heart sprang a leak. Control flowed away. The made-up Kai El could no longer hold himself back.

"Gaia, I love you. I want to be with you forever."

Only the wind heard him.

# CHAPTER 40

SURPRISES AWAITED SPIRITS NEW TO THE OTHERWORLD. The best of these, to Ashan, was the ability to travel great distances in an eyeblink. She could choose from endless places and times, moving with the speed of lightning, by the power of desire—an invisible collection of energy that was everything essential she had ever been, without the burden of a human body.

Spirit travel did not always work as Ashan expected. She couldn't be in two places at the same time. Sometimes she went places without desiring it. Unasked-for travel seemed random at times, full of purpose at others. Like humans, spirits had to sort through the meaningless to find meaning.

This time the Spirit of Ashan arrived somewhere without knowing she was coming. She found herself inside a long, narrow shelter. It was built on a mound instead of in a pit—as Teahra huts were—and was much larger. Twenty or more could sleep without touching on the swept earth floor. Foggy daylight seeped through a low door opening in the center of a long wall. Piles of skins and furs leaned against the opposite wall. Cooking fires rimmed with round stones rested near each end.

The roof of lapped cedar splits would keep rain out and warmth in. The walls were made of slabs of cedar so massive that Ashan wondered how they'd been cut. She couldn't smell without borrowing the nose of some living creature—and she was alone in this place—but she imagined the clean scent of all this cedar.

The Spirit of Ashan had never visited a finer living place. Though she didn't yet know where this was, she considered staying awhile, to learn about the people who lived here, how trees so large were cut and slabbed—

Two men crawled through the low door. They didn't look alike, but they shared a blue aura that said they were brothers. Young, healthy, bursting with mating desire, they spoke a language unlike Shahala or Tlikit. Ashan understood them, as she did everyone she visited in her new life.

The older one said, "It's crazy. What's wrong with the women of our tribe?"

The younger one rolled his eyes . . . they must have talked about the women of their tribe before.

"If you had seen these two," he said, "you would understand."

"These people don't guard their women?"

"No."

"And there are two exactly alike?"

"Exactly. Perfect beauties. A man could trade them for ten women."

"Are you sure you can find them again?"

"If not, we'll find some ugly ones to trade for beauties."

The brothers laughed.

Suddenly, the Spirit of Ashan was at her rock in the cliffs above Teahra Village.

She focused on returning to the cedar slab hut and the brothers planning evil. Instead, she found herself watching a dream that Kai El was having about his forbidden sister.

Ashan would have wept, if spirits could.

She tried desperately to enter his dream and change it, as she had done many times before, but the power of human love was too great to overcome.

She fled to a mountaintop on the other side of the world, and ran with a red wolf in the dawn-colored snow. The wolf howled to greet morning. Ashan sang with the wolf, until she forgot what she couldn't bear to remember.

# CHAPTER 41

TOR GOT WORSE. EATEN BY RAGE, DROWNING IN UN-shed tears, he danced alone on the edge of madness. He marked each day after Ashan's death with a firecoal on the hut wall. When he realized that the number of days in forever didn't matter, he stopped counting, and time blurred. He separated from the world, like a caterpillar inside an invisible cocoon. Things looked flat. Sound and taste were blunted. Nothing seemed real. He could stare at a nearby bush and a mountain behind it, and they both seemed the same distance away, as if they were *painted* on the sky. If he reached for something, he might miss it. Thinking was difficult. The smallest decision loomed gigantic. At times words made no sense. At times, he felt invisible. Unfortunately he wasn't. People saw the miserable man, but didn't know what to say to him.

Weary of inflicting himself on others, Tor spent days and nights away from Teahra Village. He wandered through markless time, as he had long ago after man-eaters massacred his Shahala tribesmen. But now there was a difference: He could go home. People would feed him. It was a good thing: No longer a youth at the mountaintop of cunning and strength, Eagle from the Light was slipping down the slope of old age.

A long way from the Great River one day, Tor hurried along a barren plateau with a strong wind at his back, using the butt of his spear as a third leg to push himself along. High, dark clouds filled the sky. "Find cover," the clouds said to all creatures, "and soon." Tor didn't know where he was, so he ran before the wind, hoping to find shelter before the coming storm's fury caught him.

*Even if I don't find shelter,* he thought, *rain won't kill me. Though all this running might.*

The clouds had turned day into almost-night when he reached a cleft between plateaus. He scrambled down a rocky decline, and into a narrow gully carved by runoff from higher ground. Farther down, where the gully widened, he saw the gray-green of a grove of trees, and ran for it.

Over the treetops, the wind howled. Inside the grove, the air was still, except for Tor's huffing. He grabbed branches and propped them against a tree trunk—leaving the side away from the wind open—then covered the frame with his sleeping skin, tied it down, and settled in to wait for the storm.

His breathing and heartbeat quieted as he looked around. Dull as he'd become, it took a while to realize the importance of what he had found.

Trees. Not just *any* trees, but *pine* trees.

No—not the majestic grandfathers of Shahala land—tall and proud, with long, limber needles in groups of three. These were old and twisted, with short, sharp needles grouped in twos. The stunted things were far from his mind's picture of pine trees, but by smell and taste, he knew they must be.

*Spirit of the tree who gives medicine for many ills, we thank you* . . . Tor remembered Ashan's song as she gathered pine in the fragrant forests of their youth. He sighed for that other life.

The only pine found in the new land was far up in the mountains, where the huckleberries grew. Tenka used what she could get for coughing sickness. There was never enough for sap tea to soothe the pains of old age, or inner bark for warriors to soak and put on their wounds.

On the side of a tree away from the wind, Tor cut pieces of rough bark with his stone blade, stripped off the thin inner bark, and replaced the outer bark so the tree could grow a scar around it. He filled his waist pouch with moist strips. His nose came alive. The inner bark smelled like health.

As wind and clouds had foretold, rain pounded the land for days and nights. Tor's shelter kept him dry. Runoff cascaded from higher ground, but missed the pine grove. The trees lived in the only place they could, proving that they were smart, as well as good medicine.

One morning Tor awoke to see the sun rising into a cloudless sky, and he knew the storm was over.

Sunlight sparkled from an ancient trunk, caught by a rounded glob stuck in the bark: a drop of hardened pitch. He pried it out, turned it over in his fingers, held it up to the sky. Smooth, clear and golden ... like sunshine seen from the bottom of a pool.

Tor could never resist the magic created by sun and water. It made him think of Kai El. The piece of golden pitch took him back to Keecha Creek—the waiting; the sound from the Home Cave that terrified him until he realized it was his child's first cries. He remembered raising his arms to the sky as men had done since the Misty Time, shouting:

"Spirits of all who love people! Kai El, Sun River, is born! Give this child a better life than mine!"

Tor sighed. So long ago ...

Inside the hard glob of pitch, a small beetle slept forever.

Once, Tor would have run to Ashan with the treasure. His curious mate had loved things with a story, and what a story *this* could tell. No one had seen such a beetle. Maybe the creature with shimmering green wings had died out like mammoths and horses.

Turning the drop of pitch over in his hands, Tor imagined the long-ago attack: the beetle crawling up the tree, stopping to sleep in the sun. The drop of pitch creeping down. Wing tip caught. Legs trapped one by one in a frantic, hopeless struggle.

"We're not so different," Tor said. He expected no answer, just wanted to talk about how he felt. But who knew? Maybe its spirit heard him.

"Like you, I get a thick, glazy crust that smothers desire, and leaves slowly swirling pain. And I get heavy, and tired, and it would be so easy to give up."

Tor's food would soon be gone. Hunger knew better than to bother him. To die by starving would be so easy, it tempted him.

As a young man, Tor had fought self-destruction more than

once. He beat the demon, but he never destroyed it. No longer powerful enough to make him kill himself, it still tormented him. He would fight this fight as long as he lived, and die the moment he stopped fighting. Like the beetle.

"How long did you fight destiny before you gave up?"

He thought he heard an answer: *As long as I could. Then longer.*

"Too long," Tor said. "Sometimes it's better just to give up, when you know what the end will be. I think of it, you know."

*But you promised.*

"Yes," he said, forced to remember. Whether he had promised the spirits or his mate, he couldn't recall, but it didn't matter. He had promised.

"A warrior's promise can be trusted," Tor said, and went to sleep with the piece of pitch in his hand.

In the morning, he was ready to head home, where someone would make sure he kept living.

Tor would never be free of his glazy crust, but the beetle could be. He crushed the pitch and the bug, made a fire, and threw the dust into it.

"You are free."

On the way home, he lost most of a day sitting on a hilltop, angry at himself. Kai El would have loved the drop of golden pitch that was like his name. It was a sign sent to Tor to give to Kai El, and he had destroyed it. Why did the son always come last in his father's thoughts?

In the late afternoon, Tor came down a trail into the canyon of the Great River, Chiawana. Heat pressed on Teahra Village like an unwelcome fur robe. Nothing stirred. He walked by his father's hut. On the shady side, Arth and his last living mate, Tashi, rested on a grass mat.

Tor greeted them in passing.

"My father and his mate, are you well?"

"I am," Tashi answered. "And you?"

"Very well," Tor lied. People didn't want the truth if you were less than well—and the man whose soulmate was dead would never be well again.

His father said nothing. Tor wanted to keep walking, but he stopped because of the guilt called "respect."

"Are you well, Arth?" he repeated.

Arth's grunt could have meant "yes" or "no." He had lived fifty-four summers—much longer than most men—but his father had never learned to say what he meant. Tor had spent his whole life guessing.

Without looking up, the old man spoke in a surly voice.

"It's not that I need younger men to take care of my hut. I'm strong as ever."

"So you would like us to think," Tashi said.

"I could do these things if I wanted to, woman, but they do it out of respect for my age! Should I steal their good feelings?"

*Arth's anger is for me, not her. What have I done now? Or forgotten to do?* Tor couldn't think. If the old man had something to say, why not just say it?

Arth looked at his son with eyes as wounded as his voice.

"You, Tor? You, of all men? I told you this was the day. Everyone came. My other sons, my friends, men I hardly know. Even my grandson Kai El came down from his high place. Tashi made everyone gifts of dry-smoked salmon. The piece behind the head she made for you. She picked out every bone."

*What are you talking about?* Tor almost asked. Then he smelled new leather. He stretched his eyes to see more than usual.

He sighed. *New skins on the old man's hut. I have defeated myself, again.* His webby cocoon returned. His vision narrowed back to the ground in front of him. Arth's accusing voice came from a distant place.

"Where were you that was more important than the roofing of your father's hut?"

Tor could have said, "Finding pine trees," but that didn't seem important anymore.

"Nowhere," he said. "I forgot. I'm sorry."

Arth sighed, huge and sad. "I know, son. I too have suffered losses."

Tor nodded.

Tashi went in the hut, brought out a bundle wrapped in grass and handed it to him.

"I made this for you, son of my mate."

Tor shook his head.

"Take it," Arth said. "You wouldn't make one good meal for a man-eater."

Tor said, "Thank you, Tashi. I know how good it will taste." He took the gift and went home.

People still called it the Moonkeeper's hut, though now it sheltered only a man and his son. He opened the doorskin, stepped into the round space dug knee deep in the ground, rested his spear near the door, and tossed the food bundle on the work shelf.

Evening light, broken into pieces by a skeleton of branched wood, showed dimly through the covering of old horsehides in need of patching. Kai El had offered a deerskin made into leather by some girl—not as good as horsehide, but there were no horses anymore.

"Fine," Tor had told him. "Do it before winter."

Of course, a boy of seventeen summers had more exciting things to do than work on his father's hut.

Tor ate as much of the salmon as he could. It should have been a blend of delicious flavors: smoke, white rock, and honey, almost covering the taste of fish. But it tasted like the dry grass wrapping. Not worth the effort of chewing. The fault was in his mouth, not in Tashi's work. He disliked food— no, he hated it. How could he enjoy eating, knowing Ashan would never eat another thing? Tor had been denying himself for so long, his mouth had forgotten how to taste.

Too bad his nose didn't forget how to smell. The hut he and the boy shared stank of old sweat. When Ashan lived here, it smelled of herbs, medicines, all kinds of things that changed with the seasons as she dried and stored the plants needed by the tribe. Tor refused to change anything, trying to keep the illusion that she might come home. But he couldn't keep her scent.

He pounded his palm with his fist. He *could not* remember her scent! Time should lessen his sense of loss. Instead, he lost more of her each day. What would go tomorrow? The depth of her eyes? The whisper of her sleep-breathing?

Stripping off his moccasins and loinskin, Tor lay on their raised earth bed. He didn't bother with the oil lamp—easier to sleep than to keep the darkness away.

*Ashan* ... Tor sighed, aching as he always did when her name ran through his mind. Ashan had slept on the inside. Danger would have to come past a fierce Shahala warrior to reach her. Now Tor lay in her place, imagining that he felt the shadow of her shape beneath him in the hard-packed dirt covered by skins, the indentation of her hip, her shoulder, from all those seasons of resting there.

The bed was too wide now, and too empty, but he lacked energy to haul the extra dirt away.

"To-or! I see you!"

Tsilka peered through the open doorway.

Exactly what he did not need!

# CHAPTER 42

TOR PULLED SOMETHING ACROSS HIS NAKED MIDDLE.

Tsilka stepped into his hut and stood there staring: A slim dark shape against the lighter sky of the open door; lines of long legs, short skirt, hair wild as the woman herself; the details of her face hidden in shadows. Turning slowly, showing herself from the side, she closed the doorskin.

Tsilka had a body that would always tempt men.

Tor was ashamed that he could even think of a woman's body.

"It's like a cave in here," she said. "I don't know which is worse, the dark or the smell, but the dark I can cure. Where is your oil lamp?"

Too tired to argue, he pointed to the shelf he had made for Ashan's work—a large, flat piece of wood thrown out by the Great River, held at waist height by two wood chunks. When her back got sore from sitting bent over, she would go to her shelf and continue to work standing up. Underneath the shelf, she kept things needed for another season. Tor's idea was so admired that other women asked their mates for a working shelf.

Crossing the hut as if she owned it, Tsilka struck the spark-stones over the lamp of hollowed stone. The firefish oil flared. In the sudden glow, Tor didn't like seeing her there among Ashan's things.

"I want you to go," he said.

Tsilka sauntered toward him carrying the oil-filled lamp. She placed it carefully on the end of his bed. Bright flames danced on the wad of fiber in the center. Comfortable shadows fled before the light.

She sat on the unswept floor, looking up at him.

"There! That's better!"

"Tsilka, I have no interest in—"

She laughed. "Don't be stupid. We're too old for that."

"Then what do you want?"

She held up a white feather, its quill wrapped with thin leather for tying in the hair.

"It's time to be friends."

The war between them was old and tired, but Tor knew she enjoyed it. Why would she want to end it? He hadn't trusted Tsilka since she speared him through the leg and kept him for a slave. Why should he trust her now?

He said, "I have many reasons *not* to be your friend."

"I know, Tor. It's for our children that I came."

He didn't believe her. Tsilka was here for her final triumph over Ashan. She must think it had been long enough, that by now any man would be starved for lovemaking.

"Go away," he said, turning his back.

The stirring he thought was the sound of leaving was Tsilka creeping onto his bed.

"You and I, Tor, each of us with half a family. It's not right. I live in a tiny hut with two girls. You live in this fine, large hut, with only Kai El. Look at all this space not being used."

Tor had an urge to strike her.

She sighed loudly. "And our young ones. You must know how Kai El and Tsagaia feel about each other."

He had an urge to *kill* her.

"Sahalie made those two for each other," she said. "What could be closer than a mate who is also your brother?"

Without thinking, Tor came up swinging. His fist smashed her jaw.

Flying from the bed, upsetting the lamp, flinging oil everywhere, Tsilka crashed into the work shelf. She yelped, swatting at spots of burning oil as though they were attacking bees, but they spread faster than she could slap them out. Her clothes ignited. Her hair, oiled for beauty, flared into a hideous orange flower. She ran blindly, shrieking, hands tearing at her face; hit a wall, flung herself around, ran the other way.

Tor dived for her and rolled her head in a sleeping skin, muffling the ear-rending shrieks. He beat the flames with his hands, gagging on the smell of burning flesh.

Fire spread along Ashan's shelf, igniting bunches of dried herbs, leapt to her feather collection woven with dusty spiderwebs, roared up and across the wood and hides of the roof. Red-orange flames raced toward the doorway, consuming the air that was so hot Tor could barely breathe.

He threw the thrashing woman over his shoulder and plunged through the fire, past the people coming to fight it. He ran to the edge of the Great River, dropped her, and poured handfuls of water on her. Howls came from the blackened sleeping skin wrapped around her head. He peeled it away. A strip of flesh clung to it. His stomach tried to come up his throat.

Tenka came running.

"She fell into the lamp and got all burned!" he babbled.

"Silence, brother!"

By the light of Tor's blazing hut, the Moonkeeper forced the struggling woman to swallow a handful of crumbled plants, made her drink the water of the Great River, bathed her seared flesh with it.

The sleeping vine did its work. Tsilka, sure to die, would sleep until she did.

The Spirit of Ashan was deeply troubled when she returned to Teahra Village.

No one would ever again make the mistake of calling Tor's home the Moonkeeper's hut, for nothing remained of it but stinking rubble and ash. Most of what Tor and Kai El lost could be replaced; but the tribe could never replace the sacred relics still kept there because Tenka's new hut wasn't finished.

As if he had worn a robe of magic, Tor suffered only blistered hands. And crushing guilt.

Tsilka was charred on the side of the heart. Face, shoulder, arm, and hand looked like meat forgotten over a cooking fire. Her other side was the glazy red of flame-dried salmon.

Swelled-up flesh oozing, burning with fever, she moaned and cried, even though Tenka kept her groggy with the sleeping vine. Everyone thought she would die.

Ashan's spirit took Tenka to some pale blue mold growing in a damp place. After several days of drinking mold tea made without heating, Tsilka's fever cooled, the swelling went down, and she stayed quiet with less sleeping vine.

When a baby was born, Ashan guided Tenka to take some of the birth sac before giving it to the mother for the ritual called This Place Will Always Know Me. Tenka put strips of the birth sac on Tsilka's burns, keeping the extra pieces soft in water for later use. She thought it was disgusting, and was glad no one asked her about it.

Because of their success, two new medicines were added to the tribe's knowledge. Blue mold would save many lives from fever. Birth sac encouraged the growth of new skin underneath it that in places looked as good as the old.

But one side of Tsilka's face would always terrify children. The fire had consumed a swath of skin from her chin to the top of her head. Eyebrow and lashes were gone, and some of her hair. The flesh of her cheek rotted away, leaving a hollow of lumpy scars. Trying to span what it couldn't, new skin stretched and pulled into ropy lines and hard, shiny patches.

The ability to smile or frown or show any kind of feeling was gone from that side of her face, while the other side showed all the feelings that it ever had, and some ugly new ones . . . because what was done to the inside of the woman would never heal.

Though she did not love Tsilka, the Spirit of Ashan couldn't help feeling pity. Tsilka's beauty was more important to her than anything. Without it, she would have nothing to offer a man. What would she do when she understood how ugly she really was?

In life—no matter how angry Tsilka made her—Ashan had never wished her a fate like this.

Why hadn't the spirit come sooner? Why not soon enough to stop the fire from happening? She asked herself until she knew.

Tsilka was still the troublemaking, man-stealing witch she'd always been. Ashan had no more use for her now than she'd

ever had. But her failure to come sooner had more to do with
ignorance than hate.

It was because of time: The passing of time in the two
different worlds could not be compared. Ashan had run with
the red wolf for a morning. But in the time of humans, two
moons had passed. Gone from Teahra Village too long, Ashan
had returned to disaster: the hut she loved, and the treasures
of her Spirit Mothers, destroyed. Tsilka, whose agony had
just begun. And Tor, in terrible guilt, living in Tsilka's hut,
obsessed with her care, ignoring everything else.

He didn't deserve this. But for one betrayal, Tor had lived
a decent life. Ashan would give anything to take his suffering
away.

... *My beloved ... You should have taken what Tsilka
offered ... found the peace I cannot give you ...*

But Tor could not hear the Spirit of Ashan.

# CHAPTER 43

Tor prowled sleep, hunting for a dream.

Full of pleasure and meaning, weighted with tabu, dreams were hard to find when you wanted one, or to escape when you were trapped in one. Of all Tor's sins, none had caused more trouble. But now, dreaming brought the only pleasure to the man waiting to join his soulmate in the only way he could: by dying.

At last Tor dreamed . . .

. . . his favorite part of the day: Almost-morning, when half-sleep makes the mind wander like smoke. Ashan snuggled close, breathing soft and slow, her long hair a blanket draped over his chest, an arm and a leg across him. He loved the feel of her skin along his body, and her gentle weight.

Dreaming, Tor knew where they were by the singing of robins outside: the Home Cave, high in the mountains of the tabu land, the first place he and Ashan had lived together. Tor had never been happier. The Home Cave had all that a man could want: perfect mate and son; kind weather; easy hunting.

In the distance a horse whinnied. Today he would hunt; tonight his family would enjoy horsemeat . . .

No.

He heard a woman's groan, not the call of a horse—ugly reality come to destroy his beautiful dream. Awakening to sounds of pain and smells of despair, Tor felt suffocated. Like

the beetle in its trap of pitch must have felt, just before it
gave up.

Tsilka moaned. Even sleep did not stop her pain. Tor reached
for her in the dark.

*I'll always be her slave.*

She was lying on her stomach. She never liked to sleep on
her back, but now she had to. If she slept too long on the
stretched, pulled skin of her face, cries would wake him
instead of groans. He nudged her. She rolled over without
waking, and stopped moaning.

Tor thanked the darkness for hiding her scars, though he
knew the shape, size, and color of each too well to forget.
Tsilka's scars were burned into his mind as surely as they
were burned into her flesh.

The dark of the little hut was crowded with heat, smells
and sounds of bodies at rest. The others were Tor's own
daughters, but he didn't like to think of them that way. Not
anymore.

To escape reality, he thought about his dream.

The Home Cave was the only home that had ever truly
belonged to him. Life there was the best it had ever been, but
it didn't last long enough. Compelled by Destiny, Tor himself
had brought it to an end. Older now, he wondered if "Destiny"
had been an excuse for his own dark desires.

Longing knifed his heart.

*The Home Cave. Where memories are.*

The knife twisted.

*If I had never left, would she still be alive?*

Questions. Guilt. Regret. None of it mattered. He knew he
would never be happy again.

But he did not have to be disgusting. Not anymore.

As an ignorant young man, Tor couldn't wait to leave the
Home Cave. Now he knew he must return. It would be a
better place to wait for death, and Ashan.

Under clouds edged with moonlight, Tor left Teahra Village
forever, taking nothing but his last shred of dignity.

On the first day of his journey home, an orak met his spear,
giving him meat, hide, bladder for a water pouch, horn for a
drinking cup, sinew, and other things he needed. That night
Tor enjoyed eating as he hadn't since he lost his mate. He

slept peacefully, knowing that no one would cry out for him in the dark.

Strengthened by food and rest, guided by sun and stars, he crossed the open plateau, and began the climb into the tabu mountains—leaving Teahra Village and its crushing responsibilities farther and farther behind.

On a windy day, a feather came from nowhere, brushed by Tor's cheek, and went on its way. He thought it was Ashan . . . a strange thought . . . Kai El was the one who sensed her spirit. Tor had never tried. It seemed a bitter substitute.

But now he was so alone. Leaning on his staff, he gazed into the sky.

"My love," he sighed to the wind. "We were together all our lives. How can I wait till I die to be with you?"

. . . *You do not have to* . . .

Tor's cheeks tingled. Shivers ran up his arms.

. . . *I have been with you, but you would not know it* . . .

He *heard*—not as sound in his ears, but as understanding in his mind.

"Ashan!"

. . . *Tor, at last* . . .

He felt her relief, as if the air had sighed. He felt her love seep into him. He clutched his chest, so full of her. He wobbled on weakening legs.

. . . *It hurt to love you, and be refused* . . . *even for a spirit, that is hard* . . .

He felt her pain enter the poisonous lake of his own, knock away the logjam of fear, and loose a never-cried flood of tears.

Tor sagged to the ground, drowning.

"Ashan, I miss you so much! I miss your body, lying with you in the dark, waking up with you in the morning!"

. . . *I don't need a body to love you, Tor* . . . *I just need you to accept me as I am* . . .

Tor wept until the sun left the sky, and was still weeping when it returned. Raw and ragged, he slept for a day and a night. From then on, he would cry when he needed to, but never like that again.

Ashan's spirit was with him the rest of the journey. Not like the first time—putting words in his mind and shaking

the air—and that was fine with him—it was almost more
than a man could stand. She was just *there*—he knew it
without any signs—an invisible, silent, comfortable compan-
ion, helping to change Tor's grief into a misery he could live
with. The old grief was made of sharpness, the new one of
weight. The other was the color of night, this one the color
of shade.

Ready for bear, cougar, or even people, Tor found the Home
Cave empty. He settled in. Living there was easier than he
remembered. Ehr's ways made sense now that he was older.
He took his food with traps and snares instead of hunting,
took more than he needed and stored it for winter.

When the Spirit of Ashan came, he talked, listened, knew
a kind of peace. But when she went wherever spirits go, he
was alone with his regrets.

*My son . . .*

Tor's love for Kai El was strong, but nothing could have
stopped his blind flight from unbearable pain.

*Couldn't you have said good-bye?* he asked himself.

Even in his foggy haze, Tor had known that Kai El was
emerging healthy on the other side of his mother's death. Now
the boy would never know what happened to his father, and
grief's journey would be harder. "When do you stop searching
and start grieving?" the boy would wonder. "What if the
crazy old man comes back?"

*I should have told him I was leaving. But I didn't even
think of him.*

Worse, Tor never told his son what the boy *had* to know
to stop the unthinkable sin.

He *should* have said, *wanted* to say, had *practiced* saying:
"The girl you love—she's your sister—she's my daughter—she's the biggest mistake of my life."

But he couldn't say those words, no matter how he tried.
The son he loved so much would have hated him. Tor wished
he'd been stronger, but all he could do now was hope that
somehow Kai El would be all right. After all, he and Ashan
had raised a strong, smart young man.

Maybe the Spirit of Ashan would be able to keep the forbidden lovers apart.

Sometimes in a long, lonely night, when Ashan would not

come to him, Tor regretted his sins with Tsilka. So long ago, but time cannot forgive. Such a small thing, it had seemed, that no one would ever know about. But ignorance does not excuse. Who could know making love with another woman was so wrong? Tor had known, even then, but he had done it. Even now, he didn't know why it was wrong, but laws were to be accepted, with or without understanding.

A father's sin: Tor would regret it, and Kai El suffer for it, for the rest of their lives.

# CHAPTER 44

HEARING EAGLES SCREAMING, KAI EL LOOKED UP. The gold-green sky pulsed with its own light, as if alive. But it was empty of eagles, though he still heard their cries. *Am I dreaming?* he wondered, as he walked up a yellow-grass hill toward an oak tree that spread its branches across the living sky. His father waited there. Feeling flowed down as a colored breeze, wrapping Kai El in the blue of family love, the green of love between friends, and the purple of spirit love. He reached the top of the hill. Tor opened his arms. They held each other as they hadn't for so long. In the peaceful silence, Kai El spoke.

"I love you."

"I know. You have been a good son."

It was the closest his father could come to words of love, and it was enough.

A cloud scudded across the autumn-colored sky. Horse-shaped creatures—a white, a gray, and a black—fell out of the cloud like magic rain. Larger than real horses, manes and tails flying, trailing strands of mist, hooves just above the ground, the creatures galloped up the hill.

"They're coming right for us!"

"I know," Tor said. "Climb."

Father and son scrambled into the lower branches. Kai El held on. Invisible eagles screamed above them. The air quaked with thunder as the horses ran beneath them.

Tor dropped out of the tree and onto the back of the white horse, driving its hooves to the earth. As if it didn't feel him, the creature kicked into the air and skimmed above the ground, flanked by the gray and the black. The man matched the rhythm of the galloping stallion as if he were part of it. Arms out, head back, he embraced the wind. Accompanied by eagle voices, Tor chanted about the deeds of warriors. His song faded as the horse carried him into the cloud.

Kai El sat straight up—confused, heart pounding, impossible images filling his mind. He couldn't catch his breath. He was up in the cliffs. It was early morning. He'd slept here—just woke up—dreamed, that was all. Still, it was hard to bring his ragged breathing under control.

*Just a dream. Think of something else.*

When his father had moved in with Rattlesnake Woman, Kai El couldn't bear to watch him turn from pathetic to disgusting; nor could he do anything about it. Distant before the fire, afterward Tor behaved as if he didn't have a son. So Kai El had been staying in the cliffs, by himself, in sight of the rock picture said to be his mother. Sleeping near the Moonkeeper's takoma brought her son many dreams. But never one like this.

*It seemed so real. Are you sure it was a dream?*

Of course it was a dream—magnificent, but completely unbelievable. Except for the hill with the oak tree—that *was* real. Once he and Tor had waited in its branches for a family of spotted deer to come to the shade, but the little animals had gone another way.

Kai El couldn't get the dream out of his mind, kept seeing his father rise into the sky on a huge white stallion, kept hearing his warrior's song.

Dreams that stayed in the mind sometimes had a message. The language of the darktime world was different and hard to understand, but Kai El tried, thinking about the ancient relationship between horses and people. In the Misty Time, Amotkan made them spirit brothers. When horses died out, the Shahala lost their winter food, and had to leave their homeland. Could the dream mean that somewhere the beautiful creatures had survived? If horses wanted men to know, his father was the one they would tell—one of Tor's names meant Brings Messages. Kai El knew of the unusual love between them. Stories told of a horse who showed Tor to dig for water under a bush when he was dying of thirst; a horse helped him find the new home at the Great River.

Or the dream might mean that Tor was in danger.

Wishing he had his mother's skill for understanding dreams, Kai El considered other meanings, but none weighed more than another. He should have gone to the village to see that his father was safe, but he couldn't resist the call of the dream place.

Except for the sky—now blue instead of golden green, and silent of eagles—everything looked the same. Crossing in and out of cloud shadows, Kai El retraced his steps up the yellow-grass hill, to the oak tree, where no one waited this time. He stood in the lonely breeze for a while, then climbed into the lower branches, and scanned the ground—

His breath caught.

There—sharp dents in the earth—four wide apart, then a leap away, four more. Then none. He jumped from the tree, and traced one with his finger: the size of a man's heel print; rounded, with a slight point in front; deep as his thumbnail; crisp-edged; fresh.

The hoofprints of a horse? Tor—who grew up with horses—would know. Kai El—who saw his last horse at three or four summers—did not. But what else could they be?

It had not been a dream. The impossible had actually happened. For Kai El, the prints were proof that Kusi, the Horse Spirit, had carried Tor into the sky.

Why, or where Kusi took his father, when or if he would return, Kai El didn't know. Tor might even be dead, but everyone had to die. It thrilled Kai El to have been there. The way it happened was so *right*. How many times had a white horse come at his father's command?

His mother had become a legend when she died. Why not a legend for his father? It might help people remember the courageous warrior Tor had once been, instead of the lump of dung he'd become.

Under thickening clouds, Kai El ran to Teahra Village, knowing his father would not be there. He couldn't wait to tell what he'd seen, to bring people and show them. He was so excited that he hardly noticed the rain beginning as he barged into Tenka's hut.

Juniper smoke smudged the air. Raindrops on the new roofskins sounded like a drum. Sitting before a small fire, Tenka did not look up.

"People ask permission to enter the Moonkeeper's hut."

"I'm sorry," he said, and stood until she told him to sit.

She stirred the coals, shaking her head.

"My boy, my boy. What has your father done?"

"You know?"

She nodded.

How could she? Kai El and Tor were the only ones there. If she could go places in her mind, maybe his father's weak sister would turn out to be a good Moonkeeper after all.

She said, "The twins were awakened by their mother's cries. Only Tor and I know how much sleeping vine to give her, but Tor was not there. The girls waited as long as they could, sure he'd only gone out to make water. When Tsilka threatened to kill them, Tahna came for me."

The Moonkeeper's long face lengthened with concern. "Your father has not returned. The way he's been, I've waited for the night he would wander off like an old man whose mind left his body without telling it to die."

So she had *not* been there.

Kai El said, "My father did not wander off."

The Moonkeeper placed dry juniper on the smudge fire and waved the smoke toward Kai El, then toward herself.

"Tell me what you know."

"I was with him last night . . ."

Kai El had thought it was a dream, but dreams didn't leave hoofprints. Yet how could it have been real? Men didn't ride horses—horses didn't fly—there *were* no horses.

Dream or reality? It did not matter. There was only one certain thing: Tor *had* disappeared. His son saw good reasons for people to believe that he'd gone to the otherworld in a glorious way. The story was grand enough to become the legend his father deserved.

Kai El took a deep breath.

"My father is dead. He left our world on Kusi's back."

He told Tenka what he had seen, adding things to make it

better. She gathered the people, who were eager to see the place where Tor died, to touch the hoofprints of the spirit horse. Kai El took them to the hilltop, but they saw nothing there: The rain had washed the hoofprints away.

Most decided to believe Kai El's story without any proof. They wanted to think their old friend Tor met a good death. They liked him, except for the time after Ashan died, and they forgave him.

Tor had brought the tribes together at the Great River. People remembered him for that.

Old ones who were drawn to things of the spirit enjoyed telling of their brother's journey to the otherworld. Told and retold, Tor's story, and Ashan's, became tribal memory and took their places among other legends. They called Ashan "She Who Watches," and Tor "Father of Teahra."

The Keepers of the Misty Time became part of the Misty Time.

# CHAPTER 45

PEOPLE FELT SORRY FOR KAI EL AFTER KUSI, THE horse spirit, took his father. He did not like the feeling.

He had overheard women talking about him, clucking like birds sitting on eggs.

"Poor Kai El. So full of promise as a boy. Now all that promise has turned to curse."

"His mother carried off by coyotes; his father by a horse."

"All his belongings gone. And that hut ... made for a Moonkeeper's family ... now it's just a burned-out, rubble-filled hole."

Many a mother had imagined a future for her daughter in that fine, large hut. The women shook their heads.

"The son of two legends living in the old Tlikit cave."

"How sad."

Most of the people of Teahra Village lived in huts of wood and skins like the Shahala had made since the Misty Time. But anyone could stay in the old Tlikit cave—if they wanted to, or had to. Men slept there after arguing with their mates; children slept there for fun. Some grayhairs liked it because, even though it smelled bad, it never leaked. When the autumn rains came early to Teahra, Kai El slept in the old Tlikit cave.

Knowing how long it would take to gather everything needed for a new hut, men offered him a place in their homes. Some offered because they still thought he'd be a good mate for their daughters. He ate and slept in one home or another, but never stayed long in one place.

Kai El thought it was sad and unfair that some girls found him so desirable, when the only one he wanted did not.

He had made Gaia angry that day in the cliffs. She wouldn't talk to him. After Tor died, she spent all her time hidden in her hut, caring for her mother.

Kai El's dreams about Gaia and their future together seemed destined to remain dreams, yet he could not give up hope, no matter how he tried in conversations with himself.

*Why Gaia,* he wondered. *Why not her twin? Or any of the others who used to excite me when I thought of seeing them naked?*

*A soulmate's love cannot be explained: Look at what your father did to be with your mother.*

*But if we are soulmates, why doesn't she know it?*

*Maybe in time she will. She can't stay angry forever. And she won't have to take care of Tsilka forever: The old witch will either get well or die.*

When the autumn rain stopped for a while, Kai El couldn't wait to get away from the village.

"Like his father," people said. "But what do you expect? An acorn doesn't grow into a pine."

Time alone refreshed Kai El, renewed his inner strength. The robe of pity people made him wear fell away. He was tired of them caring more for him than he cared for them, tired of pretending to be like everyone else. To be with his friends, to hunt, watch girls, make jokes out of everything—none of it was fun anymore. His friends seemed to have become younger, their thoughts about unimportant things, when all he wanted to do was think of Gaia and the life they would share.

Kai El found a place to go where no one bothered him.

Teahra Village hid at the bottom of a deep gorge that followed the path of the sun. To the direction Warmer, the Great River curved around a breast of land, protecting the cluster of huts from whatever lived on the other side of the water. High, rugged cliffs rose behind the village. Trails climbed through the cliffs to vast plains where the people hunted and gathered.

One trail led to the sacred place where the Moonkeeper Ashan used to speak with spirits. After her last death, the people of Teahra abandoned the Moonkeeper's Path. In life, they said, she didn't welcome others to her takoma. Why would she now? And what about the stone face that appeared up there on the day she died? The gaze of She Who Watches comforted some, frightened others. No one wanted to get close to it. Some thought the stone *was* Ashan, but her son knew better. Like all who lived in the otherworld, Ashan was free to be where she wished. Kai El knew that his mother—whose name meant Whispering Wind—would not wish to be a rock.

Partway up, the Moonkeeper's Path opened onto a piece of flat ground where Ashan would stop and rest. Behind and to the downriver side, lichen-dappled crags rose straight up to block the wind. A massive slab canted outward to keep a bit of ground dry. On the far side of the river, autumn-gold grass waved from the hills. When Kai El faced Colder looking up, the stone eyes of She Who Watches gazed back, reminding him of his mother's love.

Kai El liked the pleasant, sheltered spot. He called it the "halfway place," and spent more and more time there.

Early this morning, he'd come down to Teahra Village to gather what he could from people who had more than they needed.

He hoped to see Gaia, but she stayed in her hut, with the doorskin closed.

He hoped *not* to see Jud. His longtime friend would be full of questions he wasn't ready to answer. And—unlike most people, who didn't bring up certain things because of respect—Jud blurted whatever ran through his head.

So Kai El visited others, talked about what interested them, collected gifts to replace things lost in the fire. He didn't see Gaia or Jud. After a day among his people, with layers of pity building up, he was ready for the clean peace of the cliffs.

He passed quietly behind Jud's hut, but his friend's mother, Wachiak, heard him and stepped out, wiping her hands on her dirty dress.

*Dung*, Kai El thought.

"My favorite young man, except for Jud," Wachiak said. "Makust is making crayfish stew. Stay with us."

For a long time, Jud's mother had been trying to interest Kai El in her daughter, Makust. He could hardly stand to look at the short, fleshy girl, but the stew smelled wonderful.

"Is Jud here?"

Wachiak shook her head. "He and Talak went to see if the snakes with sucking mouths have come."

*Good,* Kai El thought.

"They waited another day for you. Did you forget?"

"I did."

It was a lie. How could he forget? Kai El and Jud had eeled together since they'd been old enough.

He was only nine summers the first time. He remembered his mother's protest . . . just because one or two had lost a son, all mothers worried about the danger.

"He's too young! Please, Tor, next autumn!"

"Do you want them to say he has weak legs?" Tor said.

Ashan knew she'd lost the argument. Even a Moonkeeper couldn't stop a boy from growing up.

Eels came with the autumn salmon. They looked like snakes and lived like fish, but seemed more simply made than either: just a piece of tasty white flesh long as an arm, in a tough, gray bag; with two small eyes, and a mouth that knew about hanging on to rock.

At a place a day's walk from Teahra Village, the Great River roared over a run of short, wide waterfalls. In the calmer water behind the cascades, eels crowded the rocks, holding on with their sucking mouths, waving in the current like animal-grass.

"Are they going upriver, or down?" people asked.

"No one knows."

"Why do they stop here and wait for us to pick them?"

"Because they need rest," older people said.

"No," boys always said. "We have seen them mating under there." That made girls giggle.

These discussions became part of a tradition growing up around the gathering of eels, which the tribes had not known in their old lands.

Kai El remembered the thrill of crawling around in the

strange world behind the falls, plucking eels from the slippery rocks, stuffing them into his creel. Cold numbed the gatherers. The raging river choked and beat them, and swept the occasional one to his death. But the honor made the punishing risk worthwhile.

Men left the work to boys eager to prove themselves, but they sat around to watch and advise. Women who cleaned the catch were given the skins to make thin, tough leather that shone. Girls came to admire the bravery of the gatherers.

The whole village looked forward to eeling time—except maybe the mothers of the boys. Not everyone went to the falls, but all loved to eat the bounty: charred like snakes on sticks before a fire; baked underground; cooked in water; or dried.

This time, Kai El's friends had gone without him. He was glad. Since he wouldn't have to see Jud, he stayed in Wachiak's hut. The crayfish stew was good, and Makust didn't try to sneak under his furs in the night.

In the morning—after hot, crisp fish cakes, and failed words to stay him—Kai El started back for his place in the cliffs with food, leather, rope, spearpoints, and a new pack to carry them in.

It had been a good visit, until now. Jud and Talak, approaching on the river trail, saw Kai El before he could hide.

# CHAPTER 46

"Kai El! Wait!"

*My spirit brother,* Kai El thought with a groan. *Just who I didn't want to see.*

Jud ran toward him. Eagle feathers flew from the staff he carried; he said they were from an already-dead eagle, but Kai El knew better. Even on a day as cold as this, Jud wore only a loinskin; he claimed to have an inner heat, and Kai El did believe that. Jud never wore moccasins; said he loved the way the ground felt under his feet. His chopped hair stood up. From a distance, it looked like a porcupine sat on his head. Kai El had teased his friend to let his hair grow, or he'd never get a woman. Jud would say he'd have ten women before Kai El had one. At seventeen summers, both were still waiting for the first.

Talak came behind Jud. He was a friend, but not a spirit brother. At fourteen summers, he was taller than Jud, but shorter than Kai El, with a thin body like a young girl's. He could act as silly as any other boy, but Kai El thought he held something back. There might be more to Talak than anyone would ever know. Who *really* understood what it meant to be the son of a Firekeeper who was once a slave?

"My friend!" Jud said. "I've been wanting to see you!"

"Me too," Kai El lied, slapping Jud's outstretched hand.

"Good to see you," Talak said, and Kai El nodded.

Willow baskets called creels hung from straps over their

shoulders. They were knee-high, round, wide at the bottom, with a small hole on top to stuff eels into, woven with open spaces to let water move around the captured eels while others were gathered.

Kai El saw light through the spaces between the willow sticks.

"No eels?"

"The boy didn't want to get wet," Jud said, casting a scornful look at Talak. "So he told them we were coming."

Talak dropped to his knees.

"I did not, oh wise one! But if you'd told me eels have ears, I would have."

"Did you ever look?" Jud said. "Do you know where their love-spears are?"

They broke into laughter. Kai El joined in, though he no longer thought their jokes were funny.

Jud pointed to Kai El's stuffed pack.

"Looks like you raided the village," he said, shaking his head. "And they gave you a new pack to carry it away in. Is there any place in there for a gift from your spirit brother?"

A gift? Kai El's mood brightened.

"If it's not too big."

"You'll like this so much, you'll throw out other things to make room."

"Well, show me!" he said, unable to hide his excitement.

In a time the young men knew of but didn't remember, the Shahala had taught the Tlikit about gifting, as Shala, the Wind Spirit, taught them in the Misty Time. People gave useful things to little ones at birth, at their first summer, and when they took their names; to girls becoming women; to new mates. When something was lost, a friend replaced it. Gifting showed the love of one for another, but was also expected— with or without love—because sharing reaffirmed the oneness of the Teahra people, as Shahala, Tlikit, and Firekeeper had come to think of themselves.

The three young men sat at the river's edge. Jud looked in his empty eel basket, turned it upside down, and shook it.

"Hmm," he said, giving Kai El a worried look. He unfolded his shoulder pouch, took everything out, poked around in the corners, put everything back.

"Hope I didn't lose it."

Gifts were too important to lose—Jud was just stirring the fire of Kai El's eagerness.

Jud thumped his head. "Now I remember where I put it!"

He opened his waist pouch, and held out a worked stone.

"A scraper!" Kai El shouted, taking it. "Mine broke in the fire!"

"Not just any scraper," Jud said with pride.

"It fits my hand perfectly."

"I know my spirit brother."

Kai El gripped it, made a motion in the air like cleaning a raw hide.

"The weight is just right—heavy enough to do the work, light enough to use all day."

Jud shrugged. "Can I help it if everything I make is perfect?"

"So smooth a girl could use it," Kai El said, fingering the top.

"I walked a long time to find the mother stone."

A man used his scraper to clean hides for his woman to make into leather—not that these three had women, but they had hope. Gray rocks from the river made the best ones. The rounded mother stone was split in half lengthwise, then sharpened along one edge. Ten spearpoints could be made before one good scraper. The rock might refuse to break, or break in many pieces, instead of splitting clean. The edge might chip dull instead of sharp. Fingers were wounded. It pleased Kai El that Jud would do this for him.

"Nice, my friend. Really nice."

Talak pointed to the faint shape of a bug etched into the top, almost worn away by the river.

"Look at this. Like a beetle died in mud, and the mud changed to rock, and the rock rolled down—"

Jud interrupted. "That's why I picked *this* rock. You know these Shahala and how they love beetles. I'd step on my sister before I stepped on a beetle, rather than make Kai El mad."

Kai El laughed—Jud didn't like his sister, Makust, any better than Kai El did.

He put his new scraping blade in his new pack.

"Thank you, Jud. Good beetle—I mean, good blade."

Jud smiled. "Now you can return mine. Someone else might want to borrow it."

"I'll bring it the next time I come to the village," Kai El said, getting up to leave.

Jud jumped to his feet.

"I never see you anymore," he said in a hurt voice. "You spend all your time alone. We never hunt or fish or talk. What happened to my old friend?"

Kai El sighed, looking away, adjusting the band of his pack against his forehead.

"Things change. People change."

"That's no answer, and I deserve one. I saved your life more than once."

"And I've saved yours. But you're right, Jud. You do deserve an answer. I just wish I knew it."

Jud pointed to the cliffs. "Why don't you take me up there where you spend all your time? Maybe that's where the answer hides."

Kai El took a deep breath. Someday, someone would have to see the halfway place. Gaia should have been first, but . . .

"Come on," he said.

With a grim look, Talak shook his head.

"I'm not going to that ghost place. When Jud doesn't come back, I'll tell his weeping mother that Spilyea turned him into a rock, too."

Kai El remembered that people of slave blood feared spirits of all kinds.

"It's just a quiet place with a good view," he said. "And no ghosts."

Jud snickered. "It can't be worse than drowning while you pick eels under a waterfall. Should we tell the girls you have weak legs?"

Talak had no choice. Once girls believed that about a boy, it was hard to convince them they were wrong.

"I may be younger, but my legs are stronger than yours," he said. But Talak couldn't help looking over his shoulder as they climbed the trail.

Kai El tried to reassure him.

"Ghosts are invisible. You couldn't see one if it came."

"*That* makes me feel better. I won't see them coming to carry me off."

"Even if a ghost comes, don't worry. They are only as mean as the people they used to be," Kai El said, thinking of his mother. She had a Moonkeeper's power, but she had never been meaner than a person deserved—though the victim might think otherwise.

"Stop talking about ghosts, and I'll feel better," Talak said. Then he jumped at a little noise somewhere behind them. The boy couldn't hide his fear.

Jud tried, but Kai El knew him too well: His bravery at the river faltered as they climbed. He tried to cover it by tricking Talak, hiding pebbles in his hand to toss when the boy wasn't looking, making him think they were being followed.

They both kept going. Male pride gave them no choice.

Kai El stopped at the halfway place.

"What do you think?"

"Good place to rest," Jud said.

"This is where I'm going to live."

"That's crazy," Talak said.

Jud said, "This is a joke, right?"

"No. I'll move these boulders—I could use your muscle, Spirit Brother—then I'll make my hut back against that overhanging slab—"

Talak cut him off. "You're crazier than your father ever was. No one's ever wanted to live away from the village. Why don't you want to live with us? Aren't we good enough?"

"You always think people think they're better, Talak, but they don't. It has nothing to do with that. It's a nice place, and I like it here, that's all."

Jud said, "You'll be lonely. You'll never get a mate."

"You're wrong," Kai El said. "The girl I love is different. We are soulmates. I like it, so she'll like it."

Jud and Talak looked at each other. Kai El hadn't told his feelings to anyone.

"What girl?" Jud asked.

"Gaia."

Their mouths dropped.

"Talak is right," Jud said. "You *are* crazy. The twins will never mate. They'll be taking care of Rattlesnake Woman until they're old and ugly themselves."

Kai El said, "Rattlesnake Woman will either get well or die. Besides, Gaia doesn't owe her life to her mother. No one does."

"Well," Talak said, "they're both good to look at, but Gaia's the one I'd take. Once I *accidentally* walked by the women's washing place. Tahna caught me and almost poked my eyes out."

The laughter of friends was a little too loud, but it sounded good. Kai El wouldn't admit it, but he *did* get lonely sometimes. He gave them antelope leathermeat and old-berry juice, and they stayed for a while. Kai El told his ideas for the place, and they seemed interested. He laughed at their jokes.

Shadows lengthened. Talak spoke in a serious voice.

"We need to get home. Ghosts are more powerful at night. If we wait any longer, we'll break our legs in the dark."

"You're right," Jud said. He nudged Kai El. "You can stay with us. You know my sister's cooking."

Kai El said, "Stay here, my friends. It's best at night. The stars are brighter, the river's quieter. I have food, and we'll make a fire. Tomorrow I'll show you trails you never knew about."

Jud shook his head. "Maybe some other time."

"Some other time," Talak agreed.

They left. Loneliness came. Kai El was not going to sit there feeling sorry for himself. He had spent enough time in the cliffs to know them. He could move silently without using the trail, knew places to hide and listen to what they *really* thought.

Following them, he caught bits of conversation.

"I don't understand him," Jud said.

"He's crazy," Talak said. "But what do you expect? Look at his parents."

"His mother wasn't crazy."

"She wasn't like anyone else. And his father—they don't get any crazier than that."

Jud didn't try to argue that Tor wasn't crazy, and Kai El didn't blame him.

Farther down the trail, he heard them again.

"Soulmates! Phht! He could have any girl. Why does he want one who's not interested?"

"I told you, Jud, he's crazy. We've heard the last of women saying what a fine mate he would make for their daughters."

"Spit on you both!" Kai El said, not caring if they heard.

He went back to the halfway place, and watched night suck light from the world.

"Jud and Talak," he yelled. "A fatherless Tlikit, and the son of a slave. Who do you think you are to judge the son of legends?"

His words bounced from the rocks and came back sounding like someone else's. Kai El was not an arrogant man, just a very angry one.

As stars took their places in the darkening sky, anger changed to discouragement. Talak didn't surprise him. But Kai El and Jud were spirit brothers. He'd been so sure Jud would understand. And so wrong.

"My best friend," Kai El said. "And he understood none of it. Not one thing."

*Now you know,* his inner voice answered. *No one will understand.*

"Except maybe Gaia," he said. Even now, he didn't give up hope. What would he have left?

"She's different, you know. We are soulmates."

But he felt so lonely.

# CHAPTER 47

KAI EL'S DEEP LONELINESS REACHED THROUGH SPACE and time, calling the spirit of his mother. She found him lying in the cliffs above Teahra Village, rolling back and forth in unsettled sleep.

*. . . If I could just talk to him . . .*

Ashan's love for people—especially her son—was as great as it had ever been. Now she knew so much more, knowledge that could make life better for people—if only there was some way to *tell* them. But people couldn't hear spirits with their ears, any more than they could see them with their eyes.

The Spirit of Ashan could enter Kai El's dreaming mind, and create pictures for him to take back to the daytime world, but this was flawed. When he awoke, Kai El kept only what he wanted, and forgot the rest. It wasn't perfect, but it pleasured her to be with her son. It allowed her to comfort him, and sometimes help him make decisions.

If Ashan kept the dream-path between them open, Kai El might someday be ready to learn that Gaia was his sister and could never be his mate.

On this night, her son felt crushed because he'd been scorned by his friends. Kai El wanted to be liked and respected. But Destiny would lead him down a different path from others, so Destiny had made him different. Sometimes being different hurt, as when you were young and could see no farther than tomorrow.

As Kai El slept, the Spirit of Ashan painted him a dream.

He dreamed that he was here at his place in the cliffs, but it was as he had imagined . . . with a large hut under the overhanging rock slab, and a wide, flat place where people could sit outside . . . a home to be proud of.

In Kai El's dream, he sat on a stone. People sat on the ground, all looking up to him. He was the chief, and they had come to ask him questions. He was glad he didn't live down in the village with them; he'd never have time for himself.

A beautiful woman stepped from the hut.

Not Gaia.

He stood with his mouth open. *I want her,* he thought.

"Kai El," said the most soothing voice he had ever heard.

Kai El woke himself up. He remembered dreaming . . .

This place . . . all finished, with a large flat spot for sitting, instead of these boulders. And a hut of wood and skins, with a rock slab roof. In the dream, people had accepted this as his home. They had come up to visit him.

Gaia had been in the dream—it didn't look like her, but he knew it was her.

Kai El looked up. A pair of hawks called to each other as they circled the cliffs.

Skaina, the Hawk Spirit, must have given him the dream. He remembered Skaina's words on his long-ago power quest.

*Amotkan wants people to listen to themselves. You are the first.*

It meant more than just picking his own name. That was only the beginning. It meant that he was to follow his own thoughts, about everything, no matter what others said.

The dream had shown Kai El that he was right about making his home up here; and that in time, others would come up to see him.

More important, the dream had shown Gaia living in his home.

Kai El sang his song to the circling birds.

"With the eyes of the hawk, I see what others can't. With the heart of the hawk, I have the courage of ten men. With the wings of the hawk, my spirit soars high above my home."

His friends may have laughed at him yesterday, but one

good thing would come from their visit. Now Gaia would know what he was doing up here, and who he was doing it for. Jud and Talak would make sure everyone knew that.

When the right time came, when Gaia was ready for him, Kai El would be ready for her. Until then, he would work on their home, and think of nothing but her.

When she saw how Kai El interpreted the dream, the Spirit of Ashan wondered if she should keep out of his sleeping mind in the future.

# CHAPTER 48

===============================================

"ALIKE AS SEEDS OF GRASS," PEOPLE SAID OF TSILKA'S daughters when they were young. Subtle contrasts emerged as they grew. At fifteen summers, the twins looked alike only at first glance.

Their dark brown eyes were shaped the same; but Tahna's flashed, Gaia's were soft. Gaia's long, midnight-colored hair rested neatly on her back, while Tahna's always looked wind-blown. Gaia dressed as if she were unaware of her beauty, but naturally knew how to enhance it. Tahna dressed for attention. Gaia walked with the grace of one who shouldn't tire herself; Tahna darted.

Firstborn Tahna, who had never faced death, had no fear of it. Secondborn Gaia, who faced death every time the Breath Ogre attacked, had beaten fear of it.

If either had reason to be jealous of the other, it was Gaia. Tahna had been blessed with a strong, healthy body. If Gaia could have anything, it would be that.

But Gaia wasn't the jealous twin.

Tahna had a secret place that no one knew about—not her mother, not even her twin. She'd been coming here since she was a girl. Not far past Teahra Village, the river trail left the water's edge. A small path led to the women's washing place. Men and boys knew better than to come down that path.

Tahna could hear the girls and women talk from her hiding place nearby; sometimes it was more fun to listen than to be one of them.

Her secret place meant more than fun now: It meant survival. Tor had been gone, dead, or whatever he was for two moons, leaving the twins to care for the demanding witch their mother had become. If Tahna couldn't be alone sometimes, she thought she'd die.

On a cold, windy day, feeling stretched like a skin pegged and forgotten, Tahna fled the village. Reached by an animal track, her secret place was just a hole in the thick brush, where boulders forced the current around a little pool. She sat on a low rock, staring at the water, thinking about her twin.

*Always the lucky one, from the beginning, when she was named for a cougar and I was named for a bug.*

Wind chopped the gray water into waves that hit the boulders behind Tahna and splashed her. Dark clouds, heavy with rain, would break open soon, but she stayed. Cold wet seemed better, cleaner, than the dry warmth of the hut.

Tahna pushed damp strings of hair from her face.

*Everyone thinks Gaia is so good . . . if they knew what I know . . . I knew her* before *the beginning.*

Being named for a bug was the second unfair thing that happened to the firstborn twin. Far worse was done to Tahna inside her mother's womb. Deer and goats might be born in pairs, but humans were born alone.

*Only one baby should have been born. Only me.*

Tahna *looked* like a whole person, but she wasn't, not on the inside where the mind and soul were. Half of her was stolen before she was even born. Sometimes she believed that her twin had willfully robbed her. Sometimes she blamed it on their mother for mating with a god—perhaps a god's staff was sharp, and could split an unborn baby in two.

Or maybe the birth of twins was simply a mistake, like the Tlikit story about a baby born with no thumbs. He learned to do everything but use a spear. Before he reached mating age, a moose killed him. The story explained how some people were doomed from the beginning.

Knowing *why* she was different wouldn't have changed

how Tahna felt about herself: less than complete, less than others. She wondered what *whole* people felt like, and wished she could feel it too.

At times, she resented her twin—then she couldn't help being mean. But she didn't hate her. What Gaia had done was long ago, and Tahna forgave her.

However it might seem, Tahna *loved* the other half of herself, love made stronger by Gaia's weakness. When they were young, Tahna found ways to make the Breath Ogre leave Gaia's body. This brought praise from her mother, thanks from her sister, and pride in herself at being smart enough to outwit a demon. Tahna never told Gaia, but in a way she was sorry the Breath Ogre stopped coming. At least the attacks had given her something of value to do.

Already wet from blowing waves, Tahna barely noticed when it began raining as she sat in her secret place.

She was fifteen summers, and what was her life supposed to be about?

Once she had dreamed of becoming a Moonkeeper, but when Ashan died, so did the dream. With a sigh, Tahna remembered how much she missed Ashan. So far Tenka had not chosen a helper, but Tahna didn't think she would be the one—even though she already knew about medicine. She felt that unlucky.

Other girls her age talked about boys, about huts of their own, and the little ones they would have. The idea of mating and babies excited Gaia. It didn't interest Tahna, but there was nothing else she could hope to do. She might not even get a mate—there weren't enough boys the right age. Not having a mate was a bad thing, as Tahna had learned so well growing up with a mother who didn't have one. No one in the tribe ever starved, but women with mates received the special things.

A few water skimmers took refuge in Tahna's secret pool. She threw a stone, scattered them, and the wild river took them.

She didn't want a mate, but it would be worse not to have one. What *did* half a person want? To be whole. But what would make Tahna whole? Maybe nothing. Maybe some people *were* doomed from the beginning.

*Why do I bother wondering what I want? My mother and my twin have decided for me, with help from Tor.*

For the rest of her miserable life, Tsilka would demand more care than a mate and a hut full of little ones. For now, Tahna had her sister's help. But eventually, Gaia and Kai El would realize that they were in love.

*Then I will be the only one to take care of the witch. Curse you, Tor, for knocking my mother into the oil lamp. Not that I haven't felt like it ...*

Tahna had been glad when Tor went away. He had disappointed her, or betrayed her—she could look at it either way.

Once, he had seemed to like the twins more than any little ones except his son. He gave them special treats, and talked about important things that adults usually saved for each other. Tahna thought he liked her because she was a clever girl who always remembered what he said. Only later did she realize that he probably came to see their mother.

Sometimes the fatherless twins played secret games in which Tor was their father.

Bad moods didn't have a chance when he came around. Tahna couldn't help laughing at his funny stories.

When coyotes took Ashan, Tor lost more than a mate. He lost what made him the person Tahna loved—especially his humor. He wanted nothing more to do with them. Gaia said she understood: Family was the most important thing. But Tahna didn't understand. True, they were not his family, but she *thought* he loved them as friends. Tor had once told her that love between friends was forever.

The line between grief and madness was thin; the fire had pushed Tor over it. His own home destroyed, he had moved into Tsilka's hut. A scary intensity drove him to keep the burned woman alive, no matter how she begged to die. Tahna never saw him sleep. His dead eyes passed by her as if she were something hanging on the wall. His ears ignored her. He took food without a word, a glance, or any sign that she existed.

The kind man Tahna thought she knew was just a disguise, like a skin worn by a warrior to penetrate a herd. The cruel man inside had been waiting for a chance to get out and make his kill. Yes, she was glad Tor was gone.

At first, Tahna enjoyed taking care of her mother.

Tor had not allowed anyone but Tenka to touch her—even though Tahna knew what to do, having learned about medicine from Ashan. After Tor disappeared, overworked Tenka was glad to turn Tsilka's care over to her daughters.

But with Tor gone, Tsilka treated her daughters like slaves. Though she recovered completely—except for her looks—she refused to do anything for herself, would not even get up from her sleeping place. Devoted to being the meanest person alive, she never ran out of work for the twins to do.

"Cover me! Uncover me! Move this! Carry that! Raise me, lower me, feed me!"

So often Tahna wanted to scream: *It's not our fault!*

Overworked and mistreated, she found herself missing Tor. So what if he'd betrayed her? At least he had taken care of the witch who used to be her mother.

Tahna gently wiped a sore on her mother's back that refused to heal because she lay on it all the time.

Tsilka snapped, "Don't be in such a hurry! You're hurting me!"

*How long do you think you can get away with this?* Tahna wished she had the courage to ask.

But she said, "I'm finished, Mother. You may lie down."

Gaia returned from the river with cooking things that their mother had insisted were filthy.

Tahna hissed, "You took your time. It's my turn to get out of here."

"See you later," Gaia said with a big sigh.

Tahna left the hut with her leatherwork under her arm. The sight of people going about their work made her smile, reminding her that normal life still went on in the world outside. She filled her chest with breezy, sunny air, and let the throb of the river calm her. She sat on a nearby rock and unrolled her leatherwork in her lap. A little more sewing, and the foldover pouch for dried herbs would be finished.

If her twin were making a pouch, it wouldn't be enough to just finish it. She would have to decorate it, too.

Saying, "Things should be pretty," Gaia might change the color of the leather, or paint on it. Gaia could make pictures that looked like things—a gift stolen from her sister in the womb. Tahna couldn't make pictures, and didn't care. What good were they? Time would deepen this amber leather to rich brown. It didn't need Tahna's help. It looked fine all by itself.

Gaia stamped out of the hut.

"Tahna! Where are my new moccasins?"

"How would I know?"

"I think you do." Her sister's voice was ugly. "I think you stole them."

There went Tahna's good mood. She had only stolen once or twice, not all the time.

She snapped, "I spent enough time with a witch today. Go find someone else to fight with."

"I want my moccasins!" Gaia shrieked. "I'm tired of making things, just to have you steal them!"

Tahna should have backed down, but she was tired of her sister's accusations. How arrogant she was! Tahna's thefts were nothing compared to Gaia's!

"I never touched your moccasins! They're so ugly, I wouldn't wear them! But if I wanted to, I'd have every right to take them, after what you stole from me before we were born!"

Gaia's fists balled. "Someday I'm going to go crazy and kill you!"

"Finish what you started in our mother's womb? It will be harder now. I'm not a helpless lump."

Gaia sputtered, then wept—great blubbering sobs—as if the black bird of tragedy had landed on her.

Disgusted, Tahna shook her head. Her sister usually put up a better fight. But Gaia—who suffered the most from their mother's rage—was falling apart like an old basket.

"Oh, stop it!" Tahna yelled.

But Gaia didn't stop. She was on her way to one of those disgusting things she *couldn't* stop until she wore herself out, or the Breath Ogre choked her. She did it for sympathy, but they weren't children anymore, and now it only made Tahna feel hard and cold.

Gaia cried, "The older we get, the less I understand you

and your stupid ideas about how we should have been *one*. I have never felt like half a person. It's so stupid!"

"But it's true, Gaia. That's exactly what you are. Together, we might have made one good person. Split apart, neither one of us is worth spit. I only wonder if you did it on purpose. And why you don't feel it yourself?"

"There is nothing to feel! We're just sisters, like any other sisters! It's not possible to steal part of someone!"

"Yes, it is. If you listened when the Moonkeeper talked about medicine, you'd know that the pain of birth is the baby tearing pieces from the mother to finish itself. So why couldn't a selfish spirit—such as *you*—hide in my mother's womb and tear off parts of me?"

"Tell me what parts you don't have! I'll cut myself open and give them to you!"

"It's too late for that!" Tahna shouted. "Why couldn't you have waited for your own time to be born?"

"My sister," Gaia said, "I've told you more times than the sky has stars: I didn't steal your soul, or any part of you. I would never do it, even if I could. I don't know why we are twins, but I had nothing to do with it. I'm glad I have a twin. I love you."

This wasn't fun anymore. Tahna ended the game.

"Look behind the firewood. I might have seen your moccasins there."

Sniffling, Gaia went in the hut.

Tahna's leatherwork wasn't interesting anymore; the sounds of people annoyed her. Her secret place called. But before she could sneak away, Gaia came out wearing a clean skirt, a cape, her new moccasins, and a frown.

"I have to get out of here or I'll die," she said.

"Well I'm sorry, but it's *your* turn to watch our mother."

"I gave our mother sleeping vine tea. She won't bother you."

Tahna jumped up. "Sleeping vine in the morning? We are trying to wean her!"

"What's one more day?" Gaia said without a trace of concern. She turned and walked toward the river trail.

"How much did you give her?" Tahna yelled. "Where are you going? When will you be back?"

Gaia kept walking without a backward glance.

Tahna went in the hut. She left the doorskin open, but the breeze didn't want to enter the place rattling with snores, and the hot air settled on her, unwelcome as a bear robe on a summer night.

Tsilka was lying on her back—at least Gaia had made sure of that. Turning her over would stop the noisy snoring, but people sleeping with the help of the vine must lie on their backs, or they might stop breathing.

Tahna knelt beside her mother, shaking her head. She couldn't believe what Gaia had done. Should she go for the Moonkeeper? Listening to the sounds of snores, the spacing of breaths, she picked up her mother's wrist and found the beating: a little slow, but strong and steady. There was no need to bother the Moonkeeper. Tsilka would sleep for a long time, but her daughter didn't think she was in danger. Maybe a good long sleep would bring relief to them all.

Sunlight came in the open door, enclosing them in a dusty glow. Tahna stared at her mother, who couldn't tolerate being stared at when she was awake. The face that a little girl had once thought the loveliest in the world was half-human, half-demon.

"They should have let you die," she whispered. "It would have been kinder than this."

Holding her hand up, Tahna made a shadow to cover the scarred half of her mother's face, and made her beautiful again. The girl gazed at her mother until her arm was tired. Then she cried and cried.

# CHAPTER 49

KAI EL THOUGHT ABOUT THE BREATH OGRE that attacked Gaia whenever it pleased, and how the Other Moonkeeper said that sage drove the demon away. He smiled as he thought . . . he could get a sage plant, and move it to the place in the cliffs where he was making their home. The Breath Ogre wouldn't try to get Gaia if its enemy lived here. It was probably a crazy idea that wouldn't work, but he had learned from Ehr that crazy ideas were sometimes the best ones.

Kai El climbed to the plateau and searched for a sage plant—a young one, because he thought the young would be stronger and have more will to live than the old. Some looked good, but he wanted only the best. He found one as tall as his knee whose round top and bare trunk had the look of a little tree, not a ragged bush like most.

He thought that plants never understood him, but he talked to them anyway.

"You are the best one," he said.

With his hands around its trunk—the size of Gaia's wrist—his face full of stiff gray leaves, he tugged gently. The sage tightened its grip on the earth. Kai El tightened his grip on the trunk.

"Come on," he grunted. "You want to help, don't you?"

He twisted and yanked, this way and that.

Like a skunk defending itself, the threatened sage gave off an eye-burning smell.

"I'm not killing you. You're just going to a new home. My woman needs you."

He pushed, pulled, wiggled the bush back and forth, getting his face scratched, squinting against the biting fumes.

"You can burn my eyes if you want. It won't stop me. This smell will save her life."

Kai El dug in his heels and threw his body behind them. Roots breaking, dirt flying, the sage tore free. He heard a screech, let go, stumbled backward; then laughed at himself—he'd heard the cry of a hawk in the sky, not the death scream of a bush.

The soaring red-tail screeched again. Kai El's Spirit Guardian had come to watch. Maybe this *would* work.

Out of the ground, lying on its side, the sage looked hurt and scared. Dirt clods hung on dangling roots. Most of the soft gray bark was stripped from the trunk. But it still had its branches and most of its leaves.

With roots cradled in his arms, Kai El carried the sage bush to his halfway place, wondering where to put it. Where would trouble come from? Human trouble would sneak along the trail, but what about the Breath Ogre? Kai El didn't know enough about Gaia's enemy. He would see the Moonkeeper Tenka again. This time he'd ask longer questions and give a better ear to her answers.

Standing at a spot on the edge of the sitting place where the dirt was soft, Kai El dug a hole with his spear, pushed the wad of roots into it, and packed dirt around them with his feet.

He stood back. The sage stood up straight, but it was shorter. At its home on the plateau, it had reached his knee—now it only came to his shin. Trying to do a good job, he'd made the hole too deep.

"Well, maybe it will keep the wind from blowing you over."

He walked around, admiring it from all sides.

"You look good," he said. "How do you feel?"

It wasn't that he expected an answer, but to acknowledge the spirit of the plant.

There he was . . . sweaty, streaked with dirt, wearing nothing but his oldest loinskin and moccasins, and talking to a bush . . . when Gaia came up the trail.

Kai El stared at her, breathless.

She wore golden doeskin too clean to have been worn before: A skirt, tight-fitting at the top, fringed from thigh to knee; a cape, painted with symbols of the four directions; knee-high moccasins with neat, crossed laces. White and blue beads at her throat. The breeze pulled strands of long, black, untied hair across her pretty face.

Kai El felt his legs under him, the ground under them. No, he wasn't dreaming.

"Look at this!" she said with delight.

He breathed again. "Isn't this beautiful? Wait until I'm finished."

"I can see that!"

He explained anyway, and it helped bring his spinning mind under control.

"This flat part here—I'm making it bigger by taking rocks out. Then I'll use dirt to make it smooth."

He pointed to the sharp-edged rocks, from huge to small, stacked on the river side—the start of a low wall.

"I put the extra ones there, so people in the village won't see up here."

"Hmm," she said.

"When it's finished, the flat place will be for sitting in good weather." He knew women liked a nice place to do their outside work.

She gave him a curious look. "You really *are* going to make your hut up here?"

"I am. Over there."

He swept his arm toward the cliff wall, where it curved around the back of a knee-deep hole, as long as three men lying head to foot, and wide as two. Kai El had spent days digging with a pointed stick and a stone ax, muscling out the rocks, carrying or rolling them out of the way. Cuts and bruises showed how hard some of them fought. Then he brought in smaller rocks, beat them into place, and filled the holes with tamped dirt.

"That will be the floor," he said with pride, pointing to the large, smooth-bottomed hole.

"Very large," she said, sounding impressed.

"I don't like to be crowded."

"I don't know anything else," she said, laughing.

He cleared his throat. "See how that stone slab hangs out? Underneath will be the sleeping place. Even the best skin roof lets rain in, but it never gets wet back there. I will never wake up with drips on my head.

"But it won't be like a cave, all dark and smelly," he said. "The front will be like any other hut, with walls of branches covered with stretched skins. My door will face Where Day Begins, for first light and warmth."

"I have never seen a more wonderful home!"

Kai El felt light-headed.

"You like it? You really do? There's nothing to see yet, but—"

"You made a good picture inside my head. Of course I like it. Who wouldn't?"

Kai El released the breath he'd been holding—a loud, unintended *whoosh*. He swallowed for courage.

"I want to show you something."

He took her to the not-yet doorway, reached under her arms, and helped her down to the floor.

"I'll put a flat rock here for you—for people—to step down on."

They stood side by side in the center of the soon-to-be hut, the cliff wall at their backs, a view to forever before them. He looked down and saw her lush hair falling smooth over her shoulders, without a whisper of wind to disturb it. She was small enough to hide under his arm. She smelled of soap leaves and new-made leather. As his senses swelled, Kai El almost forgot what he was going to show her.

"What do you notice?" he asked.

"How *big* it is."

"Not that."

"Um . . . the floor is very smooth."

He shook his head. "Your hair."

She looked up at him. "My hair?"

"It's not blowing. The cliffs keep the wind out."

"Oh, Kai El! How nice that will be in winter! Yet the wind can blow across the sitting place outside, and that will be good in summer!"

Loving her excitement, Kai El could barely control his own.

He shook out his rumpled sleeping skin—an old antelope missing most of the hair that someone gave him after the fire—and spread it over the dirt shelf he'd been using for a bed. It was a good place to sit, with smooth rock to lean against.

"You must be tired," he said with a sweep of his arm. "Will you sit?"

"I'm not tired. It's an easy trail."

It was not an easy trail, but he didn't say so.

She went on. "It would be nice to sit and . . . just talk."

He couldn't agree more.

Gaia sat cross-legged, leaning back—a pretty, young contrast to the ancient, lichened stone behind her.

Kai El sat across from her, in what would be the doorway of their hut. He remembered the time when they'd sat almost touching. Since then, it seemed like everyone and everything wanted to keep them apart.

"What were you saying to that bush?" she asked.

He wouldn't have talked about the bush; it might remind her of her weakness. He answered without mentioning his real reason.

"I love the way sage smells. I thought it would be nice to smell it all the time, so I tried something. I took this plant from its home on the plateau and moved it here. When you came up the trail, I was talking to it like you would a frightened child—you know—telling it not to worry, it will be happy here."

She laughed. "I don't think a plant would want to move."

"You're right."

"I hope I'm wrong," she said. "I love the smell of sage, too."

After a silence, she said, "I didn't know you were one who speaks with plants."

"I speak, but they don't understand. I know the sage was laughing at me."

She laughed, and he realized he was trying to say things in a funny way just to hear the tinkly sound.

"My mother tried to teach me," he said, "but plants knew me better than she did. I can hardly remember which mushroom not to eat—the red-spotted ones, or the ones that turn blue if you scratch them."

She giggled. "I'm not good with plants, but I do know that red spot kills you and blue streak makes you see things that aren't real. I don't eat either one."

"At least you know their names."

"Tahna is the one who knows about plants. She would have been Moonkeeper someday if your mother had lived."

Kai El didn't want to talk about her sister. He wanted to talk about Gaia, about love, about the life he had planned for them, but he didn't know how to start.

"What do you think of all this?" he asked with a wave of his hand.

"It will be very nice. I can see that. But why up here? Men make their huts in the village. People wonder why you don't."

Kai El had good reasons. He believed Gaia would be healthier away from her mother and sister. And it would be safer to live up here. If savages attacked the village, they wouldn't know about the hut in the cliffs. There had been no attacks since people moved to the Great River, but stories told of earlier tragedies.

*Those aren't things you say to a girl,* he told himself. *You don't want to scare her.*

"Well . . ." he said, trying to think of other reasons.

"Is it your mother? You loved her very much. This is near her favorite place."

*She* knows *me,* he thought.

"That's part of it," he said. "It's because this is a takoma."

She said, "A takoma is . . . where spirit lines cross in the sky?"

"Exactly."

"I listened when your mother talked about spirit lines, but I never understood." She looked at the sky. "I don't see anything up there."

"They're trails used by spirits, so we can't see them. Only

Moonkeepers know where they are. When many cross, like here, the land underneath is . . ." It was hard to explain.

"Blessed?" she said. "I can feel it. It has something to do with peace."

He nodded, glad that she felt it too.

"But some people wouldn't like living way up here," she said. "It would be hard to visit their friends."

"It's not far. I go to the village almost every day."

"Other people think too much time is wasted visiting that should be used for work."

Other people? Did she mean herself?

He blurted, "Would you like living here, Gaia?"

Laughing nervously, she looked at her hands.

"Mmm," she said.

Hoping that meant "yes," Kai El took his waist pouch from behind a rock. He fumbled inside with the pledge band he'd finished yesterday.

Mixed with the hard work of digging dirt and carrying rocks had been the sweet, easy work of making a pledge band for his beloved: collecting bits of antler, shell, and stone; cleaning and polishing until they pleased the eye; braiding them in with the strands of his hair. Finished with leather ties that ended in a puff of hawk down, Kai El's pledge band was every bit as beautiful as the one his father made for his mother to wear.

Kai El walked slowly to Gaia and sat beside her. Glad for all the time he'd spent to make the pledge band worthy, he put it in her hand.

She gazed at it with wide eyes, then looked up at him. Airy wonder lifted her voice.

"This is the loveliest thing I have ever seen. Is it . . . a pledge band?"

He nodded. "Shahala men have always made them."

"Who . . . who did you make it for?"

"For you, Gaia. I want you for my mate."

"Oh, Kai El! Even though—"

He touched his finger to her lips.

"Even though. No matter what. I want to be with you forever. If you want me."

"Yes!" she squealed, throwing herself at him.

His arms, loving the marvelous, new feel of womanflesh, took time enclosing her. Eyes shut, cheeks burning, breathing in all the scent her body could make, he whispered her name.

She stopped him with a kiss ... light, tentative, like a butterfly landing. They made one person in each other's arms. Shooting stars raced through him. The kiss became an urgent pressing of lips that could never get close enough. His heart beat so fast it hurt and so hard it felt like it wanted out of his body. He never wanted to stop kissing, but she finally turned her face away, saving their lives by allowing them to breathe.

She held him away from the second kiss that he wanted more than anything. Her voice was husky.

"My passion is fierce, Kai El. I won't be able to stop."

"We don't have to stop, you know. We're going to be mates. We can start right now." His voice had a catch in it, like he'd just run to the top of a mountain.

"I want to do it the Shahala way."

"Oh, please, let's just do it! It doesn't matter how!" He could no more control the choke in his voice than he could stop his desire.

"It matters to me," she said. "Since I was a little girl, I've watched the Mating Dance and pretended *I* was being carried into the night by my mate ... by you, my handsome, brave Sun River."

He sighed. Defeated, his breathing evened.

"At the Autumn Feast," she said in a dreamy voice, "on the Night of Balance, with the spirits of unborn little ones gathered for moonrise, waiting to catch moonbeams to their mothers' hearts ... Kai El, that's when I want to make love for the first time, like lovers have since the Misty Time."

She was right. More than that, she had a woman's power of "no."

"We'll do it your way," he said. "But could we kiss again sometime?"

She smiled. "Let's try now. It may be dangerous, but we're strong."

Their lips touched. He tried holding back, keeping it light, but the kiss grew of its own will. It threatened to engulf them, push them down on the sleeping shelf, force them where they didn't want to go. How could this power be fought? Why should it be?

Her voice was ripe with promise as she pushed him away.

"Wait, Kai El. The cliffs won't crumble if we don't, but it will be so much better if we do. It's already late summer. We can stop ourselves for two moons, can't we? And then . . . oh, my love, we'll belong to each other forever."

He didn't say what he *wanted* to say, but what he *had* to say.

"I'll do anything for you, Gaia. Even wait."

He tied his pledge band to her upper arm, as his Shahala ancestors had done since the Misty Time, then stood back to admire her.

"The best-made pledge band for the best-made woman, ever in all of time!"

A blush lit her dark gold cheeks. Her eyes were like mist before dawn. She reached under her hair with both hands, and untied leather thongs. Holding out her beautiful neckpiece, Gaia spoke as no woman ever had.

"This is my pledge band for you, Kai El. I want you for my mate."

Pledge bands were made by *men*. They promised not only love, but strength and courage—promises no woman could make. But these were the times and this was the place for *new* ways, even if their fathers and mothers might not understand.

Kai El took Gaia's offering, held it in his hands, gazed at every detail. He'd never seen another like it.

Some people wore beads on a string long enough to go over the head, or a special stone on a thong. His mother told of a blue neckstone Kai El had had as a baby, carved by Tor with his namesign, somehow lost. Now he didn't wear things that dangled. They could become snagged, get a man in trouble.

Gaia's neckband was different. It clung tight to the throat, held by leather thongs tied in the back. There were three rows of smooth-carved lengths of white bone, with polished beads of blue stone in between. A flat, round river stone rested in the dip of the throat. The stone's polished black face was scratched with four pointed white lines—the symbol of the Four Directions.

"It's beautiful," he said in awe, handing it back. "Will you put it on for me?" He leaned forward and lifted his hair.

She put it up to his neck. It reached halfway around. She smiled and said, "It will never go around that huge neck."

Gaia tied her band to his upper arm. Kai El felt what men had never been allowed to feel, as the band of love and power became part of him, like his skin or his heart.

That night in Teahra Village, people cheered to hear of the pledge of Gaia and Kai El.

Only two moons till the Autumn Feast . . .

# CHAPTER 50

Gaia knew she would always remember how wonderful the rest of that summer was as she waited to become Kai El's mate. The sounds, colors, and smells of crisp mornings and warm afternoons. The warmth inside her when they looked at each other. Their long talks—at the village, because she was afraid she'd give in to passion if they were alone. Awake or asleep, she dreamed of the life and love they would share: things she'd do for him; the comfortable place she'd make of their home; the little ones she would have.

Kamiulka, the Autumn Feast, finally arrived—three days and nights for celebrating beginnings. Gaia cared most about the first night, and the mating ceremony.

In the gray light before dawn, she had watched the First Warriors leave Teahra Village . . . a sight to steal the breath from any unmated woman. The seven best hunters, proud and skilled; handsome in red face paint that spoke of manhood; with spears in their hands, and bear claws hanging around their necks. Most handsome was Sun River, her Kai El. He was one of the youngest, but Gaia could see him telling others what to do—her almost-mate was that smart.

The warriors would return with antelope for the first foods ceremony. The One Drum would begin the songs that people called the heartbeat of the rituals, and the ancient celebration called Kamiulka, the Autumn Feast, would be changing people's lives as it did every time.

It was late afternoon. Gaia wondered if the First Warriors were home yet. She turned toward the village and listened for the drum. But the women's washing place was too far away; all she heard was rivernoise and the laughter of her friends.

Absently stroking the pledge band braided from Kai El's shiny black hair—she never took it off, not even to bathe—she smiled, thinking about how she would look tonight.

Gaia had never thought of her looks until three days ago. She'd dressed in her mating clothes, gone to the Great River, and stared into a quiet pool. She had made a short dress from a rare white cougar fur that Kai El had brought her. White leather fringe sewed to the bottom brushed the ground when she moved. A headdress of swan feathers trailed down her back. She wore knee-high moccasins with winter fox fur around the tops. White against dark gold skin and black hair ... there was no denying the beauty of the creature who looked back at her from the deep water.

Gaia thought about the mating dance, and her heart jumped. Her whole life had been leading to this night. All the men and women of the tribe would dance, but she and Kai El would see only each other. When the drum's slow throb rose to a mad frenzy, Kai El would wrest her from the women pretending to guard her, and carry her to his home in the cliffs. They would make love. Finally ... she would *do* what she'd been dreaming about.

Gaia had a feeling that an unborn spirit was up there in the sky, just waiting to join the new lovers. *Our baby,* she thought, touching her stomach.

"How lucky I am!" she shouted.

Her twin flung a handful of water at her, laughing.

"You'd think you were the only woman who ever got a mate."

Summer warmth lingered in the Great River canyon, as if the migrating geese barked lies. Downriver from Teahra Village, the tall willows that hid the women's washing place were still in full leaf, though the leaves had yellowed. A large flat rock at the water's edge was strewn with capes, skirts, and moccasins.

Five almost-women of fourteen and fifteen summers played

in the waist-deep water, being sillier than usual. They'd bathed together since they were little ones, but it wouldn't be the same after this. After tonight, Gaia and Bree would be women. The others would still be girls.

Sitting on a rock in swirling water, Gaia washed her toes. She was so warm from thinking of Kai El that she barely noticed the autumn-chilled water.

Bree sat on Gaia's rock and hugged her.

"Oh, Gaia! This is our day! I thought I'd be too old to care before it got here!"

"Me too!" Gaia said, as if she'd almost *died* from waiting.

Bree dissolved in giggles. Selah splashed her, and the others joined in. The river exploded in sun-bright drops, the air in girlish shrieks.

Splashing couldn't silence the two almost-brides.

"I'm the happiest woman ever born!" Gaia said.

Bree said, "I'm so happy that pain wouldn't make me cry!"

Tahna said, "Am I the only one sick of these two?"

Nissa yelled, "No!"

Selah made a throwing-up sound.

"They're just jealous," Bree said. "They wish they had men."

Tahna snorted. "I already take care of a mean old woman. Why would I want to take care of a man, too?"

Bree gave Gaia a knowing look. "I expect better rewards from a man, don't you?"

They all laughed. They were only teasing. No one was really jealous.

"Tahna, would you do my hair again?" Gaia asked.

"Yes, little sister."

Water cascading from naked skin, Tahna stepped onto the flat rock at the river's edge and took soap leaves from her waist pouch. Back in the river, she stood behind Gaia, rubbing mashed leaves into her wet hair, using a little too much fingernail on her scalp.

"Owww!"

Tahna dug harder. "You want to be *really* clean for Kai El, don't you?"

Feeling full of mischief, Gaia dived, curled under, grabbed

Tahna's ankles, and pulled her down. Tahna came up sputtering. Sometimes that would make her mad. Today she laughed, and they all laughed with her.

Laughter changed to terrified screams as two men pounced from the brush, grabbed the girls, and threw them down, thrashing and choking in the churning water.

Gaia ran on the slippery riverbottom. A hand seized her ankle. She pitched forward and cracked her head on a rock. Red light flashed behind her eyelids. She sucked in water. Yanked up by her hair—gasping, coughing—she was slammed into Bree. A rope whipped around their arms, and another around their waists, so if one fell, the other would too. Dragged through water and onto the bank, jerked to her feet, she was shoved forward in a jolting run—without ever seeing her attacker.

In front of her, another man forced Selah and Nissa down the trail.

Glancing back, she saw Tahna running away.

"Tahna! Help us!" she screamed.

Gaia was spun around, and punched in the face. She reeled, but the rope kept her from going down. With savage roughness, she and Bree were thrust after the others.

The fear of beating stopped Gaia from screaming. Bree sobbed. Jerking her hair, the savage showed her a wad of leather. But Bree couldn't stop, and he crammed it into her mouth. Branches whipped Gaia's face and cut bleeding scratches in her naked skin. Rocks cut her bare feet. The savage pushed faster than they could go. She stumbled, taking Bree down with her. He yanked them up. She tried to slow them by limping, but he kicked her, making her run. He knew as well as she did that someone must be after them.

On the trail ahead, Selah and Nissa were kicked and punched if they cried or struggled.

Terror consumed Gaia. *Where are they taking us? What will they do to us?*

*Tahna ran for help,* she told herself. *Kai El is coming. He knows this land. These men don't. He'll catch them. He'll save us.*

They came to a sandy beach. A large, flat *thing* floated in the river, made of trees lashed together with rope. Hope drained from Gaia. Her mother had seen these things. They carried men on water. Kai El would not be able to follow when it carried her away.

Now she knew: These men were Masat. Instead of a bride, Gaia would be a slave.

She yelled, "Fight!" Struck in the head, she kept yelling. "Fight for your lives!"

The savages dragged the four screaming, struggling women to the raft, threw them down, beat them into silence. One hauled on a rope and brought up a rock that held the raft in place. The other pushed with a pole against the shore.

Then they were out in the river, rolling and lurching. Gaia cowered on her stomach, stupefied with terror. Caught in an eddy, the raft spun round and round. The savages struggled to straighten it with their poles.

*So many times I thought I would die. This time I know it.*

With the thought, a strange calm settled on Gaia. Maybe they did not *all* have to die. Maybe she could save the others.

The men were too busy to see her untie the bindings holding her to the unconscious Bree. She got to her knees, glanced at the blurred shore from the spinning raft, and almost lost her balance.

Now what? The savages, used to traveling on water, stood on the raft with legs planted like tree trunks in a windstorm. She couldn't kneel without falling off. How could she overpower them?

The spinning of the raft slowed as the men pushed it out of the strong current toward calmer water near the shore. Once they got it under control, they'd be able to concentrate on the women. Gaia's chance would be gone.

She would give them something important to worry about—right now. She attacked the ropes that held the raft together—nothing but woven grass stems—working her fingers in, jerking, pulling, ripping them apart. A large piece of wood broke loose, then another.

Struck from behind, she tumbled into the water between the pieces of wood. A man caught the rope around her waist and pulled. Her head, shoulders, and arms came up.

But Gaia didn't climb onto the raft. She took a huge breath, grabbed the savage's neckpiece, and dived. Down he came, into a world with no air, a world Gaia understood.

She wrapped her hand around a rope dangling from the bottom of the raft. The water churned as he kicked and clawed her, but she barely noticed the pain. She tightened her grip, twining fingers and wrist through the leather strap around his neck. His eyes popped with terror. Looking into them, she thought, *I know about staying alive without air. Do you?*

She shoved under his chin, banging his head on the bottom of the raft. His thrashing in the roiling water became aimless, crazy. He didn't have a chance. Panic would drown him.

*Just a little longer ... I can do it ... the Breath Ogre taught me.*

The raft thudded into a tree that had fallen over the river. Gaia saw black branches through dark water. She let go of the rope she'd been holding, and locked herself around a branch.

The struggles of the drowning man weakened.

*Air, Gaia! Get to the air!*

She felt him being pulled from above.

*Dung! He was almost dead.*

Her body begged for air, but she held on tight.

The pulling stopped. The other man hit the water. Through the branches, Gaia saw the river sweep him away.

*They pushed him in! We're free!*

Under the raft, entangled in branches, she kicked the limp savage, but her hand was trapped in his neckpiece. She clawed at the strap—

With her last breath, Gaia cried out in the dark water.

"Kai El—"

# CHAPTER 51

TEAHRA WARRIORS AT HIS HEELS, KAI EL BURST ONTO the sandy beach. He saw three women—crouched, naked, weeping loudly.

"Gaia!" he cried.

The women moved away. Gaia lay on her back, eyes closed, pale flesh battered and bruised.

Kai El thrust his fists to the sky and howled.

"No-o-o-o—"

He fell to his knees, put his arm beneath her shoulders, and lifted her. Her head fell back. She was so cold. He ripped off his leather shirt and covered the nakedness that she wouldn't want others to see. Clutching her to his chest, he rocked back and forth.

"No, no, no," he wept, his face buried in her wet hair.

Jud put his arm around Kai El's shoulders.

"Let's go home, brother."

Kai El picked up the body of his woman and did as he was told. His dreams were dead, his life over. He felt as dead as the woman he carried in his arms. He barely heard the cry that went up when he walked into Teahra Village.

"Bring her to my hut," Tenka said. "She must be prepared to meet the spirits."

He didn't want to give her up, but Tenka took his arm and led him to the Moonkeeper's hut.

The wailing outside sounded like the moaning of spirits.

Kai El placed Gaia on the furs of Tenka's bed. He knelt beside her and laid his head on her breast. Silent tears ran from his eyes.

He felt Tenka's hand on his shoulder.

"Kai El, I need to be alone with her now. Do you want to keep her pledge band?"

"No. She'd want to take it with her to the otherworld."

He kissed Gaia's hand and laid it across her breast. He gazed for the last time at her beautiful face. His heart broke. The pieces fell out on the floor of the Moonkeeper's hut, and he left them lying there.

Shocked, confused, in unbearable pain, Kai El wanted to be alone. But it was the way of his people to comfort one another, and he wasn't strong enough to resist their efforts. They surrounded him, wept with him, talked to him.

"Gaia died to save the others. She's the bravest woman we have ever known. She will never be forgotten."

"It isn't how or when you die," they said. "It is how you lived your life."

But Kai El could only stare into the nightfire, thinking, *If I had run faster . . .*

They covered him, and stayed with him, and finally he slept.

He awoke to keening from the ceremonial ground.

*It's true. She is dead.* Raw pain shredded him, choked him, crushed him. He wanted to run to her, hold her one more time.

No. He couldn't bear to see his beloved lying on blackened stone, wrapped in white leather, waiting to be burned.

Jud tried to stop him from leaving Teahra Village. He failed.

"Good-bye, my spirit brother," Kai El said. "I don't know when you'll see me again. If ever."

He went to the home in the cliffs that he'd made for Gaia. He packed food, skins, furs, and weapons, and started out across the prairie in the direction Where Day Ends.

# CHAPTER 52

WHEN THE SAVAGES ATTACKED THE WOMEN'S WASHING place, Tahna fled without looking back. She slipped on the riverbottom, but didn't fall; scrambled over rocks and through bushes, running for home.

"Tahna! Help!"

Gaia's scream stopped Tahna's blind dash. She turned, and froze. Her sister and friends had been caught. Two men were forcing them down the trail.

As Tahna stared in horror, Gaia's captor punched her. He turned and glared at Tahna, as if he might come after her, then shoved the stumbling women ahead of him.

Overwhelmed with panic, she thought, *I can't fight two men! I'm lucky I got away!* She told her legs to run, run, *run* for home, but her feet were stuck to the ground. She stood there watching until they were out of sight, then control of her body returned, and she ran screaming to the village.

Teahra warriors went after the stolen women. Tahna wanted to go with them, but she couldn't. She had to take care of her mother.

Tsilka went berserk.

"My baby!" she screeched. "My Tsagaia!"

"The warriors will find her, Mother. They'll bring her back."

Tahna tried to sound calm, but her insides quivered like a clutch of frog eggs. Her eyes were ready to spout tears. Her throat felt squeezed; it was hard to breathe . . . *Like when the Breath Ogre gets Gaia,* she thought.

*Oh please let them find her!* Tahna prayed to Sahalie. *Please bring my sister back!*

Howling, "My baby! My baby!" her mother, who had not been out of her bed in moons, leapt up and threw on a robe.

"Mother, stop!"

Tahna tried to hold her. Tsilka pushed her away and dashed out of the hut. Running to a group of women who were consoling each other, she broke in yelling.

"It's the Masat! I know where they live! Give me a spear!"

Tahna ran behind her, grabbed her arm, tried to pull her away.

"Mother, come back!"

Tsilka slapped her.

"No! They took my baby! I'm going after them! Give me a spear!"

The Moonkeeper Tenka came, seized the crazed woman by the shoulders, and shook her violently.

"Tsilka! Go back to your hut and wait. You're too weak even to be standing here."

As if remembering that it was true, Tsilka slumped. Tahna caught her under an arm and helped her back to the hut.

And they waited.

Tahna knew the moment her twin died. Deep inside, part of her tore loose and was wrenched out with agonizing pain, leaving a gaping hole, all bloody and raw; as if an invisible hand plunged through her chest and ripped out her heart. She cried out and fainted.

Tahna felt crazy for a time. She was not alone. Shock and fear ran wild in the village. To think that such a thing could happen! Warriors guarded the village by day and night. Even so, people did not feel safe.

Tahna blamed herself for Gaia's death. She should *not* have panicked, should *not* have left her sister. She *should* have gone after the savages herself, not run to the village for help.

Horrible memories stuck in her mind. She couldn't think of anything else. The savages bursting from the bushes, leaping for the screaming women. Fleeing in terror. Gaia's cry for help. Looking back, seeing her twin being kicked and stumbling down the river trail. Over and over, Tahna remembered how she'd stood there stupefied, how she could not move. If she had moved sooner, would Gaia still be alive?

People said it wasn't her fault. The Moonkeeper Tenka had a talk with her. Even Tsilka, who was drowning in a mother's grief, did not blame her. But Tahna could not stop blaming herself; her guilt was a crushing weight.

She had wild thoughts, like, *Isn't it nice that half of you can experience death without the other half dying?*

And, *Now I'm not even half a person.*

Sometimes she thought sorrow would kill her. She would drown in tears or die from pain. Tahna missed Gaia, wanted so much to be with her again.

Spending most of her time in the hut, brooding and grieving, near her mother but not *with* her, Tahna barely noticed as crisp gold autumn changed to cold gray winter.

The first snowflakes drifted through still air. Ignoring her mother's angry, then pitiful, protests at being left alone, Tahna went to a sheltered place against the cliffs. Watching the snow waft down, she thought peacefully of nothing, until darkness made her go home.

In the morning, the snow was still falling. It was ankle-deep, and light as powdered herbs. Tahna made a fire and took care of her mother's needs.

Dressed in warm furs, she fluffed through the snow toward the sheltered sitting place, swept off a rock, put a fur down, and sat gazing at the village. The skin around her eyes felt stretched, as if other eyes watched through them.

All the colors were gone under white, except for dark splashes here and there—people, bits of sheltered ground, edges of rock slabs. The huts were smooth white mounds with smoke coming from their tops.

With puffs following them, little ones ran among the huts through the fresh snow; sliding, making sharp turns, diving face first, shrieking and laughing. They used the pebble-pouch in a different way—one throwing it, the others going after it. Their fur boots were caked, their skin red from cold, but they were having too much fun to notice. People came out to watch them play for a while, then went back inside snow-heaped huts to get warm.

Phoomf!

The roofskins of Chaka's hut gave way, dumping snow on his family. They were frightened, but not hurt. Women helped his mate get the snow out of her hut. Men helped him restring the roofskins. They swept snow from other roofs.

Tahna watched everything, but she felt separated from it . . . as if she were watching it from another time, or another place, or . . . she couldn't explain it.

The snow fell and fell. In the afternoon, when it was up to their knees, the last of the little ones had had enough, and went in their huts.

Only Tahna was left in the white silence. The air was still and very cold, but something that didn't want to leave kept her warm. It was very bright, as if the sun were out. The sky was almost as white as the snow. The flowing river was shiny white . . . everything so still . . .

Gaia appeared before Tahna.

She gave off golden light . . . pulsing, shimmering light so bright that the white world around her paled to gray. Her face beamed joy and peace. Black hair flowed over her shoulders. Golden leather draped her tall body. Her bare feet floated above the snow. She held out her arms in love.

Tahna held her breath. She had never seen anything so beautiful.

Gaia spoke in her mind.

"We were one before we were born. Now we are one again."

Tahna felt the empty place inside her filling. The vision of her twin faded.

The last wisp of Gaia spoke.

"You are whole, Tahna. At last, you are whole."

And Tahna knew that she was.

People missed Gaia's shy sweetness, but they hadn't known her well, because she wanted it that way. More than grief, they felt wonder at what she had done to save the others, and a great love that they'd never known during her life. Three young women were still with their families because of her sacrifice.

The memory of Gaia's brief, heroic life was on its way to becoming tribal legend.

Kai El—who had left after Gaia died, and had not been seen since—was another matter. The tribe had come to need him more than it realized. It was true that he'd spent too much time by himself, but what could they expect from the son of Tor? The Moonkeeper Tenka had relied on Kai El to help make decisions and settle arguments. He had his father's hunting skills, and more of his mother's wisdom than he knew. He could tell when herds would move, when weather would change, and many other things the tribe missed now that he was gone.

That Kai El was gone by choice angered and hurt them. They thought the son of Tor and Ashan cared more for them than that. Men argued about when and where to hunt. Sometimes they didn't hunt at all, but sat in their huts glowering, making their mates bring them this and that. A fistfight between two men threatened to spread to others. The Moonkeeper's words didn't stop them. She had to throw her body between them. Not since Elia died had men of Teahra Village struck each other.

Cold weather sickness swept through the village. Bodies ached, heads throbbed, tempers flared.

The overwhelmed Moonkeeper came to see Tahna.

"I need your help," Tenka said. "Ashan was teaching you medicine. I should have continued after she died, but I could never find the time. Now I must. There is more than I can do alone. I want you to move to the Moonkeeper's hut. I'll take you with me when I go to see people, so you, and they, will get used to it."

Tahna stood with her mouth open. Would she someday be a Moonkeeper after all?

"Well, do you want to?"

"Yes! I do!"

Closing her ears to her mother's ranting, Tahna moved her things to the Moonkeeper's hut. She felt guilty . . . it was *so good* to get away from Tsilka.

Since Gaia's death, Tsilka had been lost in a world that existed only in her mind. Half of what she said made no sense. Sometimes she awoke screaming. Sometimes she huddled against the hut wall with the eyes of doomed prey. She refused to go out, even for body needs.

Tahna went to see her twice a day. She fed and washed her, but there was nothing more she could do for her mother.

People allowed Tahna to work on their bodies, since they knew that Ashan had taught her medicine. Her hands were sure, her medicine was good, and they felt better when she left. But when it came to settling disputes, they said she was just a girl, and wouldn't listen to her.

Gaia's spirit did not appear to Tahna again, but she never forgot her words. They were so true. Her body, her mind, her entire being knew it. When her twin died, Tahna became the *whole* person she'd always dreamed of being. Complete, full, nothing missing. Gaia was what had been missing . . . Gaia, the other half, split away at birth . . . now they were reunited, one creature again.

Tahna became more than she had ever been. She knew it was because of what Gaia—who lived inside her now—gave to her. Unselfishness. Love. A way of looking at things that made them seem promising rather than hopeless, beautiful rather than ugly. Tahna worked hard, was patient with stupidity and anger. People saw that there was more to her than they'd thought, and began asking for her.

As her helper strengthened, the Moonkeeper slacked, but who could blame her? Poor Tenka was exhausted.

It was a hard winter for the people of Teahra Village, with deep snow, fear of attack, and uneasy peace among themselves.

Tahna often thought of Kai El.

*Curse you for leaving when we need you most. Just like your worthless father, Tor.*

# CHAPTER 53

BITTER, UGLY, AND ALONE, TSILKA HAD TOO MUCH time for thinking, and nothing good to think about. Only bad memories remained. Pain, humiliation, loneliness, and loss . . . life had poisoned Tsilka with enough for ten women.

Alone, alone, alone.

No more Tor to hate and love.

No more beautiful Gaia.

And now Tahna was gone. Her excuse? That stupid Moonkeeper Tenka needed help.

Tsilka despised the very word "Moonkeeper." Ashan had ruined most of her life. Now Tenka was ruining the rest by taking Tahna. Tsilka saw her daughter only twice a day. It was like having two drops of water left after your whole lake has been stolen.

This morning, the girl smiled and chatted as she stoked the fire and heated ground fish with special herbs that her mother liked. While Tsilka ate the tasty mush, Tahna took the sleeping skins outside, shook them, and smoothed them back in place. She laid out a clean dress for her mother, talking in a chirpy voice. Tsilka listened and forgot the words as soon as Tahna said them, because another part of her mind was busy watching the daughter she loved. The girl pretended they had all day together. But her mother knew she was in a hurry to be back with the Moonkeeper.

Tahna made sure there was enough food and water, and put a stack of wood by the fire.

"There. That's enough for today."

Those were the words that came before "good-bye."

"Don't go," Tsilka said, disliking the pleading in her voice, but unable to stop it.

"Mother, I have work to do. Many others need me today."

"I need you, daughter."

"You have everything you need. I've seen to that."

"I need you ... to talk to."

"If you need to talk, you should get up and visit someone."

"I'm not strong enough to walk. You know that."

"Then maybe you should think of moving to one of the old people's huts."

It felt like her daughter was choking her.

"The old people's huts stink," Tsilka said.

"Do you have any idea how this place smells? If you would open the doorskin once in a while and let some air in here—"

"It's too cold."

"Mother, I have go to now." Tahna leaned down. "Give me a kiss."

Tsilka turned her face away.

"I don't feel like kissing you."

"Then I will see you later. Good-bye."

The air in the hut was thick and smelled bad after Tahna left. Tsilka grumbled to herself.

"We don't need Moonkeepers. We never did. We should go back to the old ways, the way it was when my father lived. Timshin was chief. He did all that Moonkeepers do, and more. I should have followed him as chief. I would have, if not for Ashan."

Tsilka settled into one of her favorite ways of passing time: imagining ways she should have killed Ashan.

In her mind, Tsilka saw the enemy again for the first time: Lying on the riverbank ... unconscious, defenseless, helpless. It would have been so easy to kill her that night. While Tor was at Teahra Village getting people settled, Tsilka should have gone back to where Tenka was alone with Ashan. Tenka was just a girl then. Tsilka should have hit her in the head with a rock. And then killed Ashan.

How different life would have been, how good. Tsilka and Tor would have been mates. They would have been chiefs together. Their little ones would have been raised as brother and sisters. Maybe Gaia would still be alive.

Having tired herself thinking about killing an already-dead woman, Tsilka took a nap. She heard shouting when she awoke.

"Hummingbirds! It's spring!"

She remembered a long-ago time when she looked forward to the arrival of the tiny creatures and their promise of warmer days. First the shimmery green ones came, looking for the early flowers. Fierce brown hummingbirds with shining red throats followed later. They dived at the green birds, trying to keep the flowers for themselves, but soon there were too many flowers to guard. Then the two kinds—alike except for color and temperament—spent the rest of the summer in peace, and flew away with the vultures in autumn.

"The hummingbirds are here!" people shouted. "Come and see!"

Tsilka got up and peered outside. A beautiful day invited her to come farther. She put a robe over her dress, draped a deerskin scarf over the scarred part of her face, and took a fur to sit on. Sunshine penetrated all the way to her bones as she sat leaning against the hut. Nearby bushes showed new green leaves and red flowers. She saw green flashes of hummingbirds and heard the buzz of their wings. Black vultures soared in the stark blue sky.

People went about the work of the day. Tsilka saw them as if from the other side of smoke. They stopped at her hut to visit. Their voices sounded muffled, their questions baffling.

"Isn't the weather fine?"

"It's good to see you. Are you feeling better?"

"Tahna is doing a fine job. Aren't you proud of her?"

She forgot what they said as soon as they said it, too, but thought she answered like an ordinary person would.

After that, Tsilka left her hut on many spring days—sitting at first, then taking walks. The weakness and pain in her body lessened. Her thoughts were just as confused—even mad—but she hid them.

"Oh, Mother," her daughter said every day on her stingy little visits. "I'm so glad you're getting better."

Why would anyone think that a stronger body could help a shattered mind?

When Tsilka emerged from her isolation, she was astonished to find that her surviving daughter had become an important woman in the village. She watched Tahna work, saw respect given to her that Tsilka had always craved. She began to see her daughter as the chief *she* would have been: like Timshin, the great Tlikit chief, and the last; feared and wise; not bothered all the time with spirits. The great Timshin—Tsilka's father, Tahna's grandfather.

Tahna—not Tenka—was the rightful chief of the Tlikit people. Now her mother saw how capable she was. The girl who should be chief should have her mother to pass on Timshin's ways, to pass on what she herself had learned about power. But, no—her mother wasn't with her. Her mother was all alone in this stinking little hut.

*Moonkeepers always have what I should have. Ashan kept Tor and me apart. Now Tenka is keeping Tahna and me apart. It's wrong for someone to do that.*

If Tenka was gone, the people would look to Tahna to take her place. Tsilka would move in with her daughter, into that nice, large Moonkeeper's hut. Everything would be so nice.

If Tenka was gone . . .

"I am done with having my life ruined by Moonkeepers," the bitter, ugly, hateful woman said.

The next day, Tsilka approached the Moonkeeper. She hid quivering excitement under a calm voice.

"Tenka, I found something you should see."

"What?"

"I can't explain. I must show you."

"Where?"

She pointed to the cliffs.

Tenka said, "I wouldn't have thought you could get up there."

"I've been getting stronger."

Tenka shook her head. "I'm too busy. If it's a medicine plant, why don't you bring me some?"

"It's medicine, but not a plant. It isn't something I can bring. I can only show you. You won't believe that it was there all the time and you never saw it."

Tenka's expression said, "crazy old woman."

"Come on, Tenka," she begged. "I promise you will thank me."

"Oh, why not?"

Tsilka led the way up the Moonkeeper's Path, walking slowly, pausing often to rest, her strength still not half what it used to be. She was afraid Tenka would become impatient and go back. But Tenka stayed with her, pleased to see the progress she had made.

"Just two moons ago, you could barely walk," the Moonkeeper said. "Look at you now."

"Hummingbirds and vultures came to set me free," Tsilka said.

Tenka gave her a strange look.

"Well, I'm proud of you, Tsilka. I know it took a lot of work to get your strength back. I know how you grieved for Gaia."

*Oh do you?* Tsilka thought. *Do you know the other things I grieve for?*

But she said, "Yes, it took a lot of work."

High in the cliffs, Tsilka stopped in front of the stone seat where Ashan had disappeared. Her breathing was ragged. Every part of her hurt.

The stone picture loomed over them.

"She Who Watches doesn't frighten you?" Tenka asked.

Tsilka snorted. "It's only a picture on a rock. Come, we must go higher."

"Let's rest until you can breathe easier."

"No!" she snapped. "I'm fine."

She took off again, climbing until she came out at the flat land on top. A fierce wind howled across the open prairie, tearing at her hair and clothes. She leaned into it, walking along the edge, looking over, with the Moonkeeper behind her.

Tsilka said, "Right here. Down over the edge."

Tenka gave her a doubtful look.

"I'm starting to think you made the whole thing up. What could be down there?"

Tsilka thought fast.

"It's a stone that gives off its own light. A red light. I know it is powerful. In the hands of a powerful woman like you, who knows what it could do?"

How could a shaman resist the idea of such a stone? The Moonkeeper edged toward the precipice on her knees.

"I don't see—"

Tsilka kicked her. Tenka screamed, pitched forward, disappeared. A thump and a clatter of falling rocks cut off her scream. The only sound was the howling wind.

Tsilka crept to the edge of the cliff on her hands and knees, and looked down.

The Moonkeeper was coming back up. Tsilka lunged backward, but too late. Tenka grabbed her long hair and tried to haul herself up on it. Tsilka's elbows gave way. Her head smashed down on the rock.

"Let me go!" she screamed, grasping at the rocks with her hands, digging in with her knees against the pull on her hair.

The Moonkeeper hissed, "You evil witch! I'll kill you for this!"

Not strong enough to hold the weight of two, Tsilka was dragged to the edge, and over.

The screams of the two women mingled and died.

People heard the screaming. They found Tsilka's body first, lying broken on the Moonkeeper's Path. Farther up, they found Tenka on the Moonkeeper's stone seat, with a clump of hair clutched in her dead fingers.

Who could ever know what really happened up there?

Tahna thought she did. Evil and good fought, and both lost.

# CHAPTER 54

KAI EL HAD LEFT TEAHRA VILLAGE CARRYING A HEAVY pack of warm clothes; winter was coming. He took dried food for many days; he didn't want to waste time hunting; his weapons would kill humans, not animals. He found that he didn't need much to eat. His body fed on rage.

His anguish over the loss of his beloved could have only one cure: revenge. Gaia had taken her revenge on the ones who killed her. But the savages belonged to a tribe.

The Masat.

Kai El remembered what Tsilka said about them: people who saw no wrong in stealing the loved ones of others, keeping them as slaves, killing them for pleasure, throwing their bodies into endless water to be eaten by giant fish. Kai El was going to find this evil tribe, and kill every man, woman, and little one. People like that did not belong in Amotkan's world.

Even their name was ugly. Masat. It sounded like spitting.

They lived far away in the direction Where Day Ends, at a place where land stopped and water began. Between Kai El and his enemy lay an immense mountain range, the home of Takoma, Pahto, Lu It, Tiyak, and others whose snowy peaks touched the sky and made clouds. Between the great peaks were smaller ones. Together they made a barrier that people believed uncrossable, until Tsilka came back from her travels with Masat warriors.

Rattlesnake Woman said the Great River slashed through

this mountain range on its way to the endless water. She said the *only* way to get to the home of the Masat was to follow the Great River—a difficult, dangerous journey. Tsilka told of long times with no shore to walk on; rugged cliffs; deep gorges; vast rock slides; and many wild rivers to cross.

It would be slow to follow the Great River, and Kai El was in a hurry for his revenge. There must be other passages through the mountain range. He traveled on the high plateau where the going was easy and fast, catching sight of the distant river now and then. The plateau with its yellow autumn grass rose to hills where scattered trees were losing their leaves. Foothills rose to forested mountain slopes. Kai El did not see the Great River again. Another, higher mountain loomed beyond each mountain he climbed. Every day was colder than the one before.

The first snowstorm caught him by surprise—though there was no reason why it should have. His soulmate died on the first day of the Autumn Feast—ten and seven days ago, as his counted fingers told him many times a day. Winter followed autumn. The seasons didn't stop for death, any more than Kai El had.

The snowstorm was not a pretty or a peaceful thing. Wind howled down the mountain, blowing sharp, heavy flakes that stung his flesh. Head down, leaning into the wind, into the rising slope of the land, he plunged through ever-deeper snow until he could go no farther in the blinding, shrieking white.

Kai El huddled beneath a cedar tree, shivering in his bison robe. How stupid he'd been in his blind chase after revenge. Maybe these mountains could be crossed in summer, but not in winter. He would just freeze to death up here, and the evil Masat would go about their evil ways.

Well, then, he would try Tsilka's way, find the Great River and follow it . . . if this storm ever stopped . . . if this mountain gave him another chance . . .

He thought about the Masat to keep his blood boiling so he wouldn't freeze.

*I will kill every man, woman, and little one! Stamp them out as if they were a hill of ants! Chase down every last one!*

For now Kai El didn't worry about how one man would do this. For now it would be enough just to get there.

The blizzard went on. The sagging branches of the cedar dumped snow on him. The wind seemed to go right through his bison fur. Kai El shivered uncontrollably. His teeth chattered so hard he thought they would break.

With frozen hands and a stick, he dug a hole in a deep drift—a snow cave just high enough to sit in and wide enough to lie in. He covered it over with a thick layer of boughs, got in, and the blizzard sealed it.

In the dark, silent womb, cold and exhaustion conspired to drain off the rage he needed for revenge. Thoughts of Gaia leaked through ... his beloved Gaia ... never to be talked to, touched, held in his arms. Never again. Sorrow filled the hole inside him where rage had been. Kai El wept, holding her necklace to his face.

He didn't know how many days he had been in the snow shelter before he dug himself out. The sunshine made him squint at first, but it was beautiful, sparkling on the white world. The cold air was deliciously fresh after the stale air he'd been breathing.

Not knowing where he would go or what he would do, Kai El struggled back down the mountains through snow that, at first, reached his chest.

As he walked across a rocky ridge where the snow was as deep as his knees, he found the entrance to a cave. He went in with his spear ready. In the near-dark, he heard a deep rumble: the breathing of a bear, asleep for winter. He speared the beast, and it died without waking. He cut up the meat and put it outside where it would freeze. It was much more than he would eat that winter.

Days slipped by in the snug cave. Kai El did only what he had to do to keep warm and fed, not noticing the passing of time much more than the bear would have.

Searing rage had turned to sorrow. Sorrow's unbearable pain had given way to numbness. Now he felt hard inside, frozen up, like his heart was solid ice. He would sit and hold the necklace Gaia had given him, but no tears got through the ice. So he told himself that feeling nothing was better than feeling pain.

For all the numbness of his days, Kai El's nights were busy with dreams. Sometimes he ran and fought, but could not save Gaia from an awful fate. In other dreams they were together. She would say that it was all a mistake, she wasn't dead, and he'd scoop her into his arms and run, not touching the ground. These were the dreams that made him feel the worst when he awoke—cruel lies that they were.

One night Kai El dreamed that he was standing on a rock-strewn cliff above the Great River. He dreamed he saw his mother walking toward him, holding out her arms. They hugged long and hard.

"Look," Ashan said.

Kai El looked down. Ice covered the Great River.

His mother's voice was sad.

"The river is blocked. It can't move." She picked up a rock. "We should break the ice and get it moving again."

She lobbed the rock over the cliff. It dropped slowly, hit the ice and cracked it. She picked up another rock and handed it to Kai El. He threw it, and a crack jagged off from the first. They stood side by side, raining rocks down on the frozen river. The ice broke up and floated away.

Mother and son picked up the last rock together, and cast it over the side together. The last of the ice was gone. The river flowed free again. She hugged him, then turned and walked away.

Kai El remembered the dream with perfect clarity. He knew what it meant. His mother was telling him that the hardness inside him—the ice—was bad. She would help him break it up, help him get moving again. But he would also have to help himself. He would have to allow himself to feel, even the bad things. If he would not feel pain, then he could never feel pleasure.

Kai El held Gaia's necklace to his face, closed his eyes, and called up pictures of her into his mind. He felt something wrap around him, a slight warmth, and he imagined that it was his mother's arms. Tears came hot and blinding. After they stopped, he felt washed.

When the snow melted for the last time and green things burst to life outside the bear cave, Kai El felt life within himself.

His feet yearned to travel. But where?

Not through the great mountain range and on to the endless water. Winter had killed autumn's passion for revenge.

Not to Teahra Village, where everything would remind him of Gaia.

Kai El thought about the ancient home of his people. The Shahala homeland lay in the direction Colder, on the other side of a smaller range called the tabu mountains. He'd left there as a little one too young to remember. All he knew was what people said, and it sounded like a good place.

He wondered if other people lived in the Valley of Grandmothers now. He knew he would never mate—his soulmate was dead, and Kai El was like Samar, the goose who mates for life—but he might find a new tribe to belong to. There would never be another Gaia, but there was still life to be lived.

When hummingbirds told the coming of spring, Kai El set off to find the home of his ancestors, leaving much of his burden of grief in the bear cave. Opening up to the lushness of spring, he carried his furs on travel poles instead of wearing them, walked barefoot on green grass, found himself singing with throngs of returning bluebirds. Traveling purposefully, eating well, his young body responded with strength.

His thoughts of Gaia were less often about her loss, more often about good things he remembered, happy things, the sweetness of the love they'd known. He talked to her, and didn't mind that he sensed no answer; spirits led very busy lives.

Not that he didn't miss Gaia, and long for her. But it felt as though he could live without her. He told himself that they'd be together again in the otherworld.

# CHAPTER 55

K<small>AI</small> E<small>L FELT HE WAS BEING GUIDED BY AN UNSEEN</small> force—the same force that had led him, as a little one on his power quest, to sacred ground. Now it pulled him in a straight line, to the direction between Colder and Where Day Begins, across the spring-green prairie, into the tabu mountains.

On a mid-spring morning, Kai El crested a hill. Before him spread the valley of the grandfather Ehr, where he had lived with his mother so long ago.

"I don't believe it!" he shouted, jumping around like an excited child.

He ran down the hill to the river he and Ehr used to fish in, crossed it on a log that was still there, walked up the creek that ran into the river, past the pool where he used to feed animals. He climbed the slippery rocks to the waterfall and splashed into the Home Cave.

Kai El smelled the old good smells, saw the rays of light coming from above, heard the water dripping into the pool . . .

He saw movement from a dark recess and readied his spear.

A man stepped from the shadows.

"My son?"

"Father?"

Kai El dropped his spear, rushed to Tor, and threw his arms around him, hugging him so hard he lifted the old man off his feet.

"Father! How can this be?"

Tor gasped. Kai El put him down.

"I thought you were dead! I saw a horse carry you into the sky!"

"A horse? No, son. I . . . I just walked away one night."

Kai El was furious.

"How could you? I needed you!"

"I just couldn't stand it anymore."

"If you'd been there, maybe Gaia would still be alive!"

"Gaia?"

"She's dead."

Moaning, "Oh, no . . ." Tor put his head in his hands, sunk to his knees, and sobbed. The depth of his despair took Kai El's anger away. They held each other and cried for Gaia. Tor exhausted himself and slept. Occasional sobs shook his body but didn't wake him.

*How old he looks,* the young man thought. *How frail. How crushed to hear of Gaia's death.*

Kai El didn't sleep that night. As first light peeked through the roof of the Home Cave, he made a fire. He took dry berries and honey from the storage place—impressed by all the food his father had stored—and heated water with stones to make berry mush.

As he stirred the mush, his eyes feasted. His mother had called it the Home Cave. He always thought of it as Ehr's cave, though the beloved old grandfather died when Kai El was only three or four summers.

The sloping sides disappeared in shadow. The roof, taller than four or five men, was pierced by several holes that let in shafts of light, and gave smoke a place to go out. Water trickled from a hole in the center into a small pool. The water came from a creek that ran along the ground over the cave. His mother called it Silent Creek because it made no sound until it dropped over the waterfall that hid the cave entrance.

Kai El loved the sound of the waterfall. It was as much a part of Ehr's cave as the roof or floor, a soft splashing that had soothed him as he went to sleep.

Morning light touched the painting place, a smooth wall covered with pictures that Ehr had spent a lifetime making. Pictures that looked like the animals whose spirits they captured, their lines so graceful it seemed they might leap from the stone. Horses, wolves, and bears. A woman with lightning streaking from her head, holding a snake in one hand, releasing a bird from the other.

There was the picture that Kai El, perched on his mother's shoulders, had finished after Ehr's death—a cougar had killed the old man before he could complete it.

Tor awoke in the soft morning light.

"My son," he said in a voice full of wonder. "You really are here."

"I am."

The old man's face fell as he remembered the rest.

"And Gaia is dead."

"I'm sorry, Father. She is."

Tor crossed his arms over his chest, breathed deep, and blocked the flood of emotions that wanted out. Kai El didn't know why Gaia's death had so devastated his father, but the devastation was obvious. Tor tried to gain control of himself. Kai El saw that he was still a strong man, in the way that mattered.

Face set in grim lines, Tor asked, "How did she die?"

"It was the first day of the Autumn Feast. We would have become mates that night." Kai El sighed. "Gaia was at the women's washing place with Tahna and some others . . ."

He told the story, finishing with, ". . . and then she dived from the raft, taking the savages with her. She swam to the bottom, and held them until they died. But it took too long. She—she couldn't make it back in time."

Both men sucked in air to think what Gaia had felt.

Tor spoke after a long silence.

"The other girls—what happened to them?"

"They got the raft to the shore. They were saved."

"So Tahna is safe?"

"Tahna got away at the beginning. She ran to the village for help."

That night, Tor did the comforting. Kai El hadn't cried all his tears after all.

"I loved her so much. Why was she taken before we even began?"

"I'm sorry, son. I have no answers. For myself, I learned to stop asking questions. It becomes easier after that."

"But I'll never have a family. No mate, no sons, no daughters. We were soulmates, like you and mother, and when your soulmate dies . . ."

"I know, Kai El. I am sorry."

That night the son, exhausted from crying, slept in his father's arms.

The Spirit of Ashan entered the Home Cave, chasing out stale air, bringing in freshness and energy like a thunderstorm.

Tor's skin tingled as she slipped over him. How he loved it when she came to him like this.

"My love," he said softly.

He felt the sweet expanding as she came inside him. With his son in his arms and his mate a part of him, Tor felt complete as he had not for so long.

He whispered, "Thank you for bringing our son to me. Now I can live out my days in comfort and peace."

. . . *I brought him for you to heal. Then he must return to the people* . . .

"Oh," Tor said with a sigh. "I can do that, if you tell me what he needs."

. . . *He needs to know who Gaia really was* . . .

Tor groaned.

. . . *I forgave you long ago, but our son will never be free unless you tell him* . . .

"But he will hate me. He might kill me."

. . . *I would not blame him. You must take that chance* . . .

"I can't, Ashan. I love him too much."

. . . *You must because you love him* . . .

Tor knew she was right.

"Kai El," Tor said in the morning, "when you hear what I have to say, I fear you will hate me. If you kill me, I will understand, and forgive you."

"I don't hate you for pretending to be dead, for making me grieve. What could be worse than that?"

Tor took a deep breath.

"You and Gaia shared the same blood. She was your sister, not your soulmate."

Kai El reeled as if he'd been punctured with a spear.

"I don't believe you! You're crazy!"

"It's true. Gaia and Tahna are my daughters."

His son slumped to the floor of the cave.

"Oh, Amotkan . . ." he moaned.

Tor didn't go to him. He had inflicted this pain. His arms would only make it worse.

The explosion of rage he expected never came. Kai El listened silently, never looking in his eyes, as Tor told the story of how he'd been young and stupid and become Tsilka's lover. He hadn't known about the twins until the tribes met at the Great River. He couldn't tell Ashan, no matter how he wanted to. He forced Tsilka to keep the secret. And the twins grew up never knowing that they had a father.

Finally Kai El spoke. His voice was bitter.

"And I grew up and fell in love with my own sister. We laughed at ancient laws, played with the wrath of spirits, without ever knowing what we were doing. How could you not tell me then?"

"I was too weak," Tor said. "I prayed that something would stop it."

Kai El's eyes flashed.

"Gaia's death stopped it. Did you pray for that?"

"No, son, no. I loved her. You have to believe that. I loved all of you. I couldn't bear the thought of you hating me. That's the reason I never told you."

Without another word, Kai El took his things and left.

*As I did to him,* thought the bereft old man, much more alone now than he'd been before.

# CHAPTER 56

*I HAVE LOST GAIA TWICE,* KAI EL THOUGHT, TRAVELING again toward Shahala lands. *First her beautiful living self. Now my memories of what we were to each other.*

*Don't believe it, Kai El. Tor is a crazy old man.*

He tried to think of his father that way—wandering off, living by himself, getting crazier all the time, until one day he thought up this story, and blurted it out to the first person he saw, who happened to be his son.

Kai El had wild ideas of going to Teahra Village and choking the truth out of Rattlesnake Woman. But no—he never wanted to see that place again.

His heart knew the truth. Disbelief was an attempt to hide from the pain of loss. Only nineteen summers, Kai El knew the ways of grief. *First you don't believe it, then you want to kill, then you want to die. Then you move forward, and find that it has stayed behind.*

He wanted to hate Tor, to blame him for every hurt ever suffered. But it didn't work. Tor had been a good father, at least to him. Kai El's life had been good, until Gaia died.

He certainly couldn't blame his father for that—unless he blamed *Tor's blood* for giving her courage to sacrifice her life for others—the very blood that flowed in Kai El's own body.

What could he blame his father for? Being human?

Tor regretted his mistakes. He had suffered for them, and

he wasn't done suffering. What could be worse than dying alone?

Days away from Ehr's cave, Kai El stood on a hilltop.

"I forgive you, Father," he shouted.

Maybe Tor would sense it.

Kai El's feelings about Gaia were not so clear. He couldn't believe that he hadn't known. If it was so wrong to love your sister, why wasn't there some way to tell? He searched every memory of her for the thing that might have told him, but there was nothing. He searched memories of Tahna, his *other* sister, and there was nothing there either.

Feelings of shame tried to creep up in him ... *you held your sister in your arms, kissed her, dreamed of making love.*

"No," he told himself. "Ignorance made us innocent. How could what we did have been wrong? She was the purest creature Amotkan ever sent to the world. She was incapable of wrong."

Kai El vowed to allow nothing to spoil the memory of their love.

Once more he began to think of finding a new tribe. *And maybe,* he thought with a lump in his throat, *a new mate.* If Gaia was not his soulmate, then his soulmate was still out there somewhere, waiting for him, looking for him.

Kai El found the home of his ancestors. He'd left the Valley of Grandmothers as a small child, but he remembered the mountains on one side, the sweeping plains on the other, where they said herds of horses once grazed. After exploring for several days, he came upon a group of sunken places in the ground—all that remained of the village called Anutash. It was a strange, beautiful, lonely place: full of memories that were not his; of almost-heard laughter and weeping; of spirits.

That night, as he slept where his ancestors had once thrived, the Spirit of Ashan brought Kai El and Tahna together in a dream.

He dreamed that he entered a hut where Tahna was sitting.

"My brother?" she said.

"Yes."

"I was worried. You've been gone too long."

"I had things to do."

In the dream, Kai El loved Tahna. It was like they'd been brother and sister forever.

"I'm glad you're home," she said, sounding relieved. "I need you. These people are losing everything they had."

"I'm only here to visit. Surely you and Tenka make one good Moonkeeper."

"Tenka's dead. My mother killed her. My mother died too."

"So it's true. I dreamed it was so."

The dreamworld started coming apart. Kai El floated upward.

"Come back," Tahna said. "I need you, brother."

"Good-bye, sister."

"Please, Kai El. I need you."

That his sister might need him was not enough.

The Spirit of Ashan took her dreaming son to Teahra Village in a different time. From the sky, he saw burning huts, bloody ground, bodies of men. He saw women and little ones hiding in the cliffs.

Elia came into the dream.

"It wasn't a slave raid," he said. "They did it to each other. The peace that began when I died ended because you wouldn't come back."

Kai El was horrified.

"Things are different," Elia said. "Ashan was the last who could talk to the people. Tahna has done a good job, but she has no magic. Without magic, men need a man to control them. He must be stronger, smarter and braver than any. You were that man."

Kai El tried to fly away from the dream, from the smoking village, from Elia's accusations. But he was stuck.

Elia said, "It was meant to be. You, with the Shahala blood of Tor and Ashan. Tahna, with the blood of Tor and her grandfather, the Tlikit chief.

"You and Tahna should have led these people. The chiefs who were brother and sister ... you would have become legend.

"And what you see down there would not have happened."

Kai El awoke with certain knowledge: He was going home.

# CHAPTER 57

KAI EL HEADED BACK TOWARD TEAHRA VILLAGE, with the dream of fiery destruction putting speed in his gait. The young man didn't know how he would save his people, but he knew that he was the only one who could.

He took time to see his father on the way. What good was forgiveness if the one forgiven never knew?

On a fine spring afternoon, he found Tor in the hidden cave. Hunched by a small fire, he looked *old*.

"Hello, Father."

Tor got to his feet.

"You came back," he said, wonder lifting his voice. "She said you would."

Kai El went to him with open arms.

"How could I not come back? I love you."

Tears sparkled in Tor's eyes. "I love you, too, son."

They held each other. The grip of Tor's skinny arms was weak. He trembled. Kai El felt the bones in his back, sensing feebleness in his entire being.

"I'm so sorry for what I did to you, son. I never tried to hurt you."

Kai El patted his back.

"I understand. I forgive you."

Speaking the words felt like laying down a huge stone carried for too long.

Tor slumped against him in relief. Then he backed away,

sniffling, wiping his face. He put his hands on Kai El's shoulders.

"As a man, I am a pebble, and you are a boulder."

"You mean you're a piece of sand, and I'm a mountain," Kai El said, laughing. Tor laughed with him, and once they started, it was hard to stop.

"It's too warm in here," Kai El said. It was also dark and musty, but he didn't mention that. "Let's go out. It's a fine day."

Tor went through the waterfall, with his head covered by a stiff piece of leather. Kai El followed, letting the cold water hit him—remembering how as a little one, he seldom took time to cover his head.

They climbed down mossy rocks edging the waterfall, and sat by the shallow pool on a piece of downed wood. The splashing water laughed. There was a magic glow to the place. Kai El had happy memories of being here with the grandfather Ehr, feeding the wolf, the lynx, chipmunks, and birds who were Ehr's only company before Ashan and Kai El came. He wondered if the animals were coming again now that Tor had returned, then realized that feeding animals was not the kind of thing his father would do.

"You are right," Tor said. "The sunshine feels good."

Kai El sighed. "I love this place."

"So do I." Tor put his hand on his son's arm. "To have you here, to have your love . . . that makes it perfect."

"I believe love is the best thing to have," Kai El said. "If someone loves you—even someone who has died—you are never really alone."

Then he picked up a pebble, tossed it in the pool, and watched the water ripple away.

"I can't stay here," he said. "I'm going home to take my place with Tahna and lead the tribe."

Kai El expected Tor to argue, maybe even plead with him to stay. At least, he expected to have to explain why.

But Tor said, "I know. She told me."

"So my mother talks to you?"

Tor nodded. "I don't hear her in my ears, but in my thoughts. I feel her in the air, and within me. It's my life's greatest comfort."

"I'm glad," Kai El said, remembering the time after Ashan's death, when Tor closed in on himself so tightly that her spirit couldn't get in if she tried.

Kai El said, "She comes to me in dreams. She has, since she became a spirit. She showed me that I must go home to Teahra."

"I'm proud of you, son. You always do the right thing. It's your mother's blood in you."

"And I am proud of you."

Tor shook his head. "I'm just a man who made too many mistakes. I don't deserve your pride."

"But you do. You are a legend among our people, talked about around the nightfire. Tor, the warrior who spoke the language of horses. Tor, the man with far-seeing eyes who brought us to the Great River."

Tor was pleased.

"A legend," he said. "I'm glad they don't remember me by how I was at the end."

"They remember you with love."

Kai El tossed another pebble in the pool.

"I want you to come home with me."

"Oh, no," Tor said with a laugh. "I'm not leaving."

"Tsilka won't be there to torment you. She's dead. I dreamed it."

"That's not it." Tor waved his arm. "This is my home."

"But you'll need people to help you when you get too old to do things for yourself. I want to be there for you. It's my right as your son."

Tor was firm. "Save your arguing. Spend a day with me, then go and do what you must."

"But, Father—"

"Did Ehr leave when he got old?"

"Well, no."

"I have everything I need. I will never leave the Home Cave. *She* likes it. I know it sounds strange, but we are happy, your mother and I. Even though I don't see her, she comes from time to time. I am happy here, Kai El. And more now that you have brought me the gift of your forgiveness. I like the way people remember me. I don't want them to watch me become a doddering old man. That's no image for a legend."

Kai El knew that he had lost. Sighing, he said, "Yes, I see what you mean."

Sunshine sparkled on the water. He watched trout hatchlings swimming at the edge of the pool in the shade of a clump of grass.

"What should I tell people?" he asked.

"Tell them nothing. Let them believe I am dead."

"What about Tahna?"

Tor sighed. "You must tell her about me. She has the right to know who she truly is."

"She might want to see you."

"She might want to *kill* me," Tor said. "I hope not. I would rather die here alone and in peace. But if she wants to, you'll have to bring her."

Father and son spent two days together—sad, sweet days, rich with love. They talked about small things, important things, and things they'd never talked about before, knowing it was likely to be the last time they'd be together in this life.

They talked about *ifs*.

How would things be different if Tor in his youth had not broken the dreaming tabu, and made the man-eaters come, and with them the Time of Sorrows that tried hard to destroy the people?

What if Tor had not kidnapped Ashan? Or left her to seek his pleasure with another woman, then left that one with two unclaimed little ones? What if he'd had the courage to admit his mistakes long ago?

What if Ashan hadn't wanted to take a walk on the night they arrived at the Great River? Or Tor had stopped her, instead of showing her the way? If she hadn't fallen from the cliff, she would have had control of the Tlikit tribe from the beginning. Maybe she would have killed Tsilka with magic. Kai El agreed with Tor that it would have been a good thing.

They talked about how a single act, insignificant and innocent, of a single person can change everything and everyone around them, even people not yet met or born. And how Tor had done it over and over in his life.

What did it mean? Nothing that they could see. Tor never

meant to hurt anyone. He had stumbled through life like most men, with good—if sometimes selfish—intentions. His only flaw was recklessness; his only fear, of losing the love of his mate and son.

Did that make Tor a bad man? No. His father wasn't a bad man, but Kai El promised to be a better one.

The Spirit of Ashan had been nearby ... silent, invisible, scattering her energy so Tor and Kai El wouldn't feel her. She was proud of them. They were fine men who knew the importance of love and were willing to sacrifice for it.

After their son left the Home Cave, Ashan came to Tor. He was lying on a heap of furs on the raised earth bed they had long ago shared, his head resting on an old summer skirt of Ashan's that he'd found in a corner of the cave. On his side, he curled around a thick bear fur, holding it as if it were a woman. A blue-purple aura glowed around him, the mixed colors of family and peace.

Tor floated in a dreamy place between waking and sleeping. Ashan mingled with him, and spoke in his mind.

*... Thank you. I know what courage it took to tell our son the truth ...*

Tor answered out loud. One voice talking to itself didn't sound strange to him.

"You were right, my love. I'm glad I did it. At last, I know the peace that's been missing all my life. It feels good. It's like resting."

Tor slipped into sleep, then out again.

"Ashan, do you remember when we were young, and we lived in the mountains in the cave you found? Before Kai El was born?"

*... I remember. There was only you and me, and love ...*

"Everything was new," he said. "Sharp and clear, and sweet. I loved it all, Ashan. Do you know what I loved most? Holding you at night, going to sleep with you in my arms ..."

Wrapped in their eternal love, Tor went to sleep.

# CHAPTER 58

In Teahra Village, the late spring day dawned bright and warm, with a breeze that would keep it from getting hot. The Moonkeeper Tahna had a full day ahead, even without the unexpected things that would demand her attention. As she did every day, she wished that her mother hadn't killed Tenka, and wondered who to train as her helper.

Still, she was in a good mood. There were good feelings in being needed.

Enjoying a few moments alone behind the closed doorskin of the Moonkeeper's hut, putting new laces on old moccasins, Tahna heard shouting.

"Kai El!"

She jumped to her feet and dashed outside.

It *was* Kai El, running toward the village with Wyecat, who'd been standing guard on the plateau.

People rushed him, surrounded him, pummeled him with questions.

"Give me time to rest," he said, laughing. "Then I'll tell you everything."

The crowd opened to let Tahna through. Her smile must have taken up her whole face.

"This is wonderful!" she said. "I'm so glad to see you!"

Instead of taking her outstretched hands, Kai El hugged her.

Tahna shouted, "People! Thank the spirits. Make a feast for our brother who has come back."

Kai El grinned. "I've missed the tasty miracles cooked by you women."

Women went off chattering like birds.

"Leave us," Tahna said to the people milling around. "You may have him when I'm finished. Come, Kai El."

She took him to the Moonkeeper's hut.

He looked healthy and glad to be home.

"Look at you!" Tahna said, so happy that she laughed. "I thought I'd never see you again! I can't believe it! This is wonderful!"

"I'm glad you think so. I wasn't sure how people would feel."

"Well . . . they were angry when you left. But it's been a long time now. We've missed you. These people love you."

Kai El looked down as if embarrassed, but Tahna saw that he was pleased.

She told him to sit.

"So you are the Moonkeeper," he said.

"Yes. Since Tenka died."

She would have to tell him about that, and all the other things that had happened while he was gone.

"Did your mother kill her?"

"No one knows, but I think she did. They died together, up in the cliffs." Tahna looked at him curiously. "How do you know?"

"My mother showed me in a dream."

"A dream . . . I wish it had been that easy for me."

He shook his head. "I can't imagine how it was for you."

"It was scary . . . a hard time for everyone. That's when we missed you the most. People didn't know what to do. They were like ants in a kicked-over anthill. It was up to me to do something, so I did. I took control. They let me because Tenka had been training me. And because there was no one else."

"I'm sorry I wasn't here, but I couldn't be."

She sighed. "I lived through it, and so did everyone else."

Tahna was glad Kai El was home. She didn't want him to

feel bad about being gone. What was the use of that? It was in the past now.

"So tell me everything. Where have you been since Gaia died?"

"Running from pain. Trying to forget. When that failed, trying to find out who I am without her."

"Did you?"

Nodding, he gave her a strange look.

"I saw Tor."

"Tor? You mean in a dream?"

"No. The real man. He lives in the tabu mountains. I stayed with him."

Tahna was amazed.

"Tor is alive? I can't believe it."

"Neither could I," Kai El said. "I'm the one who *thought* I saw him carried off on the back of a horse. Now I realize that was a dream. Tor left on his own legs."

"Why didn't you bring him back?"

"I tried. He won't come."

"Well, you can take some warriors and go get him."

"He doesn't want anyone to know he's alive." Kai El paused. "Except you."

The hairs on Tahna's neck stood up.

"Me? Why me?"

"There's something I must tell you, Tahna. Something he wants you to know." Kai El took a deep breath, and it whooshed out. "Tor is . . . he's . . ."

He swallowed hard, licked his lips, looked around.

"What are you trying to say? Tell me."

"He's your father."

What could he possibly mean by that? She didn't understand.

"What?" she said, shaking her head.

Kai El looked straight in her eyes.

*"Tor is your father."*

Tahna jumped up, was going to run out, but her knees buckled. Kai El caught her and held her.

"I'm sorry, sister."

She couldn't think or breathe.

"Not sorry that you are my sister," he said, "just sorry you never knew."

Waves of shock pushed Tahna this way and that on legs made of water. She felt like throwing up.

Kai El held her tight.

"It will be all right, Tahna. I'm here."

"But why didn't he tell me?" She gasped. "How could he! I'm going to find him! I'm going to—"

*Tahna!* Gaia's voice within her shouted. *You are the Moon-keeper now. You have no time for anger and confusion, no time for tears. It's true. It happened. Let it go.*

Tahna took deep breaths. Her insides unclenched. Strength returned to her legs. She pushed away from Kai El—from her *brother*.

A wave of sickening horror washed over Tahna when she realized that her brother was also *Gaia's brother*. Had they broken the ancient tabu? Tahna pictured the god Wahawkin sucking the water from the Great River, as he had once done to the lake in the Tlikit homeland because some long-ago chief had mated with his sister.

"Oh, Kai El," she said. "That means that my sister was your sister, and the two of you were—you were going to be—did you—"

"No. We did not. We never knew each other in that way. I wanted to, but we didn't. Gaia wanted to do things the Shahala way. She wanted to wait for the Autumn Feast."

Sitting back down, Tahna motioned for him to join her.

Tahna had had a dream four times. Now she knew what it had been trying to tell her. She shared it with Kai El.

"It was a good dream. You were in it. We were friends, good friends—though I had no idea you were my *brother*. Together we led these people, like one chief made out of two. They loved and respected us. Teahra Village was a safe, happy, bountiful home for everyone of any kind of blood."

"I had a dream like that," Kai El said, with a surprised look on his face.

Tahna said, "I thought that it made no more sense than most dreams. How could you help me? I was sure you were dead. But I took comfort from it. It gave me hope. And I needed that."

She took his hands, squeezed them, looked into his eyes.

"I needed hope, Kai El. Because I need *help* so badly. I can't control everything, especially the men. I get so frustrated I think I will scream, so tired I think I will die."

It felt wonderful to say these things. Since the Moonkeeper Tenka died, Tahna had no one to talk to. Now she had Kai El.

"My brother, welcome home."

With Kai El's strong arms around her, Tahna gave in to tears of happiness and relief. She would sort out her other feelings later.

The Firekeepers made a bonfire against the cliff wall. People drummed, danced, and sang to welcome the lost one returned to them. The women had reason to be proud of the feast they prepared. Kai El let them know with every bite how happy he was to be home.

The tribe sat listening. Kai El told about the mountains, and how he almost froze to death chasing revenge; of the snow cave he dug, and the bear cave where he passed the winter. How he grieved for Gaia. How he traveled in the spring to the land of his ancestors looking for reasons to live.

Kai El said, "My mother—the Moonkeeper Ashan, who is a spirit now—came to me in dreams. She showed me many things about the past and the future. I learned that Tor had *three* children, not one."

A gasp went up.

Tahna walked past stunned people to Kai El's side. They clasped hands and raised them over their heads.

"People of Teahra, Tahna is my sister."

"Kai El is my brother."

He said, "Destiny has reunited us. We will lead our people together."

She said, "One chief who is made out of two."

People liked the idea of two chiefs, once the shock went away. It made sense. A man and a woman—brother and sister, not mates—combining their individual strengths. He would lead the men on hunts, settle their arguments, and, with the new threat of slave raids, see that the village was guarded. She would heal, tell stories, teach little ones, and speak with spirits—though Tahna did less of that than any Moonkeeper before.

He was Shahala, she was Tlikit. From their mothers came the blood of chiefs. From their father, the blood of kinship. What could be better? This was the way it should be. Everyone felt it.

# CHAPTER 59

SUMMER, AUTUMN, AND WINTER PASSED. TEAHRA VIL-
lage prospered under the leadership of the Brother and Sister
Chief, as Kai El and Tahna were called. Men respected Kai
El. With Tahna's powerful medicine, there was little sickness.
The tribe was happy, well fed, and peaceful.

Tahna lived in the Moonkeeper's hut. A girl of ten summers
lived with her, learning a Moonkeeper's ways.

Only a few old people lived in the Tlikit cave. Kai El
moved in with them, taking a place near the front where it
was light and airy. But his favorite place was the home in the
cliffs he had made for Gaia, with She Who Watches looking
down at him. He stayed up there as much as he could, but
not as much as he would have liked ... the tribe kept him
busy.

Kai El was neither happy nor unhappy. He wasn't dead to
feeling as he'd been in the bear cave; he was more like a
blade with a blunted edge. He felt good about the life his
people were living, and about his part in it. But he didn't feel
joy. He would at times brood about the past, about lost Gaia,
about the wrongs done to him by Tor. But he felt that life
was acceptable.

One spring morning, Kai El was glad to be in the village
instead of in the cliffs.

A guard came running. He had seen eleven men. Kai El
left half the warriors to protect the women and little ones,

and took the rest down the Great River. When the men of Teahra swooped down from the rocks, the intruders, caught eating their morning food, did not have a chance. Several died before Kai El shouted.

"Stop! If we kill them all, we will know nothing!"

The warriors growled, but obeyed their chief. They threw six dead bodies in the river. Jerking the ropes that bound the five survivors, being as rough as possible, they kicked and shoved them back to the village.

Women spat and threw rocks.

"Masat!" they screeched.

"Put them in the cave where I won't have to smell them," Kai El said. "Guard them."

The men needed guarding from the people of Teahra, not because they might escape.

People threw their anger at Kai El.

"Why did you bring them back?"

"Their brothers stole our women! They killed Gaia!"

"They should die for what their brothers did!"

Kai El said, "I hate them as much as you do. I kept them alive because we need to know about their tribe. Killing them won't stop others from coming."

He turned and went in the cave, with people yelling behind him.

"So let them come! We will kill them all!"

Kai El had the ropes loosened so the captives wouldn't be in pain. He had food and water brought, but they wouldn't touch it.

That night the Tlikit cave sheltered more than a few old men: On one side were the five Masat, and twice as many Teahra guards; on the other, Kai El, the chief who held the lives of everyone in his hands. No one slept.

The next day Kai El strode across the cave. The Masat— if that was who they were—sat with hands and feet bound, ropes tying one to the next; crusted with blood and dirt, stinking of body waste. Hate and disgust swept him as he looked down.

*With the vision of a hawk, I see what others can't . . .* His spirit song forced him to see beyond his personal feelings, to the future and the safety of his people.

He pointed to the huts outside the cave.

"Teahra Village," he said. Then he tapped his chest. "Kai El. Chief."

He pointed at them with a questioning look. They glared fiercely at the man standing over them, and said nothing.

Tahna came into the cave. She knelt, and spoke slowly.

"Tsilka was my mother."

The captives looked at each other.

"Squill," one said, poking his chest. "Tsilka . . . Squill . . ." He locked the fingers of both hands together, grunted, and smiled. The meaning was obvious.

Tahna looked down. Kai El saw that she was embarrassed. He knew then how proud he was of his sister. She must hate the men who killed Gaia more than anyone. But she had put it away somewhere . . . as he had.

Squill made a motion with his bound hands toward the others.

"Masat," he said.

"Masat," Kai El repeated. Ice crept around his heart. "Then we *should* kill you."

"No kill. Work."

Kai El and Tahna looked at each. How could this savage know their language?

"Tsilka you bring. Tsilka talk."

Tahna said, "Tsilka is dead."

The man didn't understand.

"Dead," Kai El said, slicing his hand across his throat.

Squill nodded. The faces of the others were blank. They didn't share his knowledge. It was limited, but Tsilka had taught him enough that they were able to communicate.

With those few words and many signs, the chiefs told the captives why they were so hated: because their brothers had stolen four women, and killed one.

Squill was sorry about the women, but it must have been some other tribe. The Masat were a peaceful tribe. They did not steal river people. Their god, Raven, forbid it.

Grabbing several necklaces around the man's throat, Kai El told him the people of Teahra were not stupid. They had seen Masat men three times, and they all wore necklaces.

Squill agreed that it must have been Masat men after all.

He spoke to the others. They remembered now: Two bad men had been chased away. It must have been them. He was glad they died. He was sorry about the women.

The Masat men took off their necklaces, to be given as gifts to the women who were stolen. Insulted, Kai El didn't take them—as if some beads could make up for what had been done. The men tossed them at his feet.

Squill said they would be good slaves, if they were allowed to live.

Kai El told him it was wrong to have slaves. Teahra gods forbid it.

He knew there were only two choices: Kill them, or let them go.

Letting them go was dangerous. Would they want revenge for their dead? Would they want what they saw at Teahra Village? Would they bring a herd of warriors to get it?

But to kill them, not in the heat of battle, but in the cold of revenge . . . how would that affect his people?

Kai El and Tahna were learning to thought-speak with each other. She let him know that she was worried about the same things.

Tsilka, who had lived with the Masat, had said they were not bad people, except for keeping slaves. Even slaves weren't treated badly, except for the killing of one or two. To Kai El's Shahala mind, the idea of slaves was horrible, and no amount of goodness could make up for it.

Tahna's Tlikit mind saw it differently. She also thought it was a bad thing, but she knew that good people could keep slaves. Her own people had since the Misty Time, until they were forced to accept Shahala ways.

The Brother and Sister Chief came to an agreement in their minds.

Their people were not killers, and never had been. The killing of these five men might be like the taste of meat to a cat. The lesser danger was to let them go.

Kai El and Tahna talked to their people around the fire that night. When they were done, people thought *they* were the ones who had decided to let the Masat go.

But first Kai El wanted to find out as much about the danger as he could. He kept them for several more days, not letting them know whether they would live or die. He asked about the number of warriors in their village, the kinds of weapons they used, how far it was, and how to get there. Squill answered, and everything he said agreed with what Tsilka had said.

The two villages were about the same size, with the same number of warriors and the same kinds of weapons. By following the Great River, then turning and following the edge of the endless water, a man could get to the Masat village in less than one moon.

Kai El asked about their slaves.

They had slaves, but they were worthless people from a tribe who lived farther up the endless water. The Hida and the Masat had been enemies since grandfathers were little ones.

Squill told him again how his tribe never bothered any other people. Especially river people. The god Raven loved his river people, and would kill the Masat for harming them.

Kai El finally told Squill that they could go, with this warning: If they or any of their kind ever came back, what Raven would do to them would be nothing compared to what Teahra warriors would do.

Tahna thought they should be allowed to give their gifts to the women who'd been stolen. Bree, Nissa, and Selah took the necklaces without looking at the men.

They left.

"Don't come back!" Kai El yelled.

The necklaces were pretty. The women couldn't help liking them. There were so many, they gave some to their friends.

Tahna took two that were alike . . . two strings of white shells, big as a fingertip . . . circles that went over her head and lay on her breast.

"One for me and one for Gaia," she told Kai El.

The Masat came back. The same five, and three more.

When Kai El took the warriors to meet them, the intruders threw down their weapons. Then they threw down large packs and opened them.

There were furs Kai El had never seen before; shells; woven hats; smoking pipes; necklaces.

"Trade," Squill said.

Kai El allowed them to come to Teahra. They stayed for several days, eating the people's food, sharing a smoking plant they had brought with them. Kai El thought it was better than kinnikinnick, not so hot in the mouth. Puffing it made his head light.

Teahra people traded roots, firefish oil, and stone beads for the wonders from the land by the endless water.

The next time the Masat came, they brought two young women who wanted to stay. The people of Teahra, who now had several kinds of blood, welcomed another kind to the tribe.

Kai El knew when he saw them that neither Masat woman was his soulmate.

# CHAPTER 60

THEY CALLED IT "FREEZING RAIN," BECAUSE IT turned to ice as soon as it hit the ground. Sometimes it was already frozen, and stung the skin as it came down. In the second winter of the Brother and Sister Chief, freezing rain fell day after day, until a thick layer of ice covered everything in Teahra Village but the tops of the warm huts. It was cold and miserable outside, and dangerous to walk, so people stayed in their huts as much as possible. Kai El hadn't been to his home in the cliffs for days.

Awakening in a deep recess of the Tlikit cave, he looked out and decided that this would be the day that he'd go to the cliffs. The ground-ice hadn't gone anywhere in the night, but for now, it wasn't raining ice. The sky was blue, and beautiful. He couldn't remember the last blue-sky day he'd seen. He hoped the sun would stay and melt the ice, but for now it was cold enough to see his breath.

As he approached the Moonkeeper's hut, Kai El slipped. He grabbed a piece of wood by the door, shaking the hut.

Inside, a girl yelped—Chopay, ten summers, who was living with Tahna now, learning Moonkeeper's ways.

Tahna said, "Who is it?"

"The hawk has landed," Kai El said as he entered.

Chopay squatted by the fire with a poking stick in her hand. "You scared me, Kai El."

He tousled her hair.

"Sorry, little one. There's too much ice out there. My feet did a dance by themselves."

Tahna stood at her work shelf.

"Smell this," she said. "It's the most wonderful smell."

He sniffed some little round seeds on a flat grinding stone.

"What? I hardly smell anything."

"It isn't on the outside. It's on the inside. That's where you find the real beauty of everything."

She mashed the seeds with the other part of her grinding stone. A sharp odor rose.

"Whew," he said. "You think that's wonderful?"

"Mmm. I do."

"Me too," Chopay said from her place by the fire. Kai El thought she'd make a good Moonkeeper someday.

He said, "After living here through fourteen winters, I thought we'd seen the worst. But I was wrong."

"I know," Tahna said. "Ice that falls like rain ... what mean spirit would make a thing like that?"

"I think you have a broken leg to tend," Kai El said. "One of the Masat women slipped as she was chipping ice for water."

"Oh," Tahna said with sympathy. "Chopay, get your furs. Poor things, they don't know about ice. It never freezes at the endless water. They don't even wear moccasins there."

Kai El shook his head. "Hard to imagine, isn't it?"

All that the Ogress—as Tsilka was called after her death—had said about the Masat people and their home had turned out to be true—though that didn't change the memory of her as a madwoman.

Kai El said, "I'm going to the cliffs."

"It's dangerous," Tahna said. "Why don't you wait until the ice melts?"

"That might not be until spring, the way this winter is going."

"The last thing I need is to have my brother all broken up."

"Sister, I'm a warrior with feet like Suda, the ram. I can climb in the dark with my eyes closed. I'll be able to tell what's happening to the Great River from up in the cliffs. We need to know."

"Yes," she admitted. "We do."

The long cold weather had changed the Great River into something that people had never seen before. First in quiet pools at the edge, then farther out, the water hardened into choppy wave shapes. Frozen chunks floating down the river snagged on boulders, and caught more chunks. Freezing rain added layer after layer, ice upon ice.

Kai El said, "I walked out there. It's solid near the shore, but as you get toward the middle, you hear water rushing underneath. The ice groans and creaks. Then you think you feel it moving, and it seems like a good idea to turn around and come back. I don't know how far it goes."

Tahna said, "I wish you'd stay off it. And keep others off. Men aren't supposed to walk on rivers. The ice could break apart and take you away."

"I can keep men off the river," he said, "but I can't keep them from asking questions. Like, 'How far out does it go? And what if it freezes all the way across?' Tahna, people have always wondered what's on the other side. I have. Haven't you?"

Tahna shrugged, but he knew she had. They had talked about it. She was just afraid of the unknown, as women had reasons to be.

"The men are talking about crossing. I will lead them. I need to know as much as I can."

"Well then, you'd better go up for a look. Please be careful."

Kai El made his way along the river trail, and began the climb up the Moonkeeper's Path, made dangerous by ice. He slipped and fell, and would have bruises to show for it.

Partway up, he could see that there were places where the ice went all the way across the Great River. It looked as if men *could* cross to the other side.

Now that Kai El knew it could be done, he would have to decide if it should be.

Having seen enough, he could have gone back to the village. But he wanted time alone to think, so he kept climbing.

He sat in front of his cliffside hut, gazing at the frozen river, and the hills rising out of it on the other side. The only colors were gray and white.

The Great River was blocked. Who could believe it?

Kai El remembered the dream where he and his mother had thrown stones on a river of ice. This ice didn't seem bad, like the ice in the dream—just different, interesting, and full of questions. He had to laugh to think of breaking it with stones.

Glancing up at She Who Watches, he said, "We could cross it, you know. Tor would if he were here. Haven't you always wondered what's on the other side?" Then he laughed at himself. "I'm sure you know by now," he said.

Looking back at the river, Kai El saw something move. He caught his breath. Far away on the other side, an animal came onto the frozen river, advancing slowly toward Teahra Village. He squinted, trying to make it out. A bear?

No. A man in a bearskin. The man crept along, then stopped, looked back, and motioned with his arm. There were others.

The question of whether Teahra warriors should cross faded. The new question was what to do about the strangers already on their way.

In a tight cluster, six or seven walked and crawled onto the frozen river. The braver one who'd tried it first waited. They came a short distance, then one fell. They turned back for the shore, and wouldn't be persuaded to try it again.

Kai El knew what it felt like to have people too afraid to do what you wanted them to.

Falling and getting up again, the brave one slowly, steadily approached.

Kai El had a strange feeling, as if he knew this one who was coming. As if his life was about to change.

The man came to an uncrossable place where the water still ran free. Kai El could see from his high place that the man needed to go down the river, where it was frozen hard. But on the vast plain of choppy white waves, he couldn't see that, and headed the wrong way.

Kai El slipped and slid down to the village without thinking of his safety.

*Who is he? This man I know but have never met?*

*Are you sure it's a man?*

*Of course it's a man. Only a man would be fool enough to do what he's doing.*

He told Tahna what he'd seen, and told her to tell everyone. The people of Teahra Village would give a peaceful welcome to the strangers.

"Since he's coming alone, I will meet him alone," Kai El said. "Unless you want to come."

Tahna shook her head. "No river-walking for me. Does he have any weapons?"

"A spear. Or maybe it's just a staff."

"I'd feel better if you took one or two warriors."

"Of course you would. You're a woman."

"At least take a spear and a blade. You don't know what kind of people they are."

"Why would one man walk up to an entire village if killing was what he had in mind?"

What could his sister say? What could women ever say to stop men from doing what they really wanted to do?

Kai El walked out on the river, heading down to where he knew it was frozen all the way across. He carried a staff for balance, but no weapons. Under his feet, the ice felt solid as stone and slippery as wet moss.

They saw each other from a distance, stopped, and stared. *Who are you,* Kai El wondered, but the bear fur covered the man from head to foot.

Kai El held up his hand in a sign of peace.

His unknown friend did the same. He was small, from the size of his hand.

Kai El walked forward, watching his feet. He stopped and looked up.

The other one stood in front of him, and pushed back the hood of the fur robe. A beautiful woman looked at him.

He swallowed, gulped, held his breath till he was dizzy. *The most beautiful woman.* Kai El had seen her in his dreams, had mistaken her for Gaia.

She seemed to be as wonder-struck as he was. Her eyes looked into his soul.

"Tosanna," she said, placing her hand on her chest.

There was no lovelier sound than her voice, Kai El was certain, not anywhere, even in the otherworld. Everything about her was perfect: face, hair, eyes . . .

"Tosanna, Last Flower," she said.

"Kai El, Sun River," he answered. Then the shock hit him. "You speak my language!"

"No, you speak mine!" she said, with a smile like sunshine inside the heart.

She pointed across the river.

"What is this place? Who are these people?"

"It is Teahra Village. We are the Teahra tribe."

"We have watched your fires. We have wondered about you."

He said, "We are peaceful."

"Good. You are many, and we are few."

Kai El wasn't cold anymore, though the wind was still blowing.

"Tosanna . . ." He forgot the rest of what he was going to say. Her name was the prettiest word. He could sit all day saying it to himself.

"What?"

"Who are you, Tosanna?"

"We are Washani. We have come a long way. There were not enough mates in our tribe, and the people who live toward Warmer are mean. So we came to see if any people lived toward Colder."

They had come looking for mates, and she was not too shy to say so. Kai El smiled.

"How many?" he asked.

"Nine now. Four died. We left in the spring, but this huge river stopped us. We followed its edge. When autumn came, we had found no people, so we decided to spend the winter in a cave, and leave again in the spring. Then one day I was out getting wood, and I saw your village."

Her soft, dark brown eyes gazing into his were like a magic spell. Kai El could not have looked away if his feet were on fire.

"And I wondered," she said. "Were you the people we had searched for? The others said, 'Too bad if they are. We are over here and they are over there, and that is not a river to be crossed.' When the spirits froze the river, I said we must come and see. But the others were afraid." She shook her head. Her long black hair swung around her shoulders. "Finally we find some people, Kai El, and they are afraid."

She talked easily, as if she'd always known him. Laughter bubbled up in him.

"You are welcome, beautiful Tosanna. Let's get your people."

Kai El brought the Washani across the ice. The people of Teahra Village gave hearty welcome to the four women and five men, amazed that they spoke the same language. A feast was prepared in the Tlikit cave—the best they could manage in the frozen conditions. Not everyone could fit, so they took turns.

Tahna told the story of when the Moonkeeper Ashan traveled in the spirit world and saw the beginning of time, when all the people of the world belonged to one tribe. It was not so strange that the Washani spoke Shahala.

Kai El did his best to pay attention and act like a chief. But he and Tosanna couldn't keep their eyes apart. It was late when the Washani settled down to sleep on the other side of the cave. Kai El imagined that he smelled Tosanna's sweet scent, and heard her breathing. And it was just as it had been in another time that he could not remember.

The day dawned bright on Teahra Village. People came out to enjoy its promise. Sunlight gleamed on melting ice. The air was a warm caress.

Kai El, whose eyes saw only Tosanna, was both happy and afraid. He heard loud pings and cracks from the Great River, like he'd heard in his dream, the sound of breaking ice.

He called her name, and she came to him.

*Last Flower,* he thought. *You are so beautiful.*

"Tosanna, listen to the river. It's thawing. Soon there will be no crossing it. I will take you back if you want to go."

She looked into his soul.

"I never want to leave."

# AFTERWORD

For thousands of years, intertribal gatherings took place at the village on the Columbia River. People came from as far as the Great Plains and the Southwest to trade for the abundant salmon. The people of the village welcomed Lewis and Clark in 1805. By the 1950s, all that remained was a mound, which was partially excavated before it was drowned in the backwaters of The Dalles Dam.

She Who Watches saw it all, and is watching today.

# AUTHOR'S NOTE

Contemporary Indians who live along the Columbia tell of the People of the Misty Time, sometimes seen as lights shining from the riverbottom; of River Devils who pull bad people into the water and drown them. Of the Ogress, a woman so ugly no man would have her, who learned magic to make herself seem beautiful in a certain kind of light. She would seduce young men, and when they made love, turn back into her ugly self. The last thing a foolish young man saw as he died of horror was the hideous face of the Ogress.

And the story that inspired this novel, the legend of She Who Watches . . .

*A woman was chief of all who lived in this region. That was a long time before Coyote came up the river and changed things, and people were not yet real people. After a time, Coyote, in his travels, came to this place and asked the inhabitants if they were living well or ill. They sent him to their chief who lived up on the rocks, where she could look down on the village and know what was going on. Coyote climbed up to the house on the rocks and asked:*

*"What kind of living do you give these people? Do you treat them well, or are you one of those evil women?"*

*"I am teaching them to live well and build good houses,"* she said.

*"Soon the world will change,"* Coyote said, *"and women will no longer be chiefs."* Then he changed her into a rock

with the command *"You shall stay here and watch over the people who live here."*

All the people know that She Who Watches sees all things, for whenever they are looking at her, large eyes are watching them.